Samuel Rutherford Crockett

Kit Kennedy

Country boy

Samuel Rutherford Crockett

Kit Kennedy
Country boy

ISBN/EAN: 9783337231477

Printed in Europe, USA, Canada, Australia, Japan

Cover: Foto ©Andreas Hilbeck / pixelio.de

More available books at **www.hansebooks.com**

" MATTHEW ARMOUR . . STILL SAT WITH THE OPEN BIBLE BEFORE HIM."

[Page 10.

KIT KENNEDY:

COUNTRY BOY.

BY

S. R. CROCKETT.

London:

JAMES CLARKE & CO., 13 & 14, FLEET STREET, E.C.

T. FISHER UNWIN, PATERNOSTER BUILDINGS.

1899.

CONTENTS.

LIST OF ILLUSTRATIONS.

KIT KENNEDY.

CHAPTER I.

The Belle of the Parish.

THE world is very fair at four of the morning during the heats of high summer. The flowers which have slept with drooping heads and during a few brief hours retracted their perfume, as a woman withdraws herself when she has ventured overmuch, prink themselves again and give forth a good smell.

So at least thought Christopher Kennedy, scholar and gentleman, as he aroused himself in the accustomed dawn to go forth to meet with Lilias Armour.

It was a strange time for wooing, yet their only; for Fate, which takes upon itself to interfere with all things, had made Christopher classical master in the academy of Cairn Edward, and Lilias the daughter of his chiefest enemy, Matthew Armour by name, farmer in the moor farm of Black Dornal, and Ruling Elder in the Cameronian congregation called the Kirk on the Hill.

For the Elder, having returned one night from the market of Dumfries, where he had both seen and heard Mr. Christopher Kennedy, had sternly forbidden one of his family to hold any further intercourse with that blasphemer and ribald, a man (so he declared) as alien from grace as he was outlaw from the Covenants.

This, had Matthew Armour known it, was an excellent device, only it came too late. For Lilias, his sole daughter and the desire of his eyes, was already so

1

holden in the toils of the schoolmaster's bright glances and loving words that not for father or mother, kirk or covenant, would she break the bond.

So, exactly at four of the old-fashioned gold-faced watch which had ticked all night by his bedstead in the house of Tibby Allen, spinster, gossip, and householder in Queen Street, Cairn Edward, Mr. Christopher Kennedy stepped out into the little white street of the burgh, clean swept of people, and with the sunshine flooding it silently and emptily from end to end, just as if it were a fine summer Sabbath day during the morning diet of worship.

That young man appeared to consider it the most natural thing in the world that he should rise with the lark, and betake himself to the heather and wood-land with his botanical case at his back. He offered no explanation when he returned at eight to his frugal breakfast, though he had not brought back a single plant and his boots were "a fair sicht to be seen," as his landlady averred. "What wi' lashin' through the dew on the meadow and splashin' through the dubs o' the moss, they are nocht less than a disgrace. And how he can for verra shame expect a professin' Christian woman to clean them in time for him to gang to the schule at nine passes' Tibby Allen's comprehension!"

But neither his landlady's caustic comment over the wall of the pig-stye at the yard-head to her neighbour Mistress Sheepshanks, nor yet the window blinds which were so gingerly put aside with one finger to enable burghers' daughters, in extreme dishabille, to speculate on what took handsome Christopher Kennedy tramping along the streets of Cairn Edward so early, had the slightest effect on that headstrong young man.

Yet despite his early rising Christopher had been late at the social club (christened by himself The Tuneful Nine) in the Cross Keys the night before. Yesterday he had wrestled all day in the grammar school with the stupidity and the yet more irritant cleverness of the rural youth. He had slept the short, broken, uneasy slumber of overheated blood and ungoverned temperament. Nevertheless, this morning he rose with a certain elastic readiness, humming a stave of a Greek song he had set to his own music as he drew on his clothes after a hasty bath. He was ready to walk ten miles before breakfast, help Lilias Armour to gather in her cows, make the prettiest and most convincing of love in the shady places of the loaning, encounter (if he had bad luck) the stern eyes of her father, and after all be back again in time to see the early 'prentices taking down their snuff-brown shutters, and stacking them in neat piles behind the shop doors in the High Street of the little town, at the exact moment when his brother teachers were turning sleepily out of their beds to the music of the morning milk-cans rattling at their doors.

So, recklessly, and yet with a sort of kingly prodigality which to many women made him irresistible, the young classical master, concerning whose future his professors had entertained such great expectations, flung away with both hands the unreturning gold of love and youth.

He was easily first at the trysting-place. For half an hour he sat alone, whistling and twirling a spray of early hawthorn in his hand, on the edge of the heathery bank above the scanty pasture fields of the farm of Black Dornal. His post of vantage was situated just at the place where the great black and purple flowe of peat-muir overlooked with sullen eyebrow the green fields, bowering trees, and white homestead buildings which till now had closed in the life of Lilias Armour. Here long day and short day she had been happy, lifting a light-heart carol level with the larks, and laying her head in as lowly a nest with the falling of the night—that is, till Christopher Kennedy came by and the song ceased.

Then in a moment all was changed. The old life grew inexpressibly dull, not to be thought of, or returned upon for a moment without a shudder—a dreary waste of time wanting alike profit, beauty, or happiness.

Lilias, too, like her lover, had slept but little and lightly that short, breathing, merciful night of latest May. She had been making up her mind to speak a word of soberest intent to the man she loved—always a difficult matter to a loving woman, who rightly and naturally would rather listen while such words are whispered in her ear.

At last she came out. The quick eyes of Christopher Kennedy saw her pass, a slender slip of a maiden enough, athwart the dusky tree-shadowed farmyard. Then she was momentarily lost to sight as she threw open the gates, ready for the cows she was to bring back with her upon her return. She reappeared presently a more indistinct flitting figure, her light summer print indefinite against the fresh whitewash of the barn wall. Then the long green loaning swallowed her, and only a fleck of shadowy sun-bonnet nodding over the hedgerows or the glimmer of swift whiteness through a gap told the classical master of the approach of the girl who was risking so many things to meet him.

Rising from his seat he went forward a hundred yards to greet her, and then stood aside in a hidden nook to feast his eyes unseen upon her eager, untouched beauty as she came towards him. For the space of a blackbird's burst of song in the coppice behind him, he saw no further sign of his sweetheart. But as the song ceased he heard the patter of quick footsteps. And lo! there she was beneath him, her wide blue eyes looking eagerly ahead, her hair confined by a single ribbon as was the custom of the place and time, then as if resenting the restraint going spraying and tendriling down her back. Her lips were parted with expectation and the haste she had made uphill. Well might a man erect himself and hasten to meet such a maid as Lilias Armour was at twenty-two.

"Why, little girl," he said, smiling easily down upon her, "you are late this morning. What kept you? I have been waiting here more than half an hour!"

At the first unexpected sound of his voice she caught her hands together upon her bosom with a little frighted

cry.   She stood still a moment while Christopher
Kennedy ran towards her down the bank.   Then with
her hands clasped and held beneath her chin she yielded
herself to be gathered against his breast.

There she rested a little while breathlessly as in a
shelter, while his hand caressed her shoulder and was
lost among her hair.   She tried to speak, but, something suddenly choking her utterance, she put her
head down, and unclasping her hands she slid them up
till they rested on the young man's shoulders.

"Lilias, Lilias—dearest," he said, reproachfully,
trying to look into her eyes, "what is the matter?
This is not like my girl—to break down like this.
What have they done to you now?   Have they been
speaking against me again?   Well, that is nothing
new!"

Then, receiving no answer, he submitted with a sigh
to the incomprehensible nature of women and let the
girl weep her fill, only at intervals touching her lightly
with his hand upon the further cheek which ran wet
with warm tears.   Once, too, he stooped and kissed
her hair, from which the sunbonnet had fallen back,
when he had first drawn her to him.   Then he took the
girl yet closer to him and was silent also.

After a little she exhausted herself, and rested quiet
with her face against Kennedy's coat, nestling as a bird
does in a safe covert in time of storm.   Her bosom
fluttered like a bird's, and a sharp dry sob clicked
recurrently in her throat, so that he felt all her slender
body shake within his arms.

"*Now* can you tell me?" he said, tenderly, and
added nothing more.   For, foolish in all else, this
young man was wise in love—that is, if the object of
love-wisdom be to win other love, not to hold it
worthily when it is won.

"Be patient with me, Chris," she whispered, "be
very patient, and I will tell you all.   It is so hard, so
hard for me at home.   I want you to take me away.
They speak against you all the time, or at least my
mother does.   My father says nothing, but I know his

heart is more and more set to hate you ever since that
night he saw you in Dumfries. O Chris, if you love
me, how can you go to such places?"

The young man moved impatiently and uneasily under
the hands which were laid upon his shoulders with so
gentle a restraint. His bold admiring gaze quailed
before the honest upward appeal of the wet blue eyes
now for the first time turned upon him. He hesitated
before he spoke.

"Why, a man must live," he said at last, with a
short laugh; "I have been used to company, and if I
did not sometimes go among men who are not afraid to
be men, I should mould and dry-rot both at once in this
place. It is all that keeps one alive in such a dull dog's
hole as Cairn Edward."

The blue eyes were still upon him with a yearning
in them that made even the selfishness of Christopher
Kennedy wince.

"And what of me?" she said, soft as a breathing,
yet with an accent that pierced to the dividing asunder
of soul and marrow.

"Lilias, Lilias," he cried, in genuine pain, "I love
you, I tell you so. That rights all. What difference
does it make what people may say? What do a parcel
of farmer folk and villagers matter to us? You know
what your Bible says, something about 'for this cause
shall a man leave father and mother and shall cleave
unto his wife!'"

She kept her eyes fixedly upon him, and their regard
was deep and steady as the sea when it is stillest.

"His wife!" She breathed the two words again, and
the wind among the waterside willow trees was not
softer, nor the dying soul's parting cry more tragic.

"*His wife!*"

The young man nerved himself, and dashed in the
rapid voice of one who fears interruption, into an
obviously premeditated speech.

"Listen, Lilias," he said, "I have told you why I
cannot marry you openly, though God knows I would
be glad and proud to do it to-morrow. My father put

me through college, and I promised to repay him before
I married. He is poor and needs the money. Besides,
it would ruin me in Cairn Edward if such a thing were
known, and I have good hopes of the headmastership.
Then again your father thinks me godless and
debauched. He told me so openly, upon the Plainstones
of Dumfries when I met him there three months ago.
He forbade me ever again to enter his door. He
forbade me to meet you. He would never consent.
But happily we live in a land where marriage is easy.
Lilias, will you marry me privately? I know it is
against your kirk rules, but it is according to the law of
the land, and to the full as binding as if twenty
ministers were present."

He paused a little breathlessly himself and looked
down upon her, smiling an anxious, forced smile.

The girl drew herself back a little way from him, and
reaching up her hands she kept his handsome head,
with its high forehead and weak irresolute mouth, at a
distance, so that she might look into his eyes.

"You have left me no choice, Chris," she said, still
looking steadily into his soul; "you have made me
love you so terribly. I must marry you when you bid
me."

"Ah, that is right," the young man cried, cheerfully,
stooping to kiss her, "that is all right. Now smile and
put your sadness away! A bride does not look like
that."

But she held him still at a distance, and her gaze did
not falter. She was a child even at two-and-twenty,
this Lilias, though she had long been climbing on the
perilous ridges which to such a temperament as hers
form the watershed of life and death.

"Tell me what it is that you propose!" she said.
"No—do not touch me—yet! I want to understand."

"I have but short time, little one," he made answer,
"and I have not yet thought it fully out. But if you
bring a friend with you I will bring another—friends
whom we can trust, I mean, and we will make the
declaration that we are man and wife before witnesses.

I, on my part, will bring Alister French the lawyer with me, and he will see that all is right and draw up the papers. Whom will you bring?"

"I do not know; I have had no one to trust, to speak to, except you; I do not want any other," she answered him, the firmness of her gaze wavering under his burning glances. She felt the weakness inherent to all loving women coming over her.

"Another we must have. Would not Bell Kirkpatrick serve?" he suggested, with a quick downward glance at her face, to see how she took the suggestion.

"I do not like Bell. I could not trust her!" said Lilias Armour, uncertainly.

"And pray why not?" he urged; "she is clever and secret. Besides, being with you in the house she could help us more than any one else!"

"I do not like her!" persisted the girl.

"Well, think it over. I must go at once or I shall be late; I am late as it is. Think it well over. I will see you again on Saturday. Be ready to tell me then what you will do. And oh! Look here, Bell is willing to help. In fact, I have spoken to her myself——"

There came a quick, leaping terror into the girl's face. She caught the classical master by the arm.

"Chris," she whispered, "what have you told her—what does she know?"

He smiled and patted her fondly on the shoulder.

"Silly one, only what I would that all the world knew," he said, "that I love you and would like to marry you!"

She was silent, but she sighed the long, weariful sigh of hope deferred.

"Good-bye!" he said, and bending a long moment to her, he was gone.

At the top of the moor, before he plunged down the long, rough, heathery steep, he turned and waved a white handkerchief. Lilias Armour stood where he had left her. She did not wave a response, but kept her hands clasped before her, looking steadfastly after her lover.

As he ran down the slope he pulled out his watch.

"An hour and ten minutes," he said; "I can do it; I shall have time to see French and look in at the Cross Keys as well. This sort of thing takes it deucedly out of a fellow whose business it is to explain the accusative and infinitive all day long."

An hour later Lilias Armour sat in her appointed place at the douce and sober morning worship of a Cameronian home. As was the daughter's duty, she had brought down the great Bible, covered with worn calf skin with the hair outside, and laid it before her father at the head of the table. Before doing so, she had taken away the breakfast dishes and respread the board with a white cloth like that which is laid upon a communion table, for the more fit offering up of the morning sacrifice.

Her mother, bustling, masterful, loquacious housewife that she was, had been so long among the poultry in the yard that the Elder was compelled to sit full five minutes silent among his family, with the Bible open before him ere he could give out the psalm to be sung. Then his wife, flustered to find them all silent and waiting, sat down and endeavoured to smooth her hair with one hand, while she found the place with the other, naturally enough failing in both. But there were tears in the eyes of one within the wide sunny house-place of Dornal as they sang to the wistful rise and fall of the Elder's favourite Coleshill the final verse of the opening song of praise :—

> I, like a lost sheep, went astray:
>   Thy servant seek and find:
> For thy commands I suffered not
>   To slip out of my mind.

CHAPTER II.

The Marriage Lines.

"Bitter are the rigours of righteousness, and by them the merciful are shamed and sinners confirmed in their evil way."

This may not be a text out of the written Word, nevertheless it embalms somewhat of the spirit of the Great Forgiver of sins.

It was the morn of the Sabbath some months after the early meeting between the classical master and Lilias Armour. The solemn Taking of the Book was over in the farmhouse of Dornal, but Matthew Armour, Ruling Elder in the Cameronian Kirk, still sat with the Bible open before him. His face, with its shock of silvering hair sweeping back from the noble cliff-like brow, was sober with more than Roman gravity. His wife gathered together the folded white handkerchief, the spectacles and the psalm-book which were her indispensables at any function of a religious character. She had learned by the experience of half a lifetime, added to her original store of woman's instinct, when it "wasna chancy" at such times to stand long in the way of her husband. Now in that hush of Sabbath silence which she knew so well, she was especially eager to be gone.

But even in the doorway the voice of the Elder arrested her.

"Margaret Armour, bid our daughter Lilias come hither to me!" he said.

"Hoot, Matthew," urged his wife, "be canny. I ken the young man is no a great professor, and his ways are no oor ain hamely ways—but dinna fret the young lass.

The lad is weel-to-do, and of a decent family enough, though they say an Episcopalian."

"Silence, woman, do as I bid you instantly," commanded the Ruling Elder; "it is with my daughter and yours that I desire to speak!"

"Mathy—Mathy, mind that we are a' sinners," the mother pleaded, "mind that ye were yince young yoursel'."

"And if so, think you not that I have suffered in the flesh for the deeds of the flesh. Think you that I do not wet my pillow many a night for the sins of my youth. And if my children must suffer, it shall not be because no warning word has been spoken, or no strong hand outstretched to deliver. Send in the lass!"

With a little helpless appeal of the hands and a sidelong sway of the head in acknowledgment of the fact that of course *her* word went for nothing, Margaret Armour took herself off to do as she was bid. She found Lilias standing with a book in her hand under the great beech tree by the house gable. But she was not reading. Her eyes, large and vague, their sometime bright blue dimmed with sadness and tears unshed, were fixed on the distant hills at the foot of which lay Cairn Edward.

She did not hear her mother come near her, and she started with a piteous gesture of fear when a large hard hand was laid on her arm.

"Lilias, my lass, ye are to gang your ways ben to your faither," she said, "and oh! mind—be kind and canny wi' him. Be not angry nor rebellious, for that is never any way with your faither. Gie up the young man gin he bids you—at least for the present. Your heart winna break, though you may think it will. And dinna forget that, whatever your faither may say, he speaks for your good."

Lilias Armour looked at her mother with so steady a gaze that the eyes of that good bustling housewife fell before them. The daughter laughed a little laugh, hard to listen to from one so young, it was so full of bitter knowledge of the past and carelessness for the future.

"Gie him up—and if I do, that will end it, will it?" she said.

"Aye, surely," said her mother, "it is the way wi' a' the young. I hae been that gait mysel'. I thocht that there was nae lad like ane that I hae mind on. For sax months I wad hae gi'en a' my shapin' claes for him. But my ain mither advised me, and I took her advice. And ye will do the like, my hinnie, like a good lass. There are better lads than him to be gotten—aye, and no that far to seek—responsible, God-fearin' men, too, wi' farms weel plenished and siller in the bank. There was ane that spak' to me Sabbath eight days nae farther gane. Ye could get him for a look—aye, and be a decent married wife within a month gin ye willed it."

Lilias Armour listened wearily to her mother, but did not answer her exhortations and appeals.

"I will go in and see my father," she said. And straightway she went in to where Matthew Armour was sitting, his head thrown back with a grave leonine action, his hand still on the open Bible, and his eyes upon the door through which Lilias was to enter.

She stood before the Elder and looked him in the face, waiting for him to speak.

"My daughter," he said at last, speaking very slowly but not unkindly, "what is the relation in which you stand to the young man of whom we have spoken once before, to him who is named Christopher Kennedy?"

"He is very dear to me," said Lilias Armour, simply.

"I asked you not as to your feelings," her father went on; "the wind does not pass more quickly over the trees than such emotions over a maiden's heart. And when it is gone it leaves as little trace of its passage. But what of him? Has he also told you that you are dear to him?"

"Ever since he came hither he has loved none but me!" said Lilias, bravely.

Her father nodded with a shade of irony and contempt mingling with the exceeding gravity of his countenance.

" Such words are a commonplace of evil and designing men," he said ; "they boast in the public places that
they are able to make any woman love them. My
daughter, that which I shall have to say will be bitter
in the mouth as gall. I pray my God that the after-
taste may be sweet. And, indeed, be that as it may, it
is my intent and bounden duty to save you from a
debased and drunken profligate, one who has already
dragged your good name through the mire, and who
would drag it deeper if he were permitted ! "

" Father ! " cried the girl, indignantly, " even you
have not the right to speak thus of the man I love ! "

" My daughter," said the Elder, a little more gently,
" the truth may be spoken by any and shame none.
Still more by a father."

" You dare not say it to his face ! " said the girl,
with a flash of angry defiance unexpected even by
herself.

The Ruling Elder smiled a calm, cold, inscrutable
smile.

" I, Matthew Armour, dare not ! Do you know your
father so little ? Listen ! Last night I heard my
daughter's name spoken by rude lips, shouted aloud in
a place of public entertainment. The door of the room
was locked. I burst it open when they refused me
entrance, and stood before your lover in the midst of
his riotous and drunken companions. I taxed him to
answer me. I accused him to his face of treachery and
depravity, and he could not answer save with oaths and
cursings. So I delivered him to Satan, that he might
learn not to blaspheme."

The girl stood pressing her hands upon her breast, as
if to keep her heart in its place, the while her father
went remorselessly on.

" Nay, more ; I was made aware last night that
Christopher Kennedy had lost his position at the
grammar school of Cairn Edward for drunkenness, and
even at that very moment with his companions he was
celebrating his way-going. This morning, with one of his
cronies, he is fled no man knows whither, and only his

creditors will trouble to inquire. He goes forth disgraced in the sight of all and in debt to half the countryside."

"No, no, father! Surely there must be some mistake," the girl faltered, the words driven from her. "Christopher Kennedy cannot have gone without seeing me, without bidding me 'Good-bye'!"

"A bad man in time of trouble thinks only of himself," said her father. "But after all, why should he not have gone to his wife?"

Lilias Armour took a swift step forward as if to silence her father's accusing voice. He stayed her with his hand extended, palm outward, with an action full of dignity and tenderness.

"Be patient, my daughter. Such dealing may be hard, but it is for your soul's health that you mate not with an evildoer. Listen! There came a man hither this morning with all the tale of his past. The man whom you call Christopher Kennedy was married half a dozen years ago, before ever he went to college, to a fisher lass in his own parish of Sandhaven. She lives there to this day."

The girl bent her nails inward upon her palms and shook with the effort to command herself.

"Who is the man who brought this news?" she asked, to outward view quietly enough.

"His name is Walter Mac Walter. He comes from Sandhaven and knew Christopher Kennedy well. His brother is farmer of Loch Spellanderie; he is a man of credit and a man who has recently bought property in this neighbourhood."

"Then Walter Mac Walter lies!" cried Lilias Armour, lifting her head very high.

The Elder took from between the leaves of the Bible a slip of blue paper. There was minute printing upon it, interspersed with larger writing.

"Walter Mac Walter brought this with him in token that he lied not," said her father. "It is a copy of certificate extracted from the registrar's book of the parish of Sandhaven, bearing that, on the twenty-fifth day of August, in the year 18—, Christopher Kennedy, son of Allan Kennedy, farmer of Mayfield in the parish of Sandhaven, was married to Mary Bisset, daughter of Alexander Bisset of Ship Row, fisherman in the same parish."

The girl came forward and put out her hand for the paper. Her father gave it to her, and she tried to read it. But the words reeled before her eyes, and her fingers trembled so violently that the paper fluttered this way and that like a leaf in the wind.

"I cannot read it," she said, "but it is not true. Why should a man bring such a thing with him from hundreds of miles away unless he hated Christopher Kennedy? And why did he go to you instead of to the man he slandered?"

"He came to ask your hand in marriage, my daughter," said the Elder with dignity.

The girl laughed—a hard grating little laugh, not good to hear.

"I thought as much," she said. "This man has pestered me at the kirk and on the way home these months back, not taking any honest answer. And now he has come from the north with this tale, when I thought that I was rid of him. Father, do not believe such a man. It is a lie. I know it to be a lie!"

"And how do you know, Lilias Armour?" said her father, speaking with great quiet.

The girl became suddenly excited, and her hand fumbled for something in her bosom.

"I know it, because I and no other am the wife of Christopher Kennedy—because he has married me in the presence of witnesses; I and I alone am his wife."

A greyer greyness settled over the face of the Elder. His firm lips paled and became more tightly compressed, but his speech was steady as ever, and the hand upon the open Bible did not quiver.

"Before what witnesses?" he asked.

"Before Alister French the lawyer, and Bell Kirkpatrick!" the girl answered fearlessly.

"Alister French it is who is fled with him, alike

shamed and in debts; his witnessing is as good as naught!" said the Elder. "Let us see what Bell Kirkpatrick will say to this!"

He rose from his seat and went to the door.

"Margaret," he cried, "send in Bell Kirkpatrick to me hastily."

His wife, who had been listening as near the door as she dared to come, obediently went into the courtyard, and in a few minutes Bell the byre-lass, a tall dark girl, with some remnant of good looks not yet coarsened out of her, entered with a kind of sullen defiance in her manner.

"What's your wull wi' me?" she said, standing her ground with her hands thumb down upon her hips.

Matthew Armour looked at her with a certain stern calmness which was not without its effect.

"Bell Kirkpatrick," he said, "is it true that you were witness to a private marriage between my daughter Lilias and a man named Christopher Kennedy?"

"Na!" said the hoyden, boldly; "it is'na true. No a single word o' it! I ken nocht aboot ony Christopher Kennedy!"

"Take care!" said the Elder; "my daughter assures me it is true!"

"Then your dochter tells a lie!" asserted Bell Kirkpatrick. "I never heard a word o' ony marriage!"

"As I thought," said Matthew Armour, turning to Lilias; "he has well chosen his witnesses, and I doubt not paid them with other people's money. He hath deceived and mocked you, my daughter. He who mocked at his Creator might well mock at the creature. But I, Matthew Armour, am your father. Fear not! I will stand beside you in the gate. You are well rid of a man so coward and forsworn, a man debauched and rotten of heart."

"It is true, it is true; what I tell you is God's own truth!" cried Lilias Armour, holding a folded paper in her hand. "See—read. Here it is, in the handwriting of Alister French, and with his name and that of

Christopher Kennedy upon it, together with Bell Kirk-patrick's mark."

"Give the paper to me, my daughter!" said her father.

With a strange reluctance to let the precious strip out of her hands, the girl gave it to her father.

The old man adjusted his spectacles, and read it as calmly as he would a text of the Scripture.

Then, without a moment's hesitation, he walked across to the fire that burned in the grate of the house-place of the Black Dornal, and thrust it deep into the midst.

With a strange, breaking cry Lilias threw herself forward towards it.

"Father, father," she cried, "give it to me. It is my all!"

Her father kept her back with his left hand, while with his right he held the paper down till it was con-sumed, and the fragments swirled up the chimney, with little fiery dots still crawling crablike across them.

"It is but the worthless forgery of a villain," he said, "and if it were not, I would burn it a thousand times rather than give you up body and soul to a man accursed and outcast like Christopher Kennedy."

The girl stood gasping, her hands still fighting to pass the strong arm that held her back, her mouth squarely open, her eyes with the wild blank terror of the utterly forsaken in them.

"Oh, you know not what you have done," she said. "I am his, body and soul; I am his! If he fail me now, I know not what I shall do!"

And without another word she turned and went slowly and heavily out of the room. Matthew Armour watched her go, and as the sound of her footsteps died down the narrow passage which led to her own little chamber, he turned swiftly on Bell Kirkpatrick.

"And now, lying woman, leave this house instantly. You have witnessed a lie and have doubtless been paid for it. Sabbath though it be, I also will pay you that which is owing between us. But God will one day give

2

you your wages in full reckoning for the evil you have
brought upon me and mine this day."

The woman stood silent and watched him, at intervals
ostentatiously humming a dance tune. Old Matthew
Armour turned upon her on his way to the little locked
drawer where he kept his money.

"Silence, woman!" he cried, "silence, lest I be
tempted to strike you to the ground."

And so threatening was his gesture that the defiance
was smitten from the face of the false witness as quickly
as a boy wipes a slate with a wet sponge. She held out
her hand mechanically for the money.

And as the last coin was told into it she made towards
the door.

On the threshold the woman turned, and with a certain fleer of bravado she said, "Matthew Armour, this is
not the end, either for you or for your daughter. I warn
you!"

The old man raised his hand, and pointed to the door
with a motion so large and commanding that the evil
woman went out without another word, like Judas,
bearing the price of innocent blood.

Then Matthew Armour laid his hand upon the open
Word of God and looked upward.

He stood a long while thus praying, his face softening
strangely as he did so with a kind of inner light shining
out from it.

"Perhaps *I* have done wrong," he said, "as well as
that poor young lassie."

And as he shut the book he said again yet more gently
than before, "My poor, poor lassie!"

CHAPTER III.

AFTER EIGHT YEARS.

IT was a mellow July afternoon nearly eight years after that Sabbath morn when Lilias Armour walked out of the house-place of Dornal with her finger nails gripped into her palms, and no marriage lines in the bosom of her dress to stir with the fluttering of her heart.

Matthew Armour sat on a bench beside the door, leaning upon the head of his staff, and looking out over the green springing corn, through the spaces of the trees in the hollow, down to the meadows by the water-side. He had grown older even to the casual eye during these last years. His hair was less abundant, and the hand that had been so strong, quavered upon the tough oaken head of the staff on which he leaned thoughtfully.

But under the heavy grey brows the eyes of the Ruling Elder were still grey and unconquerably clear. His lips were firm, and lay close one upon the other with the old precision and determination. His "yea" was still "yea," and his "nay" still "nay," to all within the precincts of the Black Dornal.

Yet withal there was something warmer and kindlier than of yore—a light from within the gates, as Mr. Osborne expressed it. Mr. Osborne was the minister of the Cameronian Kirk, and he knew his Ruling Elder well.

As Matthew Armour sat thus with his broad bonnet of blue on his head, his eye caught the glint of the mower's scythe somewhere down in the hollow. And at intervals there came to the old man a waft of song, the gay lilt of an air, the plaintive note of a psalm tune, or again, the strident *rash-whish* of the sharpening strake on the scythe as the mower set it with its point to the ground, and put an edge on the broad shining blade with long alternate sweeps of his arm.

It was very still about the old man until, sudden as a swallow's swoop, something passed behind him.

From the open door of the milk-house, which stood at the end of the farm buildings of Dornal, a little boy of six or seven came with a rush, and a brisk, stirring voice followed him with the snell Scottish scolding "tang" in it, which is ever more humorous than alarming to those whom it addresses.

"Ye ill-set blasty, Kit Kennedy, gin I catch ye in here again! I declare a body canna turn aboot for ye, but ye are at the cream. Or if ye are'na at the cream, ye are thumbing the guid fresh butter ontil your bread-piece as if it were common as clay. I hae neither rest nor peace in my life for ye—I declare, so I do!"

The figure of Mistress Armour of the Black Dornal appeared at the door of the milk-house—wrathful, gesticulant, voluble, but somewhat ineffective. For the small boy addressed as Kit Kennedy did not wait to be more nearly approached, but fled helter-skelter to the knees of the Ruling Elder. These he seized with both chubby hands and forced apart, wedging himself between them as if he had been ensconsing himself in a citadel from which it was impossible to dislodge him.

Mistress Armour stood a moment shaking her fist at the small culprit. Then she went discontentedly within, but the gist of her meditations were permitted to reach the ears of her husband, for whom doubtless they were intended.

"A bonny like thing," she went on, shrilly, among her milk pails, "that after bringin' up his ain in the fear o' God and a guid hazel stick, Matthew should be turned aboot the wee finger o' a bairn like that. It's easy seen that some folk are growin' early doited. Pre-

serve us a'—we mauna raise a finger against the brat,
as if he were a king in his ain richt and the Lord's
anointed!"

She resumed her butter-making, still muttering to
herself.

"No that he's sic an ill bairn either," she said,
relentingly, "but only that mischeevious and worritin'.
Ye'll meet the loon wi' a face on him like a thanksgivin'
service, an' ye think what a grand wiselike bairn. But
a' the same ye are safe in giein' him a daud on the side
o' the head, for I'se warrant ye that he's either on the
road to some ill-doin', or comin' direct frae a mischief!
Either way, he'll be pleased wi' himsel'!"

She fished the last of the butter out of the cool
water.

"An' his grandfaither—there, weel, he juist canna
see a faut in him. It's 'Dinna be ower sair on the
wean!' Or maybe 'Let the bairn be, Margaret; mind
ye no that he's but young?'"

And at the thought Mistress Armour gave the
wooden spoons with which she was handling the butter
a little vicious clap against each other.

"Aye, an' had it been ony o' his ain," she continued,
nodding her head, "they wad hae gotten a stick drawn
across their backs, or hae been takin' the road by the
Lang Plantin', rubbin' their lugs and scraichin' as if it
were a pigkillin'!"

But Kit Kennedy, happily unconscious of these male-
dictions, had run straight to the old man, as we have
seen, and was now beginning to venture cautiously out
of his retreat. He set his elbows first on one of his
grandfather's knees and now on the other, all the while
ceasing not to propound that steady stream of question-
ing which rises so easily to the lips of nimble-minded
youth.

"Rab Forrest lives wi' his mither, and Tam Louie
lives wi' his," he said. "What for do I no bide wi'
my mither too, g'appa?"

The Ruling Elder looked at the boy with a sudden
cessation of the smile which had beautified his counten-

ance as he watched his grandson's confidence in the safety of his city of refuge.

"Your mother comes to see ye, Kit," he said; "she was here only last Monday."

"I ken," persisted the boy; "that was because it was Monday, and Walter Mac Walter was at the market in Cairn Edward. But what for does my mither bide wi' Walter Mac Walter an' no wi' me? That's what I wad like to ken."

"Mr. Mac Walter has no one to live with," said his grandfather, diplomatically. "He has all that great house of Kirkoswald to himself. You have your grandmother and your uncles and——"

"And the dogs and the ten cats, and you, g'appa," continued the boy, putting in order and completing his catalogue of mercies. "I ken." Diverted by this thought, he made a fresh start. "But we wad be *that* glad to keep her here. For when she comes she is aye smilin' bonnily as if she had gotten oot o' the kirk, or somebody had gi'en her a sugar piece. But when she gangs awa', she pits doon her hand to her pooch and draws oot her handkerchie an' pretends to dicht her nose. But I ken fine she's greetin'. For I hae fand the water faain' *plap plap* on my heid. It was funny. But gin my minnie bode here a' the time, she wadna need sae mony handkerchiefs. It wad be a savin'. And Walter Mac Walter micht hae three o' the cats to bide wi' him—and grandma too!"

The Elder fell back on the usual reserves of age and experience.

"It's not for bairns like you to ask such questions," he said. "When you grow older you will understand all these things."

The boy fell a-thinking, and his eyes followed the hillside track by which he had seen his mother so often take her way back to the house of Kirkoswald, in which she dwelt so mysteriously with his hated rival, Walter Mac Walter.

His grandfather watched him without speaking.

"Uncle Rob will no tak' me to the back-fields to see

the rabbits an' whuttericks an' gather gowans ony mair!" he began, in a mournful tone.

"And what for that?" said his grandfather, glad on any terms to change the subject.

"Oh!" cried the boy, "juist because the last day my mither cam' to see us, after she had patted me on the head, and ta'en me on her knee, an' played hide an' seek aboot the stacks wi' me, an' gied me a' the sweeties she had (there was only nine and a broken yin), she gaed awa' ben the hoose. An' then Uncle Rob he says, 'Wad ye like a ride ower to the back-field—a ride on my back to see the rabbits and the whuttericks and pu' the gowans?' (he aye says the same thing, as if I didna ken what he meaned. Uncles is that silly; aunts, too—but I hae nane). And so I ga'ed wi' him to please him, and after a while I said, 'I think we can gang oor ways hame. My mither will be ower the hill by noo!' 'Ye blastie,' says he, 'never mair will I cairry you on my back to be oot o' the road when your mither gangs awa'. Ye can juist stop an' greet your fill!' "So," concluded the boy, "that's why Uncle Rob winna cairry me to the back-field ony mair, to see the rabbits an' whuttericks an' gather the gowans."

CHAPTER IV.

The Derelict.

Lilias Mac Walter, who had once been Lilias Armour, had parted with her son Kit at the gate of the farm loaning of the Black Dornal, and was now taking her way slowly over the hill by the little wimpling path through the heather which led to the newer and more pretentious mansion house of Kirkoswald. She walked as one easily tired, and ever and anon she stopped to take breath with her hand on her side. Each time that she did so she looked longingly back to the Black Dornal.

The little whitewashed house, one-storied, low-roofed, stretched itself out beneath her, looking hardly more imposing than a long brown-thatched potato pit. Its door stood open. She could see the marsh-mallows stand lilac and green against the wall, and almost the red house-leek that sprung thick-leaved and blossom-crowned from among the thatch.

But these were not what she most looked for. She strained her beautiful eyes—now, alas! grown somewhat dim with time and tears—to catch a glimpse of a little black figure which ran round the office house chasing the butterflies and hallooing with wild joy as the young collies pursued each other at a stretching gallop, gripped, and fell over in riotous heaps.

She sighed to think that he had so soon forgotten his mother. "But it is better so," she said, and turning, resumed her way with that slightly weary drag in her gait which was so different from the elastic tread with which ten years ago Lilias Armour used to speed to kirk and market—or, as we have seen her, scatter the morning dew on her way to bring home the kye.

The Loch of Grannoch slept blue and unruffled beneath her. The bell heather was just beginning to redden the Crae Hill opposite with a blush which showed most in the wet-shot hollows and bieldly lirks of the broad, leonine flank opposite to her.

Lilias Mac Walter breathed the summer air with a feeling of restfulness. Even at Kirkoswald she would have the house and garden to herself till nightfall of this long July day. And then—well, then she would take up again the heavy burden of her life.

So far she had followed a rough cart-track, which in the days when the onstead of Black Dornal was being built had been used for bringing down the quarried whinstone to the masons. From this point she had to follow a more winding path, roughly sketched out among the heather by the feet of the rare passer-by.

At the end of the cart-track there was a disused quarry whence the whinstone had come.

Some curious instinct, perhaps a sense of the nearness of a human being, made her go and look over the brink. Or perhaps it was only a waft of her far-off unforgotten childhood when she used to frequent that quarry hole and play with her brothers upon its margin, that blew her thither as a chance breeze blows a leaf.

She thought upon the old sweet days as she went, the days before any told her that she was beautiful—and before *he* came.

In spring, when the floods were out, and a black February filled the dyke with rainwater, she had often repaired thither to make a raft of old gates and pailing stobs along with her brothers, a vessel as wet as a modern torpedo boat, but which yet bore them safely over the black water only to wreck them on the rocks at the further side, against which the wavelets of the tiny tarn clappered and fell back dismayed. In summer she had found on its perilous ledges rock-rose and purple scabious, meadowsweet also in the little green valley through which the waste waters of the quarry trickled, with rest-harrow and field pimpernel above—the last burning, as usual, small red holes in the landscape. She remembered them all, and just where they grew.

At any rate, whatever the cause, she lifted her skirts and, with the old daintiness of step, went a little out of her way in order to look over into the quarry.

The margin on which she stood sloped perilously down, and the water slept black below, leaden and dead even on this glorious day of highest summer. But opposite there was the little green bank she knew so well, nodding with fern and queen-of-the-meadow.

On this lay a man all huddled together, a common tramp as it seemed, his clothes muddy and travel-stained, his hat of the cheapest straw, with a top that lifted like a lid and permitted a shock of greying hair to peep through. The man had obviously lain where he had fallen, for the bracken was untrampled, save in the one spot which was disfigured by that inert and unsightly body. A narrow trail, already half closed, showed the path by which the man had staggered in to rest himself on the margin of the water.

His face, upturned to the full blaze of the afternoon sun, showed mottled and blotched, every feature blunted and made grotesque by sotting intemperance, the very face which one may see among the hangers-on of many a stableyard and low bar entrance. Yet there was something else there also—some vague reminiscence of other and better things. The uncovered brow was broad and high, the features in themselves, cleared of their clouding disfigurement, excellent and even handsome, the mouth well shaped and delicate. The beard and moustache, though tangled and unkept, were yet fitted to be a glory of strength to a man.

Lilias Mac Walter stood looking down upon the huddled mass beneath her. No pulse of recognition warned her that she had ever seen or known the man who lay thus inert and unconscious at her feet. But a feeling of compassion, the instinct of one who also has suffered and sinned, and yet after all won her way through, impelled her to go down.

She would draw the man a little from the water to a place of safety. She might perhaps shelter him from the sun under that bush of alder a foot or two further back. At all events she would try.

A branch of the masking tanglement of brake and sweet gale above him half hid his features, though the meaning of the mottled complexion had been only too evident.

Bending, she moved it aside and started up with a quick cry, her hands stretched out before her in a kind of horror.

For there beneath her, his eyes slowly waking blinkingly to the outer world, lay the man whose wife Lilias Armour had once believed herself to be—Christopher Kennedy, sometime classical master in the grammar-school of Cairn Edward.

The man drew himself slowly up, first upon his elbow, then to a sitting posture with his arm set for support on the quarry's edge.

The blank July sun, shining brilliantly in his deeply-sunken eyes, blinded him for a minute, and he raised his unoccupied arm uncertainly to his brow as if to ward off a blow. Then by degress he seemed to take in the woman's figure standing above him, and the face that looked down upon him, till as he gazed his own blotched and mottled features blanched to an even grey.

"Lilias, little Lilias Armour!" he gasped. "I thought you were dead—surely they told me you were dead, Lilias!"

The tired woman stood still, grasping the clinging black skirts of her gown as if meditating flight.

"Do you not hear? They told me you were dead," he repeated peevishly; "I tell you I believed them. Do you not believe me?"

The soul of Lilias Mac Walter went whirling through a chaos of deadly thoughts and imminent terrors. She had no fear for herself, and she cared little for what her husband might say. But the boy she had left behind her down at the Black Dornal? What if this man should claim him, steal him, pervert him, make him even as himself?

Gradually out of the vortex two things rose up plainly before her mind.

She must get this drunkard out of the neighbourhood at any cost to herself, and Kit Kennedy must never know that such a man was his father. So with the wit which comes to much-tried women, so soon as they formulate distinct purpose within themselves, the words were given to her and she spoke.

"Christopher Kennedy," she said, with some of her father's manner, "what do you seek here? Why do you come back to the Black Dornal after all these years?"

The drunkard laughed with a feeble deprecation and waggled his hand amicably. The drink was leaving him rapidly, but the horror of inward emptiness and the rankling serpent's teeth that succeed debauch were biting into his very soul.

"No harm—no harm," he answered; "to get away from myself chiefly. Food, clothing, a straw loft to sleep in—these content me. I am a plain man dwelling in tents—I mean barns and lodging-houses—these days. You have not forgiven me, Lilias, I can see? Yet I think you would if you knew half I've been through since my creditors made me leave Cairn Edward at the run. I had not time even to say 'good-bye,' Lilias, but I meant to send for you—I did, indeed. But for a while I had no money and things went all awry. And then they told me you were dead!"

He paused as he came to the end of this speech, and scanned her face with a certain wistfulness for any answering sentiment.

"No," he said, without resentment or disappointment, "you have not forgiven me. And I can't wonder. Eight years ago I was a baddish sort of an egg, I admit. But I've suffered for it. And you, eh—still going on in the same old way? Your father still alive? Down on me deader than knives he was, cursed me like what's-his-name wading into the priests of Baal before he knifed them."

"My father is still alive," said Lilias, briefly.

Christopher Kennedy smiled fatuously and held out his hand for her to help him to rise. But as she apparently looked through it, he examined that member carefully on both sides as if he had never remarked it before and was wondering whence it could have come.

"Ah, that is better," he said; "you've gone off a bit in looks yourself, you know, Lilias—time, wear-and-tear and so on. But you are well dressed and prosperous-looking. Had a lot of sweethearts since Christopher Kennedy used to come from over the hills and far away to see you, when Phœbus bids arise——"

"I have been married four years!" said Lilias Mac Walter, with curt directness. "I am on my way home now!"

"What!" cried the man, with a little wince as if he had been stricken on the face by an unseen hand, "married? You cannot be married. You and I were married. You cannot have forgotten. Why, poor French and that maid of yours (a piece she was!) witnessed it, and French wrote out the lines—wrote them in style, too."

Without the least feeling in her face Lilias Mac Walter eyed the man, who now stood up unsteadily on his feet, with one hand on the stem of the alder bush. As he stammered his shambling sentences she confronted him with a calmness which astonished herself.

"Perhaps you never heard of Mary Bisset, daughter of Alexander Bisset, of Ship Row, in the town and parish of Sandhaven?" she said, quoting readily a name and style that was graven upon her heart. She had often wondered what Mary Bisset was like and what became of her.

"Mary Bisset," said the man, doubtfully, passing his hand across his brow, as if to clear his mind and keep it from wandering; "yes, yes—certainly I knew Mary Bisset when I was a lad. That was the bonny fisher lass that Walter Mac Walter——"

"Do not lie to me again, Christopher Kennedy," said the woman; "the man you name is my husband."

"Your husband—Walter Mac Walter?" the sobered drunkard almost gasped. Then he recovered himself, and for the first time a spasm of anger crossed his face. "Curse him! He has crossed me twice. Let Walter Mac Walter have a care. There is still something here that can strike!"

He brought his hand with a large gesture down upon his breast, a movement which in such a wreck of a man appeared merely pitiful. Then he turned swiftly upon the woman.

"Aye," he cried, in a shrill, wavering voice, "and you, Lilias—you are twice married, and your husbands both alive. Bigamy, that's the name for it. It has an ugly sound. They give ten years for bigamy, Lilias Kennedy, *alias* Lilias Mac Walter."

The woman smiled bitterly.

"It is Christopher Kennedy, not Lilias Mac Walter, who stands within the danger of that," she said, with a chill scorn. "Think rather of Mary Bisset, whom you married and deserted, as afterwards you married and deserted me. That marriage made a plaything of my marriage lines—and broke my heart as well!"

"I—marry Mary Bisset," cried Christopher Kennedy in blank astonishment, "why, it was Walter——"

He stopped suddenly, as if he had found that way blocked and had perforce to try another.

"But after all why should I fret you?" he said; "I am derelict, castaway, bound for the darkness, and he who would keep me blind and insensible till I die would be my best friend. Yes, yes, of course I married Mary Bisset. But long, long ago, poor thing, has Mary Bisset been in her resting-grave, as says old Patrick the Pedlar. Forgive me, Lilias, I had forgotten for the moment. I forget all things now!"

He steadied himself on his feet, and lifting stiffly

a bundle done up in a blue handkerchief, and a well-worn stick which lay among the sedges where he had fallen, he addressed himself to the path over the hill.

Lilias Mac Walter walked silently by his side till they came to the crest of the moorland where they had parted that summer morning eight years ago. Then with one accord they stopped, and facing about looked at each other. The man retained his grey pallor. The marked blotches were now scarcely visible. The puffy swelling beneath the eyes had fallen in, and instead of the rubicund countenance, purple as a plum, the withered skin hung loosely about a haggard and desperate face.

"Forty years of age this day, Lilias," he said, smiling; "it was luck that brought us together on my birthday. Say that you forgive me before I go. You will never see me again."

A sudden light of joy flashed into full glow over the woman's weary face.

"Ah," he said, sadly, "that makes you glad, does it! Once the thought of it would have brought the tears starting from your eyes."

"I do forgive you, God knows," she said, gently, "but now, go. And God Himself keep and forgive you, and bring you to better things than these!"

"Do not fear. I have made me like a brute and worse, but I am not brutal; I will betake me far enough away out of your sight, that a respectable woman like Mistress Mac Walter of Kirkoswald may never again be offended by the sight of that which I have made of myself."

He looked down with a curiously sheepish air, and rubbed a boot through which a stockingless toe looked with broadly farcical effect, in the dust of the little turn of highway where the cart-track of the quarry ended.

"You do not happen to have any money about you?" he ventured, looking slyly sideways at her. Lilias started, and put her hand into her pocket.

"You will not drink it?" she said, quaveringly

She felt that she could not refuse. Yet what could a promise mean from Christopher Kennedy?

"No," he said, firmly. Then, with a weakening of the voice, "That is, I will try not."

Lilias Mac Walter took out her purse.

"For the boy's sake," she murmured to herself; "I cannot afford to quarrel with him."

There were two pounds in the purse and some silver. She put one of the notes in his shaking palm. His eyes were fixed on the other in her unshut purse.

"You will go away if I give you this?" she queried, her mind divided between hope and fear. "You will promise to go straight to Cairn Edward and to-morrow to Dumfries if I give you this other? It is all I have."

"I swear it," said the drunkard. And he meant to keep his word.

As Christopher Kennedy took the second pound from her hand he gripped her fingers and held them a moment in his. For the space of a heart's beat she tried to withdraw them. But finally she let them remain.

"For the boy's sake!" she thought in the ashen deeps of her heart.

"*Vive memor amoris nostri—et vale!*" said Christopher Kennedy in his old drolling voice, but with a firm grip of his fingers upon hers.

"What does that mean?" said the woman, just as she used to do.

"It means 'Good-bye, and do not quite forget'!" he said, and let her hand drop. He looked at her a long while before saying another word. "The fire is burned out. And the ashes of it have made all the waters bitter. Marah—Marah, let them be called! For they are exceeding bitter!"

And again he made the large gesture of one who sows the wind.

"Good-bye!" she said, simply. And with bowed head she took her way towards the distant bunch of trees, under which nestled the mansion-house of

Kirkoswald, its frontage all aglitter with plate-glass and dusky with red sandstone.

The man stood watching her as she went down the moor edges. He watched her as she came to the stile at the head of the old grass parks. His eyes did not leave her for a moment till she became a black dot scarce discernible above the green of the corn, and so passed on towards the house.

When she had vanished finally from his sight, Christopher Kennedy lifted his hand and kissed it towards her with something of his old graceful manner.

"Why should you bear the burden, Love Lilias," he said, "when such a wreck as I am can bear it for you?"

He turned again at the top of the hill, and looked once more at the green clump of trees behind which Kirkoswald was hidden.

"*Ave atque vale!*" said the classical master; "being (as I hope) about to die—my love, I salute you!"

His hand stole to his pocket. He fingered the two notes, and as he did so his mood changed. "Now, I wonder where the nearest public-house is?" he added.

For the classical master had once more become the tramp.

CHAPTER V.

THE RED LION.

IT was six o'clock at the hostelry of the Red Lion in the village of Whinnyliggate. This well-known inn was held, as all must know, by the Misses Barbara and Keturah Heartshorn. The village had long boasted of but one house of public refreshment, and the Red Lion, a comfortable two-story house, with a commodious yard behind enclosed on three sides by stabling and barns, was that one.

It had been left equally to his two daughters by Job Heartshorn, a man from the Anglican fenland who having wandered to Galloway to buy cattle, had lived to amass a very cosy little fortune by stabling other people's.

Miss Barbara Heartshorn, the elder of the sisters, was tall, many angled, muscular, and withal somewhat assertive. Her sister Keturah, on the other hand, was persuasive, yielding, and carried the easy evenness of her temper reflected on a plumply smiling face.

The elder sister drilled the company in her parlours as a sergeant breaks in an awkward squad. The younger brought them good measure on the sly. Thus was the hostelry of the Red Lion carried on with a success far greater than that obtained by any other in four neighbouring parishes, and so busy were its present owners and occupiers in conducting it that they had reached middle life without even having had time to think of marrying. Miss Barbara usually acknowledged any approach to familiar and personal discourse on love and matrimony with a sound box on the ear of the speaker, to which was added an admonition to " Mind now!" While as for Miss Keturah, though doubtless she had listened to much lovemaking in the course of her life, and turned the dimples of her rosy cheeks and a pair of not unappreciative ears to the charming of many male serpents, she stood too much in awe of the indignation of her sister, and was too afraid of hurting the Red Lion by deserting the colours, to permit matters to go any further.

Besides, the younger sister had not forgotten the awful occasion when Archibald Girmory (commonly known as Big Bauldy), the farmer of High Creochs, had informed her for the fiftieth time that she was the " heartsomest, bonniest, most tasty bit lassie in a' the countryside."

In her bed at night she still flushed to remember how upon their startled ears had broken the voice of her sister Barbara: "Keturah Heartshorn, I bid you remember that praise to the face is an open disgrace. Come your ways ben the hoose this minute and peel the potatoes!"

  *   *   *   *   *

In order to preserve the immaculate character of the house, the sisters had added an outer bar-room at the back within call of the ostler on duty in the yard and stables. This was reserved for " transients "—that is, guests who had not the "freedom of the parlour " and who might not aspire to that comfortable inner room in which, during the forenight, Miss Keturah might occasionally sit down with her crocheting, and even Miss Barbara herself deign to stand a moment with a tray in her hand, ere she hurried to another apartment to dispense stores or lay down the law.

To the Red Lion therefore came the tramp in the lidded straw hat, the same who earlier in the afternoon had lain in the quarry hole on the muir above Black Dornal. He had cleansed some of the mud off his clothes, yet his appearance was even more desolate and forlorn than when Lilias Mac Walter had come upon him sleeping under the alder-bush.

But—he had two pounds in his pocket.

He limped thankfully into the outer room, bare of board, severely furnished with bench set along the wall and round the small central table. At one end was a zinc-covered bar, shining like silver, and a square spy-hole through which liquors were served and at which appeared upon occasion the dimpling cheeks of Miss Keturah, or, with a stern rapping of steel knife handle, the reproving and obedience-compelling visage of her elder sister.

It was to the latter that the tramp appealed.

"Whisky, indeed? Bread and cheese will set ye better, my lad. Keturah, a pennyworth of bread and cheese for a gaun chiel in the outer parlour. What—drink ye will have also? You can pay for it? Well, if you can, and that honestly, it consorts but ill with your onputting. Yet, after all, we keep a house of public entertainment, and we cannot be choosers any more than the beggars. But keep the peace, my lad, or out you go from the Red Lion, money or no money. And mind ye that, no swaggerers within my doors! There shall be no complaint of unruly house or noisy brawling go forth from this house so long as I am its mistress. I speak for Keturah also!"

She added the last clause as an after-thought.

The tramp's hand mechanically sought the brim of his battered hat with a grace which to Miss Barbara's experienced eye instantly betrayed that too common type, the "man who had seen better days." He was therefore more than ever a man to be suspected, to be watched, to be got out of the way of her sister. For to such Miss Keturah was often both over-kind and unwisely liberal.

"Madam," said the tramp, courteously, "you need not fear that I shall not behave myself in your house."

"See that ye do, then!" was Miss Barbara's un-compromising retort, as, having filled the order, she shut down the panel of the bar with a decisive snap and went to see what her sister Keturah was doing.

Presently in the outer parlour of the Red Lion, as

the "casual" room was called by a very latitudinarian
courtesy of language, gathered a large and, for Whinnyliggate, a most representative company.

At the corner of the deal table there sat, by
immemorial right, Geordie Breerie the packman, a man
fully as broad as he was long, with a face smoothed
and jollified with good living, and made russet and
purple by exposure to many a summer sun and winter
gale. His huge pack stood in the corner, done up in
black American cloth, flaccid and inert, with a comical
lurch forward of its upper part, out of which he had
extracted a number of dress pieces to show Miss
Keturah, when Miss Barbara should happen to be out
of the way—an opportunity which had not yet
occurred.

Geordie Breerie, it was reported among his professional brethren, could frighten the fiercest dog in Scotland, and that by a very simple plan. As he walked
along the packman presented a very curious appearance.
First and nearest the ground there were two short and
thick legs, squat like the props of a corn stack. Next
came an equally short but much thicker body, as nearly
square, indeed, as might be. ("A big sack o' cauf
(chaff) on the tap o' twa wee sacks o' cauf," was the
description of Geordie by a local humourist.) Then,
driven by the weight and height of his pack almost into
the middle of his body, came Geordie's head, crowned
by its broad blue bonnet. While above all, black and
square, towered the pack, the whole combination being
enough to drive the most unsuspicious farm dog into
hysterics of rage and noisy denunciation.

Nevertheless, George Breerie was never harmed. He
had a way of bending himself double from the thigh
and looking through between his legs at his barking
enemy, which was more effective than a field piece
loaded to the muzzle.

For so soon as that vast purple face and bristling red
hair appeared upside down between Geordie's legs, and
the whole apparition began to approach backwards
"like a partan," the bravest and most reckless collie

tucked tail inward like a steel spring, and stood no longer upon the order of his going.

On this and other counts Geordie was an important person in the outer parlour of the Red Lion, and was, besides, the only man who dared to hammer on the table with his pint stoup to call the attention of the austere divinity behind the veil.

Upon his frequent visits to the Red Lion Geordie presumed a little upon being the only person at whose jests Miss Barbara had ever been known to laugh, and he derived much consolation from the distinction, even building a little upon it in confidential converse with his cronies.

"I tell ye what, Geordie, ye will stan' at the back o' that coonter some day yet," Rab Irvine the journey-man smith, would say, jocularly. "The auld runt Babby is fell fond o' ye, that's plain to everybody. Did ye no see what a laugh she took to hersel' when ye gied the table siccan a drive wi' your neive that ye spilled the jug o' tippenny doon your breeks. It was fair compromisin', yon."

"O no so verra," said Geordie, much flattered; "the like micht hae happened to ony body, even yoursel', Rab, though you haena' my personal advantages. A weel-made unmarried man has his privileges—as is weel-kenned."

"Aye, aye, it's a sair warl' ony way ye tak' it!" said Rab Irvine, shaking his head with feeling mournfulness. "Did ye hear that my brither Tam's wife was deid!"

"But what for need ye fret aboot that?" asked Geordie Breerie, resentfully. He was angry that the subject should be changed, for he liked nothing better than to be joked about Miss Barbara Heartshorn and his chances of one day becoming landlord of the Red Lion.

Rab Irvine shook his head still more lugubriously.

"It's no that," he said, "it's no that ava! She was a besom, and Tam's well rid o' her. But what gars me greet is juist that everybody is gettin' a change but me!"

CHAPTER VI.

LILIAS ARMOUR'S TWO HUSBANDS.

THE tramp sat in the corner most remote from observation. He did not wish to be recognised—though, indeed, there was no one in the company who had known him when he was classical master in the Academy of Cairn Edward. Nor was it likely that any one of his ancient cronies would recognise in the ragged tramp the smartly-attired young college man who had fluttered the hearts of many an orthodox civic dovecot by a careless wave of his hand, as he took the hill road to the Black Dornal with his green botanical case over his shoulder.

"A worthy young man—a diligent young man; learned and hopeful, sure to rise!" declared the parents, peeping through the first floor blinds immediately over the shop.

"A handsome young man! Did you see how he waved his hand to me?" said the eldest daughter at the narrower windows of the floor above.

"No; it was to me!" said the younger, but secretly, thinking of certain glances exchanged at the last Choral Union.

And now the worthy young man, the handsome eye-glancer, the collector of botanical specimens, the lover of Lilias Armour, belle of six parishes, sat unknown and unknowable on a wooden bench in the outer parlour of the Red Lion, drinking by himself, none paying heed to him.

Upon this jocund company, enter a well-attired, well-groomed figure, leather-breeched, riding-whipped, blatantly assertive, floridly prosperous.

"And ye are welcome; come awa ben, sir!" cried Miss Barbara through the wicket gate, whence she spied upon her guests, and from whence she rebuked the evildoer and bade the worthy Pharisee come up to the higher seats in the Red Lion synagogue.

But Walter MacWalter was jovial from the market, and willing to stand well with the company as a free-handed, open-hearted landed proprietor.

"Thank you, Miss Barbara; presently, presently!" he answered, taking off his hat politely to the divinity within the veil, "when I have spoken with these excellent fellows here, I will accept your kind invitation!"

He opened out his coat and sat down beside Geordie Breerie, calling jovially for glasses round as he did so.

All complied with his invitation except the tramp in the dark corner, who sat moodily drinking by himself. At the first entrance of the prosperous man of means the tramp had shaded his brow with his hand, only stealthily peering at him when his back was turned.

Walter Mac Walter looked gaily round.

"Are your glasses all charged?" he cried. "All at my expense, remember. I will give you a toast—'the health of the Misses Barbara and Keturah Heartshorn!' Stop though, there is a man in the corner not standing up!"

"Hoots," said Geordie Breerie with contempt, "dinna bide for him. It's only a puir feckless gaun body that's been sittin' there tipplin' by himsel' the hale forenicht!"

"One man is as good to me as another," cried Mac Walter, whose strong suit was an affectation of republican equality; "beggar or laird, he shall never leave this house without drinking this toast. Hey, man, come to the bar and get your glass like a man. All's free when Walter Mac Walter pays."

"I would rather be excused," said the Classical Master, quietly.

"Excused! Nonsense! Drink it, man. And if you cannot rise to get it, faith I will bring it to you, and have a look at your physiognomy as well, which you hide like a bashful bride!"

And as he spoke he rose from his seat and made his way between the chairs to the corner where sat Christopher Kennedy.

The tramp bode still till his would-be entertainer was within a yard of him. His head was more deeply sunk than ever on his breast, and his eyes further retired under the shade of his brown hand.

Walter Mac Walter set his palm with rough freedom upon the man's shoulders, the whole company looking on silently to see what would happen.

Suddenly the tramp lifted his head and looked straight into Mac Walter's eyes. For a moment the two men kept their positions, giving and taking glance for glance. Then Walter Mac Walter lifted his palm from the tramp's shoulder and stood upright, with his hand still uplifted in the air. The tramp sat motionless, but did not remove the fixed intensity of his gaze from the other's face.

"Do you still wish me to drink with you?" he said, in a low, restrained voice.

Astonished and unsettled Mac Walter stammered some inarticulate explanation to the company, and then turning again to Christopher Kennedy he hissed out, "What in the fiend's name are you doing here?"

"I am drinking what I am able to pay for!" returned the tramp, without moving from his seat.

"Drunken dog!" cried Mac Walter, "for a quart of ale I would strike you as dead as——"

"As Mary Bisset!" put in the sitting man, very clearly and distinctly. There ensued a stir among the company.

"What did he say? What name did he mention?" went round the room.

Walter Mac Walter turned white under his tan, and the purple bloom produced by good marketing cheer died out of his cheek. He did not answer, but went back to the bar and faced the company.

"Gentlemen," he said, as if desirous of ignoring what had gone before, "I give you my toast again, and every well-wisher of the house will drink it—'the health and prosperity of the Misses Heartshorn!'"

The company stood up with an irregular cheer, to which followed contending shouts of "Miss Barbara" and "Miss Keturah," according to whether love of beauty or self-interest ruled their hearts.

Then every one sat down amid the awkward pause which always comes after social ebullition.

Then Mr. Mac Walter of Kirkoswald rapped on the door which led from the outer to the inner parlour through the bar which separated the two. Miss Barbara opened it for him. He passed within and the company were left to themselves. They whispered low one to the other, and many were the glances directed to the corner where the tramp sat. Presently he went to refill his glass, and being asked to settle his score he tendered one of the pound notes in payment.

Through the little wicket every eye followed the crackling paper to its destination in the till, and took in the jingle of the change as it dropped nonchalantly into the tramp's pocket. Suspicion sat lowering on every brow, and a cabal was instantly formed at the centre table to find out where this very doubtful character came from, and how he happened to be in possession of so much money as a whole undivided pound note.

"Mair than a well-to-do-man can make in a week about fairtime," said Geordie Breerie; "it's clean impossible he can hae come by it honestly."

"We'll hear news o' this yet!" said Rab Irvine, nodding his head sagely.

"I wadna wonder gin he will hae murdered somebody and sunk their body in a moss hole. He's a' ower glaur!" whispered the road-man, by name "Gleyed" Charlie, who had imagination.

"Stealed it oot o' some decent man's pooch, mair like. A craitur like yon wadna hae the pluck to murder onybody!" retorted Geordie Breere, who liked to have the monopoly of wisdom in any company.

But they were soon to hear news of the pound note, as Rab Irvine had predicted.

Even as they were speaking the inner door opened, and Miss Barbara stood in it, tall and imposing. She held a pound note in her hand. Behind her could be seen the sturdy, prosperous figure of Mac Walter, with several other statutory occupants of the bar-parlour. Every eye except those of the tramp was fixed upon her. Not a jaw but dropped in expectation, nor a rustic mouth which was not opened in a universal gape. But the tramp alone sat in his corner with his hand again above his brow. He fingered his glass with the air of a man who has been accustomed to wear dress clothes and toy with a glass of port after dinner.

"Let the doors be closed," cried the hostess. "Davit Dick, are ye there?"

"Aye, Miss Barbara," came from the other side of the entrance which communicated with the stable yard, and the shoulder of the ostler was heard rubbing against the panels without.

"Are ye armed, Davit?"

"I hae the hay-fork!" came the answer. "I'll no let a leevin' sowl gang by!"

"It is well," said Miss Barbara, solemnly, with the air of a judge pronouncing sentence.

"I have here a pound note which has been handed over the bar by some one of this company. Bell Kirkpatrick, my servant, took it, and I changed it. But the careless limmer says that she cannot identify the man that gave it into her hand at the bar. No one has left the room since this took place. I demand to know who tendered this pound note, and who received seven half-crowns and some coppers in change?"

The tramp stood up in his corner, thrusting back as he did so the small round table on which he had been leaning.

"The note in question was mine," he said, quietly.

"It is stolen—seize him instantly," commanded Miss

Barbara, while her sister caught her arm and besought
her to come in and shut the door, lest the thief should
murder them all. And indeed for a moment or two it
looked like it. For the tramp swept the high-backed
wooden bench on which he had been sitting round in
front of him, and drawing a long sheath knife out of
his pocket, he opened it with a vicious click.

"The note was mine," he said, "honestly obtained
from a friend. I am innocent, and will not be taken.
Let the first man approach at his peril."

Walter Mac Walter stepped in front of Miss Barbara
Heartshorn.

"Gentlemen," he said, "the pound note which I see
in Miss Barbara's hand is mine. I had it in my pocket
when I came in. The man must have stolen it from
me as I stood speaking to him, asking him to drink the
toast which I had the honour to propose to you. I
remember now that I felt a twitch at my pocket, and
looked down, but could see nothing. If, as he says, the
note came honestly into his possession, let him give us
the name of the kind friend who supplied a ragged
tramp with so much money."

"Aye, let him tell us," cried many hangers-on about
the room.

"That I can easily do, if you desire it," said the
tramp, standing up with a certain dignity behind his
defences. "It was given me by——"

He hesitated before giving the name. A vision of the
piteous face of Lilias Armour when she had spoken of
her husband came upon him.

"I will *not* tell the name of the friend from whom I
got the money," he said; "that concerns no one here
except myself alone!"

A great shout of ridicule swept up from the inner to
the outer parlour of the Red Lion as the men heard
his answer.

"A likely story, friends," sneered Walter Mac
Walter, "he will not tell. He stands upon his honest
character. Well, listen, I can prove this note to be
mine. Miss Barbara, will you tell the company what is

marked with a printed date-stamp in the left-hand corner of the back?"

Miss Barbara deliberately took her spectacles out of their worn shagreen case, and mounted them with circumspection upon her nose.

"There is printed upon the note the letters W. Mac W. 1. VII. 18—," she said.

Walter Mac Walter nodded with a satisfied expression.

"I can prove that that is my ordinary way of marking with my initials and a date every note that comes into my possession. I have a sheaf of notes similarly stamped in my pocket. I cannot have stamped them since I came here, for my dye is on my study table at Kirkoswald. Again I demand this thief shall tell us from whom he obtained this note marked with my name and style—that is, if he can clear himself of this charge."

"I decline to answer," said the tramp, throwing down his knife upon the little table.

At this point Rob Irvine bravely and nobly kicked it underneath, and secured the weapon after it had rolled ringing upon the floor.

"Seize him, hold him!" cried the village tailor, getting as far behind the others as he could, but being as usual most valorous and even vain-glorious with his mouth.

The tramp stood with his hands behind him.

Then the entire company, led by Walter Mac Walter, rushed upon him and threw him by mere weight upon the floor. They held his hands; they knelt upon his poor hollow chest; their hands explored his pockets.

"Hurrah," cried the big packman, who had become suddenly prominent as soon as he saw the tramp on the floor, "I hae gotten anither ane, and here's the same mark—Mr. Mac Walter's ain stamp on the corner!"

They raised him to his feet, and the prisoner stood swaying, held erect by a dozen hands. A thin stream of red was flowing from his mouth.

"Now," said Walter Mac Walter, standing before the captive, truculently, "will you or will you not confess your theft, or tell us from whom you received these notes?"

"I will do neither," said the tramp. "I cannot. A theft I never committed; and I will not tell from whom I received them, for it is no business of yours!"

CHAPTER VII.

A Woman Despised and Forsaken.

There was a certain power which Lilias Mac Walter
had over her husband, a power all the more effective
because she was unconscious of exercising it.

Her strength was the strength of the Quiet Eye.

It was this which met and countered him as he came
to the hall door of the house of Kirkoswald, heated
after company, hectoring with victory, and eager to
begin one of those quarrels of recrimination in which
he could vent upon his wife his furious jealousy of her
past, and his hatred of the boy at the Black Dornal.

Walter Mac Walter was a man nominally generous,
outwardly freehanded, a man anxious for popularity,
who was yet conscious that he stood naked and bare
before his wife's eye, maskless, pretenceless, without
chiaroscuro or perspective, revealed as pitilessly as a
geometrical drawing in which meanness and brutality
have been reduced to lines and letters.

Lilias was sewing in the little parlour when Walter
Mac Walter trampled in, his brows red with the angry
jamming of his hat upon them, as he rode over from
Whinnyliggate after seeing the thief locked up for the
night in the single cell of which the village constabulary
could boast.

He had meant to begin with the question, "Where
are those two pounds which I gave you this morning?"
The words had been on his lips all the way home. But
when his wife looked up from her work something
sprang from her eye, and for that time at least the
insult was shut within him. The quarrel must run
upon other lines.

"Well, are you glad to see me?" he cried. "It does not look very like it. I suppose there are many others you would welcome more effusively than your husband?"

"I am glad you have come," said Lilias Mac Walter, quietly, rising to put away her work. "Will you have supper now?"

"I do not want any supper. I want to talk," said her husband. "Do you know that it is poor cheer for a man to come back to a home like this, a wife like you, and a welcome as cold as dead fish on an ice block?"

"I am sorry I do not please you, Walter," said his wife slowly, without, however, looking at him. "I will try to amend."

He was growing rapidly angry, his own evil temper finding fuel in the expression of itself in words. His mood of elated triumph had passed.

"If I had known what a wife you would have made, I should never have come near you. I declare to heaven I would not," he cried, striding up and down. "And I should have let the bond take its course. I would have bankrupted your canting dog of a father. But I listened to your mother. You were young. You were pretty. Yes, I thought so years ago. You had been ill-used by a villain. You would forget it, your mother told me. Your heart would turn fully to me. Well, I did what not one man in a hundred would have done. I married you—I, a landed proprietor, a man against whom nothing could be alleged. On the wedding day I handed your father the bond on his farm and stock. I wish to God I had sold him up and sent you all to the workhouse. It would have been better for both of us!"

"Better for me, certainly, Walter," she made answer, "for you paid money for that which money cannot purchase. Coined gold can buy the body of a woman, but not her soul. I promised you nothing else than that which you have obtained."

"Your love would answer mine in time, so your mother assured me. Other children would take your mind from the brat at Black Dornal. Heavens, how

I have been cheated! Your heart is still with the blackguard who deceived you. You run over every spare hour to see that nameless loon at your father's."

"The boy is not nameless; he has his father's name," said Lilias Mac Walter, quietly; "that he has not a right to it is no fault of his or mine. All these things you knew long before you married me. And if I love my son, is it not natural? But a childless man cannot understand the feelings of a parent."

The man flushed at the low-spoken words. He took them as a taunt.

"You are laughing at me," he cried, clenching his fist and striding over to where she stood; "woman, take care! Some have laughed at Walter Mac Walter who have lived to regret it. Others have not even lived to repent. One of the former is your lover. He rests in a prison cell to-night because he laughed at your husband."

He watched her keenly, but Lilian's face did not betray her. Its grave quiet had grown with suffering and repression into something like her father's calm. It made the brutal man long to strike her down. Once, but only once, had he done so during their ill-starred wedded life.

Seeing that she did not mean to answer he began again.

"Yes, Christopher Kennedy is in gaol for stealing. And as I know the sheriff personally, I will see to it that he gets a long sentence. He will do well if he escape the assizes and seven years."

Once more Walter Mac Walter had it on his tongue-tip to ask concerning the pound notes. But with the cunning of hate he discerned that it would be more bitter to Lilias Armour to know that her former lover, the man whom she had once believed to be her husband, was suffering for her act, while for very shame she was unable to speak the word which would clear him.

The woman rose, still without making answer, and began to remove the unused supper. Her husband threw himself down in a chair, miscalled an easy chair,

4

of black and shiny haircloth. He lit a short black pipe and puffed vigorously, watching his wife all the time out of his small, deeply-set eyes.

Presently he grunted, thrust his fingers into the bowl of his pipe, and turned the red-hot contents out upon the polished mahogany of the dining table. Then he capped it, and thrust it still hot into his waistcoat pocket.

Without a word more he trampled noisily up the stairs, and along the passage to his bedroom. She heard the door slam loudly. Then came the click of the lock as she stood with the bread tray in her hands listening. The tang of a coarse and brutal presence hung about the room, together with the fumes of a tobacco scarcely less crude. Lilias threw up the windows and opened the outer door. Then she sat down in the window seat, and looked long into the dusk of the summer night.

At the persuasion of her mother she had consented to marry Walter Mac Walter—to save her father (as it was put to her) and the old place of Dornal. She did not regret her act, only the price had been longer in the paying than she had expected. After the desertion of Christopher Kennedy and the birth of her boy she had not expected to live. But Death comes not to those who most desire him, and her father had tended her with grave and deep affection during the days of darkness which were so many. He had laid his hand upon the boy's head, and promised that he should be to him even as one of his own. So to marry Walter Mac Walter seemed the only thing that she could do for her family, and she did it.

But now trouble had come upon her to make the way more difficult. Christopher Kennedy had returned, like a ghost out of the darkness which had swallowed him. He was accused of stealing the money she had given him, and being the wreck he was he would doubtless reveal from whom he had received the money. She would be called upon to testify. For herself or even her husband she cared little. Nothing could make matters much worse at Kirkoswald. But her father—and the boy. She could see the look on the Elder's face if he were to hear of it, and the disgrace would cling to her son through life.

Out of the open window she could hear the birds calling fitfully on the moors, and the sound went to her lonely heart with a sense of kinship. She rose, closed the window and went upstairs, dry-eyed and stony cold.

When she had been Christopher Kennedy's sweetheart she had wept for nothing at all. Now that she was Walter Mac Walter's wife nothing could make her weep.

*　　　*　　　*　　　*

The Sheriff Substitute of the Stewartry sat easily in his official chair. He had seen to it that it was a comfortable chair.

"If I must sit here and make my bread by listening to liars," he was wont to remark—"no, I do not mean lawyers—I may as well sit easy."

Sheriff Nicoll was a man of parts, of wit and of heart, accounted the soundest lawyer and the best company for a hundred miles. He was kindly and shrewd, filled also with charity and understanding. Not a poacher but felt a certain community of sentiment between himself and the Sheriff as he stood before him.

"Shure an' it's your hanour that knows the rules," said Mick Donelly, who was up for having in his possession four pheasants of which he could give no better account than that they had "flewn agin' a telegraft wire," and that "to keep down sour reek" he had put them in his pocket. "And ye won't be hard on a poor man, for shure manny's the dainty long-tail your hanour has wiled from the branch when the moon was in the sky!"

"I wad raither tak' a month 'with' frae yersel'—I declare to a merciful Providence—than three days '_withoot_' frae Sherra Howp, the ill-stammacked, soor-faced reprobate that he is!" was the verdict of Mary Purdie, as she stood up to receive her sixty-fifth conviction for behaving in a riotous manner (under the

influence) and resisting the police in the exercise of
their duty.

And Mary ought to have been an authority upon the
subject.

The windows of the Sheriff's court looked up the
long street of St. Cuthbert's Town. The court sat at
ten o'clock, and the tramp was brought in with several
casual cases from Cairn Edward and Urrston.

As soon as the court had been opened the tramp
spoke out in the voice of an educated man.

"Your honour, I am anxious that my case should be
taken first. Is it in order that I be tried now?"

"Who may you be that are in such a hurry—John
Smith your name is, I see by the sheet. Fiscal, what
has John been doing? Stealing two pounds. That is
serious, John. Well, John Smith, we may as well get
it over soon as syne!"

"The chief witness, Mr. Walter Mac Walter, is not
yet in court," objected the Procurator Fiscal.

"He will be here in a moment," said the Sheriff,
easily; "I saw him at the King's Arms with his wife."

A tremor of anxiety passed over the shattered frame
of the accused.

"I do not want any evidence led," he said; "I plead
guilty to the charge!"

The Sheriff leaned forward in astonishment.

"Did I understand you to say that you plead guilty
to having stolen these two pound notes here produced
from the pocket of Mr. Mac Walter in the parlour of
the Red Lion in the village of Whinnyliggate?"

"I plead guilty!" said the tramp, with his eye
anxiously cast up the long High-street of St. Cuthbert's.
He could see a woman coming down it alone, a woman
slender and clad in black, yet with a certain swing in
her carriage and a set of the head which even yet came
back to him in his dreams.

"Well," mused the Sheriff, "this is your first offence,
John. The police know nothing against you except
that you are overfond of the bottle. The fondness is
not uncommon among all classes" (here the Sheriff

sighed). "The only difference is that we don't all put our hands into our neighbours' pockets. I am willing to believe that you had a drop too much that night, and your frank confession takes me by surprise, and— would you like it 'with' or 'without'?—I prefer 'with' myself; you get better food and more of it."

"With? Then I think three months will meet the case. Officer, remove the prisoner. Ah, Mary! you haven't been here for two whole months. I was missing you, Mary. What is it this time, Mary?"

But ere he could take up Mary Purdie's sixty-sixth breach of the peace Lilias Mac Walter had entered the court.

"My lord," she began, breathlessly, "there is a mistake. I know this man, I——"

But she got no further. She was stopped by the convicted criminal.

"The lady is mistaken," he said, firmly; "she means to be kind. But she is entirely mistaken. I never set eyes on her before!"

"I am afraid that the case is settled," said the Sheriff, kindly. "But be quite at ease, Mrs. Mac Walter. John Smith pled guilty, and I let him off easily. I can quite understand your regret that your husband should, by his careless habit of carrying notes loose in his overcoat pocket, have thrown temptation in this poor man's way. I daresay he had a drop too much, and in any case he has got the benefit of the doubt. May we all get the same when our time comes; God knows we shall need it! Next, Fiscal."

Such was the ordinary course of justice in the very informal tribunal presided over by Sheriff Nicoll.

CHAPTER VIII.

HEATHER JOCK AND HIS BILLY-O.

HEATHER JOCK lived at the Back o' Beyont. Jock's name was baptismally John Kinstrae, but he had so long borne the appellation of Heather Jock that he actually started when any one called him John. And it is on record that when a new minister with a copy of the communion roll in his pocket asked him by the wayside where "Mr. Kinstrae" lived, Jock replied, "Fegs, sir, I dinna ken him—he's no a here-aboots man!"

Jock's business in life was the manufacture of heather "besoms," otherwise brooms. With these he supplied the good wives of half the Stewartry, and had been known to venture as far as Wigtonshire with his produce. Here, however, he found his goods out of line with the local taste, which preferred a shorter and scrubbier article as more generally effective.

"Awfu' pernikkety fowk as they are on the Shireside," he would say to the parliament gathered in Hutcheon's smithy at nights when the boys had set him on to tell his perilous 'scapes. "They are no content wi' giein' a pot a bit syne wi' a jaw o' water. They maun hae a scrubber made special-like for gettin' intil a' the lirks and corners. Siccan a fyke! And they caa' peas 'pays' an' peats 'pates' as if they were a' Paddies. Aye, they do that!"

To the manufacture of besoms of ling Heather Jock added some traffic in eggs and the toothsome salted mutton hams of the moorland districts. The Back o' Beyont was a solitary place, and being situated on a led farm (that is, a farm held by a non-resident farmer), Jock was permitted by the favour of his land-

lord to keep a score of black-faced sheep on the shaggy
slopes of the Yont hill. For this he was trysted to give
what help he could to the herd of the Black House o'
Beyont in lambing time, and generally to be to him a
good and not unprofitable neighbour on the face of the
moorland.

It was furthermore curious that, though according to
the revenue reports smuggling had long been as extinct
in Galloway as the cave bear or the wolf, yet nevertheless Heather Jock could produce upon occasion a
thickish beverage, oily and yellow as a liqueur, and
as fragrant of peat reek as his own homespun clothing.
Of course Heather Jock did not retail this article,
which was understood to have grand stomachic qualities.
But when a farmer or well-to-do cottier asked if it
would be possible to get a dose or two of his famous
"yerb" cordial, Heather Jock would say that fennel
and henbane were scarce this year, but, seeing it was
himsel'—why, he thought the thing could be managed.

Heather Jock had lived long all alone by himself in a
low-thatched but-and-ben cot-house, lying so close to
the brown moorland that its whereabout could only be
made out by the "pew" of blue reek which rose from the
rough chimney in the gable, to be promptly blown down
again over the heath and green "quakkin' quaas."*

At this time Heather Jock was a hearty, good-looking,
loquacious man of forty, sound as a hazel-nut out of the
Glen Wood, and keen-bitten as a dust-scattering wind of
March. He was naturally not averse from the society of
women-kind, but he had hitherto fought shy of offering
any of them the use of his name. He had never made
up to any of the country lasses, and it was one of the
recognised, and, indeed, expected jests of the glen and
strath to rally Jock on his prolonged bachelordom, and
to ask him when he thought of taking a mistress up to
the Back o' Beyont.

"Deed," he would answer, "there's fools enough up
on the muir wi' me, an' the cuddy, and Davit Caruthers

---

* Shaking bogs dangerous to cattle and wandering men.

the herd o' Yont. What need o' a woman to mak' a fourth? Aye, an' she michtna stop there. She micht maybes breed mair. I hae kenned as muckle. Na, na ; I ken what I hae, but I dinna ken what I micht get if I began thae capers."

There was no better known or gladsomer sight than Heather Jock and his donkey on all the drove-roads and farm-loanings of the Stewartry, nor one more welcome to gentle and simple alike. He had a heartsome word for everybody, and even the revenue officers who suspected him, and the tinkers whom he alternately fought and shared his bite of bread and dish of tea with, liked him and would wave their hands as soon as Heather Jock and his companion hove in sight.

Specially all children loved him. Heather Jock could clear a school green at any time.

"Wha has coupit the boy-hoose?" he would ask, as a whole village green came tagging after him and his donkey. Duncan Duncanson, deposed minister and schoolmaster in the village of Whinnyliggate, was the only man who hated the sight of Heather Jock. He knew that there would be a thin school that day and many court-martials on the morrow for the high mis-demeanour of truancy.

But in every relation of life Heather Jock was eminently a man who could be trusted. Many errands he performed that could not be given to any other. His wandering habits and uncertain purpose kept him unsuspected, and Jock, though himself not only celibate, but on the subject of his own feelings almost cynical, had carried and delivered safely more love-letters than any other dozen men in the parish.

He called regularly at the house of Kirkoswald to buy the mistress's butter and eggs, and to ask if any besoms were needed for the stable yard, any scrubbers for the kitchen, or any peesweep's eggs, cranberries, blacberries, raspberries, blackberries—all which he was prepared to supply according to the season and the abundance or scarcity of these moorland delicacies.

On such occasions he often come across the master

of the house, and Walter Mac Walter had tried
his wit and bluster against Jock's triple armour of
shrewd secrecy and unfailing good humour.   He had,
in fact, on more than one occasion ordered Jock off the
premises as a wandering gipsy fellow who could be
after no good.   But Jock, while never refusing to obey,
had so punctuated his retreat with caustic sayings, and
so revenged himself the next time he chanced to
encounter his enemy at market, kirk-door, or public
house, that Mac Walter, a man to whom popularity was
as the breath of life, had long fallen back upon valour's
better part, and now permitted Heather Jock to come
and go about Kirkoswald without notice or protest.

Lilias on every occasion interviewed Jock herself.
She neither trusted her indoor handmaid Kate nor any
of the outdoor servants to arrange matters with the
"general dealer," as Heather Jock described himself
in the census paper.

"Aye, mistress," he would say, "and that's the last
fardin' that I can allow ye for eggs.   There's a sair
glut o' them in the Dumfries market.   I declare I
think that the fowk maun be eatin' puddocks and asks.
They winna buy good honest meat, or if they buy it,
they winna pay a price for it, but expect ye to cairry it
to their doors and then pay them to tak' it aff your
hand ! "

At that moment Walter Mac Walter was passing
along the path which led from the back door at which
this colloquy took place.   He happened to be going in
the direction of the stable, and so long as he was in
ear-shot so long Heather Jock continued to denounce
the short-sighted folly and stupidity of "town-buyers."

But when there was no longer any danger of a
listening ear, Heather Jock spoke in a lower tone of
quite other matters.

"I am gaun ower by to the Black Dornal," he said.
"Ye'll maybe hae nae word to gang there, hae ye,
mistress ? "

From a small wall-cupboard Lilias produced a bundle
apparently tied up in a linen handkerchief.   At least,

there was a flash of something wrapped in white, which passed so quickly into the great inner pocket of Heather Jock's coat that no clear account of it can be given.

"And as I was sayin' to you, mistress, aboot thae eggs, it's juist no possible——"

The voice of Heather Jock took up the former topic with zest and in a high key as Mac Walter's head appeared at the stable door. Then, with a sudden confidential drop, he ran over his instructions as soon as it had again disappeared within.

"Aye, hinnie, rest ye easy in your mind. I'll see till the boy, and tell ye what like he is, a fine callant as ever ran on legs. I'll let your mither ken that ye canna come to the Dornal this week. And she shall hae the package safe frae my ain hand. Then this is Tuesday, and I'll be back by Friday on my rounds. And gin ye be at the white sands by the lochside at ten o' the clock, the bairn shall be there withouten ony fail. He will come wi' me for a word. The boy is no born that winna rin till he draps after Heather Jock and his bit cuddy."

A heavy step was heard on the gravel of the path, and with it came an alteration in Jock's tones and subject-matter.

"An' I'll be this gate on Friday, mistress, an' bring ye the siller change faithfully. And the twa crocks and the white sugar as weel—or else puir Jock will be laired in a moss-hole. It is a fine day, Maister Mac Walter, and a bonny bit ye hae here. And my service to you, mistress, and thank ye for your kindly custom."

Heather Jock took the village of Whinnyliggate on his way to the Dornal. He did not wish to be seen going straight from Kirkoswald to the farm of the Elder. For it was one of Walter Mac Walter's most distasteful and unpopular peculiarities that he was wont to keep track of his workers, and others in whose movements he was interested, with the assistance of a pocket pair of field glasses.

Jock's cuddy was generally addressed familiarly as

" Billy-O," and one of Billy-O's duties was to carry salt to the good wives of Whinnyliggate.

At the lower end of the village the street fell away sharply towards the smithy and the school gate, and here the houses were built high on the bank, with a kind of terrace of stone slabs in front. Along this Heather Jock took his way, rapping with his knuckles loudly on every shut door, and then with the free habit of the countryside opening without waiting for any answer and crying in his wares to the busy goodwives within.

Meanwhile Billy-O stood below patiently waiting his master's orders, and as Heather Jock passed from house to house on the terrace above, Billy-O kept exact pace with him on the roadway beneath.

The progression of events was something as follows:

" Rat-tat-tat! Ony saut—grand saut—clean saut! A new crap juist in, fresh as this morning's milk, and fresher than last Sabbath's sermon—for that was nae chicken. What's that ye say, Mistress Mac Nab? Faith I said to the minister that he should hae pitten it doon at the manse door, and it wad hae kenned the way to the pulpit itsel'. It had been there sae aften ! "

" What, nae saut the day ! What's wrang, Mistress Landsborough ? Saut's no that dear that ye should spare it oot o' the porridge. D'ye tell me sae —ye havena finished the last ye got? What, nae saut ? "

At this point Mistress Landsborough's door was closed with a sharp report, and in a loud voice apparently continuous with the previous colloquy Heather Jock went on.

" What, nae saut ! Then *go-o* on, thou baist, Billy-O ! "

And at the word Billy-O obediently moved on to the next house while his master attacked the door on the terrace.

" Ony saut—what? No? Then go-o on thou baist, Billy-O ! "

CHAPTER IX

THE SPOILS OF WAR.

IT was ever a great day and a bright for Kit Kennedy when Heather Jock came up the loaning to the Black Dornal. It was indeed the one thing which instigated him to keep track of the days of the week. Wednesdays and Saturdays were Jock's statutory festivals, but sometimes he would arrive on another day, mostly, alas! in the gloaming when Kit was going to bed under the determined superintendence of his grandmother, a lady who stood no nonsense on the subject of baths, or apples under the bedclothes—the last mentioned of which had been known to be connived at by the Elder.

But as surely as the Wednesday and Saturday came round Kit would be found at play on the heights of the Craigs, rolling heathery wildernesses with the most fascinating nooks and corners, hiding-places and rocky watch-towers, that could possibly be imagined by the mind of boy. Here with Royal and Tweed, his satellite dogs, Kit kept his vigil, and was always the first to discern, far down the dusty road, the advent of Heather Jock and his donkey. From that point Kit would keep up a succession of wild war whoops, intended to announce that Sir Kit the Kennedy was on the look-out for his enemies, and that whoever attacked his fortress of Craigs Castle did so at his peril.

But secretly and within himself, during all his wild charges and multiplied flourishings of wooden swords and wavings of red petticoat banners, Kit was secretly thinking how he would spend his bi-weekly penny, which he received from his grandfather each

day that Heather Jock's travelling emporium came
that way.

As he overran the possibilities in his mind, the
charms of four farthing biscuits were first of all balanced
by the superior toothsomeness of two halfpenny cookies.
To this succeeded what might be termed the study of
the arts in the shape of gingerbread elephants and
rabbits with bulbous currant eyes. These last were
delightful to pull to pieces, but the extraction of the
fruitage (apparently dry fragments of old boots) was a
joy fleeting though acute. Again he would call to mind
the extended satisfaction of a penny Cairn Edward loaf,
a production of human skill which gave as much crust
in proportion to as little bread as has ever yet been
compassed by merely human baker.

If Kit were hungry (which happened nine days out of
ten), the penny loaf would win the day. But during
the season of gooseberries and apples, or when the blackberries were hanging in clusters all along the Dornal
Bank and down by the lochside, Kit could afford to
treat himself to a daintier gingerbread rabbit or the
pennyworth of farthing biscuits which made exactly
four bites and no more.

On the morning of this day, the Wednesday after
Heather Jock's visit to the house of Kirkoswald, Kit
Kennedy was early astir. The problem needed more
than usually careful consideration. It was true that it
was not likely that he would be very hungry. His
grandmother, in conjunction with Betty Landsborough
her maid, was known to be meditating the great fort-
nightly baking of 'cake.' Now 'cake' in Scotland
does not mean the stolid overladen indigestible pudding-
stone compound of Christmas England, but the crisp
homely farle of thin oatmeal, kneaded and rolled to the
thickness of good blotting paper, and thereafter toasted
on an iron 'girdle' to such a miracle of fresh 'crumpi-
ness' that the pen refuses to describe and the mere
thought of it secretes appetite.

Now Kit did not steal. Who indeed could be supposed to steal with the approbation and under the

instruction of an Elder of the Cameronian Kirk?
Sometimes it seemed as if Kit had changed his grandfather's nature. Perhaps the old man felt he must
make up to the son for that wherein he had erred in
over-severity to the mother. So it chanced that a boy
of less than Kit Kennedy's invariably cheerful optimism
and sturdy acceptance of the facts of life, would have
run a good chance of being spoiled.

But Kit Kennedy was not spoilt. True, he did not
steal, but then again he certainly made raids upon the
kitchen at intervals. And when his grandmother
opened the door of the milk-house, he had even been
known to follow close at her back, the soft pads of his
bare brown feet making no more sound than a cat's on
the stone floor. He would stop when she stopped, turn
when she turned, and finally slip out behind her when
like a full-canvassed, deep-cargoed ship she went about
to lock the door. But Kit did not leave the milk-house
alone. He brought a pat of butter or a jug of cream
with him, still following stealthily in the wake of that
stately caravel, Mistress Matthew Armour.

Then, the raid having been successfully carried out,
Kit would right gleefully repair to the seat, on which
under the great beech trees sat the Ruling Elder.
Upon this, all unreproved, he would deposit his hoard,
and his grandfather, an accessory before the fact, would
become still further art and part in the crime by condescending to partake of the spoils of war.

"I wonder ye arena shamed, Matthew Armour," his
wife would say, "an' you at a session meetin' yestreen
at the manse, nae farther gane. Forbye next Sabbath
day ye will cairry in the communion cups frae the
vestry wi' a' the ither elders walkin' ahint ye. And
yet ye are aye encouragin' that ill-set loon to plunder and
torment your ain married wife—the impident, graceless
young reprobate that he is!"

"Aweel, aweel, wife," Matthew Armour would say,
tolerantly, "I ken that the laddie does me mair guid
than I am likely to do him harm."

"Matthew, Matthew," his wife would persist, shak-

"YE ARE AYE ENCOURAGIN' THAT ILL-SET LOON." [Page 62.

ing her head, "mind what ye do. Think, oot o' whatna pit the laddie has been digged. Ye ought to be stricter wi' him than ever ye were wi' your ain, and ye are the verra reverse. The sun maunna shine ower warm on him, nor a shadow fa' cauld on him. He maunna be reproved nor meddled wi' whatever mischief he does. I bid you bethink yoursel', Matthew Armour, lest ye reap in heaviness that which ye have sowed sae lichtly wi' your hand."

"Margaret," said her husband more seriously, "yince and for a' I hae learned my lesson. That boy has showed to me that the warst bairn is better than the best man."

Mistress Armour held up her hands in silent protest against such sentiments. Then, feeling that the matter was far beyond her words, and having a life-time's experience of the uselessness of arguing with her husband, she fell back upon her cake-baking, and her proven ability to take it out of Betty Landsborough.

"Betty," she would cry, as she went into the kitchen, "ye are but a feather-headed lassie. Ye think o' naething but the vain adornment o' your frail taber- nacle, and aiblins what lads will come up the loanin' courtin' ye this nicht. Mind ye, there are mair eternal verities to be considered than lads and bonnets wi' gum- floo'ers. And " (in a louder tone, as being more pressing matter for consideration than even the eternal verities) " mind the scones on the girdle. Gin ye frizzle them up into fair sole leather, I declare to peace that I will gie ye a daud on the side o' the head that will pit ye by looking at a lad till September fair. Noo, ye hear me, Betty Landsborough."

Then Mistress Armour, active as at twenty in spite of her sixty-five years, would whisk about quickly with a sense of some unseen presence behind her. Sometimes she would catch a glimpse of a small boy in a tattered pair of knickerbockers with a couple of ravished cakes of oatmeal in his hand, making desperate attempts to keep directly behind her, so as to be out of her line of vision, or, alternatively, to reach the outer door before she could take in the situation and rally her forces.

"O ye blastie!" she would cry, "ye are at it again. And me no done speakin' to your grandfaither aboot your ongangin's! Think shame! I'll gar ye sup sorrow for this. Gin I catch ye ye shall never sit on an easy seat for a month and mair! Lay doon that cake. Wad ye, then?"

As she spoke she made desperate attempts to head him off from the door.

"Catch him, Betty! There—ye hae him! Oh, the loon!"

Almost Kit had been caught, but the very desperation of his case supplied him with wit.

"Oh, granny, granny!" he cried, pointing behind her with a sudden stop and a scared expression on his face; "there's a fire in the lum——"

"Save us!" cried his grandmother; "d'ye tell me that? I aye kenned that something wad happen that lum——"

She wheeled about with more alacrity than seemed possible to one so solid of frame and compendious of garmenture. The fire was indeed burning on the hearth and reaching up the "lum," but only as it had done every baking day since the beginning of the world. Mistress Armour recognised that she had been taken in, and turned with speed to recover her advantage. But naturally she was just a moment too late.

Kit had dived under her uplifted arm, and dodging the amused Betty, who was vainly trying to control her mirth, he had carried off his spoils. He was now well on his way to the seat under the beech trees, breaking off alternate bits for himself and for Royal, his great lolloping red collie as he went.

"Betty Landsborough, ye are a useless, handless besom. I'se warrant ye are in league with the ill-set young vaigabond. Certes, lass, but ye shall walk at the term. I rede ye tak' your warnin' noo, and never a character will ye get, ye guid-for-naething, ungratefu' besom that ye are!"

Wisely Betty Landsborough made no answer, knowing

well that the energetic old lady would forget all about her warning in half an hour, and would, if taxed with it, even deny ever having said such a word.

On such an occasion Mistress Armour cooled gradually. At first she declared that nothing would induce her to keep such a rascal a moment longer about the house—a threat which, so long as Kit's grandfather remained his ally, was knowingly and notoriously empty and vain. Then, alternately, she went on to upbraid the ill-setness of Betty, and to remind her of the fact that in the time of trial she had even laughed at her mistress. But as nobody was much affected these manifestations soon ceased, and she confined herself to such propositions as that it was high time the young vaigabond went to school, and that "in her young days weans were not spoiled—no, and servants had more respect for their mistresses!" So it came about that from much dropping the stone was worn away at last, and Kit Kennedy was in good earnest to be sent to school.

It chanced, however, that this resolve of Mistress Armour's, falling in with a letter which her daughter Lilias had sent by Heather Jock, decided the fate of Master Kit more sharply than might otherwise have been the case.

Dear Mother (so the hurried note ran). "I have been thinking much of Kit. As you know. I dare not mention his name here. My husband hates him, and would gladly have him out of the country. Besides, it is high time that he should go to school. I shall be alone next Wednesday all day, and I should like to come over to the Dornal and take him to the dominie myself. I send herewith some things that I have made for him. He can have his Sunday clothes to go to school in, and afterwards we shall manage about getting him some others for the kirk.

Your LILIAS."

It was a simple letter, but with pitifulness under it deep as the sea. That which Lilias Armour had obtained of the happiness of earth was so much less than she had expected, or indeed deserved, that her every word was like a poem. Love and life had gone so pitifully wrong with her that baldness of language only threw into relief the bitter tragedy of the fact.

CHAPTER X.

THE SPRIG OF HEATHER.

Now Kit Kennedy had never been at school before, though his age was eight years all told. Never had the leathern " taws " of reproof tickled his palm, nor yet had instruction's warning voice disturbed his hours of play. True it was Kit had always been able to read. How he learned he could not have told you. Ever since he could remember he had made A's and B's in the thick white mealy dust of the bakeboard where his grandmother was rolling out the "farles" of cake, presently to be erected, crisped and curved into toothsomeness, by the side of the fire.

At all events he had certainly learned to read, and his first book, as we know, was "The Traditions of the Covenanters," his second "The Pilgrim's Progress." Kit Kennedy had not yet read "Paradise Lost." But even thus early he discovered the capacities of the devil as a hero, and his favourite character in Bunyan's book was Apollyon. So presently it was no wonder that he frightened the byre lass into fits by stripping himself naked, staining his body red with "keel," and picking out his ribs with sheep tar—a grisly spectacle to leap out of a hedge in the grey of a September gloaming.

Indeed, it was this prank, taken in connection with several others still more daringly imaginative, which at last caused Kit to be sent to school, where (as his uncles pointed out to him with unnecessary detail and a savoury sense of enjoyment which Kit felt to be little less than infernal), such pleasant and merry pranks as that of the byre lass would be rewarded with stripes of quite another colour.

For old Dominie Duncanson had no sense ot any humour save his own—a humour of which every one of his pupils frequently felt the point.

His mode of repartee was always considered to be most pungent and convincing upon cold frosty mornings, when the finger-tips were blue with cold, and the application of the "taws" felt like handling so many red-hot nails in Hutcheon's smithy down by the old village well.

Nevertheless to school Kit Kennedy was bound to go. So he went, as most of us go to the dentist, because he had no choice.

His mother was going over the hill with her boy in order to put him into the care of Titty Cameron, a buxom and self-possessed young lady of ten, who had to tramp all the way to Whinnyliggate school five days out of every week. But his mother did not tell Kit this. For if he had so much as suspected that his well-grown manhood was to be put into the care of any "lassie," Kit would promptly have made a bee-line for the fastnesses of the Hazel Banks. And from these it would have taken a long summer's day to dislodge him, and even then only hunger or the absence of ripe nuts would have driven him forth.

So his mother was compelled to resort to guile, and that bribery which appeals to the sweet universal tooth of childhood.

"Kit," she said, soon after she arrived from Kirkoswald, "I'm gaun over the hill to Whinnyliggate. I'll be lonely and it's a lang road. I'll hae to tak' a big sugar piece wi' me."

"Will ye so, mither?" said the boy, coming closer to her. Then in a wheedling, coaxing tone he added, "Will ye let me look at the piece?"

Whereupon his mother, with great circumspection, drew from her black reticule basket two noble "whangs" of baker's bread, thick with butter, the brown sugar dusted upon the top like silver sand on a mower's sharpening strake. And at the sight Kit's teeth watered so that he had to swallow steadily to keep the cistern from running over.

" Preserve us, mither ! " he cried enraptured, " I'll
come. Man, that sugar's fair encitin' ! "

So presently mother and son were to be seen wending
their way over the heathery wilderness of crag and moor
which lay about the farm of Dornal. Kit's mother's face
was full of a great still sweetness like that of a woman who
has indeed won her way to an isle of rest, but through an
ocean of pain. And the washing of the waves of sorrow
had swept that countenance clean of self. Her cheeks
were softly pale, and she stooped a little when she walked
as if she were bearing an unseen burden. But she was
still young, and her eyes remained as frankly and win-
somely blue as when no such lass as Lilias Armour
stepped demurely into the Kirk-on-the-Hill five minutes
before the service began.

Kit Kennedy admired his mother above anything on
earth —and loved her too, almost as much as his red dog
Trusty. So they went out over the heather, only they
two together. Lilias stepped sedately and stilly along
the rude moorland track, her head a little bent, her eyes
but vaguely taking in the purple of the hillsides and
the misty blue of the valley lakes.

And as she looked a sob rose in her throat, like water
in a well which communicates with some great subterranean reservoir.

"Oh, it's bonny, bonny," she murmured to herself.
" It's far ower bonny for the like of me to see."

Kit Kennedy gambolled about over the moor, looking
for belated birds' nests, pulling " hardheads " and
chance bits of white heather. Presently he brought a
sprig of the latter to his mother.

"Hae, mither ! " he said, carelessly, "see what Kit
has gotten for ye. Set it in your frock there below the
neck, as the lasses do at the Kirk on Sabbaths."

Lilias had been thinking deep within her bosom of
things and days that it hurt to remember, when the
boy's words called her back to herself. The sprig of
white heather lay in her palm, and she raised it towards
her eyes in the uncertain manner common to the short-
sighted and the absent-minded. I think she supposed

it to be a bit of sweet-scented southernwood, which Kit had brought with him from the garden.

But so soon as she saw what it was that her fingers held, she cast the sprig of white heather from her on the path and stamped upon it, grinding it into the black peaty soil with the heel of her small strongly-made shoe.

"What mean ye by the like o' that, laddie?" she cried, catching at her breast as if she felt a sudden spasm of pain there. "How dare ye?"

Then she saw the wonder leap into the boy's face and the colour ebb from his lips. For Kit had never seen his mother moved to anger before.

"Wi' mither," he faltered, "it's nocht but a sprig o' white heather that I gat ower there by the dyke-back! There's plenty mair. Come and see it growing sae blithely."

But the water in the caverns of the woman's heart had now risen surging up, and all her will could not keep the wells in her blue eyes from over-brimming. She sat down on a tussock of yellow bent-grass, which like an island rose defiantly in the midst of the red heather. Then she put her head into her hands and sobbed aloud in the hill silence of that great blue empty September day.

Kit was deadly afraid. He had never before seen his mother thus give way. Indeed, sorrow was not connected in Kit's mind with anything less concrete than a hungry stomach, a tumble from a tree higher than those which he usually selected for the purpose of falling off—or, at the worst, with a crack on the side of the head from the nearest of his uncles when he was caught in some unusually outrageous piece of mischief. These, as it seemed to Kit, were all provided for in the scheme of life. But that his mother—who was too old to get a "cuff on the lug," and too staid to climb trees and fall off them—should cry was a dispensation unaccountable and mysterious—like those decrees of Providence of which he had heard in the Catechism. The matter must certainly be looked into at once.

Lilias bent her head further upon her breast and sobbed—the sob of a woman who tastes the bitterness of once-sweet memories which time and circumstance have turned to gall.

"Oh, how could he do it?" she wailed, half to herself.

Kit went forward to his mother.

"Mither, mither, hearken to me!" he said, wistfully; "dinna greet, mither! Are ye hungry? Tak' a bit o' my sugar piece. It's in your black basket there under your hand. And I would fain hae a bite mysel'."

But his mother did not answer, or even respond in the least to the invitation, which in Kit's opinion was the worst symptom of all. So with the fear of a child in the presence of an unknown sorrow, he clutched at her arm and tried to pull the hand away from her face.

"Minnie," he cried, using the pet name that he would have sunk into the earth with shame rather than let any one else hear him utter, "Minnie, what ails ye? What garred ye greet? Tell your ain Kit."

Then, finding that he could neither pull away the hand nor still his mother's grief, the boy gave way utterly. He burst into a howl of childish suffering, the tears presently running down his face and dripping freely from his chin. "Oh, Minnie, Minnie, drop it, stop it!" he cried. "D'ye hear me? Gin ye dinna, by my faith, I'll greet too. And how will ye like that?"

Lilias stilled her sobs. The magnificent selfishness of male childhood braced her. She reached out her hand and patted the boy on the cheek as he bent towards her.

"We maun gang on to the schule, and see the maister," she said, rising to her feet and lifting her basket. "If we dinna make haste we will be ower late."

Kit's spirits rose triumphantly.

"Come on, Minnie," he cried; "there's Titty Cameron gangin' by the black yett (gate) the noo.

We'll no let a lassie bairn wi' petticoats flappin' aboot her shanks beat us."

But as Lilias Mac Walter passed on after the boy, her eyes went back to the spray of white heather crushed by her own heel into the black crumbly peat. She glanced once after her son. He was in full career, with his bonnet in his hand, chasing a gay yellow butterfly which had come flirting and prancing along the path, and, being greeted with a shout, had deflected across the moor with irrelevant infirmity of purpose.

The woman hastily stooped and tock up the tattered spray of white heather in her hand. With her eye on Kit she dusted it tenderly and placed it in her basket. Then, apparently recollecting that Kit would before long explore the basket for the "sugar piece," she furtively withdrew the sprig again, and unbuttoning the top fastenings of her faded black merino bodice she thrust the battered and broken twigs within, and refastened the buttons with fingers that trembled with eager haste. Then she looked again at the distant figure of her boy as he leaped high into the air in his eagerness to prevent the butterfly from escaping him. Lilias sighed, and a sweet half-satisfied look rose in her eyes. Something like a smile passed over her features. She went demurely over the heather with her eyes once more on the vague blurred blue, which was all she saw of the sparkling lake beneath. Her shoulders were still a little bent, but the burden seemed to be partly lifted from them.

Presently Kit and his mother overtook Titty Cameron. That young lady was nothing loath to accept their company. She would indeed have preferred to travel with Kit alone. But even with the escort of the swain's mother, much may be done. Friendship of the most intimate kind was soon established between Kit and Titty. The lady put out her tongue at the gentleman, and the gentleman dropped a sharp stone down the lady's back when she was not looking. What more was necessary to immediate marriage?

They also talked a little in whispers, and pulled each other's hair when they could, but the only time they were really caught was when Kit said to Titty, "Stand wide, and I'll buzz a stane between your legs." Then Lilias, whose hearing was acute, heard the "buzz" as the rough-edged piece of whinstone took the hard road between Titty Cameron's feet and boomed away at a new angle.

"Kit," she said, turning reproachfully, "can ye no be douce and behave? Come and walk by me. Ye will hurt the bairn wi' your stanes."

"Mither," said Kit, "I am no a lassie. I just couldna miss. It was as easy a shot as hittin' a barn door, and Tittie can stand stride legs frae yae side o' the road to the ither if she tries, though she is but a lassie in coats to her knees."

So in good time they arrived at the school, Titty going in safely under the escort of the parent of a new scholar, though she was nearly one hour late—whole sixty precious minutes snatched from the infernal gods.

CHAPTER XI.

KIT KENNEDY'S FIRST FIGHT.

DOMINIE DUNCANSON—grey, dour, self-opinionated, with a really kind heart overlaid with habitual crustiness, and the edge of his sympathies dulled by the hourly practice of flagellation—came to the door with a book in one hand and the "taws" in the other. He seemed to flush a little when he saw his visitors. But the traditional courtesy due to a neophyte brought the regulation smile to his face.

"Ye are welcome, Mistress Mac Walter," he said, making Lilias a stiff little formal bow, which affected no part of his frame but his head and necktie, "ye are welcome and your brave laddie. I trust we will make him a guid scholar, and that he will turn out a credit to this seeminary o' learnin'."

Dominie Duncanson did not waste any time in supposing that boys might possibly be good by nature. Forty years of mingled experience in the instruction of the boys of Whinnyliggate had made him fully confident that goodness is always instilled into boys by vigorous physical exercise. He had, indeed, kept himself all that time in excellent training, and even now at sixty-five he was accustomed to say that though in his best days he could perhaps have kept on longer—indeed, till the whole boydom of Whinnyliggate was reluctant to sit down—yet it was only recently that he had compassed the secret of how to make one "pawmie" do the work of two; and how to produce a finer moral result by one judicious flick upon a well-stretched and rotund curvature than by exertions like those of two men flailing corn in a barn.

The ceremony of introduction was soon over. Kit was solemnly delivered to the Dominie. The door was shut, and the lad found himself for the first time within the walls of a school. He looked nervously round, not from any fear of his fellow-scholars, but with the natural instinct of a newly-trapped animal. However, upon a second look he was somewhat reassured. He thought he could manage the door before the Dominie could catch him, if he got anything like a fair start.

Presently the hum of the school droned lower and lower. The arithmetic pupils along the wall communed as to results in subdued tones. The writing classes joggled each others' arms and elbows with cautious circumspection. Dominie Duncanson leaned back in his desk and bethought him of his new pupil.

"New boy, what's your name?" he said.

"Kit Kennedy, sir," said Kit, the polite son of his father, rising to his feet.

The action instantly aroused the deepest resentment in the breast of every boy in Whinnyliggate School. They gazed at him in amazed horror.

"Did ye hear him?"—the whisper ran swiftly as ill news athwart the school—"he said 'Sir!' And he stood up to answer the maister."

And then heads were shaken, and resolves were taken that betokened no good to Kit Kennedy. Such a disgrace had not been heard of in Whinnyliggate School within the memory of boy. Who was this upstart that had come off the heather to take away their good name?

"Come here, my boy," said the master, more kindly still—for he loved gentle breeding, though, indeed, he did little to inculcate it among the boors of Whinnyliggate, "and let me hear what you can do in the way of lessons."

Kit marched towards the master's desk, heedless of the nips and pinches which took effect upon his legs, the sly kicks aimed at his shins and the feet thrust privily out to trip him, so that he might fall from his supposed high place of "maister's favourite."

A boy at a side desk dropped a slate with a great clatter.

"What's that?" cried the Dominie angrily, looking in the direction of the culprit.

"Please, it was the new boy that joggled me," said the noisemaker, with a prompt mendacity which endeared him to the whole school—or, at least, to the male portion of it.

The Dominie looked severely at Kit.

"He is a liar," said Kit, calmly, giving back glance for glance.

Now, in Whinnyliggate, to call your enemy a "lee-er," the ordinary pronunciation of commerce, is less than nothing. But the assertion that he is a "liar" must be backed with your knuckles on his nose.

"Silence, sir," cried the master; "let me not hear that word used in my school again, or——" He paused grimly, and fingered the taws, while for the first time Kit rose in the estimation of the school.

After a long and severe gaze, which Kit bore unflinchingly, the master said, "Read." Kit looked about for a book, and, not seeing a school-book handy, he calmly lifted a pamphlet which had been laid face downwards on the sacred desk of state itself. He turned it deftly in his hand, with the manner of one well accustomed to books, and began to read. It was "Macaulay's History of England," just then being published in a cheap form and in monthly numbers, with double columns. Kit plunged straight into the famous chapter on the state of England in 1685, while the master gaped, and the school paused in its scufflings to listen in an amazed contempt, which slowly sank into a kind of dull uncomprehending disgust.

At the end of the first page the master seemed about to speak, but Kit, detecting his intention by means of the same instinct by which he knew that the minister in the Kirk was tacking for the port of "Finally, my brethren," dodged under the master's intended command to stop, and proceeded to the end of the long paragraph.

"Eh, maister," he said, enthusiastically, "but that's

grand! Will ye lend me the buik when ye hae done wi' it ? "

Duncan Duncanson absolutely gasped. Such a thing had not happened during all his forty years in Whinnyliggate. A new boy—a wild colt from the hills—to read Macaulay at sight and ask for the loan of the book when he had done! His first instinct was to " whale " the boy soundly for " cheek," that being the only plausible explanation of such a phenomenal request coming from any boy in Whinnyliggate. But one look at the clear eyes and innocently eager face of Kit Kennedy convinced the master that the request was genuine. Macaulay, however, was a very precious possession. The Dominie was poor.

Kit saw his hesitation, and at once put it down to the true cause. He had noticed the same hesitation in one of his uncles, who was a buyer of books, on every occasion when Peter Siboe, the New Galloway " bookman," passed that way, and Kit asked for the loan of his latest purchase.

" I'll no dirty it," he exclaimed with earnestness, "and I tell ye what, I'll lend you my ' Gleanings among the Mountains.' "

Dominie Duncanson smiled. After all, he also had an enthusiasm for letters, and had sent many a good scholar out of that low, gloomy, mud-floored cart-shed miscalled Whinnyliggate Schoolhouse.

" You *shall* have the loan of the book," he said; " I will walk over to the Dornal with it myself! "

Kit went back to his place calmly elate. He had got the promise of a new book to read—a happiness only known to those who have been reared with a mighty desire for reading and few opportunities of gratifying it.

Kit had not been many moments at his place in the class nominated the " tenpenny," to which his proficiency in Macaulay had raised him—a bad eminence, indeed, in that it made him the mark of envy, when a paper appeared on the desk before him. It came mysteriously, dropping apparently from the roof, or perhaps materialising itself out of the solid wood. For

no hand laid it there, nor was any forefinger seen to
project it flippingly from the cover of a book by that
deft universal post which all schoolboys know so well.
The manuscript was exceedingly dirty, and bore in
large, irregular, straggling pencil capitals the following
threatening message :

"SUCK IN WITH THE MAISTER !—WE'LL WARM YE
WHEN WE GET YE OOT."

Kit gazed at the writing, and recognised, with the
quick instinct of youth, that he had rough times immediately in front of him.   But he was undismayed, for
if he had anything like fair-play he thought he could
give at least as good as he got.   But he was to walk
home with his mother, and he did not wish to fight that
day.   So he turned the paper and laboriously printed the
words " THE MORN " upon the reverse, as an indication
of the date of the battle.   Then he despatched the missive to his unknown challenger by the simple process of
handing the grimy cartel of defiance to the nearest boy,
who forwarded it round the desks, avoiding those
occupied by girls, who according to their nature
would certainly " tell."

At last came the welcome noonday interval common
to all schools, and known in Whinnyligate by the
sufficiently descriptive appellation of "denner-time."
Kit was a little late in getting out.   The Dominie detained him to ask a few questions as to who had taught
him to read, and what books he had mastered.   Kit
answered at random, with his eyes hungrily on the
paper-covered number of Macaulay which told such
wonderful things.   At last he escaped from the teacher
and ran down the little playground—which was so
steep that when any one fell on it they never stopped
rolling till they came to the gutter in the roadway
beneath.   The children had all vanished.   So Kit ran
along under the tall Lombardy poplars to find his
mother, who had promised to wait his coming there
to ask him of his experiences.   But it chanced that
Lilias also had been detained.

She had gone to a white house by the bridge where lived one Jane Little, an old maid who had never been seen except with two ringlets at either side of her thin white cheeks, and who had never been known to wear anything but a black "bettermous" dress, such as the other women-folk of the village reserved for Sundays. On this account Jane Little was thought to be setting up for a lady, and the parish gossips counted on their fingers how often the black dress had been turned.

Kit walked quickly up the village street looking for his mother. However, he did not at once find her. But at the bridge-end, where the great beech tree stoops with a pleasant sound of rustling leaves over the still water, close to the raised earthen mound whereon Andrew Hutcheon, the blacksmith, welded on his cart-wheels, Kit saw a crowd of boys shouting in that irregular and cruelly playful way, which is the wont of boys all the world over when they are tormenting something that cannot escape them—yet affords them sport by flying out in impotent anger at their insults.

The crowd of boys surrounded a man who half reclined and half stood in the angle of the bridge wall. He was a tall man, with closely-cropped hair and a certain native dignity which he strove hard to maintain even when being baited by village boys. He was not drunk, only stupid and mazed—with, perhaps, some suspicion of the staple of the village inn, acted upon in his empty stomach by the heat of the mid-day sun.

He balanced himself judicially, and made futile rushes with his stick at the closing and scattering crowd of his tormentors, ending, tragically enough however, by stumbling and falling headlong upon the hard stones of the causeway. Then Pete Tamson, the "ill deil" of the junior classes, jumped upon him and proceeded to execute the simple double-shuffle which represented dancing to the boys of Duncanson's school.

But in the very midst, when the plaudits of his companions were rising in pleasing music to his ear, Pete Tamson received a blow on the cheek from a hand as hard as a mason's mallet, a blow which knocked him off the body of the tramp, and sent him staggering half-a-dozen yards away in dazed astonishment.

"A fecht! A fecht! The New Boy and Pete Tamson! Make a ring!" shouted the knowing. So in a trice a ring was made and the combatants were stripped for the fray. The man with the hollow face and closely-cropped hair, the original cause of the disagreement was instantly forgotten. He struggled indeed to his feet, and balanced himself in the corner of the wall where he had stood at first. He pointed unsteadily to the combatants, and delivered himself of moral remarks upon the future career of those who would fight with their fellow-creatures.

"Boys," he said, severely, "shake hands and be friendly. I am willing to be friendly. Boys will be boys, but it is a sin to fight. I have always inculcated this principle, though, alas! I myself have not always followed my own advice. Shun the wine-cup, lads——"

"Shut up, they are beginning!" cried Nathan Girmory, the biggest boy in the school, who attended all fights to see fair and official play.

Kit and his enemy were not equally matched, for Pete Tamson was at least a head taller. But Kit was wiry and active as his own pet goat, and Pete's first blow produced no effect. Kit flickered aside like a sunbeam dancing on the pebbles in clear running water.

Pete was furious.

"That's no fair! Stand still!" he cried, as he made another terrible rush.

"Aye, stand still!" cried the school. "How can he hit ye if ye dance aboot like that?"

Kit was so astonished at the request that he did stand still, and Pete's fist met him in the eye with a sudden sharp and most surprising pain. In a moment Kit forgot everything. He heard not the shouts of the school calling on Pete Tamson to go in and "finish the muirland brat." He did not hear the warning voice of half-drunken wisdom from the man whose quarrel he had taken upon himself. A thin red whirling vapour

seemed to smoke before his eyes, and he saw the face of
his enemy through it, flushed with triumph. Anger
boiled black in his heart. He cared for only one thing
in the world—to kill Pete Tamson, and to kill him
quick. He had never seen boys fighting. He had had
his only lesson in the art from the collies, which growl-
ingly arched their backs, and gripped and tore at any
unfortunate visiting stranger "tyke" that might chance
to come up the Dornal loaning; while his sole idea of
boxing had been obtained from Black Billy his goat,
as he assisted a tramp across the green quadrangle
of the farmyard.

So not only Pete Tamson, but the whole of Whinnyliggate School was astonished by the fury of Kit's
assault. Like a wild cat he seemed to spring
bodily into the air, and to strike his opponent with his
head, his hands, and his feet all at once. Pete was
instantly overborne to the earth, and Kit had his fingers
on his enemy's throat and his teeth in his arm before
the shouting throng realised what had happened. And
if there had been none to loosen that grip it might have
fared very ill indeed with Pete. But with one united
yell the school pulled Kit off—kicking, biting, and
scratching at every one who came within his reach.

They punched him for a "tearing teegur." They
cuffed him for a "young savage." They pulled him
hither and thither, while Pete lay on the ground and
howled that he was killed. But Kit was wholly unconscious of the blows that hailed upon him. His whole
soul was taken up with the problem of how to get at
Pete again.

But so far as he was concerned Pete desired no more
getting at. As soon as he saw that the instinct of
sport in the minds of his companions would quickly
overmaster any considerations of fair play, and that Kit
was within measurable distance of breaking loose, he
rose from the ground, and with his cap in his hand he
raced for home, *boo-hooing* lustily all the way the tale
of how he had been "killed dead" by the young savage
from the Black Dornal.

A hand was laid on Kit's head—an unsteady hand—a hand with long lithe fingers, a gentleman's hand spite of the signs of recent manual labour. It was the drunken tramp who had straightened himself, and now stood with a certain wayward swaying dignity by Kit's side.

Kit's anger melted and his pity came back.

"Can I help ye?" he said; "tell me where you are going."

"To the last refuge of the unwise," the man answered, smiling wistfully; "the hotel of the misfortunate, the sanatorium of those who have lived not wisely but too well. Set me on the way to the poorhouse, and I will bless you, my boy; but first I will shake off the mud of this ungrateful village from my feet."

Kit surrendered his shoulder to the man's hand. The tramp leaned heavily upon it and hurt him a good deal; but Kit bore the strain manfully. The shouting throng of children had melted as quickly as it had gathered, some having gone home to dinner and the rest scattered to play.

Kit and his new friend walked slowly up the street together, the tramp still holding forth in a strain of lofty moral precept. At the door of the public-house the man paused, and with solemn voice and uplifted finger warned the boy against the seductions of bad company.

"For myself," he said, "I must e'en but once more—only this once—enter these dangerous portals that I may obtain a modicum of fictitious strength to carry me on to my quiet resting-place. But for you, my lad, I beseech you take advice, and never—never——"

He would have proceeded further with his somewhat scholastic declamation, but at that moment Miss Barbara Heartshorn appeared in the doorway and motioned him abruptly away.

"Ye are no coming into my hoose again the day. Ye hae gotten mair than is guid for ye already. If ye dinna gang quietly I'll set the dogs on you."

The man wagged his head with grave, pathetic resignation, and then nodded to Kit with a kind of smile, as if he had expected it.

"The application of my sermon!" he said. "So soon as your pockets are empty it is: 'Away—get hence—the police—the dogs'! Take heed, my good lad; note well the end from the beginning and be wise."

At that moment Kit's mother was seen coming down the white road towards them. The tramp gazed a moment at her, standing as if petrified, and then instantly a wondrous change passed over his countenance. His cheeks seemed to fall in, his jaw dropped, he put his hands unsteadily to his head, and pulled the brim of his hat low over his eyes. His wrist had bled in his fall, and the action left a broad stain of blood across his face. He closed one eye as if it had suddenly become blind.

"Come away, Kit," cried Lilias, "come away from that man!"

For though she would not have been intentionally cruel, the terrible appearance of the tramp—so helpless, debased, forlorn—frightened her. She did not repeat the one hurried glance she had given him.

Kit withdrew his shoulder gently from the man's reluctant clutch.

"And good-day to you; I maun be gangin'! There's my mither cryin' to me!" said Kit, and ran off.

The tramp squared his shoulders and straightened his face. He limped determinedly down the long leafy way towards the gaunt "Combination" poorhouse, till he came to a burn that trickled underneath a little bridge. He went slowly down to a reef of pebbles, and taking off his coat he proceeded to make a thorough toilet. When he had finished and put on his coat again he gazed at his finger-tips critically, sighed, washed them again, and let them dry in the sun. Then he put them gently into an inner pocket and drew out a faded pocket-book, pitifully grey and frayed at the edges, where the

cartridge-paper lining showed through. It bore the
inscription :

CHRIST——R KENN—DY, B.A.

Several of the letters were blurred and missing. He
opened it with his slim, clean fingers, and the tears
flooded over in his eyes and rained down on the leather.
Tremblingly he took out a packet, and, unfolding the
paper, he found some stray fragments of stalk and
greyish powder, with a few petals of heather bells still
adhering to the largest piece. On the paper was
written "Given me by Lilias," and an undecipherable
date.

"Bless God she did not know me to-day, as she did by
the quarry," muttered the tramp as he sat and gazed.
He lifted the paper half-way to his face, as if to kiss the
heather; but before he had touched it he snatched the
packet away.

"No," he said, "I will not—I will not. A man of
unclean lips—a man of unclean lips !"

Then he restored the whole with reverend care to his
pocket, and, regaining the perpendicular with stiff
dignity, he set his eyes again to the road, and dragged
his feet down through the dust to the poorhouse.

And as she and her son walked homeward, talking
almost gaily, the hand of Lilias Mac Walter was fingering at the bosom of her dress, that it might touch the
trampled spray of white heather, which she had placed
there after grinding it into the soil with her heel.

CHAPTER XII.

A Royal Road to Learning.

KIT's schooling, so far as the mere acquisition of the orthodox amount of learning was concerned, was easily gotten. He had the natural faculty for letters which makes nothing difficult. He was possessed of a good general idea of the next day's lesson before the other scholars had done marking the place. He listened with wonder to the slower rustics at the age of seven and eight still wrestling with the alphabet. He never remembered the time when he could not read any book which came in his way. To this hour he never knows who first taught him to read, but one of his earliest memories is connected with stealing out of a bottom drawer in the "ben" room a copy of "Simpson's Traditions of the Covenanters; or, Gleanings among the Mountains," and, couched prone on his stomach, of reading the small-printed green-covered volume by the light of the fire, spelling out the most difficult words, and so dwelling for hours in an enchanted fairyland of hunted wanderers and fierce marauding dragoons—actually stealing back to his cradle to dream of Clavers and Lag, of battles by rushing rivers and shootings on lonely mountain sides.

Indeed, Kit remembers how it was at this time still the custom that he should be put to sleep in the middle of the day in the old cradle which had rocked his mother, and his mother's mother. One such occasion recurs to his memory with a curious persistence.

It was a quiet summer afternoon in the fulness of July. The day was hot. Flies hummed high up under the roof, where among the unceiled rafters it was dusky

and cool. The house-place seemed very large and vague
to his childish eyes, because the windows and doors were
so bright that the sight could not dwell on them long.
Kit lay quietly in the cradle, which had become so small
for him that when his "granny" was not looking he put
his feet over the oval bar at the end to give them a rest.
He had the "Gleanings among the Mountains" under
his pillow. He had been spelling out the all-fascinating
tale of a boy who, crawling up a hillside, had suddenly
come upon a fierce chase—fleeing wanderers of the hills,
God's folk hunted like the partridge upon the mountains,
the dragoons full tilt after them. He was crying because
he, too, had seen the poor lads weltering in their blood.
He could not sleep for thinking of them. Very cautiously he drew the volume out, and there, in the too
brief space of the cradle, he laboriously spelled out
the remainder of the tale, and was just assuring himself
of the ultimate safety of the original witness (boggling
much over the unknown word "sequestered," a favourite
one with the fine old-fashioned Seceder minister of
Sanquhar) when he saw a hand he knew well hovering
in the air above him.

For at this moment it chanced that his grandmother,
slippering about in loose "hoshens" on the floor of cool
blue whinstone flags, must needs come to his cradle-
side to make sure that the boy was sleeping. Kit tried
to run the book secretly back under his pillow. But it
was too late. That eagle eye fastened upon it. The
firm hand descended, secured the volume, removed it
to a place of safety, and returned to investigate
the reality of Kit's slumbers. The sleep of the just
in six-foot resting grave was nothing to the invin-
cible depth of his unconsciousness. But that was
the last Kit saw of the "Gleanings" for many a day,
in spite of a hundred spirited hunts, until one never-to-
be-forgotten day when (the grown-up faction busy preparing for the Sabbath journey to the Kirk on the Hill)
Kit ran the green octavo to earth in the far corner of a
drawer, which his grandmother had opened to take out
the week's linen. To slip the book under his pinafore

and convey it and himself to the safe shelter behind the corn mow was the simplest of Kit's achievements. To such a student, therefore, the routine of scholarship in the village school of Whinnyliggate presented no difficulties.

Upon the first day he had, as we have seen, been put into the "Tenpenny," school books being in Galloway known by their prices as far as the "Shillin'-book." After that came the "Series of Lessons," and that admirable compendium of knowledge and excellent reading, McCulloch's Collection, of which (and vainly*) I have long desired to possess a copy. In this only the very oldest pupils were exercised, but Kit soon found it worth while to stay in school during the dinner hour in order to spell over the lessons in a purloined copy till he had mastered them, carefully avoiding, however, the numerous scientific and philosophical disquisitions.

Duncan Duncanson, deposed minister, chanced to be in a good humour during the first days of Kit's pupilage in the little schoolhouse of Whinnyliggate. No dark red bar crossed his brow. He had been disposing of his harvest of honeycomb, and there still remained in the corner cupboard so much of the silver coin of exchange as sufficed for three trips to the "Red Lion" every day—"to change his breath," as the neighbours said. The schoolmaster was so regular till the hoard was done that the neighbours looked at their clocks as he passed by to see if they were keeping anywhere near the mark, and surmised a catastrophe when he was five minutes late.

One of the first lessons Kit learned in school was that of "Brave Bobby," the Newfoundland Dog of educational fiction. In ten minutes after the calling of the class Kit had won his way to the top by dint of correct spelling and "trapping" in the reading lesson —that is, informing a stumbling neighbour of the correct pronunciation of a word. But his crowning achievement came last.

---

* No longer in vain! These two words, appearing in serial form, procured me over 300 copies, for which I render thanks to the generous donors.

The master, whose strong point was not geography, which he looked upon as a vain thing, rose to point out the mist-veiled island of Newfoundland, Bobbie's aboriginal home. But finding that his short-sighted eyes could not discern the name, he was tracing the coast line of America with the short pointer, hoping to arrive at his desire by force of a policy of exclusion, when Kit broke in abruptly:

"Eh, man, can ye no find it? It's juist that elkuck (elbow) that sticks oot there into the sea on your richt hand. Ye're glowering straight at it, man!"

And while the other pupils of Whinnyliggate sat dumb at his daring, Master Kit Kennedy went forward to take the pointer from the master's hand, and finish the job himself.

He got the pointer in due course, but it was across the shoulders.

"Sit down, sir," cried the angry master, "I was not looking for Newfoundland, but for the Gulf Stream!"

And as the scholars retired they gazed with awe upon Kit, and pointed him out to chance passers-by as "the boy that had trappit the maister!"

But in spite of the dominie's search for the Gulf Stream, he was so much impressed by the boy's general knowledge that he immediately removed him into the "Series" (full title, McCulloch's Series of Lessons) where Kit underwent a most wholesome discipline from his elders and betters.

"Gin ye daur to trap us that's bigger than you, we'll thresh ye like a sheaf o' corn—hear ye that?" cried half-a-dozen of the senior pupils, after the promotion had taken effect.

"We are no gaun to be trappit by a wean like you!"

The command was punctuated by sundry admonitory "punces" in the ribs, and the exhibition of half-a-dozen grimy fists in immediate proximity to Kit's nose. Then it was that for the first time Kit felt the path of learning to be a thorny one.

But soon he was so interested in the school games and especially in that eternal one of dodging the master and

learning as little as possible, that he cared no more
about trapping, and so escaped many troubles.

As was the custom among all the country scholars he
took his dinner with him in a leather bag. For the
most part it consisted of scone and butter with a piece of
oatcake and cheese added thereto. Semi-occasionally a
piece of cold bacon would be enclosed and a tin flask of
new milk was always placed in a separate compartment,
which beverage, when consumed shortly after noon, had a
strong and composite flavour of tin and newly tanned
leather. But Kit did not complain, for the natural hunger of healthy youth furnished as good sauce as any
cook, however celebrated, could have invented.

Kit took his meals with a kind and gentle old lady,
the wife of the smith in the little house down the lane
from the schoolhouse.

Kit's hostess was a friend and gossip of the goodwife
of the Black Dornal. And she had a great and con-
suming interest in Master Kit.

It was understood the Mistress Hutcheon, the wife of
the Whinnyliggate smith, was to keep a more than
maternal eye over the young man's morals, and to report
any transgression at headquarters. Whereupon his
grandmother would reckon with him in the gate.

This arrangement was an admirable one—in theory.
But in practice it had its drawbacks. For Kit possessed
one of those heedless, cheerful, happy-go-lucky dispositions, which since the world began have commended
their owners to the hearts of all women-folk. Mistress
Hutcheon, a thin-faced, sweet-eyed woman, with an
air of being perpetually tired, did her part, so far as
personal reproof went, with admirable firmness. It was
in the report stage that she failed most conspicuously.

At the first reading this was somewhat her form:

"Kit Kennedy, ye are a regardless, mischeevious
loon. Ye troaned (*i.e.*, truantised) the schule yesterday,
and as true as daith I'll tell your grandmither on you
the very first time she comes to Whinnyliggate. Forbye I hae heard o' your ill gangings on at the schule,
and how the maister lickit ye for cuttin' the taws into

finger-lengths and flingin' them up the ventilator.
Dinna think that I'll conceal your evil deeds. Na,
they shall rise in judgment against ye. Your
granny shall hear it every word, as sure as my name is
Nannie Hutcheon. Ye shall sup sorra,' ye misleart
young reprobate, that wad bring disgrace on a God-
fearin' hoose, and especially on your ain grand-faither,
that's ruling elder in the Kirk! Think shame o' yoursel', Kit Kinnedy!"

This sounded threatening enough, but Kit knew his
entertainer too well to be very anxious. For when at
last his grandmother did come into Whinnyliggate,
riding in state in a red cart, driven by her strong son
Robert Armour, the fashion of the speech of Mistress
Hutcheon was changed.

Instead of cursing, like Balaam, she blessed.

After the necessary and essential discussions of the
price of eggs, the new tune the precentor put up last
Sabbath at the first diet of worship, the remarkable
and shamelessly gaudy bonnet worn by Mistress
Allardyce, the grocer's young wife ("a fair peevce wi'
pride an' gumflooers"), the goodwife of the Black
Dornal turned to home topics, and instantly a wary look
in Mistress Hutcheon's eye told that she was on her
guard.

"And hoo's that ill boy o' mine behavin' doon here at
Whinnyliggate? I can get naething oot o' him at nicht,
except that he won a dozen and a half 'stanies' at the
bools (marbles), and maybes an 'alley'—but is he aught
o' a guid boy, think ye, Mistress?"

Then the smith's wife would lift up her hands in a
sort of perfervid ecstasy of admiration.

"Margaret Armour," she would cry, "to tell ye the
truth there never was siccan a guid boy as that Kit o'
yours. I wad gie a pound note (or mair) gin ony o' my
ain were like him. He's juist the best laddie, clever at
his lessons, an' quaite—indeed, quaite is nae name for
him."

And "quiet" was indeed no name for Master Kit
Kennedy, in that said the smith's wife aright. But to

herself she added, "I hope this is no ta'en doon Up Abune, or I'll hae a heap to answer for!"

"I am pleased to hear ye think sae weel o' the lad," said his grandmother, eyeing her gossip, however, to see if there was any trace of guile in her eyes. But the pale, tired face of Nannie Hutcheon told nothing. There came even a kind of eager enthusiasm in her expression when she spoke of Kit Kennedy.

"I tell ye, Margit," she would say, "whiles I think there is given me the spirit o' prophesy, and the time will come when ye will be prood, prood o' that laddie. To see him sittin' hotchin' on his hunkers, feedin' his dowg wi' bits o' scone, an' learnin' him to growl when he says "Duncan Duncanson," and bark when he says "Kit Kennedy"—it's fair cowes a'. He'll come to something, that laddie, I'se warrant!"

"He'll come to the gallows gin he disna behave better than he does at hame," declared his grandmother, decisively. "And his grandfaither spoiling him at every turn—as weel as you, Nannie Hutcheon, that should ken better, praisin' him up to the skies; I wonder at ye, Nannie, at your time o' life."

"'Deed, Marget Armour," the smith's wife would reply, "ye needna talk. Ye ken that ye are juist as fond o' him as ony o' us, for your puir lassie's sake as weel as the bairn's ain. And what maitters a wee bit wildness? Faith, I wad raither hae him that, than ane o' the unco' guid weans that are aye rinnin' *baain'* to their mithers wi' some tale o' their companions. Aye, an' sae wad ye for a' your talk, my woman!"

This brought out a very pertinent question, and one which it needed all the wit and readiness of Kit's champion to answer.

"The boy never brings either buik or copy to the Dornal," said Mistress Armour. "Does he leave them wi' you, and learn his lessons afore he starts for hame? The maister tells me that he disna allow ony o' his scholars to leave their buiks in the schule!"

Previously the smith's wife had always thought that Kit took his scholastic outfit home in his bag. But in a moment she had faced the sad truth, and replied, "I daresay he leaves them aboot the smiddy, but I dinna ken for certain. He's great wi' my Andrew, and I hear the twa o' them aye speak—speakin' about learnin' and lessons!"

This also was true. For every night Andrew Hutcheon looked up from the fore-hammer, and said to the little boy who lingered about the red-belching door of the forge, loath to undertake the long homeward way in loneliness and weariness, "Kit, hae ye learned your lessons for the morn?"

"No!" Kit would reply, as cheerfully as if he had every page letter-perfect.

"Are ye gaun to learn them the morn's mornin'?"

"No," said Kit again with equal serenity.

"Then," cried Andrew Hutcheon, "as sure as daith, Duncan will gie ye your pawmies the morn richt nippily! I hope it will be frost."

Whereat Kit Kennedy laughed scornfully.

"I wad like to see auld Duncan layin' a hand on me. Faith I wad set Royal on him!"

Then he would stoop to pat the great red collie which generally kept vigil outside the school all the time of lessons.

Mistress Hutcheon therefore was quite within the truth when she declared that she had heard her son Andrew and Kit Kennedy talking about lessons every night in the smiddy, as she went and came for water to the well at the gable end.

What Kit really did with his books was curious. Yet when taxed with the matter by Mistress Hutcheon after the departure of his grandmother, he replied that they were in his bag, which proved to be true. For he opened that composite-smelling receptacle of scones, tinny milk, tarry twine, sweatmeats, and dead moles. There on the top lay Kit's school books duly tied together.

"Aweel, see that ye carry them hame this time," complained Mistress Hutcheon only half convinced, "and no hae me obleeged to threep lees by the dizzen to your granny, honest woman. The Lord forgi'e me for a' that I had to tell this nicht. But I think He will, as it was dune for no ill-setness, but to keep doon din."

With hypocritical deliberation Kit closed up his bag, and strapped it down with an air of finality which completely imposed upon his good easy hostess. Then he proceeded along the road to a ruined saw-mill which stood deep in the howe of the narrow Grannoch glen. Here was an old mill half unroofed, and still containing much of the machinery which had once driven the whirling blades, and sent a little line of brightness before the cutting edge through the rifting tree boles.

In one corner, sheltered by the sole remaining angle of the roof, was a hearthstone. Kit had prised up one end of it, and in a space excavated beneath he stored his school books till his return upon the morrow. Then he filled up his bag with stones from the first roadside pile, and gave every animate object on both sides of the way home a nice interesting time dodging them.

But one morning a sudden burst of storm, and the continual decay inherent to an unsupported roof brought a ton or two of rafter, slates, and plaster down on the stone which covered his ill-used books. It took Kit three days to dig them out—days during which he never went near the school, preferring like most of the sons of men any amount of future punishment to the least present discomfort.

When he did get back to school with the recovered books Duncan Duncanson asked where he had been.

"I have been quarrying!" replied Kit, calmly.

Now a rural schoolmaster is accustomed to his scholars being kept at home to help with all sorts of labour, domestic and agricultural. But a boy who had been employed quarrying was new to him.

"What were you quarrying?" he demanded, sharply.

"Books?" said Kit Kennedy.

And was duly licked for sticking to a lie. So thus by a side wind substantial justice was done in the end.

CHAPTER XIII.

WHEELS WITHIN WHEELS.

WALTER MAC WALTER was a man who hid, under a blunt and bluff affectation of rough honesty, the revengeful heart and restless suspiciousness of a jealous woman. He had married Lilias Armour after successfully separating her from the classical master of Cairn Edward Academy, married her because his heart had resolved upon possessing her from the first time he set eyes on the girl at the Kirk-on-the-Hill.

But the possession of years had only made more poignant his early disappointment. He had long known that never could he hope to reach this woman's heart, who in the trust and innocence of youth had bestowed her love upon another.

That the other had proved unworthy, that he had been blotted out of Lilias Armour's life, had but increased the jealousy and hatred natural to a rude bullying man of secretive instincts. It was an ever-growing offence to his pride that Kit Kennedy should be upon the same earth with him. The fact of his own childlessness still further embittered Walter Mac Walter, and when he saw the boy trudging schoolward with his bag of brown leather on his back he hated him with the hatred of hell.

He had to grip the reins of his black horse tightly lest he should be tempted to ride over his small unconscious enemy. And on one occasion when his horse slightly started at Kit Kennedy's sudden apparition behind a bush of broom, the Laird of Kirkoswald exploded into a sudden storm-break of passion, and even lashed the boy furiously across the face with his riding whip.

But he never again so forgot himself. For when next day he rode past the little loaning which led up to the farm-steading of the Black Dornal, he found the Ruling Elder waiting for him by the posts of the gate.

"I require you, Walter Mac Walter," said Matthew Armour, with all his ancient dignity, "to tell me the cause of your striking the boy Kit Kennedy with your whip on his way home from school yestereven."

"I do not know why I should be accountable to you for this or anything else," said the bully, "but since you ask me I will tell you. The rascal jumped from behind a bush and startled my horse. For this I laid my whip across his back, and for the like will do as much again."

"Nay, Walter Mac Walter," returned the Elder, "you do not speak the truth. The boy was seated at the foot of a tree reading his book. Your horse coming quickly along started of its own accord. And you struck the boy, not on the back as you say, but across the face with your whip. Let me tell you that for this you have to reckon with me, Matthew Armour, and with my three sons."

The proprietor of Kirkoswald laughed harshly.

"It is true, good sir," he said, sneeringly, "that I married your daughter, but I did not marry the whole Armour family connection. I have not troubled you much for many years, and now I will inform you that it would be well for you to keep your nameless brats more closely at home, or a worse thing than the lash of a whip may befall them."

"Sir," said the Elder, calmly, "I count this child more my own son than any that bear my name, and I will call you to account for aught that may befall him. And if you revenge yourself upon Lilias, my daughter, I have three sons and she three brothers who shall not hold you guiltless. Also she is not ignorant that her father's door stands open to her night and day."

"Some day you shall not crow so loud on the rigging, my venerable father of the Kirk," said Walter Mac Walter. "And pray do not forget that one day, not so long ago, I forgave you a debt of some extent, putting your bond of six hundred pounds into your hand on the happy day I married your daughter. But when next I settle accounts with you, my dear kinsman, I may not be quite so lenient."

"I owe neither you nor any man anything!" said Matthew Armour.

"We shall see, we shall see," the bully answered. "And do you, who talk so bravely and boldly of your door standing open to your daughter, look to it that you have any door to shut or open, except that which shuts you out of the Black Dornal, or any roof save that of the common poorhouse to cover your head."

"If it be the Lord's will," said the Elder, solemnly, "it may be even so. But the evil shall not come because you wish it, Walter Mac Walter!"

The Ruling Elder parted without further word from his son-in-law, the former retracing his steps with bowed head and heavy tread to the farm of Dornal. The other took his way at the full stretch of his horse's speed to the house of his crony, Richard Wandale, factor on the joint estates of Glenkells and Dornal.

Wandale was a man of similar social habits to the laird of Kirkoswald, but less given to savage gloom and mad freaks. Wandale was an Englishman, and had known Mac Walter in that manufacturing district of Yorkshire, where the purchaser of Kirkoswald was reputed to have made his money. What their relations there had been was not known to any except themselves, but they were obviously united by some strong common bond of interest.

"Hillo, Wandale," cried Walter Mac Walter, so soon as he reached the house of the factor, "where are you off to? I want to see you. Put up your beast for a while and let us have a talk."

****

The laird of Kirkoswald and his friend the factor of Glenkells had a long and very interesting private conversation, carried on behind the locked door of the business room. These were the concluding sentences of it. The pair were on the point of leaving the room. Mr. Wandale stood with his hand on the knob, ushering his guest out.

"Well," he was saying, meditatively, "it will be a difficult job. I need not tell you that. You know my lord's temper and prejudices as well as I—or better. But he is in such a hole that he will do anything— nearly—for money. And you can count on me to manage it for you, if any man can. You know my good-will."

"I know it is to your advantage, Wandale," said Mac Walter, with a loud laugh, "and with Dickie Wandale that is far better security!"

Wandale smiled a wry, stomach-ache smile, and as he went a few steps down the passage behind his friend's back, he turned upon his broad shoulders such a look of hatred that it justified the shrewd insight of Mac Walter's last words.

There might be honour among these two rascals, but there was little love to lose betwixt them.

CHAPTER XIV.

A Strip of Blue Paper.

THE farm of Black Dornal was of the value of fifty pounds a year. On it the Elder had been born, and his father before him. Lord Glenkells knew that the Armours of Dornal were by far the oldest tenants on the estate, and Matthew had ever been a diligent man and ready with his rent.

But my lord was in sad want of money. He was a widower, and, being a man fond of company, he saw a good deal of that sort which it costs the most to see, and from which there is the least return. More than once had his creditors attempted a compulsory settlement with him, but his lawyers had so far been able to persuade them that they would be no gainers by pushing my lord through the courts.

Still, every pound was now of consequence to the proprietor of Glenkells, and he had a strong belief in Wandale as the man who could conjure the largest number of these out of the rocks and scanty pastures of his Galloway estate.

To Wandale, for instance, was entrusted the difficult task of selling wood quietly, and selecting trees which could be cut and conveyed away without attracting any great attention.

"Wandale, mark a thousand pounds' worth of timber," would be an order twice or thrice repeated in the course of a year. And it was obvious that on such an encumbered property this could not go on for ever.

My lord came but seldom to the countryside, contenting himself with writing a long letter to Wandale once or twice a month, or, in case of emergency, sum-

7

moning him forthwith up to London to give an account
of his stewardship.

There was nothing of the bold rascal about Dicky
Wandale. He trembled in his lowest shoe-leather each
time he appeared before his passionate master. In his
anger Glenkells would sometimes shake his steward as
a terrier shakes a rat. He had even been known to kick
him completely round the house, ending by throwing
him neck and crop into the Kells water before an entire
house party. But Wandale, completely satisfied with
his own position, took these ebullitions merely as
troubles incident to the pleasant factorship of Dornal
and Glenkells. After all, he did what he pleased nine
times out of the ten, and Mr. Richard Wandale
emphatically preferred the substance to the shadow.

Lord Glenkells was a sinful and a passionate but
not a bad man. His infirmity, whatever it might be,
came quickly upon him and departed as swiftly. It
chanced that on one of his visits to the great house
among the pines my lord was in the park on a
summer's day. He walked with his hands behind him
on the shady side of a tall hedge of yew. On the other
a young under-gardener was talking to one of the maids,
who on her part had been on an errand to the village.
I know not if matters of old acquaintance or springing
affection detained them overlong in oblivious converse.
But the sight of the pair of them wasting his lordship's
time (and perhaps also the fact that for the moment he
himself lacked any one to waste his own with) so
wrought upon Lord Glenkells that he grasped his
walking-stick fiercely, and ran out upon the embryo
lovers.

He struck fiercely at the young man with his cane,
cursing him for a lazy good-for-nothing. The girl
screamed and ran towards the house. But it chanced
that in the assaulted youth my lord had lit upon one
who was his equal in passionateness, and very much his
superior in youth and strength. The assaulted not only
stood his ground, provoked by being thus put to shame
before the maid of his fancy, but, wresting the stick

from his assailant, he laid it about his lordly back and
legs with zeal and efficiency.

Then, breaking the weapon across his knee, and
leaving Lord Glenkells raging on the ground with pain
and inarticulate anger, the youth walked back to his
bothy to pack his box and set it ready to be called for
by the common carrier. Then he went over to the
house of the head gardener to tell him what he had
done and to say farewell. While his chief was holding
up his hands and exclaiming, there came a messenger
all breathless from the great house with an order that
the head gardener was to go up at once to speak to his
lordship.

The youth who had wrought the deed looked pitifully
at his friend, for his anger had died out quickly within
him.

" This will be a court job," he said, "and I was never
in gaol in my life before ! "

" Gang doon to the porter-lodge and wait till I come
till ye," said his more experienced chief; "I'll bring
ye word what says my lord ! "

The youth waited trembling at the appointed place.
At last the head gardener approached, shaking his head.

" Is he like to dee ? Are there ony banes broken ? "
cried the assailant before his friend came near.

" No," answered the gardener. " His lordship says
that here is a pound for you. But I am to give you
a good talking to, for you are a somewhat over-hasty
young man. So pit the note in your pooch and back to
your work with you before his lordship comes oot for
his afternoon walk."

The youth did as he was bid, and my Lord Glenkells
never made the least further allusion to the matter.

It will be understood that, with such a temperament,
continued suggestion working upon the necessities of
an indigent and extravagant man could accomplish much.

" Well, Wandale," cried my lord, looking up from
where he lay in an easy chair with his swathed feet
tenderly posited upon another, "what can you do for
me ? I want money devilishly, Wandale. These

women—they are always crying for something, and the less you have to give them the more they want. I wish to high heaven I had never seen one of them. Can you let me have that thousand?"

Wandale shook his head sadly.

"My lord," he began, diplomatically, " I have been all over the woods near and far with the head forester, and there is not a thousand pounds' worth of trees fit to cut on the estate."

"Hark ye, sirrah," cried his lordship. "I did not ask you for your opinion as to the value of my property. I gave you my orders."

"My lord," answered the land steward, meekly, "were it a thing even remotely possible I would obey. But even if we were to cut down the best trees in the park, we could not raise a thousand pounds on the timber. What with the last great storm, wood is so cheap that the wood merchants make a favour of taking it away for nothing!"

Lord Glenkells rubbed his head thoughtfully, ending upon the bridge of his nose with a rueful air.

"Well," he said, "I suppose it must be the court this time. I can't raise a single penny in London, and I've had a dozen letters from the bank about my overdraft."

At this moment Wandale struck in with the suggestion he had been waiting to make.

"My lord," he said, suavely, "I think I see a way of raising the money. There is one of your smaller detached farms, which, as it is not an integral part of the estate, it is in your lordship's power to sell. I have an excellent offer for it from a sure hand."

"What is the name of the farm?" said Lord Glenkells, glowering at his factor, yet with an eager look in his bold injected eyes which was not lost upon his tempter.

"The farm of Black Dornal," said the land steward, with submission; "it is detached from the rest of the estate. It is of small extent, rocky, and little capable of improvement. I have an offer of £1,600, which is the best we could ever expect to get for it."

"I tell you, Wandale," cried Lord Glenkells, "I will not split the property. And I won't have my old tenants put out. The Armours have been in the Dornal ever since I can remember. I've often got my tea there when I was a boy and out shooting—aye, and my dinner too. I am not going to have old Matthew shifted at his time of life!"

"There is no thought of such a thing, I assure you," said Wandale. "The offerer is Armour's own son-in-law, the Yorkshire merchant who bought the little estate of Kirkoswald, which came into the market half-a-dozen years ago. As your lordship knows, he is a very respectable man. Mac Walter is naturally anxious to acquire his wife's birthplace. And of course there is no thought of putting the old folk to any inconvenience, but quite the reserve. I had it from himself that he never intends that they shall pay another half year's rent so long as they live, if the sale is put through. And your lordship may remember that it was Mac Walter who paid off that bond which was in our hands for so long, indeed, from the time when some former Armour took over the stock in your father's time."

His lordship nodded.

"I remember; yes, yes, I remember, Wandale," he said, as if considering. "I hate to part with a field. But there is no doubt that the money would be a vast convenience. And that cub Reginald will have plenty when he succeeds. It is best that a young fellow should be kept a little tight on the curb—in his youth, at any rate."

"I have a provisional cheque here, my lord," said Wandale. "I met Mr. Mac Walter to-day, and he was so anxious for the bargain that he entrusted me with half the purchase money against your lordship's mere acknowledgment."

"Oh, hang it—but I say, that was somewhat cool. The rascal took my consent for granted. See here, Wandale, I've warned you, I won't have my affairs——"

"My lord," purred the land steward, very deferentially, "the man is indubitably anxious to buy the place. It lies well to his own little property, and is of no importance to us. Your lordship knows that I have always advocated the consolidation of the estate——"

"Tut-tut, Wandale, don't prose! Let me see the cheque!" cried Lord Glenkells, stretching out his hand.

It was for £800, payable on sight and at a local bank.

"Hang the fellow!" cried he, irritably, shaking the cheque at Wandale, "where do these pedlars get all their ready money? They never spend it like men. Fancy being able to keep a balance of £800 in a local bank! That hasn't happened to me for thirty years, eh, Wandale?"

"No, my lord!" said Wandale, acquiescing, as he was meant to do. His manner in unguarded moments was that of a butler in fear of dismissal.

A queer straggling smile passed over the features of his master.

"And yet, Wandale, all things considered, I have not had at all a bad time of it. I may fry for it later, but never mind—for the present——"

He considered a moment, the smile broadening.

"But I say, Wandale, that fellow Mac Walter must be rather of a sentimental turn for a money grubber. His wife's birthplace—and be willing to give good coined money for it! I was a jolly sight more glad to see the vault where—but, there—I won't be a blackguard. Well, Wandale, you had better see about the transfer. Make young Hewitson, down in Cairn Edward, do it. I always liked old Dickie, his father—a gentleman, Dickie. Understood a gentleman's feelings and requirements, hang me if he didn't."

He waved the cheque in the air.

"I'll keep this," he cried, bringing his leg to the floor with a muffled sound. "*Whe-e-ew!*" he whistled, "that was a bad one. But after all, a little bit of blue paper like this is the best plaster for the gout. I'm off to Paris, Wandale. Urgent business, you know! Paris is the place, I tell you. London is stupid, and I don't want quite to forget my French."

He was at the door as he spoke, and the land steward stood bowing deferentially with his hat in his hand.

" Expedite the matter, Wandale," he cried, turning and waving the cheque once more, " make young Hewitson hurry. And I say, Wandale, send me the fellow to this as fast as you can! I need it, Wandale, I do indeed."

The member of the House of Peers vanished. The door swung to on noiseless hinges, and the factor was left winking to himself in the tall pierglass.

CHAPTER XV.

THE SHERIFF'S OFFICER.

WILLIE GILROY, sheriff's officer in Cairn Edward, was a well-known residenter in that compact little burgh of Barony. He held, perhaps, the most extraordinary plurality of offices ever filled by one man. He was town officer, and rang the mid-steeple bell at eight in the morning and six in the evening—except on Saturdays, when for unknown reasons he rang it at twenty minutes to seven.

He kept the library of the Mechanics' Institute, and doled out books twice a week on a curious system. When he did not like a borrower Willie never had a book in, no matter if the volume had been that moment returned, and lay contiguous to the borrower's elbow with the title in plain sight.

"I tell ye it's no in," he would say. "Gin ye canna tak' a plain answer I'll get the poliss to pit ye oot for obstructin' the traffic!"

The borrower was usually doubtful as to the powers of a sheriff's officer, and at the least credited Willie with an extensive knowledge of the law. If he was wise he tried mild courses.

"Weel, ye micht keep it for me, and I'll no forget ye, Willie!" he would say.

"Humph," the official within would object, "there's no date to that bill."

Whereupon not unfrequently a surreptitious half-crown passed, and the borrower was on the tariff of the most favoured nations for the year.

Willie owned a large block of houses at the lower end of High Street in Cairn Edward, a somewhat dank

and out-at-elbows block, which apparently began to fall
into disrepair from the very day it was finished. These
domiciles were known indifferently as Gilroy's Buildings
or Willie's Rickle o' Brick, and were probably the only
houses in the town the rent of which was never pressed
for. For Willie Gilroy had a curious feeling that it
was not "sportsmanlike" to "peace-warn" his own
tenants—perhaps on the principle that a doctor of right
professional feeling will not attend his own wife in case
of sickness.

"What for should I steer the craiturs," said Willie;
"I'm no needing the siller the noo. And if I was to be
comin' hame wi' warrants and warnin's in my pooch, a'
my tenants wad rin like rabbits every time they saw me.
I'm a puir man, but I like to be neighbourly. But I
tak' it oot o' them—gin they dinna pay their rents—
faith, I make them execute their ain repairs!"

Which was perhaps the reason why Gilroy's Buildings
had more broken windows, missing bannisters, jagged
and gap-toothed railings, ragged clothes' lines a-flutter,
twisted chimney-stacks askew on the sky-line than all
the rest of the town put together.

Willie had married thrice—no, to be exact, four times.
Yet there was no desirable beauty of person about him.
He explained his remarkable success thus:

"Ye see the way o't is this—I gang a heap aboot the
country in the exercise o' my profession. And like a
doctor I maistly see fowk when they are in trouble.
Then I hae aye had a sympathetic way o' servin' a sum-
mons. That tak's weel! Noo, there's Christie
Culshangie o' Kirkubree—the crature sticks the blue
paper under a man's nose as if it was a dish o' salts, or
hauds it at his head like a pistol. Mony a time I wad
hae warned oot thae tenants o' mine—an idle, shiftless
lot—if I could hae gotten a man to do the job to my
mind. But I couldna bide to see it made sic a hash o'
as Christie wad mak' o't. And of coorse I couldna for
shame do it mysel'. So the gypsies sit on and on, and
think nae mair o' payin' their rent than they do o'
gangin' to the Kirk. An' faith, it is maybe as weel,

for I ken wha I hae on my property, but I dinna ken wha I micht get! "

Now it chanced that a blue paper had been put into Willie's hand to serve on a sad day of his life—that of his fourth wife's funeral—and Willie had put it in his pocket to be delivered after the solemn occasion.

" It'll keep till she's happit! " was the form in which he put the case to his brother, the well-to-do sweep of the town.

" Ye tak' it weel, Willie! " said Gib Gilroy, gazing regretfully down at his own hand. He looked as if he, too, had had a loss. So he had, for he had washed.

" Aye, Gib, I do tak' it weel," said the sheriff's officer. " Ye can use wi' onythin', Gib. This is my fourth time, ye ken! "

The funeral was over, and after eight spadefuls the sexton (who in consideration of Willie's being a good and steady customer did the job reasonable) lifted his bonnet exactly one-quarter of an inch, and the whole body of the mourners instantly faced about and began to discuss the weather, the crops, and how soon Willie would " tak' anither."

The bereaved and his brother were left standing alone at the grave-head. James Burt, the sexton, was filling up the last home of mortality in the most matter-of-fact way, as if he had been shovelling coals and sick of the job. He grunted resentfully at each spadeful. After putting him to the trouble of digging a grave, the " corp " might have been very well content without the superfluity of requiring to be covered up again.

Said Gib Gilroy, sweep, to his brother, the present chief mourner, " Willie, were ye thinkin' o' onybody yet? "

" How could I, Gib Gilroy," returned the afflicted with his handkerchief to his eyes, " I wonder at ye, and Margit doon there no richt happit."

James Burt unsympathetically continued to clap down the mould with the back of his spade, making a gruesome jarring sound with the loose shank.

" It's a mortal world an' we're no lang for it, Willie,"

continued his brother, "but supposin' that it was the morn, what wad ye say to Grace Mac Cubbin?"

"Supposin' it was the morn," answered his brother, with some speculative show of interest, "I wad say she was ower auld. I'm no keepin' an infirmary!"

"Mistress Martin then, Samul's weedow?"

"Kens ower muckle," said Margit's chief mourner, "she has been married twice hersel'!"

"Margit Lonie?"

"Twa Margits followin' ane after the ither is no lucky. Forbye it wad confuse the names on the stane there!"

"Weel, ye are ill to fit, Willie. But I suppose ye hae had sae mony, a man is bound to be particular. There's Lang David Geddes's dochter—I forget her name—Elspeth, I'm thinkin'!"

"Nae siller!" Elspeth's case was settled abruptly.

The sweep considered a long time before offering another suggestion. "I can think o' nae mair the noo," he confessed mournfully. "But I'll tak' anither thocht in the Kirk the morn."

"Aye," said his brother, shaking his head, "it's a business that needs a poo'er o' thocht. Look ye here, Gib, ye see what it is to be a forehanded man. Gin I had been a common ram-stam, deevil-may-care character that juist took a woman like a whurl-wund, wad I hae had as bonny a stane as that to cover them a', think ye?"

He pointed to the long and heavy grave-stone, shaped like a turnip-pit, and called a "thruch" stone (rhyming with loch), which had been temporarily set out of the way to make room for Margit underneath it.

"No?" said his brother, doubtfully, feeling that he must not contradict the bereaved on such a day, yet not seeing whither he was being led.

"Na, I trow not," continued Willie Gilroy, swinging his long arms excitedly as he pointed to the rows and rows of inscriptions.

"It's bonny, fower o' them a' in a row. Gib, d'ye ken I often wondered what I never had ony bairns for?

I thocht that it was a Divine dispensation. But the reason o't is clear noo. Wonderfu' are the works o' a kind Providence! It's juist that Mary and Susan and Jean and Margit micht a' lie cosy and caigy thegither like fower pitatie-pits weel covered, wi' nae weans to dibble in atween to spoil the symmetry, as it were. Forbye, there's the inscription. It's getting a wee scant o' room, as ye see, Gib, and had there been bairns ye wad hae needed to say what ane they belanged to. Na, it's juist won'erfu' weel arranged as it is!"

"Are ye gaun to pit up a new stane to Margit, Willie?" said his brother.

The chief mourner took a long look at the sweep as if he had suddenly taken leave of his senses.

"It's weel seen ye are no yersel' the day, Gib, or ye wadna speak like that. What's the maitter wi' ye? It maun be because ye hae ta'en soap and water to your face. Ye should be carefu', man, you wi' a young family to bring up. Shocks like that are no canny at your age. I yince kenned o' a man that washed his face and neck—and him no used to it like. And " (here the sheriff's officer lowered his voice and spoke very slowly and impressively) "that verra day a slate fell aff a roof and killed him dead on the spot!"

"Save us!" cried Gib, "d'ye tell me sae? Gin I had kenned that I wad hae ta'en a thocht. But I did it oot o' respec', Willie."

"I ken, I ken," said his brother, holding out his hand; "ye never were forehanded, Gib, but aye ram-stam and rideeklus! But bless ye, Margit there wadna hae cared a fardin' gin ye had comed to her funeral as black as the pot. But as I was sayin', I was richt thoughtfu' and farseein' aboot the 'thruch' there. I bocht that stane in Mary's lifetime (she was my first and a clever, ready-handed woman Mary was)—weel, when she left me a lone weedow I laid it langwise on Mary, an' mony were the folk that quarrelled me for being at siccan an expense, and Mary and me only five years marriet. But I said naethin', only keepit my thochts to mysel'.

"An' then when Susan (that was my second an' a ceevil body) was ta'en away I made nae change—no, nor yet for Jean, though I was fell fond o' Jean. For, ye see, a man never kens what may happen. But noo that Margit has gane the way we maun a' gang, Gib, faith, I'll turn the stane round aboot and lay it cross-wise abune the fower. *And it'll hauld them a' doon!*"

Willie looked triumphantly up at his brother. "Ye see what 't is to be a forehanded man, Gib!"

Gib saw, and the brothers went down the street, silently ruminating on the mysteries of Providence, and especially on the benefits of being a before-handed man.

CHAPTER XVI.

FRATERNAL CONSOLATION.

AT the cross Willie Gilroy put his hand in his pocket. He gave a little dramatic start and said, " Gib, I am no doin' richt. I am lettin' my natural feelin's interfere wi' my bounden duty ! "

" Oh, Willie," said Gib, " on a day like this the fiscal himsel' wud surely make allowances. Come on into the Commercial and hae a glass. I'll—I'll pay for't."

Willie hesitated a moment, dividing the swift mind.

" It's kind o' ye, Gib ; ye mean weel," he said.

" It's oot o' respec' to her that's gane," said Gib, with much emotion, holding out his hand to his brother and shaking it solemnly, till all the people who were on the watch said to each other, " Did ye think that Willie and the sweep had as muckle feelin' in them ? "

" Come your ways, Willie, and we'll e'en hae a glass —o' tippenny ale ! " he added, with a gasp.

Willie had been wavering, but upon his brother condescending upon the particular beverage he hesitated no longer.

" Na," he said, " Gib, it wadna be decent—indeed, hardly law-abiding. I'm away wi' a bit of blue paper to Matthew Armour, the Cameronian elder up at the Black Dornal. I'll no be back till late. Ye can ring the six o'clock bell for me, gin ye want to show your respect for the departed ! "

A sudden thought seemed to flash across Gib the sweep. He cracked the clenched knuckles of his right hand suddenly into the palm of his left.

" Dod, man," he cried, " that was the very thing I

was tryin' to bring to my mind when we were speakin' awhile since aboot your prospects, as yin micht say. It was Betty Landsborough that I had in my mind. What think ye o' Betty?"

" Ower licht-headed and young!" said his brother. "And thinks hersel' ower bonny."

His brother gave the chief mourner a little semi-festive, half-mourning poke in the ribs.

"Hoot, Willie, ye are a guid-lookin' chiel eneuch yet. And ye ken what lasses are——"

Willie smiled.

"The lass may be young, though she'll mend ower soon o' that. But she is through-gaun, clean, strong, and they say her auld faither has a pickle siller. Ye micht do waur, Willie."

" I'll cast my mind ower Betty on the road up, Gib," said the bereaved. " But I misdoot, I misdoot!"

" What do ye misdoot, Willie? Surely no whether she wad hae ye or no?"

" Na, it's no that," said Willie; "it's juist that I hae my doots whether there's room eneugh on the ' thruch ' there for anither name."

"Hoot, aye, Willie," said his brother, cheeringly, " besides ye'll hae to pit up a new upricht ane for yoursel', to stand at the head. That wad look awfu' tasty wi' a' the five lying below, and your stane lookin' doon on them. There wadna be the like o' it in a' Galloway. Fowk wad come miles to see it. It wad mak' the fortune o' ony sacrament!"

" There's something in that, Gib, but it canna be!"

" And what for no, Willie?"

" It's easy seen that ye are a puir weak vessel, Gib, and has only been marriet yince. Ye forget the Judgment Day, Gib!" said Willie, solemnly.

Gib experienced a sudden shock. His mouth fell with that quick jerk which comes to men when a grave topic is needlessly introduced.

" Save us, Willie; what need hae ye to speak o' the Judgment Day? What in a' the warld has that to do wi' puttin' up a standin' stane to yoursel' at the head o' your ain grave that ye bocht and paid for ? "

" It has everything to do wi' it, Gib! Did ye never think on what will happen when the trumpet of the Angel Gawbriel blaws yon awfu' wakening blast ? "

" Na," said Gib ; " it hasna juist occurred to me ! "

" Weel," said Willie, pausing in the midst of the street and demonstrating a case upon his finger, " here's me—ye see ? "

Gib nodded; he saw his brother as a grimy thumb which would have done credit to his own profession even on non-festal and funeral days.

" And there's yer fower wives—we'll say fower for the sake o' argument, Betty Landsborough being for the present oot o' the reckoning," added Gib, parenthetically.

" Exactly," said Willie, beginning to tell off the fingers of his right hand. " Weel, there's Mary, and Susie, an' Jean, and here's puir Margit. They are all quaite and sleeping soond the noo. But when they rise, a' fower o' them, and get the poo'er o' their tongues after a' that rest, there'll be a noise, I'm tellin' ye. I hae leeved wi' them, and I ken! "

The Sheriff's officer recurred to his thumb. He folded it down on the palm of his hand with a gesture of putting something out of the way.

" And here's Willie Gilroy," he said. " Mary, and Susan, and Jean, and Margit (and Betty Landsborough if she's spared) can settle it amang themselves. But as for me, I hae bocht me a plot o' grund in a retired spot they caa' Carsphairn. And I'm to be buried there, wi' a minister on ilka side o' me and a paper in my hand declarin' wi' chapter and verse on it oot o' the Scriptur', that in heaven there is neither marriage nor giving in marriage! "

CHAPTER XVII.

An Offer of Marriage.

When employed upon the business of the law Willie Gilroy's customs did not alter with the weather or the seasons. He was a small man, with very long arms that hung level with his knees. He wore a battered stovepipe hat as straight up and down as if it had been made with a gross of others in one tube and then cut into lengths to suit the wearer's stature. His legs were out of proportion to the length of his body, and he walked with a long stretching stride which did not vary either up or down hill.

What the Sheriff's officer's meditations were on the way to the Black Dornal it would be hard to tell. Certainly they had nothing to do with the message that took him there, which was to serve a certain legal paper upon Matthew Armour.

Kit had gone to bed when Willie Gilroy arrived. The kye were just leaving the byre after milking-time, under the capable superintendence of Miss Betty Landsborough. Now cows are dignified and matronly animals. They do not like to be hurried, and there is a sympathetic and an unsympathetic way of putting them out of the byre.

Rob Armour's way was the unsympathetic—not so Betty's.

Rob, a general squire of dames, always wanted to get away to visit at the neighbouring farmhouses. So he let the chains fall one after another with a rattle into the stalls, brought down his hand with a surprising "flap" upon each cow's flank, and said in a loud, stable-yard voice, " Hup, you beast! " The motherly, cud-chewing

8

matron so dealt with turned about with surprise and
resentment in her slow-moving heart. She gave her
tail a flick of protest, and immediately pushed her
horns into the flank of her neighbour in front, who in
her turn slid on the threshold, in the place where it is
always slippery. Thus, according to the methods of
Rob Armour, the black Galloway and flecked Ayrshire
cows poured tumultuously into the Dornal yard, and
took their ways to the hill pastures strangely disturbed
in their minds. It had always an effect on the milk
next morning when Rob Armour undertook the putting
out of the milk-givers the night before.

But with Betty Landsborough on the quarter-deck
how different both method and result!

She had milked them with a hand light as a caress.

"Now, Flora," she would say, as it came to the turn
of some placid and glossy beauty—as it were at the
bovine climateric of "fair, fat and forty"—at any rate
in the plentitude of her milk.

Then Flora would move a little to make room at her
side, and Betty would sit down upon her stool and lean
her brow against a soft flank. There was no holding
back of milk under such a persuasive hand, which
could humour a cow as well as a gallant, and yet could
set bounds to both that neither might pass.

Then when the milking was done, and the reaming
luggies of white milk carried to the milkhouse for the
mistress of Black Dornal to deal with according to her
art, Betty came back to the byre. Every cow—Flora,
Meg, Blossom, Hettie, Beauty, Specklie—turned her
head, red horned Ayrshire and black curly-polled
Galloway alike, to see if it was Rob Armour or another
who was to put them out. When it was "another" a
perfumed sigh of bovine thankfulness pervaded the
byre. Each cow knew that the deed would be done
sympathetically, and that they would go forth out of
the byre and up into the croft so quietly that (a great
point with a self-respecting animal) they could discuss
both their cuds and their neighbours' morals all the way.

"Gently the-n-n!" said Betty, as each neck chain

fell into its place, not with loud clank, but with a faint musical clinking. "Gently, beauties!"

And so all in order, as if milking had been a pleasure, each Flora and Blossom and Specklie took her even way out of the byre, orderly and calm, giving her head a little shake just to settle the neck hair, where the links of the chain had irked its glossy surface.

Only once the voice of Betty Landsborough rang out determinedly.

"Gae way frae there, Rob Armour," she cried; "gin the puir beasts set their e'en on you they will no gang quietly to their pasture. Ye are a ram-stam, over-grown, headstrong bullock. Get awa' wi' you!"

"Oh, Betty," said the voice of Bob Armour from the stables to which he had retreated, "haste ye wi' the kye and I'll walk wi' you doon to Whinnyliggate. I ken that ye are gaun to the shop there the nicht!'

"Deed, I'll gang nae sic gait wi' you, Rob Armour! Tak' yoursel' aff to the Crae and get Leezie to gang wi' you to the shop o' Whinnyliggate. She's no particular!"

"Betty, I'll never speak to Leezie again, gin you will come wi' me the nicht!'

"Come wi' you I will not, so gang your ways, Bob Armour!' answered Betty Landsborough with finality.

Service in a countryside so primitive as Whinnyliggate argued nothing of social inequality. And Betty Landsborough, the daughter of the cooper in the village, a man with a good business connection, took her place not as servant but as helper, almost as daughter, in the house of Black Dornal. She was a handsome girl with dark rippling hair, a pretty, firm mouth, a clear complexion, and the dark blue Irish eyes which, like the sky reflected in a hill tarn, light up a plain face and ennoble a beautiful one.

Betty took her way to the High Croft behind her cattle, humming a heart-free snatch of song and twirling a little slip of willow in her hand. She carried the wand for form's sake, but she never laid it upon one of the meek file of cows before her, which, observing precedence as completely as humans at a state reception, had each their appointed order of coming and going, not to be departed from on pain of horning and forfeiture of social standing.

Betty Landsborough put up the bars, slipping them into their slots with a little familiar clatter, and fastening the cross pin of each. And now with her face to the brown moorlands she stood awhile thoughtfully gazing into the west, thinking the sweetly tangled thoughts of a young maid before " he " comes to gather all the strands into one, and to make sky and earth, the night and the day, the flower and the tree, the sun, the moon and the stars of heaven speak only of " him, him——" of what he will say next time, of what he said last time, of what he is doing now, and in especial when he will come again !

Barring a flirtation or two with lads whose names, as far as her affections were concerned, were certainly writ in water, Betty was heart-whole, untouched by love, ignorant as yet of the breathing of that divine breath, which goes round the world stirring to good and evil after their kind the hearts of men, yet making either preferable to the dead stagnation of selfishness.

As she stood looking into the sunset across the pasture bars the lately bereaved Willie Gilroy, sheriff's officer and proven expert in matrimony, came down the heather, walking as it were in six-leagued boots—so disproportionate to his size, and especially to the sagging and swaying mourning " weeper " in his hat, were the strides with which he conquered the breathless miles.

" A guid and heartsome evening to you, Betty ! " said Willie, cheerfully ; " ye are takin' the air ? "

Betty turned and looked at the little man with the large tolerance which in moments of good nature we may extend to a spider—even to an earwig.

She was a perfectly healthy and healthily perfect country lass, well aware of being pretty enough to choose whom she would marry, but who was not in any hurry to finish the job.

Betty was completely happy at the Dornal. She was fond of her mistress, afraid (but not too much afraid) of her master. In matters of the heart she took it out of her master's sons, and especially out of Rob the eldest, and she was devoted to Kit Kennedy. She considered herself with justice a fortunate young woman.

"Guid e'en to you, Mr. Gilroy!" she said, coldly, recognising the Sheriff's officer. "I heard o' your loss and I'm vexed for it. But what brings ye sae far frae Cairn Edward at this time o' nicht?"

"Business, business, Betty, nothing less," said the little man; "my work will not permit me a day's rest even at this trying time. The Queen's service must be attended to."

"Aye, it maun come hard on you—at your time o' life!" said Betty, who, like all her sex, could not get up any sympathy for the too frequently bereaved.

The Sheriff's officer, with the remembrance of his brother's advice in his mind, did not relish the allusion to his age.

"Betty," he said, "I hae kenned you a lang time——"

"Aye," interrupted Betty, "I hae heard my mither say that ye were a man weel up in years at my christening. I dinna mind whether she said ye were at hers as weel!"

"Na," said Willie Gilroy, "I am no near your mither's age—no near!"

"Some folk age quicker than ithers, Maister Gilroy," said the girl, with sympathy in her voice but mockery in her eyes, "and we a' ken that ye hae had your experiences. Let me see, was Margit your fifth or your sixth?"

"Fourth!" cried the Sheriff's officer, eagerly, "only my fourth!"

Betty did not deign to answer, but turned and began to walk slowly back to the farm, swinging her willow wand to and fro in her hand daintily as she did so.

"Ye'll hae far to gang," she said; "I wadna be keepin' you!"

"Oh, nae hurry," said Willie, "nae hurry ava! I am gaun nae farther than the Black Dornal." He paused to give effect to what he was going to say. "I'm some dootfu' that ye will be wanting a new place at the term, Betty!"

Betty Landsborough turned upon him sharply.

"Ye dinna dare to tell me," she cried, with the inconsequence of all women with regard to the instrument of affairs legal, "ye dinna dare to say that ye hae brocht ony o' your nesty law-papers to vex my maister. Rob Armour will wring your neck like a chuckie's if ye hae."

The little man wagged his head.

"Neither Rob Armour nor half a dozen Robs dare deforce the messenger o' Her Maijesty the Queen when in the performance o' his duty," he said, grandly. "I cannot help the errand on which I am sent."

"It's a puir, puir business," said Betty.

"Maybe, maybe," the Sheriff's officer went on, with offended dignity, "but it's an honest business. And yin that brings in a fair share o' guid siller. Aye, it boils the pot, and that is mair than all the stock on the farm o' Black Dornal will do. I hae a peace-warning to deliver to Mathy Armour, elder though he be, that will send him oot o' this comfortable doonsittin'. An' I hae it frae a creditable source that he's sair behindhand at the bank."

Betty Landsborough said nothing. With a sinking heart she contemplated the ruin of that worthy household where she had been so happy. She knew well what servant lasses had often to put up with in other places, and the house of the Ruling Elder had been a haven of security and peace to her.

But the Sheriff's officer had yet more to say.

"Aye," he continued, insinuatingly, "ye'll be wantin' a new place, Betty, and that afore lang. Weel, ye ken me. I'm a man that weemen folk has been partial to a' my life, though I say it mysel'. Noo, Betty, I speak to you as a freend, do you think that ye wad like to come an' keep hoose for me?"

"A FIRM HAND, IMPELLED BY A STRONG RIGHT ARM."

[Page 119.

Betty turned upon him a regard so fixed and stern that the least sensitive man might have taken warning. But Willie Gilroy was completely panoplied in the armour of his own conceit.

"Dinna be bashfu', Betty ; I ken it's kind o' overcomin' at first, but I assure ye that I mean it seriously," he said, trying to subdue a certain condescension.

"To be your hoosekeeper—ye want *me* to be your hoosekeeper—and Margit (your sixth) hardly cauld in her grave! What do you tak' me for ? "

Betty finished her sentence with a vehement question, and bent towards the little man as if she would have annihilated him on the spot.

But Willie Gilroy was not warned even by this. He expected that Betty would be overcome.

"I tak' ye for a sensible lass," he went on, "that kens a guid offer when she gets it. Faith and mind I dinna say, but if ye are a guid lass and biddable, and your faither (wha is weel-to-do) does the richt thing by ye, I michtna e'en mak' ye in time Mistress Gilroy. Of coorse I dinna promise that, till we see hoo ye turn oot. The offer is 'withoot prejudice,' as we say in our business. But still I'll no say but what I micht. Ye are a snod bit lass, a guid worker and no that ill to look upon! "

The Sheriff's officer put his head a little to the side after the manner of a cock sparrow.

"Eh, what say ye to that ? " he asked, perkily. "That's a fair offer, Betty, is it na? Ye didna expect the like o' that when ye left the onstead o' the Black Dornal to caa' oot the kye. What say ye to that— what say ye to that, my bonnie woman ? "

" *That !* " cried Betty Landsborough, briefly.

And as the word left her mouth a firm hand, impelled by a strong right arm, took the astonished Willie on the ear with a bang that cracked like a pistol shot, and he staggered across the road to the hedge before he could recover himself.

"That's my answer to an impident atomy that ought by richts to be on the tap o' a barrel organ wi' a red jacket on and a brass plate for pennies in his hand. Ye wad ask Betty Landsborough to be your ninth or tenth, after comin' like a corbie in the gloamin' to pyke oot her master's e'en. Gin ye dinna want mair and waur, Willie Gilroy, never daur to speak to Betty Landsborough again! "

CHAPTER XVIII.

The Taking of the Buik.

" Come your ways in, sir,' said the quiet, steady voice
of the Ruling Elder, as sitting waiting for the completion
of the family circle he observed a visitor stand at his
door.

"I have business with you, Mr. Armour," said the
Sheriff's officer, gravely, in his most professional tone.
"I have here a paper——"

"It is the hour of worship," returned the Elder; "let
business wait."

"I have here a paper——'

"Let it wait, sir," said the Elder, with firmness. "I
bid you to sit down."

And the man sat down with an ill-enough grace, for
he was smarting from the treatment he had received
from Betty Landsborough.

"Are we all here present?" said Matthew Armour,
looking reverently about.

His wife nodded her head, a little placid bow which
rustled the crisp white linen of her mutch.

"Then let us worship God in the 124th Psalm at the
fifth verse." And the Elder read the psalm of the
night.

Then rang out like a battle chant the noble
rugged numbers of Old Hundred and Twenty-fourth,
throbbing over the moorlands even as in days of
the Covenant. With such fervours quickening their
pulses and steadying their souls, Matthew Armour's
forefathers had stood in line at Drumclog, or made
ready to ride into the smother of that last charge

at Ayrsmoss. And none can ever understand Scotland from whom these things are hidden.

> The raging streams,
>> With their proud swelling waves,
> Had then our souls
>> O'erwhelméd in the deep.
> But bless'd be God,
>> Who doth us safely keep,
> And hath not given,
>> Us for a living prey
> Unto their teeth
>> And bloody cruelty.

The lines were rude, almost like the improvised song of some Celtic bard stormily triumphing over a battle-field of slain enemies.

Then succeeded a gentler strain, in which the voice of Betty Landsborough thrilled like a mavis singing in the springtime copses.

> Even as a bird
>> Out of the fowler's snare
> Escapes away,
>> So is our soul set free.
> Broke are our nets
>> And thus escaped we.
> Therefore our help
>> Is in the Lord's Great Name,
> Who heaven and earth
>> By His great power did frame.

In the after silence followed the reading of the word, the story of Gideon's night surprise and victory, and the simple and dignified prayer ending with these words:—

"And keep thou the stranger within these our gates. Console and succour him, bringing good to Thy cause and Thy servants from his presence and errand. And to thee be all the glory. Amen!"

The family rose, and the Sheriff's officer with them. He did not now seem to be in any such hurry to deliver his missive. He sat down on a chair in a frame of mind palpably ill at ease.

"And now, Maister Gilroy," said the goodman of

Dornal, "ye shall hae some some supper before we consider your message. Margaret, will you set the table?"

For the Elder held to the old Scottish saying that there can be no suitable discourse between a full man and a fasting.

When the Sheriff's officer had finished his repast, Matthew Armour smiled upon him and said, "And now, sir, you will bide with us this night. The room and bed are ready, the night is dark, and you have far to go before you reach your home."

At this Willie Gilroy, who had done so many messages of pain and brought trouble into so many houses, found himself embarrassed for the first time in his life.

"You had better see this first," he said, and handing him the folded paper he leaned back in his chair intently watching the face of the Elder.

The goodman of Dornal took the long blue legal document, and straightening it out upon the rough calf skin cover of the Bible he carefully wiped his spectacles and set them on his nose with the natural dignity which marked all his actions.

Then, drawing the candles nearer, he began to peruse the contents. The writing set forth with much circumlocution that upon the twenty-fourth day of November, being Michaelmas term day, Matthew Armour was called upon to quit the farm of Black Dornal and to remove therefrom all his stock, implements, furniture, bestial, and everything belonging or appertaining to him from the lands, outhouses, dwelling-houses and all other places upon the said lands. This he was to do at the instance of Walter Mac Walter of Kirkoswald, proprietor of the land aforesaid and of the steading and offices of the aforesaid Black Dornal.

Having read it through twice very calmly, Matthew Armour folded the paper and placed it between the pages of the Bible from which he had been reading.

"This will await consideration till morning," he said aloud. And with equal composure he engaged his guest in talk about the weather and the prospects of the crops.

Presently the goodwife came in with a candle in her hand.

"The room is ready," she said, smiling upon the Sheriff's officer with hospitable goodwill. Willie Gilroy felt more crushed and miserable than he had done when Marget, his wife, died. Yet he told himself that he had done no more than his duty. Which was true enough; but conscience, when it awakes, is an engine wholly irrational and does not care even for the best excuses.

"What was the man's business?" asked the goodwife of her husband when the door had closed upon their guest.

"Nothing that need vex us," answered her husband, calmly, "so being that we carry it to a throne of grace. We will take our sleep first. In the morning we will consider it together."

And being accustomed all her life to depend upon her husband's judgment, Margaret Armour laid her head down upon the pillow and slept. But the Elder lay all the night with unshut eye, praying to his God, till the grey light came creeping round the edges of the window-blind and the early bird cried in the rustling beech-trees.

Then he rose and went out. The sun was rising and making of the east a broad and even glory. A vane upon the roof of the new house of Kirkoswald, all that could be seen of it from the farm steading of Dornal, glittered coppery in the red light.

"*As we forgive them that trespass against us!*" said the Ruling Elder, and went like a man with his mind at ease, to do the morning duties of the farm.

CHAPTER XIX.

The Roup of the Armours.

BITTERLY the wind piped across the moorlands. It rushed upon the onstead of the Black Dornal, singing one high level note like an express whistling as it rushes into a tunnel. It was the Tuesday before the Martinmas term, and the day of the Armours' roup.

From far and near the people had gathered to give Matthew Armour a good send-off. As the harvest had been an excellent one, their pockets were well lined with siller and their hearts with pity; for by this time all the world knew that it was his son-in-law who was putting the Elder out of his ancient holding.

His three sons, Rob, Allen, and Archibald, busied themselves with bringing forward the horses and cattle into the yard where Muckle Jock Bennett, the auctioneer from Cairn Edward, had been playing his oldest and most successful jokes for three long hours, and getting the best prices for everything from the good and kindly folk of the united parishes of Dullarg and Whinnyliggate.

There were others present at the auction besides the country folk, Souter (of Snellgrove and Souter, the agents for the present proprietor) being the most prominent. He was a little bow-shouldered man, with a reputation for great sharpness. He went hither and thither, pushing through the press about the " nowt-beasts," and peering cynically at the cattle under the elbows of some gigantic farmer, as if mentally estimating how worthless a lot they were.

Also, standing shyly on the outskirts of the crowd with a certain calm reserve of dignity, Henry March-

banks, the Cairn Edward banker, was often pointed out
as the best man in the countryside, ministers not
excepted.

Mr. Osborne, of the Kirk on the Hill, by general
consent the best minister, nodded his head approvingly
when he heard the verdict of the popular mouth.

Mr. Marchbanks was a fellow elder of Matthew
Armour's, though a man of not quite half his years.
He had few social comings and goings, save with the
like-minded and like-hearted intimates whom he had
drawn about him.   But there was no man of such good
and approven counsel in twenty parishes.   The row of
red leather Oliver and Boyd's Edinburgh almanacks in
his little consulting room at the Bank of Scotland had
listened to more secrets than any score of lawyers' desks
in the South Country.   Wherever there was a widow
in trouble, a good man in the toils, an orphan left
alone, there was Henry Marchbanks, his tall, slender
figure and calm face lifting him above common men.
And if you stood watching him in any gathering of
folk in his own or a neighbouring parish, you would see
grim faces soften as they came near him.   Strong
hands were silently stretched out to shake his, with the
grip which means that the tongue may say little but the
heart has not forgotten.   The salt water would stand in
some woman's eyes as she minded her of the hour of
her calamity, and thought of what had been done for her
in that day and of the man who did it.

Yet no one dared to thank Henry Marchbanks in
public, hardly even in private.   But the general heart
approved him as the man who in all the county
stood most out of reach of selfish ends, the one friend
whose motives were above suspicion, the helper to
whom those in trouble went straight as dove to its
window.

Yet Henry Marchbanks was not a rich man, and
could give little money away in comparison with others
of far inferior popularity.   For " banker " in Scotland
means bank agent, and Mr. Marchbanks' income had
never in all his life equalled that of a tradesman in a

good way of business in the town. Yet, when in the
fulness of time the first School Board came to Cairn
Edward, and the people considered the probabilities,
they never speculated about who would be top of the
poll. They only discussed the second place—for, "of
coorse, Maister Marchbanks will be at the head o' the
poll. No a craitur that can scart wi' a callevine but
will gie him a vote!" Which thing in due time befell.
And Henry Marchbanks became for a season the chair-
man of the board, and piloted that crank and unsea-
worthy bark with rare judgment through perils of waters,
ecclesiastical and political. Then after three somewhat
barren and thankless years he retired, and never again
could be induced to assume public duties; for, as he
said when pressed, after all these things were not his
sphere.

Such was the man who now stood by Matthew
Armour in the day of trouble.

The sale proceeded to its somewhat sombre end. The
cows one by one went under the hammer. The horses
were brought into the ring and led out. Rob Armour's
lip quivered strangely at the thought that never again
would he lead Bess and Jean to the plough, in the
morning when the birds were twittering their brief little
winter song of thanksgiving for open weather and the
seagulls were sweeping aloft—nor ever again ride them
home with outstretched necks of weariness, their chain-
gear clanking in the evening stillness as they turned
their feet gladly towards stable and supper.

Betty Landsborough wept without disguise in a corner
of the empty byre in the intervals of serving refresh-
ments, and paid no heed to the compliments of her many
admirers. The stalls, already void and cold, where Fleckie
and Bell would stand no more, were too much for her.

"What for are ye a' forgrutten?" said handsome
Eckie Fergusson of Langbarns; "ye'll sune get anither
place. Faith, lass, I wad gie ye yin mysel' that ye
wadna be easy pitten oot o'!"

But Betty passed on her way without so much as a
saucy look, and that meant much from a maid so

ready of retort and so willing to exercise both her charms and her repartee as Mistress Elizabeth Landsborough.

In the milk-house to the north Margaret Armour was sitting by herself on the stone shelf, which looked bare and forlorn without its shining white wood basins and cool blue delf. She rocked herself to and fro.

"Ochanee—ochanee!" she said softly to herself, using the old half-Erse keening cry of Galloway which most have now fogotten, but which still comes uppermost on the lips of the old when they mourn to themselves and think that none are near. "Ochanee—that I should leave the bonny bit. Here I cam' a bride forty years since. Forty years last May on the face o' thae craigs Matthew lifted me doon frae the beast's back, and I grat on his shooder because I was sae young to hae the care o' a hale farm toon, and I thocht he wad be disappointed in me.

"And there by the saugh tree was oor wee Lilias's garden, and she was that fond o' her bit flooers. I mind she had a bank o' daisies an' muckle white gowans an none-so-pretty. Aye, an' when I gaed to the kirk she wad bring me a bit sidderwood for my kerchief frae that bush there, that she hersel' planted. She caa'ed it 'mither's snuff.' Aye, but she was a lichtsome bit thing as she flichtered by like a butterflee among the flooers. Bless the Lord that I never foresaw this day, nor a' the sorrow that was to licht on her young life!"

She had not heard the step behind her as she sat on the cold stone seat drowned in sorrow and misery. But a hand was laid on her shoulder—the hand of the Ruling Elder.

"Come your ways ben, Marget," he said; "we will go in and shut to the door. There is that to be done that only you can help me with this day—a sacrifice that shall clear our hearts and let us hae the richt to look every man in the face, owing no man anything. Yet I will not do it without your approval. We haena faced the warl' sae lang thegither, you and me, Marget

Armour, to be divided now, when the lift is dark and the thunder wakens up there amang the hills."

"Mathy, Mathy," said his wife, catching at the old man's hand and holding it in hers, "what for does the Lord use us this way? It is juist as if we hadna tried to serve Him. Yet for forty year we hae striven, and never forgotten to call morning and evening on His name. And after a' He has forgotten us. Is it richt o' Him, Mathy — d'ye think it is richt o' the Almighty?"

The face of the Ruling Elder was filled with greatness at that moment. Yet it was tender also. He felt the tears of the wife of his youth fall upon his hand after they had run down her withered face.

There was a dangerous break in his own voice as he tried to answer her.

"Marget, Marget, my ain lassie," he said, even as he used to do when he came to her father's house courting Margaret MacBryde half a century before, and she convoyed him in the gloaming as far as the horse-watering place, "ye mauna speak that gate. Do we serve the Lord of Hosts for what we can get? Shall we, the creatures of a day, keep count and reckoning wi' Him? Nay, Marget, dinna fret on God. Have we had fifty years o' the wonders o' His providence, and now shall we rebel when for a little time we underlie His chastening hand?"

"I never thocht to leave this bonny bit—to forsake the first nest, whereto ye brocht me a bride, Mathy. We hae been sae happy—sae happy, and ye hae been kind to me aye, kinder noo when I am auld and grey-headed that ye were when I was a lassie—and ye thocht me bonny."

The Elder's hand patted his wife's cheek.

"Hush thee then, lassie," he said. "I have never thocht ye bonnier than this darksome day, and when His hand is heavy upon us. But we will bide its liftin' and win through. Think, wife, He micht hae ta'en the yin or the t'ither o' us, even as He did our three bonny bairns, and left the ither to battle through by

9

their lane. But the Lord has tempered His judgments. Mercy is His attribute, and justice only His law. And we winna mourn ower sair as if we mistrusted Him! He wadna like that."

"I ken, I ken," she said, bending her brow till it rested against his hand, "I do wrang to fret ye this day, Mathy, but I canna help it, I canna help it. Ye maun juist bear wi' the heart o' a woman. It's no reasonable or richt, I ken, to mourn like this. And yet——"

"Come your ways, Marget," said her husband, gently raising her; "come your ways ben, and we will gang into the closet and shut to the door. This trial shall not break our faith. I hae thocht ower muckle o' this world, and maybe the Accuser of the Brethren came also to present himself before the Lord, and said of me, 'Doth Matthew Armour serve God for naught?'"

*   *   *   *   *

"*For twenty-three pound going, this valuable coo!*" It was the voice of Muckle Jock Bennet in loud announcement which came to them from the outer yard. "Have ye a' dune at twenty-three? Thank ye, Airieland! Twenty-four is bid. No advance on twenty-four? At twenty-four this excellent Ayrshire coo in full milk, going—going—gone! She's yours, Airieland, and I wish ye joy o' her."

The milkhouse door burst open, and Kit Kennedy came flying in.

"They are selling the kye, granny; come quick. And they say there never were sic prices as they are gettin'!"

To Kit the roup was a day of high excitement. He had no sentiment about leaving the Dornal save that he would see new things at last, and in his secret heart he hoped that perhaps his grandmother and grandfather might flit somewhere where he would not have to go to school any more. He did not mind the lessons, but he hated sitting still so long. So Kit alone, of all the family, actually enjoyed the sale. He drove forward the calves with hearty goodwill. He helped at the "buchts" with the sheep. He rode upon the iron roller as it was taken away. Pennies, even shillings, were showered upon him, till he had quite a hoard in his pocket.

Suddenly he noticed the serene gravity on his grand-father's face, the traces of recent tears on that of his grandmother. He stared amazed, vaguely compre-hending that there might be another standpoint than his own, from which to view all this excitement and commotion.

"Ye are vexed, grandfaither," he said, anxiously; "what is it? Is it siller? Dinna greet, granny. I'll gie ye a' mine. I hae lots and lots!"

He pulled out a double handful of mingled silver and copper. "Hae," he cried, eagerly, "tak' that; I dinna want it. I hae mair in the bank. And ye can hae my bools and my green missionary box and my wee cairt wi' the blue wheels. I'll gie ye them a', but dinna greet, grandmither! Grown folk shouldna greet!"

The old man patted the boy on the head and smiled down at his wife.

"I telled ye the Lord had been guid to us," he said; "this laddie will make it up to us. Mind that we are suffering in his cause. You and me, Marget, may not live to see it, but in the time to come this boy will make glad many hearts. Show, therefore, a com-fortable face before the friends who have come in the day of our calamity, and let us give thanks for our many mercies!"

And with this the Ruling Elder and his wife went out of the little milk-house, both of them together, and passing through the crowd of buyers and sympathisers, they entered into their own chamber. But when Matthew Armour knelt down there was nothing but thanksgiving in all his prayer. For as he said after-wards, "Shall we not trust the Lord to do that which is best without directing Him? Have we received good from His hand, and shall we not receive evil?"

So with well-assured hearts the pair made them ready for that which yet remained to be done.

CHAPTER XX.

KIT KENNEDY'S SALE BY AUCTION.

PRESENTLY Matthew Armour and his wife went out and stood on the doorstep, looking down on the crowd with calm and smiling countenances, from which every appearance of emotion had passed away.

They could see at the entering in of the courtyard the dark burly figure of Walter Mac Walter. "He had ridden over to be in at the death," as the crowd put it. His horse was tethered to the gatepost, and whinnied fitfully as the Dornal plough teams were led away by their new owners.

At this moment there came a burst of laughter from the crowd, and a pressure of heads forward toward the auctioneer. He was talking to some one down near the ground, and the bystanders were evidently listening with eager amusement.

Then the voice of Kit Kennedy rose above the tumult, its childish treble piping out clear and distinct.

"But ye maun sell them—I tell ye that ye will sell them. My grandfaither needs the siller. And my grandmither was greetin' sair. I will part wi' them and gie her the siller. And then maybe granny will no greet ony mair!"

With a half-humorous shake of the head Muckle Bennet gave in to the boy's persistence. And presently upon the broad rough platform of planking before him appeared the blue go-cart which Geordie Elphinstone, the neat-handed Irish surface-man, had made for Kit, a peck measure half full of marbles, a wooden horse with three legs, and a large clasp-knife with one blade broken.

Margaret Armour would have spoken, but her husband stayed her.

"Let be," he said; "this may be from the Lord. It is an answer to our prayer. If we have lost something for His sake, surely we also gain much."

There was no laughter among the crowd now. On the outskirts some poor women who had lingered to pick up odd household gear were sobbing without disguise. The men looked shamefacedly at the ground, at the tree-tops, over the platform—anywhere but at one another.

Even the auctioneer, who had the repute of being copper-fastened as to cheek, and iron as to nerve, who united the voice of a brazen bull to the sentimentality of a horse-dealer, did not seem quite to achieve his customary fluency or raciness in description. It was felt that he was not doing himself justice.

"Now, gentlemen," he said, "here is the closing bargain of the sale, and it is a collection of gems. Never in all my experience have I had such a recherchey lot to offer. A coach and harness all complete, carefully upholstered in blue paint, and with a window in the back in case any lady should want to faint. I do not conceal from you that one wheel comes off, and the harness is mended with string. But I can recommend the turnout to any family wanting a reliable article to take them to the kirk on Sabbaths. How much, gentlemen, is bid for this valuable family coach, with trimmings all complete?"

Then from the crowd there came a curious wavering cry, as one and another with children of their own spoke out their hearts.

"Dinna sell it! Let the laddie keep his muckle cairt! It's a cryin' shame, so it is."

Once more rose the treble of Kit Kennedy high above the growl and murmur of the assembly.

"They are my ain to sell if I like. I will sell them, and granny shallna greet ony mair."

Then over the heads of the people came the gruff voice of Walter Mac Walter. "Quit this fooling," he said. "Auctioneer, I call upon you to go on with the sale, or to declare it closed if it is finished."

For he had caught the rumble of the people's anger, and he noticed with a curiously vivid resentment that whenever he came near any man or woman they had instantly business in another quarter. Being a man constitutionally eager for popularity, this cut him to the quick.

But Muckle Jock Bennet did not like the laird of Kirkoswald. "I am here to sell the entire stock and plenishing at my own discretion as to time. And the last item in this bill is sundries. Now these articles evidently come under that head. So the sale is not over till they be disposed of to the highest bidder. How much is offered for this coach?"

The murmur suddenly exploded into a series of sharp bids, some half laughingly given, others with a certain shamefacedness characteristic of Whinnyliggate when it was foolish enough to do a kind action. A whisper also went round, "Let us buy them and gie them back to the laddie."

"Half-a-croon!" "Three shillin'!" "And thrip!" "And six." So ran the bidding.

"I bid a pound," said the quiet voice of Henry Marchbanks over the shoulders of the throng, and the coach was knocked down to him. The keynote was struck. The peck measure with the marbles was disposed of for twelve shillings to the parish minister. A top went for eight shillings—"going at a sacrifice to clear out!" said the auctioneer as he knocked it down to a swarthy bachelor farmer. "Ye'll hae to set aboot getting the bairns to play with it at yince, Urioch," he added.

At this the people had begun to laugh with the curious hysterical laughter which may sometimes be heard in sacred places in hot weather. And when Kit, dissatisfied with the auctioneer's praises of his favourite possessions, mounted the platform, there was a general shout of welcome.

"This is a grand horse. Dapple Grey is its name,"

said Kit. "I want a lot for it. And I'll no let it gang unless the man that gets it promises to be kind to Dapple and fodder him every nicht and gie him fresh beddin'. For he's a prood horse, and has been used to kindness a' his life. Noo, bid awa'."

And bid they did, fast and furious, betwixt laughter and tears. The ball was set rolling by an offer of ten shillings for Dapple. It was offered by the mother of ten, and though she could ill afford it, she followed bravely on till the noble steed had reached eighteen shillings. Then, recognising that there was keen competition, she dropped quietly out. But Mr. Marchbanks gave her an approving nod which made her a proud woman that day.

The young farmer of Urioch, Gavin Black, was perhaps the most determined and enterprising, but he was closely followed by the auctioneer's brother, a notable horse-dealer from Cairn Edward, known to all the world as "Muckle Jock Bennet's Muckler Brither," who examined Dapple Grey's points with professional straw in mouth, hissing as he did so.

"Three pounds is offered—only three pounds for this excellent draught-horse. He has certainly had the misfortune to lose one of his legs. But as he runs on wheels this does not in the least interfere either with his action or his usefulness."

So for one of the most interesting quarter-hours that Whinnyliggate had ever known Dapple Grey continued skying, till finally he was knocked down to the cattle dealer for five pounds ten, "the cheapest beast I ever bought in all my life," said Barney Bennet, smiling broadly as the whole circle of his friends congratulated him on his purchase, and asked him if he had got a pedigree and warranty with Dapple, and if he did not mean personally to "travel" the country with him. When Kit came down from the rostrum he was nearly swamped with the coinage (ranging from pennies to half-crowns) which was poured into his pockets. All the women wanted to pet him. The men felt his muscle, and prophesied well of his gameness. The boys present waxed green with envy of his notoriety, and resolved to lick it out of him on the first favourable occasion. There were no girls present or they would have worshipped him—that is, except Betty Landsborough, and she did that already. Betty did not count.

*   *   *   *   *

The people still lingered about, some of them settling with the auctioneer, others only talking upon general subjects, but most with a strange feeling that all was not yet over. For one thing Henry Marchbanks stood behind the auctioneer's clerk as he totted up the figures with a look of satisfaction on his face. Then, taking something out of his pocket, he went to Matthew Armour, and without a word put a sheaf of notes into his hand.

Walter Mac Walter was talking to his agent, Souter the lawyer, with an affectation of ostentatious ease. He slapped his riding breeches with his switch, and occasionally laughed aloud as at some rare jest. All the same his gaiety sounded a little forced, like bravado.

But for all that he kept his eyes uneasily about him, and when he saw his father-in-law come towards him, he started and dropped both his whip and the sentence he had begun, leaving the latter suspended in the air like the unfinished arch of a bridge.

So strained was the attention of the people that, when the Ruling Elder approached Walter Mac Walter, every conversation died a natural death, and men drifted towards the centre of the yard where the new proprietor and the outgoing tenant of the farm of Black Dornal had met each other.

Matthew Armour stood in front of his son-in-law.

" I have somewhat to say to you, sir," he began. " I make no complaint of what you have done. A man has a right to do what he will with his own. But in one thing I must liberate my own conscience. Eight years ago I was called upon unexpectedly to pay a debt of six hundred pounds which had been incurred when my father took over the stock many years ago. This debt had always been allowed to remain upon the yearly

payment of the interest, but eight years ago my lord
needed the money and I was suddenly called upon to
pay it. Again a man may do what he will, and there is
no wrong in asking for one's own. But at the time,
without denuding the farm of stock, I had not the where-
withal to pay, and you, sir, came forward with an offer
of money. You took no acknowledgment from me. You
asked me to consider the money as a gift. But neither
then nor now have I ever been able to do so. The stock
upon the Black Dornal has always been yours in my
eyes, and I have looked upon myself as keeping it in
trust for you. Now that it is sold, I desire to repay
you the money I owe you, with interest at five per cent.
that all may be clear between us. And I thank you,
sir, before these our neighbours, for every forbearing
kindness you have showed me and mine in the past.
And may the Most High, in whose hands are riches and
poverty, bless and advantage you in your new possessions."

Walter Mac Walter had automatically drawn back
his hand when Matthew Armour offered him the sheaf
of crisp and rustling notes. He was about to refuse,
for he was not wholly destitute of human feeling.
Indeed, had his hatred of Kit Kennedy not embittered
him, he would certainly not have taken the money.

But his agent was at his elbow, and whispered something to him. At the same moment he caught sight of
Kit Kennedy, who had just come into the yard, leading
his pet lamb Donald. Instantly black hatred, and the
jealousy that is cruel as the grave, hardened his heart
and smothered all generosity.

He reached out his hand and took the notes.

"I never expected to set eyes on the money," he said,
brutally, "but I'll not deny that the feeling does you
credit in the circumstances. My lawyer will write you
a receipt."

"He need not trouble himself," said the Elder;
"these good friends will bear me witness. I bid you
good day, sir!"

As has been recorded, Kit Kennedy came into the

ring dragging after him his pet lamb Donald. He had put a rope round its neck, and Donald was objecting furiously.

"I forgot," he cried, "this is my ain. I'm gaun to sell him to get siller for granny. But Donald is no to be killed for mutton. He maun be keepit for his fleece, and he maun hae milk for his breakfast every mornin'. And he winna gang wi' the ither sheep, but wi' the kye. For he's a prood beast and very particular. Noo, hoo muckle for Donald?"

All the time the black pet lamb was making furious rushes this way and that, and in one of them he happened to knock slightly against Walter Mac Walter. He raised his heavy riding boot and kicked the pet lamb on the side, so that Donald emitted a piteous little shivering bleat of pain.

And then the assembled parish had its first glimpse of the true character of Kit Kennedy. The boy's face went suddenly white. Fury gleamed in his eyes. He was standing on the wooden platform, up the steps of which he had been endeavouring to haul his recalcitrant property. He dropped the rope instantly and sprang like a cat at the throat of Walter Mac Walter, fastening his teeth in his neck and gripping both hands into his full black beard. The force of the assault and its unexpectedness together brought Donald's enemy to the ground.

The lawyer tried to pull him off, but though battered with powerful fists in front, and pulled at least adequately from behind, Kit held his grip with a fierce blind determination.

At last he was thrown off, only to rush again to the assault. But the big cattle-dealer gathered him up with a hand in his collar, as he might have done a small game dog that had no chance in a battle with one greatly its superior in size.

"Bide ye, bide ye," he whispered to Kit, "ye've dune weel. Let him alane noo!"

Walter Mac Walter rose with the marks of Kit's hands and teeth upon him, and strode furiously forward to seize him. But Muckle Jock's Muckler Brither stood in the way, and the larger half of Whinnyliggate edged its way between.

"I'll have the law on the young scoundrel! I'll ruin him yet!" he cried. "Come, Souter, let us get out of this!"

And he went through the farmyard of Dornal, amid the low murmur of hatred and contempt which had been following him all day, toward the place where his horse stood tethered.

When he was fairly gone Kit disengaged himself from the grip of the cattle-dealer. "And noo," he said, as if nothing had happened, "hoo muckle for Donald? But he's no to be killed. Mind ye that!"

The young farmer of Urioch finally bought him for five pounds—"as an ornament," he said. And Kit collected the money on the spot.

He handed the whole proceeds of his small private auction—thirty-one pounds, eight and a penny—to his grandmother.

"Hae," he said, "dinna greet ony mair! We can leeve on this till it be done, and by that time I'll be a man and makin' plenty o' siller!"

"Are we not more than rewarded, Marget?" said his grandfather, looking fondly down at him, and touching his hair lightly. "Verily, out of Zion, the perfection of beauty, God hath shined!"

CHAPTER XXI.

Ruling Elder and Stone-breaker.

With a clear conscience, a hundred pounds in the bank (without counting Kit's treasure-trove) and the universal respect of his neighbours, Matthew Armour, with Margaret his wife, Kit Kennedy, and Betty Landsborough, retired to the Crae cottage, a little house under shelter of a wood at the other side of the Loch of Grannoch. The laird of Crae was, as he said himself, neither great kirk-goer or kirk lover; but he admired honesty and uprightness of dealing as between man and man. · Also he had disliked Walter Mac Walter ever since he came into the country-side, with the half-contemptuous aversion of a man of old family for one whom he looks upon as a merely vulgar and moneyed interloper. Mr. Kinmont Bruce was not sorry, therefore, to have it in his power to annoy his enemy without great cost to himself.

He was comparatively a poor man, and his farms and moors were all let. The shooting tenant lived in the mansion-house, and Mr. Kinmont Bruce himself, a bachelor and a great traveller, occupied the factor's lodge and discharged his duties.

Now the laird of Crae was a road trustee, and his word had power with the surveyor. So in a few days Matthew Armour, with an equal mind and with his natural strength yet unabated by the creeping chills of age, went out to break stones upon the roadsides of Whinnyliggate. And that strong-hearted community, permeated to the core with the republican equalities of three hundred years of Presbytery, thought neither the better nor the worse of him for the change.

His sons scattered, two of them becoming porters on

the railway at Cairn Edward, and Rob, who for various reasons desired to remain near his father and mother, entering into the employ of the laird of Crae as junior forester.

Betty Landsborough accompanied her master and mistress to their new abode. She had her own views upon the matter, though perhaps she did not reveal all her motives to the world at large.

"I ken brawly that I could get anither place," she said, when her mistress remonstrated with her; "but I'm no gaun hame where I'm no wanted and no needed. I can do bravely withoot wages in the meantime. There is a decent garret at the Crae, for I hae seen it. And ye are neither so young nor yet so able to work as ye were. So to the Crae I'm comin', and ye'll surely never put me to the door."

To her master she said, "Maister Armour, I hae been in your hoose since I was a bit bairn leavin' the schule. I hae learned whatever guid I hae in me frae you. What ill I hae dune has been mysel', but the guid—an' I'm dootfu', there's no muckle to speak aboot—has been juist you and the mistress. If ye can be doin' wi' me, I will work my fingers to the bane for you and yours, and for that bonnie laddie there, puir faitherless thing. Leave the mistress an' you! Na, fegs, no likely; that's never Betty Landsborough!"

So in a week's time Crae Cottage had a new face put on it without and within, and Betty Landsborough went about with a sharper tongue than ever and a glow of honest pride on her face. When Rob came home at nights from his work in the Crae woods she gave him no rest, but set him to chop wood and stack it in the little peat-house. She sent him to the well for water, and refused to accompany him thither so much as one single step on his way. She set Mrs. Armour down in the rocking-chair with her knitting, bidding her take her rest, for that she was just in the way anywhere else, and it was time that she should take things easy with young arms and legs to run and work for her. And in every way Betty Landsborough was quite another

Betty from the girl she had been in the old thoughtless days at the Dornal before the coming of the trouble.

It chanced one day that Matthew Armour worked in his sheltered roadside nook at his growing stone pile. His arms, strong as oaken boughs, gnarled from wrestling with winter gales, soon struck firm and true at the stubborn rock. And though for the first few days he was weary with a deadly weariness and almost fainted by the way, yet now he was learning how to strike with the least effort and with the greatest effect.

Geordie Elphinstone, an old and experienced adept at the art, showed the Elder how and where to take the stone. He pointed out the line of least resistance, and how, when the tap was rightly driven home, the stone would fall apart of itself.

"It's no strength that does it, it's airt," said Geordie And Matthew Armour was learning the "airt."

Geordie would willingly have showed him various other paying things connected with the method of making up a stone-heap to look more than its size. But the surprise in the old man's eyes caused him to change his mind.

"Of coorse," he said, "that's what the ill fowk do. I was only warnin' you. There are some gye coorse boys knappin' on this section."

Mr. Osborne walked out from Cairn Edward to visit his elder at his work, and knew better than to condole with him. But he blistered his hands, soft with sermon-writing, in trying to reduce the stubborn block of whinstone to the standard size. Matthew let him thrash his fill, and then told him that the one he had chosen had been thrown aside as impervious to treatment.

"And what for did not you warn me, Elder?" said his minister, ruefully glancing at his damaged hands.

"It is whiles for our souls' guid to break ourselves against that which we cannot accomplish," said Matthew Armour, quoting from last week's sermon at the Kirk on the Hill.

Then the well-mated pair proceeded to hold high discourse of fate and freewill, the decrees of God, of fore-

knowledge and predestination, while the Ruling Elder,
with his wire goggles on the stubborn stone, brought
down his hammer with the steady *crack*, *crack* of a
master of the trade, and the minister sucked tart
" sourocks " and gave God thanks that he was privileged
to have such a man as Matthew Armour to measure
himself against, as it were, shoulder to shoulder.

" I have a ' piece ' here ; I told the wife I might not
be back to dinner," said Mr. Osborne, diplomatically ;
" will ye join me, Elder ? "

" For me also Betty Landsborough put up something," returned the Elder. " I kenna what it was,
but we'll see."

And so, at the hour of noon, by the side of the
common highway, these two Christian gentlemen bared
their heads, and the Elder said grace at the request of
his minister. They were cheerily happy, too, with the
fine sauce which comes of hunger and a good conscience
as kitchen to their dry bread.

For along with his trouble there had arrived to the
Elder a yet rarer gentleness. His ultra-sternness
seemed to have passed away, and a kindly tolerance
had taken its place.

" It is good for me to be here," said the minister at
last ; " but old Marget Elshioner is waiting for me at
the Cross Roads, puir body. And, moreover, I am only
keeping you from your work."

Elder and minister parted with a friendly nod, but no
handshake, and for an hour only the rise and fall of
the hammer broke the stillness, till a whinchat came
near and perched upon the dyke near by where lay
Matthew's coat. So regular were the old man's movements that the bird sang its little song two or three
times over before stepping down and beginning to peck
at the crumbs that had fallen from the table of these
two rich men, the minister of the Kirk on the Hill and
the extruded farmer of Black Dornal.

It was three of the afternoon before another wayfarer came along the turnpike by the side of the loch.

Walter Mac Walter was on his way to visit his friend

Wandale. The factor had done his work and would be wanting his pay. The Laird of Kirkoswald and Dornal was in a good humour. His dark spirit looked out of his eyes over the moors of his new possession and pleased itself with victory. He had lunched, and during that repast had asked his wife over and over again whether he had not now fully repaid her father for his trick of keeping that boy about the country. As he put it, in his delicate way, he had "rubbed it into him."

He had not seen his father-in-law since the day of the roup. As he went, jogging comfortably on his beast, conscious of his own importance and the excellence of his balance at the bank, he came in sight of a figure in the little square indentation cut from the side of the road, which, in all parts of the empire, is sacred to the priesthood of Macadam.

He did not recognise Matthew Armour till he came quite near. The stoop of the shoulders and the disfiguring wire barnacles which shielded the Elder's eyes produced, at first sight, a strange effect. But as his son-in-law came up, Matthew Armour took the latter off to wipe his brow, and stood up leaning upon his hammer.

Instantly Mac Walter brought his horse to a stand, and set himself to enjoy the sight.

"You see what you have brought upon yourself, Armour," he said. "I warned you long ago that if you did not get rid of that brat you would live to repent it."

The old man looked Mac Walter in the face with even more than his ancient gravity and dignity. "Have I ever told you that I have repented that which I did?" he said.

Walter Mac Walter, flushed from the table, laughed a short, scornful laugh.

"I think your occupation shows that you cannot do anything else!" he said.

"I have not seen the righteous forsaken, nor his seed begging bread!" answered Matthew Armour, lifting his blue bonnet, and letting the wind wave his grey locks.

" I think even your friend, King David, would have admitted that breaking stones on the roadside is not far from it."

" It is so very far from it, sir," returned the Elder, " that I desire nothing better till I die, than to be able thus to provide for the wants of those who are dependent upon me ! "

" If you had been reasonable and done as I wished, you might have lived and died somewhat more comfortably in the house of Dornal ! " said his son-in-law, with another quick laugh. As the old man did not answer immediately he proceeded : " Perhaps you would be willing to have your daughter also to provide for; she is welcome to go from my house when she will ! "

The Elder answered him with a grave, sweet directness.

" Day and night my door stands open for her. Even as at the Dornal, so to the cot which God has given me to lay my head in, Lilias Armour may come when she will. There will be a place and a welcome for her."

" Then why do you not take her altogether, as you have taken the boy ? "

" Because," said the Elder, " a woman's duty is to abide with her husband while she may. But in the end, if she be unequally yoked, and there is no remedy, she may return to her father's house."

A sudden fierce anger burnt up in Walter Mac Walter. At times hatred and jealousy made him almost insane. Yet it was not that he loved his wife, but only that the boy, Kit Kennedy, hurt his newly-born pride of position and consideration.

" Hark ye, Armour," he said; " you have thwarted me when you might have met me fairly as man to man. I might have made something, too, of the boy. I would have placed him on a training ship and looked after him there. But you kept him here, in this place, where all knew his mother and himself. You have not scrupled to shame me before my neighbours. I tell you I will ruin him sooner or later. You will yet live to see him even as that drunken sot, his father,

10

who was lately in gaol for theft. I have brought the Ruling Elder from independence to—this. I will also bring down your pride in this boy. You know that I do not boast without being able to perform."

The Elder stood still, calmly surveying his adversary.

"The evil as well as the good is in God's hand, not in yours, Walter Mac Walter. I pray that these threatenings come not home to your own door. Sometimes I have observed the wicked suddenly stricken to the ground, when the whole world was filled with the pride of his shoutings. 1 have seen the worm at the root of his green bay tree in a moment laid bare. Yea, I have seen the wicked perish from the earth, quick as a light that is quenched in the sea!"

As he spoke the Ruling Elder stood suddenly erect, and pointed eastward to the sharp turn of the road, where it bridges a little brooklet which furrows the brow of the heather.

Palpitating with anger, Walter Mac Walter raised his whip to strike. But the old man did not move. He kept his hand outstretched, pointing down the road as if he saw a vision rising out of the white dust of the highway. And for a moment Walter Mac Walter paled and his eyes were compelled to the same spot. He stared as if he also saw somewhat, and was stricken cold at the sight. Then he leaped from his horse.

"You threaten me," he cried; "not even your age shall protect you. I have borne much from you and yours. I will bear no more."

And with his bridle on his left arm he advanced upon the old man, who stood motionless as he came nearer. His eyes glared like those of a wild beast, his purple face was injected and his fist clenched to strike.

"Why should not I throttle you, Matthew Armour," he cried, "and throw your carcase in the loch?"

"Because you are afraid of the justice of man," said the Elder, calmly, "and because the Almighty holds your hand!"

"Then in spite of both the law and your friend the

Almighty I will thrash you like a dog; I have borne
more than enough!" cried the furious bully.

"And I can never bear enough because that I was so
blinded as to give my daughter to such a man!" said
the Elder, with quiet incision.

The hand of the assailant was drawn back, his face
was set for the stroke, but yet he did not strike. For
out of a bush of broom rose a tall, gaunt figure, and the
shining muzzle of a pistol looked coldly into the face of
the Elder's adversary. It was the tramp.

"Stand back, Walter Mac Walter!" he said, with
some of his old distinction of manner. "I was silent
before you once for another's sake in the parlour of the
Red Lion. But, by Heaven, I will not be silent now!
Stand back, I say! For at least *I* have no fear of being
hung!".

So the three men stood for several seconds, Matthew
Armour leaning on his stonebreaker's hammer, Mac
Walter with his arm drawn tense to strike, and the
ex-prisoner and classical master with his pistol pointed
at the head of his enemy.

It was the last of these three who spoke first. He
dropped his weapon to his side and laughed a little
scornfully.

"But I know well that you will not strike," he said.
"Walter Mac Walter only strikes behind men's backs—
as you struck at me years ago when first you came from
Sandhaven, as lately you have struck at Matthew
Armour from behind your friend the factor."

The laird of Kirkoswald and Dornal glared savagely
at his former rival.

"My man," he said, with an attempt at calmness,
"you forget that I am a magistrate, and that I can soon
have you back where you came from—and that is in the
prison of Kirkcudbright."

"But you will not," said the tramp, coolly.

"And what is there to hinder me?" he retorted.
"Matthew Armour here shall bear witness that you
threatened my life with a pistol. The Sheriff knows
what reason you have to hate me."

"I know that Matthew Armour would bear true witness were it against himself," said the tramp, "but yet you will not put me again in prison."

"And wherefore, pray?"

The tramp leaned nearer to Mac Walter and uttered a few words in a low tone.

"*Because of Mary Bisset!*" he said.

CHAPTER XXII.

The Two Truants.

KIT KENNEDY was playing truant. The fact is sad, but it must not be blinked. It was a glorious day in June, and the water of Loch Grenoch basked blue and warm in the eighteen-hour-long sunshine. Also Royal was with him, his great red collie, whose left-hand connection with the laird of Crae's Newfoundland was suspected on strong presumptive and circumstantial evidence. Royal however, like most mixed races, was of a joyous disposition, and questions of pedigree did not trouble him. That he should have a blue-blooded Newfoundland or another to his father was all the same to Royal. He had even been known to "down" his putative parent on the open street of Whinnyliggate and to take unfilial toll of his ear, for the first commandment with promise is not of any canine acceptation.

This day, however, he had assuredly led Kit Kennedy astray. The boy had left the cottage in the wood in the most meek and obedient frame of mind. He even ran over the multiplication table as far as nine times nine so quickly that it sounded like the gurring of a sewing machine in rapid action. It was no use going further, for ten, eleven, and twelve times are too easy to be required seriously of babes, while thirteen times is impossible even to chartered accountants.

Kit proceeded as far as the road end of Crae before letting his good intentions falter. This was the precise distance that Betty Landsborough's sugar "piece" lasted him. Mistress Armour did not approve of spoiling boys, and would have sent Kit off empty-handed. But Betty thought otherwise. She continued the plan

of Kit's mother on his first day of school, and her
foolish extravagance was connived at by Matthew the
Elder.

So every morning when Kit set out for Whinnyliggate,
that is, every day except Saturday and Sunday, Betty
spread a scone with butter, and upon the butter, with
no illiberal hand, she showered a coating of sugar,
thick, brown, and gritty as the desert of Sahara. To
Kit's unsophisticated palate the combination constituted the food on which angels grew their wings.

But at the end of the little straight avenue, which
led from the cottage door to the pine-edged road, the
tempter was was lying in wait. Royal, whose position
in the family was now purely supernumerary, had
vanished from the green in front upon the first
appearance of Kit Kennedy at the door with Betty,
who was concealing the sugar piece under her apron
from Mistress Armour, while that shrewd lady occupied
a position of observation in the rear.

So at the end of the road Royal waited on his prey.

Kit caught sight of him and whistled joyously. The
dog curved his tail and came bounding up to the boy to
beg for " scone." He had had his breakfast, and he
privately despised sugar, except perhaps in lumps and
of the best white quality.

But he wanted Kit Kennedy to come down and play
with him on the lochside. And so, as Kit himself
would have said, Royal " let on " to like it.

The tempter gambolled in front, barking joyously.
He said as plain as print, " Now then, we're off!
Hurrah for the water! "

But for awhile—for at least as much as a quarter of
an hour—Kit manfully resisted. By that time a considerable distance had been put between the cottage
and the wayfarers. The loch was very blue beneath.
The little waves sparkled distractingly. The wind
waved the yellow broom in a way it really ought not to.
The universe was ill-arranged for a small boy attending school that day.

Kit thought of the hot and breathless schoolroom at

Whinnyliggate, of Duncan Duncanson and his leathern taws (not that he cared much for those—he would back his granny's palm against them any day)—the smell of spilt ink, the mussy gritty slates and smutty copy-books, the bouquet of crowded and perspiring village childhood, the buzz of flies, the infrequency of so much as a wasp in a girl's class by way of entertainment. And—well, he followed Royal down to the edge of the loch.

He would stay just a minute—not more. He could easily make it up. He knew he could. He had started early that morning. And Royal would be so disappointed. See how he ran on before, saying "Come along. I want a swim. And I know where there is a lovely stick for you to throw in!"

And so Kit succumbed to temptation, telling himself (like certain wiser and older people who shall be nameless) that it was only this once, and just to see what it was like.

"*Splash!*" went Royal into the water, his eyes fixed on the stick, his head rising and falling steadily with the power of his mighty chest-strokes and the lift of the little in-coming waves. "*Jerk!*" he had it, with a snap of the jaws and a snort to clear his windpipe of the water he could not swallow. He was coming back hand over hand. Now he touched ground, and his back appeared above the loch. Royal scorned to pretend he was swimming when his feet were upon the bottom. Kit respected him for this. He was not always so conscientious himself. Who is, at the age of eleven, if it comes to that?

"*Stand clear all! Shake!*" The crystal drops flashed every way as Royal dropped the stick and stood ready again. Head a little forward, legs fixed on hair springs, eyes intently watching Kit's hand as he lifted the wet branch, tail switching a little nervily—it was high summer time with Royal Armour.

"*Ouch!* Get on," he said in his own language, "don't keep me waiting. I can't bear it. If you knew how nice it was in the water, you wouldn't like to stop out here either."

Kit swung the branch over his head, but instead of throwing it far into the water, he flung it up the green bank with a great heave into the waving broom on the slope. Then he laughed heartlessly.

Royal gave him one look—contempt mingled with a most painful surprise.

"*Et tu, Brute!*" he remarked, plain as Cæsar at the foot of Pompey's statue.

"Ha! ha! ha!" laughed Kit.

"*Ouch!*" snorted Royal, in quite a different key, with his nose in the air, as who would say, "Ha! ha! Aren't you funny?"

Then he went slowly and without joyousness up the hill. With a grave submission he brought the branch back and dropped it in dejected fashion at Kit's feet.

"I wouldn't have expected this from you," he said, reproachfully. "You treat me as if I were not more than half a water dog. And the nicest half of me, too, on a day like this!"

Whereat being shame-stricken, Kit again cast the branch into the clear brown water of the loch—clear, that is, but with a little amber in its depths decocted from the peat bogs at its upper end and from the green water meadows of Dornal and Crae.

It looked so cool that in a trice Kit had off his clothes, and he and Royal were tumbling hither and thither in a wild wrestle about the sandy shallows. The crystal drops flew every way. Laughter and splashings were mingled with joyous barking. The sun shone down with a broad grin upon the pleasant saturnalia.

Kit could swim a little. Geordie Elphinstone had taught him the breast stroke, but it was pleasanter and more interesting to wrestle near the shore with Royal, because at swimming he had no chance, whereas near the beach he was on more equal terms. The sun poured down upon his white glistening body. He shouted aloud in the young gladness of his heart. Duty, schoolmasters, lesson-books hid under broad stones, hours of exits and entrances, leathern taws and the moral law, were all alike forgotten.

" *Ouch*—let's have another ! " barked Royal, lumbering outwards like a great pot-walloping elephant through the shallows to become instantly perfectly graceful in the amber deeps, " come and have another ! " And Kit went. The water was still chillish, for it was early in the year. But the violence of the exercise and the racing of the young blood through his veins kept Kit warm for the better part of an hour.

Then he began to think of putting on his clothes. He waded ashore, feeling as the water fell away from him and the fanning wind blew, as if he had left part of himself behind in the water. He wished he had kept his sugar piece till now.

" *Ouff—ouff* ! " barked Royal behind him, " call yourself a swimmer and going out already—look at me ! "

And the doubtful Newfoundland pushed right across the loch for the woods on the further side.

" Oh, no doubt," said Kit in reply, turning to watch him, " it's very easy for you, staying in the water with all that hair on. Try it in your bare skin and see how you like it."

Then he held up his foot to try how it felt to have the water run between his toes. This proved interesting with the right foot, so Kit repeated the operation on the left. A little shiver of cold began to strike downward along his spine. He would put on his clothes. Where were they? Oh, yes, he remembered, behind that broom bush on the bank. He sprang up the short turf and rounded the waving green and gold of the obstacle.

There sat his mother beside them.

CHAPTER XXIII

Kit's Eyes are Opened.

KIT stopped abashed and ashamed. There is, doubtless, a disembodied moral law, a spiritual essence of right somewhere in the air about us, but we seldom let it alight on us till it comes in human guise. We rather *shoo* it off like a troublesome fly.

Kit Kennedy remembered for the first time that he ought to have gone to school.

"Kit," said Lilias Mac Walter, with sad directness, "you are playing truant!"

"Yes," said Kit, hanging his head, and standing meanwhile like a spare young Apollo erect before his mother. The moral law had alighted now.

There was a basket by his mother's side covered with a white napkin. She had been on her way to meet Heather Jock and his donkey as he passed along the highway, that he might take it to the Crae Cottage. She had not seen her father or her mother for many months.

Without saying a word Lilias took the napkin from the basket, and calling Kit to her she began, with strange thrills and upleapings of her mother's heart, to rub some warmth into the boy's chilled limbs. She had not done so much since he was a little lad of three years old. This made her glad that she had chanced upon him that morning, though she meant to speak seriously to the boy all the same. For the space of five long minutes both were silent, the tears welling up in the woman's averted eyes, and the boy casting about for some non-committal subject of conversation.

Then, garment by garment, she helped him on with

his clothes, till he stood completely arrayed before her.

Royal had swum and barked, and barked and swum between the deeps and and the shallows ever since Kit's desertion. But now he came up the bank, sheepishly wagging his lank wet tail, keeping meanwhile one eye on the intentions of Lilias's hand and one on her uncovered basket.

"Kit," said his mother, gravely, "sit down. I want to speak to you."

Much subdued Kit sat down. He wished that he had been suffering under Dominie Duncanson's taws instead. But he sat meekly down as he was bidden.

Royal settled himself upon his haunches a few yards below on a spit of broiling shingle, cocking his ears alternately at these inexplicable humans, who on such a morning preferred the land to the water, and, having a basket of delicacies such as he could see plainly with his nose, went on making foolish noises with their mouths. Royal could have shown them a better use for these last.

"Kit," said his mother, "I have been thinking for a long while that you are old enough to be told what is before you. You are nearly eleven, and older than most boys of twelve or fourteen. I did not mean to trouble you yet, for Mr. Duncanson says that you are doing well at school. But now I must speak. You are getting wild and playing truant. I will not rage upon you, Kit. I will only tell you that if you go on in the way you are doing you will break your mother's heart."

"Oh, mither!" cried Kit, tears springing into eyes which would not have been wet for the best whipping that Duncan Duncanson could have given, "I forgot. I did not mean to—at least, I didna ken ye were comin' this road."

"No," said his mother, gently, "that is just it. You did not think; you did not mean any wrong. You did not expect to be found out. That is exactly the way to break a mother's heart."

Kit hung his head. The moral law was biting steadily now.

"Kit," she went on, after a pause of strengthening silence and upward appeal, "Kit, laddie mine, I want you to be a good man, a true man. I think you will be a clever man—you have it in you. Listen, Kit. Once I knew a very clever man—not a bad man, but one who, like you, did not think, did not mean, did not care, so long as he was not found out. Kit, your mother would have been the happiest woman in the world if that man had thought, had meant, had remembered. But—he broke my heart and made my life a living death. Now my heart grows alive again to look at you. But, oh! Kit, I see something of that man in you. I would rather see you lie dead before me than that you should break any woman's heart as that man broke mine!"

"Was he my faither?" asked Kit, in a low awed tone, not looking at his mother, but down at the loch, which somehow seemed suddenly to have grown misty and far away.

"He was your father," said the woman Lilias, very softly.

There was a long silence between them twain, so long that Royal dropped his head and pretended to go to sleep.

"Is he dead, mither?" said Kit at last, the realities of life humming in his ears and making his heart like chill water within him.

"No, he is not dead," said Lilias Mac Walter, her face looking ashen grey and drawn in the insolent optimism of the morning sunshine.

Kit thought a while, and then said, with an indignant ring in his voice, "How you must hate him, mither!"

There was a little rustling beyond the dyke in the broom into which Kit had thrown the stick. A thrush which had flown in as if to visit its nest flew out again, "cherking" crossly.

His mother did not answer, so Kit repeated his words, "How you must hate that man, mither!"

With eyes pulsing and misty, like the sky over the Northern sea where the ice floats, Lilias replied. She did not sigh—sighing is for hopeful people who are only temporarily unhappy. But this woman was hopeless, expectationless, convicted on a life sentence from which she did not mean to appeal.

"Hate him—no. I do not hate that man, Kit," she said, slowly, but very distinctly. "Rather, God forgive him and me—I love him still. For a woman who once loves truly, Kit, as I loved your father, there is in this life no escape, no hope. I do not know about the next. At any rate she loves to the end. You do not understand. Nor can any man fully understand. Like a wasp that is crushed a man turns to sting that which hurts him. But when a woman is bruised, wounded to the death, ground to powder, if the heel be the heel of the man she loves, it cannot grind the great love out of her heart. Such love as this, Kit, does not come at will. It does not go at bidding. It is there, Kit. You do not understand. You never will wholly, for you are a man. But that is the truth. God has made woman so that because I loved that man once I must love him always!"

The relieving tears welled up silently in the grey-blue eyes. There they stood for a moment like water in an over-full glass held by a sort of surface tension. Then they ran slowly over and dripped unheeded one by one upon her lap. One fell on Kit's hand. It was warm.

"Oh, mither, dinna!" he cried, agonised, snatching his hand away with the swift intolerance of youth for mental suffering—an unknown and foolish thing to healthy childhood.

"Do you love Walter MacWalter?" said Kit presently, with the remorseless curiosity of youth, whose inquiries sometimes sting like lashes, sometimes cut like knives.

Lilias started at his words. She formed her lips for some vehement answer. But it was unspoken. The fire that leaped into her eyes died out as swiftly. For a space she was silent, and when she spoke it was in a low, even, colourless voice.

"No!" she said, "I do not love Walter Mac Walter."

"Did you never love him?" pursued pitiless youth.

"I never loved him!"

"Then why did you marry him?"

In all her life's trials Lilias never had to endure (save once) any moment so terrible as this.

She tried to speak, but a pulsing check rose rebelliously in her throat, and she stammered like a speaker who has suddenly forgotten his next sentence.

"Kit—Kit! Oh, Kit," she gasped, "you are cruel. My lad—my lad—but you do not mean to be. I will tell you—yes, you shall know. I married Walter Mac Walter because I thought my heart was dead—because of the man, your father. I thought he did not love me, that he had deceived me. My mother said, 'Marry the man for your father's sake. The debt crushes him to the ground. He is a good man. Love will come afterwards.' I did wrong, Kit, I sinned against love. But do not hate me, Kit. I will die if you hate me. I have gotten so little out of life—I who expected so much. I cannot bear that you should hate me, Kit. At least, I have not deserved that."

The boy felt the tears well up in his own eyes. He did not understand. He could not. Yet Lilias was wise, for the effort to understand made a deeper impression on Kit's mind than if he had understood all. The mystery of suffering sobered him. He grew older and wiser each moment. By instinct this woman had reached the truth that to make children trust you, you must appeal to their understandings as well as to their hearts.

Kit Kennedy reached his hand across to his mother and laid it on hers. She took her left hand and gently patted it. Then she went on again.

"My boy," she said, "I did wrong. I sinned against love. But I have been punished, and God, I think, looks upon it so. 'Whom He loveth He chasteneth.' I heard Mr. Osborne say it. But not as if he knew it. Not as I know it. If I have sinned greatly

I have also been greatly punished, and God does not exact the penalty in both worlds. Kit, be a good man. Be true. Speak the truth and take the consequences. If you do wrong, as you will, stand up to the punishment. Kit, do not run from trouble, as—as *he* did. If he had remained God knows how proudly, how gladly I would have stood by his side—aye, through disgrace, penury, and death. But he was afraid and went away. Oh, Kit, do not flinch, stand up to the storm, and be sure that the woman who loves you will stand beside you. I tell you her heart will be proud and rejoicing because she knows it is done for the man she loves!"

A rabbit or some wild thing stirred in the broom bush. Kit turned his head quickly, but saw nothing.

Having spoken out, Lilias Mac Walter's heart was happier than it had been for years. The burden was eased. An unseen hand seemed to lift it from her shoulders.

"You do not hate me for this, Kit?" she said, with a yearning pitifulness in her eyes.

The boy sobbed one great sob, felt his face go cold, and then fell on his mother's neck.

"Mither!" was all he said.

And from the heart of Lilias, the sinned-against, the year-long pain ebbed away.

*　　　*　　　*　　　*　　　*

It was some time before these two friends found articulate words again. When they did it was the woman who began to speak in a hushed tone. Kit had forgotten his eleven years, his adult superiority, his dignity of man. He lay with his head on his mother's breast. She kissed his hair and brow as often as she would. And that was not seldom. God did not grudge her this season and slowed the universe to make it longer. He had done as much for Joshua upon a less important occasion. But overhead a dark and threatening cloud drew down from the Girthon Hills, thunder brooding within its blue-black bosom.

"Kit," the woman said, gently, "you are a clever

boy. I want you to be something in the world. I am
sure you can be if you like. For your mother's sake,
try. You must do it for yourself. I cannot help you.
Your grandfather and grandmother are too poor to aid
you. You must help yourself. I do not want you to
be only a ploughman. There is more in you than that.
Only remember that mere money-making is nothing,
Kit; I want you to be a scholar, like your father. But
with the strength he had not. Perhaps one day, who
knows, God may repent Him of the evil. No, I
must not think of it. It is impossible ! " She paused,
and was silent a long while.

Kit did not interrupt or ask any questions this time.
He was pillowed contentedly under his mother's chin.
He liked it—when he was sure that no one could see
him. Also he was forming great resolves within him.
For a boy of eleven can make resolves—and sometimes
keep them better than a man of forty.

"Mother, I am going to be a great man," said the
reformed truant. And even as he spoke there came a
vivid flash, and the thunder broke above in sonorous
mirth at Kit's daring !

"All right, we'll see ! " said Kit Kennedy, leaping up
and shaking his fist at the elements.

CHAPTER XXIV.

Kit Begins to be a Great Man.

HEEDLESS of the rain Kit went off to school, much belated, but jubilant in his heart. He saw life before him now, and he meant, as his mother had bidden him, to stand up to it.

He made a beginning by standing up to the consequences of his truantry in the shape of the frown on the brow of Duncan Duncanson, deposed minister and schoolmaster in the parish of Whinnyliggate.

"Where have you been, sir?" demanded the stern pedagogue. He had had a "cast out" with his daughter Flora that morning on the subject of going to the Red Lion with a black bag which contained an empty bottle.

"I have been swimming in the loch with my dog Royal," said Kit, calmly. He had learned his lesson.

The dominie could not believe his ears. Denial of imputed iniquity was so much the rule in Whinnyliggate school that any other course was paralysing. Something must be concealed under such superfluous candour.

"Wha—at!" cried Duncan Duncanson, lifting the taws threateningly.

"I have been swimming in the loch with my dog Royal," Kit repeated. His head not yet dry testified that his witness was true.

"Stand out," cried the enraged dominie, snapping the lid of his desk.

Thus Kit began his course as a reformed character by enduring without wincing, and even with a considerable amount of mental satisfaction, a larger number of

11

"pawmies" than had ever been known previously even to the liberal arithmetic of the deposed minister. He did not feel them very much, and when the master had exhausted himself, Kit still further astonished the school by still holding out his hand and saying, "Is that a'?"

"Go to your seat, sir," thundered the master, and Kit went, rubbing the palm of his right hand against that of his left, with an appearance of enjoyment which made him the envy of every boy and the adoration of every girl.

Kit sat down on the worn "form," and glanced at the lesson-book which he had exhumed on his way to school. He knew it from beginning to end. An idea came to him.

He rose from his seat and marched straight up to the master.

Duncan Duncanson glared at him in amazed surprise.

"What do you want?" he thundered. He had an idea also. He thought that the boy was outbraving him.

"If ye please, sir," said Kit, whose English had departed from him with the relaxation of the tension, "I want to gang into the 'Coorse o' Readin'.' I ken a' that's in MacCulloch's 'Series.' It is silly bairn's book onyway. I dinna care to gang blatterin' it ower and ower again. Let me gang into the 'Coorse' and I winna troan the schule (play truant) for a year!"

"You are too young—far too young for the 'Course,'" said the astonished teacher, scratching his head. Marvels came too thick that morning.

"Try me," said Kit, boldly and succinctly.

Duncan Duncanson stared. "Give me a 'Course of Reading,' somebody!" he cried. He had a certain respect for that fine school-book, and felt himself personally insulted (as well as the editorial MacCulloch) by this boy's insolent request.

"And if you fail, the licking that you have had will be child's play to what you will get. Make your count with that, my clever young man."

Kit said nothing whatever in reply. He only stretched out his hand for the book.

"Where will ye hae her ? " he asked.

Mr. Duncanson pointed out a lesson in which the properties of the atmosphere were illustrated with a wealth of scientific "jaw-breakers." "Read!" he cried, ferociously, and he tightened his fingers about a hazel stick usually reserved for the grown-up youths who frequented the school in winter. He felt that the most indurated and leaden-toed "taws" would not meet the case if Kit so much as stumbled. But the son of the classical master had a natural affinity for words. Also the master did not know that there was an old copy of Johnson's Dictionary in two big volumes bound in calf that Kit considered the best reading in his grandfather's house, and the transport of which to Crae Cottage he had personally superintended. Therefore the properties of oxygen and other probably wholly imaginary substances concealed no terrors for him.

The master listened, at first with surprise, then with a wavering tolerance, lastly with a rapidly rising admiration. But he could not give in before the school. He did not believe in " cockering up" boys.

"That will do," he said, austerely. "You can stand up at the foot of the 'Course' class."

Thus was Kennedy promoted to the highest seats in the synagogue for having gone in swimming with a red collie of indifferent character and more than doubtful antecedents.

At the end of school a little girl came up to Kit. She was sweet of face and her eyes were full of compassion.

" Did it hurt much ? " she asked.

Kit laughed. "What? Oh, the taws. They didna hurt at a'. You should get a lickin' frae Granny when she is doin' hersel' justice ! "

"I think you are very brave ! " she said, with a certain shyness very grateful to the hero.

Kit thought so too, but he was not going to confess it to a mere lassie. "Yon's naething," he said,

modestly, in an off-hand manner. Then he added,
" I say, lassie, what do they caa' ye?"

"My name," said the girl, "is Meysie Mac Walter!"

"Do ye like it?" said Kit, looking doubtfully at her.

" Like it—why should I no like my ain name?" said
the girl, with surprise. She was a year or two older
than Kit, which of course made her praise and interest
much more acceptable.

" Weel," said Kit, "my mither's name is Mac
Walter noo, and I dinna think she likes it muckle."

A curious light shone upon the girl's face. " Did
your mither marry my uncle Walter Mac Walter?"

Kit looked down and scrabbled in the dust with his
toe. He did not like to answer that question. It
seemed like betraying his mother's confidence.

" He married her!" answered Kit, turning the
corner of the question.

The girl held out her hand. "Then I like her. I
have come to stay at Kirkoswald with my uncle Walter.
But I live at a place called Loch Spellanderie!"

" Lord—a' that!" said Kit Kennedy.

Thus it chanced that our hero, having set out to
play the truant, received a lesson more enduring in its
results than any he had ever learned, and in addition
obtained promotion in his classes—all which convinced
him that honesty was the best policy. Besides which
he had had his swim and a play with Royal as well. A
still further blessing of Providence befell him.

The alternate shine and shower which began with
the thunder plump at the lochside had settled into a
fixed and determinate downpour.

At first sight it may be difficult to see why this should
be classed as a benefit. But to Kit's mind the matter
was very clear. For had he remained at the lochside
with Royal instead of coming on to school and getting
the consequences well over, he would have had to choose
between an afternoon in the rain and going home with
the evidence of his truantry rank and obvious upon him.
But as it was, he sat talking with this new girl, swinging
his legs comfortably over the ledge of a window in the

school during the short dinner-hour. When the school reassembled he devoted himself to the study of his lessons with a diligence which, when the hour of recitation arrived, delivered boy after boy and girl after girl into his hands. Indeed, he was in a fair way of "trapping" his way to the head of the class, when all unexpectedly he found himself beside Meysie Mac Walter.

"Dinna 'trap' me, or I will never speak to you again as long as I live. Besides, I shall greet. I won't be taken down by a boy more than two years younger than me! I'm gangin' awa' hame in a week, so then ye can get to the head o' the class."

"A' richt, lassie," said Kit, who was distinctly precocious, "it's a' richt. I'll tell ye if ye dinna ken. Auld Bottlenose is as deaf as a post."

"But I dinna want to be telled—I want to ken!" said the girl, rebelliously.

So all the afternoon Kit prompted the young lady, and despite her protest—after the first time, when another girl passed above them both—she answered when in doubt according to Kit's instructions. She did not, of course, demean herself by showing any gratitude, but took the credit of all the good shots, and cast upon Kit the ignominy of all the bad, according to the wont of her sex when they are becoming conscious of their power.

"Meysie Mac Walter!" said Kit, "what an awesome funny name ye hae gotten. Whatever garred them caa' ye that? Ye maun hae been brocht up in a verra outlandish-like place."

"I was going to let you call me 'May' for short, but noo I winna. You are not a nice boy, and very ignorant. You let Grace Turner get above me for spelling 'awry.'"

"It's a silly word onyway," said Kit, scornfully. "What's the use o' sayin' 'awry' when ye mean twisted? But I'll caa' ye 'May' whether ye let me or no. So there!"

By all which things we can see that Kit was getting on bravely with his learning. For most that is really

valuable in a man's education is the work of those great
natural wit-sharpeners, women.   And Kit was in hands
with four of them, his grandmother, his mother, Betty,
and now this tan-faced, white-toothed, sweet-eyed
schoolgirl, Mistress Meysie Mac Walter of Loch Spellanderie, niece to his arch-enemy, the Laird of Kirkoswald.

CHAPTER XXV.

A Broken Heart.

But Kit was fated to have yet another adventure, and to place himself the second time under the sting of the moral gadfly.

It chanced that his strong Uncle Rob, the woodforester, had come down that morning early to the sawmill in the village with a load of birchwood to be transformed into "bobbins" and "pirns." Rob Armour was not so long out of his own schooldays, at least in the winter season, and he thought of the prisoned schoolboy when the thunder broke over the village and the first plump descended. He looked out of the bobbin mill door, and said to himself, "It's gaun to be a stormy day. I declare I'll look in at the schule and get Dominie Duncanson to let the wean aff. I'll gie him a ride hame, and he'll no be vexed to win away at this time o' the day. I can easy mak' it a' richt wi' my mither."

So as he was driving homewards through the village he went round by the school and asked for Kit Kennedy.

The master seemed surprised.

"He has not been here to-day," said Duncan Duncanson. "Perhaps they have kept him at home to help with some work."

Rob Armour said nothing, because he did not wish to get Kit into further trouble.

But within him he said, "The young rascal is troanin' the schule. He'll catch it when he gets to the Crae."

Then he drove off, missing Kit by just five minutes.

For that youth had taken the path over the fields as a shorter cut through the rain.

*　　　　*　　　　*　　　　*　　　　*

When Kit reached home that night he came in with the bright smile and the cheerful countenance of one whose mind and conscience are wholly at rest.

But he had hardly looked about him before he became aware of a painful chill of restraint which was visible upon every face. His grandfather sat in his chair, more erect than usual. He said no word of greeting, and Kit cared more for that than for his grandmother's most voluble angers. Kit laid down his bag on the window-sill with a certain dreary foreboding of evil to come, the tin flask echoing emptily in it. Then he went to the white wooden "dresser," on which the blue delf plates were arranged symmetrically, to get his evening's drink of milk.

Now there were two points along the lochside road from Whinnyliggate to the Black Dornal from which he could see the chimneys of his home. And Kit being a boy full of all manner of sentiment, a connoisseur in sensations even before his teens, always climbed to the top of the bank to look at them. That is as he was returning from school. On the outward journey the prospect of milk on the dresser was too remote to come, as it were, within the sphere of practical politics. He called these vista-heights Pisgah and the Delectable Mountains.

" It will hae turned wi' the thunder," he observed by way of breaking the painful silence as he stood at the "dresser." Then a sharp voice, surely not that of his grandmother, told him curtly to "stand away frae there!"

Kit was excessively astonished. He knew in a moment that something was very far wrong, and in his whirling mind he ran over the catalogue of his most recent misdemeanours. There were the eggs (Kit got a halfpenny a dozen from his grandmother for the eggs of "outlaying" hens—that is of hens which, disdaining their appointed nests, wandered off and laid in the woods) ; no, he had always been careful when arranging one of these treasure-troves not to include any ducks' eggs. For Kit was in the habit of taking occasional tribute from the official nests in the outhouses, in order that after a day or two he might find them as "out-layers" and receive his copper.

On the whole he did not think it could be the eggs. The gooseberries? No, again he thought not. Nobody knew of that hole in the garden hedge except himself. And he had always kept modestly at the back of the bushes whilst he was eating his fill. The broken bowl he had buried in the midden—again no. He had blamed the loss of that on the cat, and his grandmother had thrown the dish-clout at Baudrons that very morning with such excellent feminine aim that it had knocked down other two bowls from the shelf!

He had it. The swimming!

He had been forbidden to swim in the loch unless one of his uncles were with him. Well, he would forestall criticism. It might be too late, but still he would try, in any event.

"Granny," he said, "the water was awfu' warm this mornin'; I took aff my shoon and dabbled my feet in the water."

He looked up to see how this was received. It contained the truth, he told himself, only a trifle understated. The silence in the Crae cottage became only more stony than before.

"I waded up to my knees," he added, with the air of one who makes a last concession for the sake of peace. No one spoke. His uncle, Rob Armour, was deeply interested in the "Wee Paper," as *The Cairn Edward Advertiser* was at that time somewhat slightingly called.

Kit was in despair. He resolved that when he grew up and had nephews and grandchildren, he would know better how to treat them when they had something on their minds. These people never helped a little boy who wanted only to make sure which crime it was he had been found out in. They might at least give a fellow a friendly lead, and then he would know what to do. But this dead silence was inhuman, to say the least of it. How would they like it themselves?

Then with a burst came his complete confession.

"I strippit and gaed into the water this mornin' on my road to the schule!"

His grandmother stopped and looked at him as he sat swinging his legs with counterfeit ease on the great wooden meal-ark which had come to the Cottage from the Black Dornal. Then she went on again without making any remark. She was brushing the floor with that quick, uncertain stroke which with Mistress Armour was good evidence of a perturbed mind. But now his grandfather spoke.

"You were at the school to-day?" he said, looking at Kit for the first time.

"Aye," answered Kit, cheerfully; "I got to the head o' my class!"

He felt himself on firm ground now.

"Let me see, what was the lesson this afternoon?" said his grandfather, with a distance and calmness which Kit felt to be of the worst augury.

He saw it all now. They had found out about his leaving his books under the flag-stone of the old mill.

"I forgot to bring hame my books, grandfaither!" he said.

"Enough!" said the Elder, rising as if the matter were ended, "more than enough. Boy, do not lie to me any more. We know that you were not at school to-day. You played truant!"

Kit was more aggrieved than if he had been soundly beaten. To be accused of having successfully done that which he had only intended to do—it was unbearable.

"But I was at the schule! As sure as daith, grandfaither!" he cried, with his most solemn oath.

"You were not," said his grandfather. "Your uncle was in Whinnyliggate. He asked at the school for you, and the master said you had never been near the place that day."

It was a tight corner for Master Kit, but he made the best of it. He told the whole truth, which after all, licking or no licking, considerably simplifies matters.

"Grandfaither," he said, "this is the way o't—I gaed into the loch wi' Royal, but my mither fand me and sent me to the schule. The maister lickit me for coming late. But I got a' my lessons, grandfaither!"

"What time did ye get to the school, sir?" continued Kit's inquisitor.

"I couldna tell. It was after the Bible lesson!"

"I am sorry that I cannot believe you," said his grandfaither; "you began by saying that you only dabbled in the water—then that you waded, finally you admit that you went in to swim. Your uncle was told by the master that you had not been near the school all day!"

Tears sprang into Kit's eyes, a kind of ghastly surprise settled down on his spirit. "Do ye mean that ye winna believe me when I tell you, grandfaither?"

"I am grieved that you have not given me cause to believe you, sir," answered his grandfather. His heart was wae for the boy, but he believed that he was being severe for his good.

"Aweel!" said Kit, and rose to go out without saying another word.

His grandmother called him to come back and get his tea. Her heart was smiting her already.

"I dinna want ony tea," said Kit, who was beginning to glory in the injustice done him.

"Then come in for your supper in an hour. The parritch will be ready a wee bit earlier the nicht."

"I dinna want ony parritch," said Kit, with a certain ring of triumph in his voice.

What did a broken heart want with porridge? Kit was wounded in his tenderest affections. His grandfather had hitherto been his standby, and now even he had refused to believe him. Kit was under the impression that he was a truthful boy. And so, all things considered, perhaps he was. That is, he would not tell a direct lie. He would rather be whipped ever so. He did not count a little judicious hedging to be "lying," and, after all, on this occasion he had told the truth about the swimming. Like many older folk, Kit discriminated severely between the truth and the whole truth. The truth was a duty—the whole truth often an inconvenience, always an impertinence.

Kit wandered away through the little glen where the alders and willows were swaying their slender stems and silver-grey leaves, sighing over the dreariness of the world. The mist was collecting in white pools down in the hollows of the meadow. The waters of the loch drowsed purple-black under the shadow of the hills. Yonder was the Dornal where he had been so happy.

Now no one loved him. He was alone in the world. He wished he could go away over the hills and never return. Perhaps somewhere in the wide world he would find someone to care for him—to believe in him.

His mind flew to Meysie Mac Walter, the new girl from Kirkoswald, with a certain comfort. She would understand and she would help him. He would slip round that way. Perhaps he might see her. He started without a moment's hesitation, though it was getting dark, with the ready alacrity of healthy country boyhood. At any rate he would put his grandfather and his cruel words out of his head.

Kit went on up the hill-track, past the quarry, through the wet bracken in the midst of which the glow-worms were already shining and the crickets *cherk-cherking*. The dark-green branching fronds, wet with dew, touched his bare hands. He could feel the coolness of them through his summer clothes. *Swish-swish* went his feet through the dew-drenched grass, which had yet nothing of that dankness which comes with rain.

The stile over which his mother had disappeared the day she found the tramp was before him. Kit did not look up, interested in thinking how deep he was wading through the bracken. Suddenly the keen acrid tang of strong tobacco came to him on the resinous air of night. At the same moment a rabbit startled him, scurrying in prodigious but half-pretended fright across his path and into the firwood.

He glanced up. A gun was leaning against the stone dyke, and on the stile, smoking a short black pipe, sat Walter Mac Walter, the new laird of the Black Dornal.

CHAPTER XXVI

Kit's Kind Friend.

Kit's heart stood still. He knew that this was the arch-enemy of his race, the man who had tried to lash him with his whip, and who had put his grandfather out of the farm. He turned to run, conscious how useless it would be if the man should try to catch him. But the man did not move.

"Don't be frightened, boy," he said instead, in a kind voice, "come here, I want to speak to you."

Whereupon Kit, more from a feeling of helpless curiosity than anything else, stopped and looked back over his shoulder.

"Come here," said the man again, "I want to have a talk with you."

Walter Mac Walter sat smoking without a movement. Kit dragged himself foot by foot back through the bracken till he was within half-a-dozen yards of the stile. Nearer than that he could not bring himself to go.

A wild thought came into his head that the man might have grown sorry about the farm, and that he was going to tell him that his grandfather might go back again. How fine that would be! Then he could return to the cottage and paralyse them all with the news—he, the boy whom they had refused to believe and had cast out a little while before. Ah, they would be sorry then.

Walter Mac Walter sat a long while with his eyes fixed on the boy's face, perusing his features like the pages of a book.

"You are a clever boy, they tell me?" he said.

"Aye," replied Kit Kennedy, not heeding much what

he answered. He wanted him to begin about the farm.

"The schoolmaster has a good account of you," continued Mac Walter.

"It's different to what he tells mysel' then!" said Kit, finding his tongue, "for he's aye fechtin' at me the day by the length!"

The man with the black pipe laughed a short laugh.

"I wonder at you"—his speech flowed slowly, yet with a friendliness which Kit felt the more because it was so wholly unexpected—"how old are you, boy?"

"Gangin' on for twelve," said Kit, with the optimism of spendthrift youth in the matter of years.

"I wonder at you, Kit," repeated Mac Walter, taking his pipe meditatively from his mouth; "you are twelve, you say, and as far up in the school as the master can put you, so they tell me. Did you never think what a care and burden you are to your—your grandfather and grandmother? They are poor and cannot afford to keep a great fellow like you idle!"

"I'm no' idle!" said Kit, indignantly.

"What do you do then?"

"I cut the sticks, I brick the steps at the door. I gather the eggs, I look after the chuckies when they lay away——!"

Kit faltered, for at best it was a poor catalogue, and even during its brief course his conscience had smitten him several times—especially in the matter of gathering the eggs.

"These are all nothing! Your grandmother could easily do them herself," said the man. "But it takes food and clothing and money to keep you. Your school fees are to pay for and your books—the very bread and milk you carry with you in your bag. And you never help to bring in a penny. You should be at work, man. I had a father with money, and yet I was sent to work before I was either as big or as old as you!"

"I never thocht o' that!" said Kit, his heart mis-

giving him. It was evidently true. He saw it all
now. They were tired of him at the cottage or they
would never have disbelieved him that night. He
was a burden to them and they wanted to be rid of
him. Yes, that was it. Well, he would rid them of
that burden as soon as ever he could.

"But how can a boy like me get work?" said Kit.
"I hae never learned onything in particular!"

"If I was to find you work," said the man with
the black pipe, "would you promise to bide away and
never tell anybody that you got it through me?"

"Aye," cried Kit, eagerly, "I wad that! As sure
as daith and dooble daith!"

"Then," said Walter Mac Walter, "meet me here
to-morrow morning on your way to school, and I will
give you a letter to a man who will find you work and
pay you well for doing it too! Is it a bargain?"

"I'll come!" answered the boy, pleasing himself with
a curious feeling of vengeance upon those he loved.
He would make them sorry for refusing to believe Kit
Kennedy. Play truant—yes, he would play truant for
a very long time. Then when he came back with
money of his own, they would not grudge him anything.
It was true what the man said. He did not earn anything and he was a burden upon them. But it would
not be for long.

"When will I come?" he asked.

"As early as you like," answered the man with the
black pipe; "I will be on the outlook for you."

Kit was turning away when the man suddenly called
to him. "Come and shake hands, boy!"

Kit turned and walked fearlessly to Walter Mac
Walter, holding out his hand.

"Guidnicht to ye, sir, and thank ye kindly!" he
said, more cheerfully and gratefully than he had yet
spoken.

The man looked into the boy's eyes, and drew him
closer to him. Then he said in a low voice with a
sudden fierce hiss in it, "Mind, do not deceive me.
Keep your promise."

" MIND, DO NOT DECEIVE ME."

[*Page* 177.

"I always keep my promises!" said Kit, with the same bright fearlessness.

To this the man answered nothing, but dropped the boy's hand and resumed his pipe.

"Guidnicht!" said Kit again, with great hope in his heart. The man only nodded, and continued to smoke as Kit went homeward through the wet bracken. At the quarry edge where his father had lain, Kit turned to wave a hand to his newly-found friend.

CHAPTER XXVII.

Kit Runs Away from Home.

There was a general air of cheerfulness in the air when Kit entered the little cottage under the wood of Crae.

"Come your ways up to the fire, Kit," said the Elder, "it's gettin' cauld thae nichts."

He had had time to bethink himself during his grandson's absence, and it had occurred to him that in spite of evidence to the contrary, the boy might after all be telling the truth. And at any rate, he, Matthew Armour, had been too great a sinner to make him a good hand at casting the first stone. So in absence his mind was drawn to the lad, and when Kit came in his grandfather spoke the countryside talk to mark the difference.

But the boy instinctively felt his advantage, and nursed his grievance with the redoubled assiduity of youth, when it feels at once misunderstood and afraid of giving in.

"I'm no cauld!" he said, with chill evasion, and went and sat on the edge of the settle at the point nearest the door.

"Your parritch hae been waitin' for ye this hour and mair—I hae keepit them warm by the fire for ye," put in his grandmother, anxiously.

Kit was on the point of saying that he did not want any porridge, but the hunger at his stomach and the thought of the long waiting hours before the morning induced him to think that sacrifice to wounded pride unnecessary. So he did not speak but moved dourly to the table. He was afraid of giving in too soon, so as he took bite and sup of the porridge and milk, the latter yet warm from their one cow, he kept repeating over to himself all his grandfather's cruel aspersions on his truthfulness, and fortifying himself with the new ideas that he was a burden to them, and that they must consider him so to treat him as they had done. It was a comfort to Kit even in thought to call his grandfather and grandmother "they."

Betty Landsborough moved about with a quaint smile on her face, which was half contempt for Kit's fit of the sulks, and half occasioned by a vision of Rob Armour waiting in vain for her at the end of the loaning, where she had no intention of joining him. For, sad to relate, to make a promise with a lad was with Betty by no means synonymous with keeping it.

Presently Mistress Armour went into the little side room, where she and her husband slept, to put things in order for the night. The Elder was looking out of the window. He had gone in before her.

As soon as they were safely out of the kitchen Betty came behind Kit and gave him a sound pinch on the soft part of his arm.

"Tak' that for a silly sulky brat!' she said, and passed on her way. She was not a commonplace girl, Betty Landsborough.

"*Ouch!*" said Kit Kennedy.

"Did you speak, laddie?" said his grandmother, looking out from the closet door.

"No," said Kit, instantly relapsing, and waiting for Betty to come near enough for him to kick her under the table.

He was really suffering to make it all up, but he would not say so while no apology was made. His grandfather and grandmother were just as anxious to be friends as he, but with the Scottish dourness of relative with relative they could not bring their minds to own themselves definitely in the wrong. Such a capitulation subverted discipline. So the chance passed and the candles were lighted for bed.

"Guid-nicht, Kit!" said his grandfather.

"Good-night!" answered Offended Dignity—their
several forms of speech marking their moods of mind.
So without reconciliation and with sore hearts the
friends parted for the night.

And on the morrow Kit meant to keep his promise
to Walter Mac Walter.

*   *   *   *   *

In the morning Kit made ready to meet his new
benefactor, the man with the pipe. He rose before
daybreak, and stole down from his little garret so softly
that he did not even awake Betty, who slept near him.
He listened a moment at his grandfather's door to make
sure that all was safe. He was on the point of lifting
the latch and going out when he heard the Elder stir.
He held his breath, and in a moment all was still again.
The small-paned window of the little kitchen only
admitted a feeble grey light which diffused itself somewhat dismally over the floor with its whorls of whiting,
and upon the ashes of last night's peats in the dis-
hevelled grate.

Kit had a stubby pencil in his pocket. He found it,
and approached the deal table. In the corner he found
a "funeral letter"—that is, in the Scottish language, an
invitation to attend a funeral. He tore off the back,
and began to scrawl some words on the broad white
space within the heavy mourning borders.

DEAR GRANDFAITHER [so the letter ran], I am run away to
make my own leeving and not be a burden on you and grandmother and Betty no more. I have got a place. At least a man
says he will get me one. But I am not to tell who he is, nor
where I am going. He says I would be a coward and greedy if
I stayed and ate off you any longer. Dear grandpa, I am sorry
if I have been a greedy wretch, though I ken that I do eat a lot.
And grandfaither, I *did* gang to the school yesterday, but was
late, and auld Duncan licked me for it. I didna care for that, no
a flee. But I love you and will write you from my new place,
and I hope to send you some money to make up for what I have
eat. So no more from your loving

KIT.

This composition took quite a while to write, and the
boy was on pins and needles lest someone should come

and find him at his task. He stuck this note, folded together neatly and sealed by a thumb mark, upon the latch of his grandfather's little side closet, and then, stealing to the outer door, he ran with all his might through the wood, crossed the Grannoch lane at the stepping-stones, and made his way up to the trysting place on the march between Dornal and Kirkoswald.

Mr. Mac Walter was not at the stile. The sun was just rising, and Kit had quite a while to wait. But he remembered that he had omitted to say his prayers that morning. So he made up arrears by repeating the Lord's Prayer twice over, and the " Chief End of Man " no less than seventeen times.

Kit grew uneasy as it neared six o'clock, and he watched the green depths of the Crae wood for the light streamer of Betty's morning wood fire which would mean that his flight had been discovered.

But Mac Walter had seen the little figure waiting on the stile, and it was not long before he arrived along the edge of the stone dyke, striking unexpectedly up from the deep gloom of the plantation. He had the same gun over his shoulder, and a setter dog followed at his heel. As before he was smoking his black pipe, and at every half-dozen steps, regular as a minute gun, a solid blue curl of reek swept over his shoulder and thinned out to grey behind him.

"Good morning, boy!" said he without taking his pipe out of his mouth ; "you are in time, and have kept your word. Here is the letter to your new master, Mr. John Mac Walter at Loch Spellanderie on the water of Ken. And here is a pound to help you on your way. You will go down this hill, and through the wood towards the railway cutting. At the bridge head of the Dee you must wait till a red cart comes past. You will know it by seeing " Kirkoswald " printed on the panels. The man will give you a ride. He is going to my brother's farm. I am giving you a chance not many boys have had at your age—a chance to make their own living and to rise in the world."

Kit said nothing, but looked down from the stile on

the waving fern. He could have sworn that he caught sight of a face looking out from it, the keen white face of a man with short-cut grey hair. But when he looked again it had vanished, and only the bracken swayed and soughed as before in the breeze of morning.

He took the money, and at Mac Walter's request he repeated mechanically the directions he had received. Then he prepared to depart, the man with the black pipe pointing out the way by which he could best escape observation.

" Whatever comes, mind you are to tell no one that it was I who helped you to do this ! " he said.

Kit promised with alacrity. He would not disoblige so kind and unselfish a friend.

Besides he was now most anxious to be gone. For even as he stood, and looked over the green tangle of the bracken, a faint blue smoke rose straight up from among the trees in the Crae wood under which the cottage nestled. And as he watched it Kit knew that his absence would be discovered. He longed to go back, but his pride and his promise alike bound him.

Briefly he bade his benefactor good-bye, and went down the hillside, a forlorn little figure striding through the tall brackens in the clear cherry-coloured morning light—the eternal type of youth going forth to seek its fortune, ignorant of life, eager for adventure, prodigal of sentiment, and—foredoomed to disillusion and dis-appointment.

Kit reached the bridge over Dee Water without mishap, and presently stood in the breathing gloom of the hazel copse, bending the elastic branches sufficiently aside to command a view of the road by which the red cart was to come.

At last, after watching some twenty minutes, far away he heard the rattle of its loose axle, then the jog and sway of the plodding farm horse, and lastly the musical clink and tinkle of head harness.

He kept in the covert till he could see the " Kirk-oswald " on the panel and then came out.

A taciturn man was driving, a man with a slouch hat,

who wore in addition a pair of yellowish-brown and exceeding rusty mole-skin trowsers. A jean waistcoat, and boots so large and heavy that they seemed to tilt the cart to the side as he planted them on the shaft, completed his easy attire. "Get in," he cried without stopping the red cart or turning his head. And Kit scrambled easily in over the back-board without waiting for any further invitation.

"The master said ye were to cover yourself with thae corn sacks when we were drivin' through New Dalry," said the serving man, still without turning his head, "and ye maun lie down when we meet onybody."

Kit did as he was bid, and so, alternately sitting up and lying at full length on his pile of cornbags, he travelled forth somewhat unheroically into the world. Occasionally the man put a question to him and grunted when Kit answered it. At other times he gave vent to a short disconcerting laugh for no cause at all that the boy could see.

"You are to serve at Loch Spellanderie?" he put the question sharply, as he might have cracked his whip.

"Aye," said Kit.

The man produced a crackling noise from somewhere near the red "shilbin" of the cart on which he rode.

"Micht ye be acquainted wi' Mistress Mac Walter?" Again he shot the question as from a pop-gun.

"No," said Kit, as briefly as before.

Again the man produced the curious mechanical sound, which in some way seemed to be an attempt at laughter.

"I thocht sae," he said. "But ye will! Oh! yes, ye will be better acquainted with Mistress Mac Walter o' Loch Spellanderie before a' be done. Lie down, here's a man coming!"

Then in a little, as they passed up the long and fertile strath of the Ken, the man broke forth with yet another question.

"What do you think you are going to be?"

"A great man," said Kit, as easily as if he had been declaring his intention of becoming a stonebreaker like

his grandfather or a forester like Rob.   Kit had always
known that he would be a great man one day, and had
already begun to be anxious about the writing of his
biography.   There were various matters he felt that he
would like to conceal from his biographer—the affair
of the hens for instance, the truantry by the lochside—
indeed, all the interesting revelations which make the
modern biographer the terror of his race, Kit, being
old-fashioned, began early to provide against.

But the taciturn driver from Kirkoswald had once
been tickled and now could not contain his mirth.   At
every new turn of the winding road up the green valley
he chuckled to himself.

" A great man—and going to Mistress Mac Walter
o' Loch Spellanderie.   Ho ! Ho ! "

But neither he nor Kit Kennedy saw a figure which
kept the cart in sight all the way from the bridge-head
of Dee to the loaning gate of Loch Spellanderie, a figure
which dodged darkly through bracken patches and
behind stone dykes—that kept a beeline through
the hazel coppice of the Dornal Bank, and was waiting
within a hundred yards of Kit when the red cart
reached the further bend—that skulked among the
heather on the purple side of Bennan when there was
no shelter by the wayside and the highway ran long
and straight into the north.

Kit Kennedy was less alone than he knew in his
great adventure.

CHAPTER XXVIII.

After Many Days.

But we have now to turn back some considerable distance in order that the tale may run plain and clear.

The tramp was at last clear of both prison and hospital. Physically his three months' hard labour and six of nursing and nourishing food in the hospital of the combination poor-house had infinitely improved him. The unhealthy, mottled appearance had gone from his face. It was still a pale face certainly, but with a look of health and vigour strange to it for many days.

The Sheriff had not forgotten him, and when Christopher Kennedy, B.A., laid aside his hospital attire he received in exchange, not the stained and ragged suit of odds and ends in which he had been convicted, but a rig-out of Skye homespun, woven for Sheriff Macleod himself by the good women of his native island. It was rough and loose, too large at chest and infinitely too liberal of waist-girth for the spare hunger-hollowed figure of the tramp. But all the same a certain natural gift for the wearing of clothes enabled him to remedy these defects, so that the white shirt a little frayed at the cuffs which had accompanied the tweed suit, and a black tie provided by the kindly poor-house matron, constituted a rig-out which, as Nurse Hetherington said, "was a deal mair respectable than the Earl himsel' in shootin' time."

Curiously enough the suit acted as a complete disguise. For the tramp in rags caused every eye to turn suspiciously upon him, but the tramp in another man's good clothes, though they fitted him little better than a sack might fit a pea-stick, attracted no attention whatever. He wore his deerstalker's cap as a laird might have done, and none would have suspected that the tall man in loose grey had done three months "with," and thereafter lain six months in hospital.

During these long months Christopher Kennedy had been doing a great deal of thinking, and, like others before him, he had resolved that his future should not copy fair his past.

His feet had turned instinctively northward when, with ten of the good Sheriff's shillings in his pocket, he had been discharged as cured from the county hospital, and found himself upon the road at six in the morning. He was clear of the country town in ten minutes thereafter. He got his breakfast of porridge at a wayside house near Tongland Bridge.

"Ye're welcome to them," the good dame said. "Siller for a wheen parritch! Preserve us, I never heard o' siccan a thing. Na, faith—sup them up. I was e'en gaun to gie them to the dowg. But the tyke's gettin' ower fat onyway. He'll be far better wantin' them. But they will no be thrown awa' on you, I'm thinkin', my man. Ye look as if ye could stand a bow or twa o' meal for paddin' to your ribs. Man, there's room for twa like ye in thae claes o' yours!"

* * * * *

It was many months afterwards that the tramp laid him down for a sleep on the verge of Loch Grannoch. It was a little flat place half-way down a steep bank, a sweet spot equally sheltered from above and from below. Here the broom grew high and golden, the stone-chats cried *spink-spink-spink*, and the bumblebees hummed like the horns of Fairyland all day long in that sunny sylvan solitude.

The sound of voices awakened the tramp, and he peeped out with the caution which soon becomes habitual to a hunted man. He saw Lilias Mac Walter, and with her a boy, slim, tall, and active of body. The boy was putting on his clothes. A large yellowish collie was barking on the pebbly beach, running a little way into the water, and then squattering out again apparently in order to entice the boy back.

The tramp lay down again and listened with all his ears. Once he would have scorned to listen. But all such extra moralities are conventional and on the level of napkins for dinner. Once definitely left behind, the need of them is no longer felt.

As the tramp listened his heart began to beat fast. His pale face flushed to the brow, and then grew paler than before. He could scarcely contain himself. He buried his face in the damp sod, and bit on the soft part of his hand to help him to keep silence. At the sound of that excellently low voice the universe reeled, swayed, and resolved itself into whirling mist. The wreckage of his life floated by stick by stick. He saw the thing which might have been, and bit harder to repress a cry. He saw what he had brought on others, and his impulse was to be quiet till Lilias and the boy had gone away, and then to fling himself into the deep peaty waters of Loch Grannoch.

At last the boy, completely dressed by his mother's lingering hands, took his way up the bankside, and made all haste in the direction of Whinnyliggate school. Lilias, the woman, was left alone. The tramp gripped himself tighter and crouched lower in the broom. He meant never to let her know of his presence. But, as the Galloway folk say, " it hadna been to be."

Lilias Mac Walter rose to her feet and shaded her eyes with her hand, in order to watch her lad as he stood waving his hand cheerfully to his mother before vanishing from her sight.

With a sudden instinct of her lost youth she bent down to pull a sprig of the yellow broom. It had always been a favourite of hers. As she stooped she saw the tramp. Instinctively she caught her hand to her heart, but this time she was not afraid. She looked about; the green lakeside strip, the scanty pasture-fields, the heathery knowes were all void and empty save for a scattered score of nibbling sheep and one or two grazing cattle.

"Christopher," she said, softly, scarce knowing even that she spoke.

The man did not move, but lay with his face concealed. She went timidly and laid her fingers on his shoulder.

"Chris!" she said, speaking still more softly.

The man in the suit of grey rose slowly to his feet and stood before her.

"I did not know you were here," he began, with swift breathless apology. "I walked all the way from Kirkcudbright this morning and had fallen asleep."

She looked long at his face. It was again colourless, and Christopher Kennedy appeared a different man from the drunken loafer she had found in the quarry on the Dornal Hill.

"You have been ill?" she said, her voice asking the question, but her eyes perusing his face.

"Yes," he said, a little wearily, "but I am better now. I am going away for ever. I was on my road. But I ought never to have come here. I only trouble you. I have troubled you all my life."

"No," she said, calmly; "you do not trouble me now, Christopher."

"I am glad," said the tramp. "Do not think worse of me than you can help. And believe that when I married you, I thought I had a right to marry you. Also that when I went away I meant to come back."

"I will try," said Lilias, wearily, as if she had thought more than enough already upon the subject. "It does not matter," she added, as the hopelessness of their lives hemmed her in.

But a fresh thought struck Lilias and made her flush crimson. It was not fear of her husband, for that day he had gone to market with Wandale the factor and would not be back till evening.

"Did you see any one here with me?" she asked the tramp, keeping her eyes upon his face.

"No one," he assured her steadily. "I was sound asleep."

"Nor hear anything?"

" I heard the linties singing when I fell asleep, and I heard you calling me by name when I awoke ! "

" Nothing more ? "

" Nothing more ! "

Lilias drew a long breath and took her gaze from his face. She was wondering how he came to marry Mary Bisset, and what kind of eyes and hair she had. She would have liked to ask him that very moment, but she dared not.

And within himself the tramp was saying over and over in his heart, " And that is my son—my boy—hers and mine. And she is my wife. Yet I dare not claim her. I have ruined myself. I will not ruin her also. But, by God's grace, I will not lose sight of this lad. He shall yet be all that I might have been and have failed to be ! "

Lilias Mac Walter began to go slowly up the hill, and the tramp walked beside her. They did not speak much. They did not tell each other of the withered sprigs of white heather which both carried with them at that moment. All was past, done with ; their hearts that had been as fire were only grey ashes now, chill and empty even in the sunshine of the high new summer. Anger was not in the heart of Lilias—only a great patient hopelessness. Pain was not pain for her any more. She seemed as if under the influence of some spiritual anæsthetic. She found herself in situations which ought to have been exquisitely painful to a woman in her position. But somehow she felt nothing. Something about her heart seemed permanently frozen and dead.

" Lilias," said the tramp, at last, " I did not mean to speak to you to-day, though I own it was in my mind to watch from the wood for you and look once more upon your face. I will come no further with you now, lest a bird of the air carry the matter. God be good to you, little Lilias. You have been most hardly treated, and I the cause. Yet believe it—I never meant you wrong. And late or early, now or then, I have never loved any but you ! "

"Christopher Kennedy," she answered, "it is a strangely late day for you to speak of love to Lilias Mac Walter!"

"I know—I know," he said; "it is my wretched enfeebled will. I had not meant to trouble you with it."

"Whether you love me or not has long ceased to concern me," said the woman, with her eyes on the ground. She was weary and longed to be alone. But though her words sounded hard, her hand was in the pocket of the dress where within the folds of her purse lay the spray of white heather.

They came to the end of the woodland and with one mind they stopped. They must part here. Up there on the hillside, under its belt of trees, stood the new freestone house of Kirkoswald. There on the other side lay the wide garish world, empty under its blue arch of sky. She must go to her narrow duties, her sordid cares, her unloved husband. He must wander out, whither he knew not nor greatly cared. The Love Eternal had come to this.

Or at least Christopher Kennedy had not cared when he lay down under the golden torches of the broom. But now all was different. He had come alive again.

The tramp stood looking at the woman a while without speaking, but his mouth was working curiously.

"I do not ask you to take my hand now, Lilias," he said at last, "I am not worthy. But some day—some day you will forget all that I have made you suffer, and only remember that I loved you."

A short dry sob choked his utterance. The storm after long threatening broke overhead and the rain began to patter down on the leaves. She saw his face drawn and eager in the pale blue flame of the summer lightning. Something moved in the heart she had thought dead. She went quickly to him and laid her hand upon his shoulder with a gesture she had been wont to use in other days.

"Chris, be a man! For my sake!" she said.

They were the words she had used that morning she

would never forget, the morning when the trouble came upon them—the trouble of which she had known, but not he.

"Lilias!" he cried, and stood shaking and trembling before her.

Then turning, without a word he strode away across the heather, the lightning flickering about him and little fitful wafts of hot wind blowing the thunder spume low over the moorlands of the Black Dornal.

CHAPTER XXIX.

ON THE TRAIL.

BUT Christopher Kennedy, Master of Arts, late Her Majesty's prisoner in the gaol of St. Cuthbert's, had lied when he declared that he had heard nothing.

The veil that had hidden his spirit so long was at last lifted. He had learned, lying hidden behind the bush of broom, that the boy Kit Kennedy was the son of Lilias Kennedy and therefore his.

For years he had thought this woman dead. A man, he knew not his name, had told him on his first visit to Sandhaven after his flight that Lilias Armour was dead! Dead—yes, he thought it likely enough. He left little Lilias, whom he had made his wife, without a word. He had not meant to go without telling her. But the crisis had come upon him quickly. And Nick French said that they must both leave Cairn Edward that night. So he fled, meaning, with that easy shifting of responsibility which breaks more hearts than plain wickedness, to come back soon.

After he heard that Lilias was dead all things grew mixed. Nothing mattered, and the succeeding years brought him ever lower—lower—lower!

Then all suddenly, like one awaking with a start from a hideous nightmare, he had found himself on his elbow above the old quarry, with another Lilias, one older and more weary, looking down upon him.

After the prison he had wished to die. In the poorhouse hospital he had almost resolved with a leap to end all. But not in Galloway. He would go to some great city in which one tramp the less would not matter, where they would take a dead waif to the mortuary as nonchalantly as if he were a dead dog.

Then, a long time after, he had lain down behind that bush of broom. He had heard what he had heard; and with his recreated brain, set up anew by the discipline of many months' total abstinence, he had reconstructed with acute and appalling vividness all that Lilias, little Lilias, had undergone after he had left her alone in those great blindingly bright, horribly empty summer days.

His son! The son of his wife Lilias. But now she was another's—for she, too, had thought him dead. Well, he would never vex her nor let her know that he had any claim upon her. But this boy, his son—he would watch over him. Here was something for him to do. He was not yet an old man. He could still work, think, plan. He would sin no more. He had now something to live for.

So, at first afar off, he followed and watched. During the dark years he had spent in the Pit of Life, he had learned the vast liberty which being on the lowest level of humanity gives a man.

Of old, when he was classical master in the Academy of Cairn Edward, he could not go along the High Street without fifty people wondering where he had been and whither he might be going. But John Smith the tramp! Who speculated as to his outgoings or incomings? Whether he slept in his fourpenny lodging, or froze to death at a dyke-back, who cared? A stray policeman might cry to him sharply to move on. But that did not matter when he was moving on anyway. A gamekeeper, more zealous or more keen of sight than his fellows, might turn him out of a plantation if he caught sight of him entering it. No matter, there was another equally thick half a mile further on! But mostly he could do what he would, watch where he liked, go where his liking took him, with none to interest themselves in his movements, without suspicion, surmise, or question on the part of any human soul. Thus on the ground floor of life many stiff problems resolve themselves.

So the tramp watched the boy Kit Kennedy.

He was present at his interview with Walter Mac Walter. It was his approach that stirred like the passing of a breeze the tall bracken on the Dornal side of the stile. And as the red farm cart with the taciturn driver took its rattling road towards Loch Spellanderie and the abode of Kit's new master, there might have been seen at intervals, trickling round some distant curve, at gaze upon a bold bluff, waiting under a hedge after some short cut through fields, a certain ragged tramp, to whom all routes were the same, to whom time was no object, whose meals were always assured in that hospitable lowland countryside, and who could sleep under any stack or outhouse, or if need be in the short summer heats under the grey coverlet of night itself.

That shadow was Kit Kennedy's newly-appointed guardian angel. The classical master knew well enough that Kit Kennedy was running away from home. And he did not mean to prevent him. He saw that so long as the boy remained with his grandfather in the little cottage, his goings and comings carefully watched and noted, he could do but little for him. Besides he wanted to find out what object Mac Walter had in thus secretly getting rid of Kit.

So it happened that when the cart turned into the farmyard of Loch Spellanderie with Kit asleep upon the cornsacks, a tramp halted with his bundle at the road-end which led up to the out-at-elbows pile occupied by the brother of the laird of Kirkoswald and his wife.

As the tramp sat there it chanced that he heard a sound of singing along the long vacant road to the north. The afternoon sun was still hot, and the tramp rested under a wide-sheltering ash, the shadows of whose leaves swept the grass with a soft sidelong movement like the caressing of a woman's hand.

> Come, Love, let's walk in yonder spring,
> Where we may hear the blackbird sing,
> The robin-redbreast and the thrush,
> The nichtingale in thorny bush,

The mavis sweetly carolling.
This to my love, this to my love,
   Content will bring.

Heather Jock was on his way home from the uplands
of Carsphairn, whither he had gone to peddle his
besoms. Already he could smell the good smell of his
native air, and as he was wont to say, pointing proudly
to his donkey as one might put forward a favourite
child, "As soon as ever Billy-O gets his nose by Snuffy
point and the wind o' Whinnyliggate blaws roond the
hip o' the Bennan, he's a different beast. It's graund
air, that o' the muirlands. Fowk canna dee up there.
There's naebody has died fairly, up amang thae Carsphairn Hills, within the memory o' man."

"And how," someone would put in, "how is it that
whiles we will see a funeral comin' doon frae that gate?"

Heather Jock would shake his head sagely, then nod
a little knowing nod.

"There's ways—aye, there's ways. Whiles fowk has
leeved lang eneuch. Whiles it's better that they should
slip awa'! But that's no what ye wad caa deein'! Na!
na! That's just what they caa in Carsphairn 'a kind
providence'!"

Heather Jock was in good humour. He had no wife
waiting for him at home. Billy-O would be the better
of a rest—he himself of a pipe. Here was company
ready to his hand under a commodious tree. So
Heather Jock, a universally adaptive man, sat down
beside the tramp.

"Will ye hae a draw, honest man?" he said. "No,
ye're richt. No on an empty stammack! Stand still,
Billy-O! I'll tak' aff your creels. Ye're mair trouble
than twa wives that willna' gree. I'll no say but ye
are mair solid comfort too, though that's neither here
nor there!"

The tramp watched the pedlar as he busied himself
with his creels.

"I'se warrant, my lad, ye'll no be ony the waur o'
a bit whang o' mutton ham. It's rare stuff, as I can
tell ye, for this is nae braxy, but a graund auld yow

(ewe). A rale snaw-breaker, abune fifty year auld, they say she was. I gat it up at the Glenhead frae Mistress Mac Millan, and says she, 'Jock, that'll haud your teeth gaun tell ye win hame—that is, if ye hae guid teeth and they last oot. We hae a' had a turn at Auld Granny, and the teeth in this hoose is a' dune!' she says.

"But I daresay ye'll no quarrel wi' it. They are awfu' particular fowk aboot their eatin' up in the Glen o' Trool. Kind fowk too. There was the guidwife o' the Trostan. She fair fleeched on me to bide wi' her. 'I wad hae gien ye a bed, and welcome, Jock,' says she, "but there is a horse in 't!" Terrible kind fowk they are up at the head end o' yon glen. How are ye managing wi' the mutton ham—no that ill, I houp? Aye, man, I wish I had teeth like you. I declare to peace ye could tak' to stanebreakin' withoot a hammer. It's fair divertin' to watch ye!"

So Heather Jock plied the tramp with provender and local information crouched in the raciest form o' Scots, only spoken by the folk of the western uplands, where it is still free from the defilements of Glasgow Irish, and shines with a lustre undimmed by secondary education.

The tramp put a question.

"Wha leeves up there, say ye?" cried Heather Jock, "and what like fowk are they? Weel, I'll tell ye. Ye maun be a sore stranger no to ken, though. John Mac Walter leeves there, a decent man, and the name o' the bit farm is Loch Spellanderie. John wad gie ye a bed and your breakfast—that is, gin he wasna hadden doon wi' a wife. But to tell ye the truth, John, honest man, is o' nae mair accoont up at Loch Spellanderie than you or me—or as a yin micht say, puir Billy-O!"

"O, she's a tairger, Mistress Mac Walter. She wadna gie ye ony mutton ham, though ye micht hae a chance to get the shank bane on the side o' your head."

"Would they be kind, think you, to someone in service there?" asked the tramp.

"Ye needna think on't, my man!" said Heather Jock.

"They keep nae man at Loch Spellanderie. A bit boy
(Guid peety him!) and a slip o' a lassie indoors to provide Mistress Mac Walter wi' employment for her hands
and tongue. That's a' the service that they hae ony
use for up at Loch Spellanderie."

Heather Jock was eyeing the tramp carefully.

"Ye hae seen trouble in your day," he said at length;
"were ye seekin' wark? I think I can put you in the
way o' some. D'ye see you white hoose on the hillside
yonder? That's Rogerson's o' Cairnharrow. They are
wantin' an orra man, for the guidman has a sair hand,
and fowk are ill to get up here. I think ye might hae
a chance, though ye dinna look verra strong—and mair
like your bed than takin' on wi' farm wark.'

"I have been ill—very ill," acknowledged the tramp,"
"but I am better now."

"Fegs, I was thinkin' that, by the haun ye hae made
o' the mutton ham. It's fair astonishin'! Honest
Geordie Breerie himsel' couldna hae beat ye!

"Weel, guid-day till ye—What did ye say your name
was? Smith? Dod, I yince kenned a man o' the name
o' Smith. Maybe he was some friend of yours. It's no
a common name here awa'—Smith. They's a' Mac
Millans and Mac Quhirrs an' Mac Landsboroughs. Aye,
man, and ye're a Smith. Weel, a heap o' decent fowk
hae had queer ootlandish names in their day. And I
daresay ye'll no be a penny the waur o' yours!"

And so with this farewell, uttered in all sincerity,
Heather Jock took his way down the strath of Kells,
and soon Billy-O was sniffing the fine Whinnyliggate air,
and beginning to think how good it would be to get off
creels and saddles and leathern bellybands and indulge
in a long scratchy satisfactory roll among the heather.

The tramp sat awhile at the foot of the little loaning
that wound its way from the main road up to the farm
of Loch Spellanderie. He was thinking whether he
should accept the advice Heather Jock had given him,
or remain in a position of greater freedom, when he
heard heavy footsteps coming down the avenue. He
could not see the wearer of these weighty boots, but

presently the black-pitched gate was opened, and a tall, dark-browed, masculine-looking woman came out with the swing of a grenadier. She caught sight of the tramp's grey coat and instantly stopped.

"Get awa oot o' here!" she cried, pointing to his little bundle, which lay on the grass beside him. "We want nane o' your kind here. There's thieves and useless reprobates eneugh comin' intil a decent woman's hoose without gangrel vaigabonds sitting on her verra doorstep. Aye, an' whaur gat ye that mutton ham? I missed yin the day before yesterday. I wish there was a polissman here. Tak' your ways up the road, my man, and look as slippy as ye can, or I'll set the dowgs after ye!"

The tramp said nothing, but rose to his feet, and pocketing his package and the affront together he went quietly up the road. The wrathful voice pursued him.

"Dinna let me see or hear o' you in this countryside again, my man—you that hasna a ceevil word in your head an' a stolen mutton ham in your hand—gaun aboot the land burnin' ricks wi' your matches and abusing decent women wi' your black looks, vermin that ye are!"

And the mistress of Loch Spellanderie took her way with the consciousness of having done a worthy and eminently Christian action, in thus ridding the bounds of so disreputable and even dangerous an element as the tramp in grey.

CHAPTER XXX.

The Ne'er-Do-Weel.

A stormy voice broke the morning silence of the farmhouse of Loch Spellanderie some months thereafter.

"Kit Kennedy, ye are a lazy ne'er-do-weel, lyin' snorin' there in your bed on the back o' five o'clock. Think shame o' yoursel'."

And Kit did.

He was informed on an average ten times a day that he was lazy, a skulker, a burden on the world, and especially on the household of his mother's sister-in-law, Mistress Mac Walter of Loch Spellanderie. So, being an easy-minded boy, and moderately cheerful, he accepted the fact, and shaped his life accordingly.

"Get up this instant, ye scoondrel!" came again the sharp voice. It was speaking from under three ply of blankets, in the ceiled room beneath. That is why it seemed a trifle more muffled than usual. It even sounded kindly, but Kit Kennedy was not deceived. He knew better than that.

"Gin ye dinna be stirrin', I'll be up to ye wi' a stick!" cried Mistress Mac Walter.

It was a greyish, glimmering twilight when Kit Kennedy awoke. It seemed such a short time since he went to bed that he thought that surely his mistress had called him the night before. Kit was not surprised. She was capable of anything in the way of extracting work out of him.

The moon, getting old, and yawning in the middle as if tired of being out so late, set a crumbly horn past the edge of his little skylight. Her straggling, pallid rays fell on something white on Kit's bed. He put out his hand, and it went into a cold wreath of snow up to the wrist.

"*Ouch!*" said Kit Kennedy.

"I'm comin' to ye," repeated his mistress, "ye lazy, pampered, guid-for-naething! Dinna think I canna hear ye grumblin' and speakin' ill words against your betters!"

Yet all he had said was "Ouch!"—in the circumstances, a somewhat natural remark.

Kit took the corner of the scanty coverlet, and, with a well-accustomed arm-sweep, sent the whole swirl of snow over the end of his bed, getting across the side at the same time himself. He did not complain. All he said, as he blew upon his hands and slapped them against his sides, was, "Michty, it'll be cauld at the turnip pits this mornin'!"

It had been snowing in the night since Kit lay down, and the snow had sifted in through the open tiles of the farmhouse of Loch Spellanderie. That was nothing. It often did that, but sometimes it rained, and that was worse. Yet Kit Kennedy did not much mind even that. He had a cunning arrangement in old umbrellas and corn-sacks that could beat the rain any day. Snow, in his own words, he did not give a "buckie" for.

Then there was a stirring on the floor, a creaking of the ancient joists. It was Kit putting on his clothes. He always knew where each article lay—dark or shine, it made no matter to him. He had not an embarrassment of apparel. He had a suit for wearing—and his "other clothes." These latter were, however, now too small for him, and so he could not go to the kirk at Whinnyliggate. But his mistress had laid them aside for her son Tammas, a growing lad. She was a thoughtful, provident woman.

"Be gettin' doon the stair, my man, and look slippy," cried Mistress Mac Walter, as a parting shot, "and see carefully to the kye. It'll be as weel for ye."

Kit had on his trousers by this time. His waistcoat

followed. But before he put on his coat he knelt down
to say his prayer. He had promised his mother to say
it then. If he put on his coat he was apt to forget it, in
his haste to get out of doors, where at least the beasts
were friendly. So between his waistcoat and his coat
he prayed. The angels were up at the time and they
heard, and went and told One who hears prayer. They
said that in a garret at a hill farm a boy was praying
with his knees in snow-drift, a boy without father or
mother near to help or listen to him.

"Ye lazy guid-for-naething! Gin ye are no doon the
stairs in three meenits, no a drap o' porridge or a sup
o' milk shall ye get this day!"

So Kit got on his feet, and made a queer little shuffling noise on the floor with them, to induce his mistress
to think that he was bestirring himself. So that is the
way he had to finish his prayers—on his feet, shuffling
and dancing a breakdown.

The angels saw and smiled. But they took it up and
up, just the same as if Kit Kennedy had been praying
in church with the best. All save one, who stopped
above the garret to drop something that might have
been a pearl and might have been a tear. Then he
also went within the Inner Court, and told that which
he had seen.

But to Kit's mind there was nothing to grumble
about. He was pleased if any one was. His clogs did
not let in the snow. His coat was rough but warm.
If any one was well off, and knew it, it was Kit
Kennedy.

So he came downstairs, if stairs they could be called
that were but the broken rounds of a stable ladder.
His mistress heard him.

"Keep awa' frae the kitchen, ye thievin' loon!
There's nocht there for ye—takin' the bairns' meat
afore they're up!"

But Kit was not hungry, which, in the circumstances,
was as well. Mistress Mac Walter had caught him red-
handed on one occasion. He was taking a bit of hard
oatcake out of the basket of "farles" which swung

from the black, smoked beam in the corner. Kit had cause to remember the occasion. Ever since she had cast it up to him. She was a master hand at " casting up," as her husband knew. But Kit was used to it, and he did not care. A thick stick was all he cared for, and that only for three minutes ; but he minded when Mistress Mac Walter abused his mother.

Kit Kennedy made for the front door, direct from the foot of the ladder. Mrs. Mac Walter raised herself on one elbow in bed to assure herself that he did not go into the kitchen after all. She heard the click of the bolt shot back, and the stir of the dogs as Tweed and Tyke rose from the fireside to follow him. There was still a little red ash gleaming between the bars, and Kit would dearly have liked to go in and thaw out his toes on the still warm hearthstone. But he knew that his task-mistress was listening. He was twelve now, and big for his age, so he wasted no pity on himself, but opened the door and went out. Self-pity is bad at any time. It is fatal at twelve.

At the door one of the dogs stopped, sniffed the keen, frosty air, turned quietly and went back to the hearthstone. That was Tweed. But Tyke was already out rolling in the snow when Kit Kennedy shut the door.

Then his mistress went to sleep. She knew how Kit Kennedy did his work, and that there would be no cause to complain. But she meant to complain all the same. Was he not a lazy, deceitful hound, an encumbrance, and an interloper among her bairns ?

Kit slapped his long arms against his sides. He stood beneath his employer's window, and crowed so like a cock that Mistress Mac Walter jumped out of her bed.

"Save us ! " she said. " What's that keckling beast doin' there at this time in the mornin' ? "

She got out of bed to look, but she could see nothing, certainly not Kit. But Kit saw her, as she stood shivering at the window in her night-gear. Kit hoped that her legs were cold. This was his revenge. He was a revengeful boy.

As for himself he was as warm as a toast. The stars tingled above with frost. The moon lay over on her back and yawned still more ungracefully. She seemed more tired than ever.

Kit had an idea. He stopped and cried up at her, "Get up, ye lazy guid-for-naething! I'll come up wi' a stick to ye!"

But the moon did not come down. On the contrary, she made no sign. Kit laughed. He had to stop in the snow to do it. The imitation of his mistress pleased him. He fancied himself climbing up a rung ladder to the moon, with a broomstick in his hand. He would start that old moon if he fell down and broke his neck. Kit was hungry now. It was a long time since supper-time. Porridge is, no doubt, good feeding; but it vanishes away like the morning cloud, and leaves behind it only an aching void. Kit felt the void, but he could not help it. Instead, however, of dwelling upon it, his mind was full of queer thoughts and funny imaginings. It is a strange thing that the thought of rattling on the ribs of a lazy, sleepy moon with a besom-shank pleased him more than a plate of porridge and as much milk as he could sup to it. But such was the fact.

Kit next went into the stable to get a lantern. The horses were moving about restlessly, but Kit had nothing to do with them. He only went in for the lantern. It stood on the great wooden corn crib in the corner. Kit lighted it and pulled down his cap over his ears.

Then he crossed over to the cattle-sheds. The snow was crisp under foot. His feet went through the light drift which had fallen during the night, and crackled frostily upon the older and harder undercrust. At the barn door Kit paused to put fresh straw in his iron-shod clogs. Fresh straw every morning in the bottom of one's clogs is a great luxury. It keeps the feet warm. Who can afford a new sole of fleecy wool every morning to his shoe? Kit could, for straw is cheap, and even his mistress did not grudge a handful. Not that it would have mattered if she had.

The cattle rattled their chains in a friendly and

companionable way as he crossed the yard, Tyke following a little more sedately than before. Kit's first morning job was to fodder the cattle. He went to the hay-mow and carried out a huge armful, filling the manger before the bullocks, and giving each a friendly pat as he went by. Great Jock, the bull in the pen by himself in the corner, pushed a moist nose over the bars, and dribbled upon Kit with slobbering amicability.

Kit put down his head and pretended to run at him, whereat Jock, whom nobody else dared go near, beamed upon him with the solemn affection of "bestial" for those whom they love, his great eyes shining in the light of the lamp with unlovely but genuine affection.

Then came the cows' turn. Kit Kennedy took a milking-pail, which he would have called a "luggie," set his knee to Crummie, his favourite, who was munching her fodder, and soon had a warm draught. He pledged Crummie in her own milk, wishing her good health and many happy returns. Then, for his mistress's sake, he carefully wiped the luggie dry, and set it where he had found it. He had got his breakfast —no mean or poor one.

But he did not doubt that he was, as Mistress MacWalter had said, "a lazy, deceitful, thieving hound."

Kit Kennedy came out of the byre, and trudged away out over the field at the back of the barn to the sheep in the park. He heard one of them cough as a human being does behind his hand. The lantern threw dancing reflections on the snow. Tyke grovelled and rolled in the light drift, barking loudly. He bit at his own tail. Kit set down the lantern, and fell upon him for a tussle. The two of them had rolled one another into a snow-drift in exactly ten seconds, from which they rose glowing with heat—the heat of young things when the blood runs fast.

Tyke, being excited, scoured away wildly, and circled the park at a hand-gallop before his return. But Kit only lifted the lantern and made for the turnip-pits.

The turnip-cutter stood there, with great square mouth black against the sky. That mouth must be filled and emptied many times. Kit went to the end of the barrow-like mound of the turnip-pit. It was covered with snow, so that it hardly showed above the level of the field. Kit threw back the coverings of old sacks and straw which kept the turnips from the frost. There lay the great green-and-yellow globes, full of sap. The snow had slid down upon them from the top of the pit. The frost grasped them from without. It was a chilly job to handle them, but Kit did not hesitate a moment.

He filled his arms with "swedes" and went to the turnip-cutter. Soon the "*crunch-crunch*" of the knives was to be heard as Kit drove round the handle, and afterwards the frosty sound of the oblong finger-lengths of cut turnip falling into the basket. The sheep had gathered about him, silently for the most part. Tyke sat still and dignified now, guarding the lantern, which the sheep were inclined to butt over. Kit heard the animals knocking against the empty troughs with their hard little trotters, and snuffing about them with their nostrils.

He lifted the heavy basket, heaved it against his breast, and made his way down the long line of troughs. The sheep crowded about him, shoving and elbowing each other like so many human beings, as callously and selfishly. His first basket did not go far, as he shovelled it in great handfuls into the troughs, and Kit came back for another. It was tiring work, and the day was dawning grey when he had finished. Then he made the circuit of the field, to assure himself that all was right, and that there were no stragglers lying frozen in corners, or turned "avel" in the dusty lirks of the knowes.

Then he went back to the onstead of Loch Spellanderie. The moon had gone down, and the farm buildings loomed very cold and bleak out of the frost-fog.

Mistress Mac Walter was on foot. She had slept nearly two hours, being half an hour too long, after wearying herself with raising Kit; and furthermore she had risen with a very bad temper. But this was no uncommon occurrence. She was now in the byre with a lantern of her own. She was talking to herself, and "flyting" on the patient cows, who now stood chewing the cuds of their breakfast. She slapped them apart with her stool, applying it savagely to their flanks. She even lifted her foot to them, which affronts a self-respecting cow as much as a human being.

In this spirit she greeted Kit when he appeared.

"Where hae ye been, ye careless deevil, ye? A guid mind hae I to gie ye my milking-stool owre yer crown, ye senseless, menseless blastie! What ill-contriving tricks hae ye been at that ye haena gotten the kye milkit?"

"I hae been feeding the sheep at the pits, mistress," said Kit Kennedy.

"Dinna 'mistress' me," cried his employer; "ye hae been wasting your time at some o' your thievin' ploys. What do ye think that John Mac Walter, silly man, feeds you for? He has plenty o' weans o' his ain to provide for withoot meddling wi' the likes o' you—careless, useless, fushionless blaygaird that ye are."

Mistress Mac Walter had sat down on her stool to the milking by this time. But her temper was such that she was milking harshly and unkindly, and Crummie felt it. Also she had not forgotten in her slow-moving bovine way that she had been kicked. So in her turn she lifted her foot and let drive, punctuating a gigantic semicolon with her cloven hoof just on that part of the person of Mistress Mac Walter where it was fitted to take most effect.

Mistress Mac Walter found herself on her back, with the warm froth of the milk running all over her. She picked herself up, helped by Kit, who had come to her assistance.

Her words were few, but not at all well-ordered. She went to the byre door to get the driving-stick to lay on Crummie. Kit stopped her.

"Ye'll pit a' the kye to that o't that they'll no let

doon a drap o' milk this morning. An' the morn's kirning-day."

Mistress Mac Walter knew that the boy was right; but she could only turn, not subdue her anger. So she turned it on Kit Kennedy, for there was no one else there.

"Ye meddlin' curse,' she cried, "it was a' your blame." She had the shank of the byre besom in her hand as she spoke. With this she struck at the boy, who ducked his head and hollowed his back in a manner which showed great practice and dexterity. The blow fell obliquely on his coat, making a resounding noise, but doing no great harm.

Then Mistress Mac Walter picked up her stool and sat down to another cow. Kit drew in to Crummie, and the twain comforted one another. Kit bore no malice, but he hoped that his mistress would not keep back his porridge. That was what he feared. No other word of good or bad said the goodwife of Loch Spellanderie by the Water of Ken. Kit carried the two great reaming cans of fresh milk into the milkhouse; and as he came out empty-handed Mistress Mac Walter waited for him, and with a hand both hard and heavy fetched him a ringing blow on the side of the head, which made his teeth clack together and his eyes water.

"Tak' that, ye gangrel loon!" she said, "ye are aye in some mischief!"

Kit Kennedy went into the barn with fell purpose in his heart. He set up on end a bag of chaff, which had been laid aside to fill a bed. He squared up to it in a deadly way, dancing lightly on his feet, his hands revolving in a most knowing manner.

His left hand shot out, and the sack of chaff went over in the corner.

"Stand up, Mistress Mac Walter," said Kit, "an' we'll see wha's the better man."

It was evidently Kit who was the better man, for the sack subsided repeatedly and flaccidly on the hard-beaten earthern floor. So in effigy Kit mauled Mistress Mac Walter exceeding shamefully, and obtained so many victories over that lady that he grew quite pleased with himself, and in time gat him into such a glow that he forgot all about the tingling on his ear which had so suddenly begun at the milk-house door.

"After a', she keeps me!" said Kit Kennedy, cheerfully.

There was another angel up aloft who went into the inner court at that moment and told that Kit Kennedy had forgiven his enemies. Being a sympathetic recorder he said nothing about the chaff sack. So Kit Kennedy began the day with a clean slate and a ringing ear.

He went to the kitchen door to go in and get his breakfast.

"Gae 'way wi' ye! Hoo daur ye come to my door after what yer wark has been this mornin'?" cried Mistress Mac Walter as soon as she heard him. "Aff to the schule wi' ye! Ye get neither bite nor sup in my hoose the day."

The three Mac Walter children were sitting at the table taking their porridge and milk with horn spoons. The ham was skirling and frizzling in the pan. It gave out a good smell, but that did not cost Kit Kennedy a thought. He knew that that was not for the like of him. He would as soon have thought of wearing a white linen shirt or having the lairdship of a barony as of getting ham to his breakfast. But after his morning's work he had a sore heart enough to miss his porridge.

But he knew that it was no use to argue with Mistress Mac Walter. So he went outside and walked up and down in the snow. He heard the clatter of dishes as the children Rob, Jock, and Meysie Mac Walter finished their eating, and Meysie set their bowls one within the other and carried them into the back-kitchen to be ready for the washing. Meysie was now nearly fourteen and was Kit's very good friend. Jock and Rob, on the other hand, ran races who should have most tales to tell of his misdoings at home and also at the village school.

"Kit Kennedy, ye scoondrel, come in this meenit an' get the dishes washen afore yer maister tak's the 'Buik,'" cried Mistress Mac Walter, who was a religious woman, and "came forward" regularly at the half-yearly communion in the kirk of Duntochar. She did not so much grudge Kit his meal of meat, but she had her own theories of punishment. So she called Kit in to wash the dishes from which he had never eaten. Meysie stood beside them and dried for him, and her little heart was sore. There was something in the bottom of some of them, and this Kit ate quickly and furtively, Meysie keeping a watch that her mother was not looking. The day was now fairly broken, but the sun had not yet risen.

"Tak' the pot oot an' clean it. Gie the scrapin's to the dogs!" ordered Mistress Mac Walter.

Kit obeyed. Tyke and Tweed followed with their tails over their backs. The white wastes glimmered in the grey of the morning. It was rosy where the sun was going to rise behind the great ridge of Ben Gairn, which looked, smoothly covered with snow as it was, exactly like a gigantic turnip-pit. At the back of the milk-house Kit set down the pot, and with a horn spoon which he took from his pocket he shared the 'scrapings' of the pot equally into three parts, dividing it mathematically by lines drawn up from the bottom. It was a good big pot, and there was a good deal of scrapings, which was lucky for both Tweed and Tyke, as well as good for Kit Kennedy.

Now this was the way that Kit Kennedy—that kinless loon, without father or name — won his breakfast.

He had hardly finished and licked the spoon, the dogs sitting on their haunches and watching every rise and fall of the horn, when a well-known voice shrilled through the air.

"Kit Kennedy, ye lazy, ungrateful hound, come ben to the 'Buik.' Ye are no better than the beasts that perish, regardless baith o' God and man!"

So Kit Kennedy cheerfully went in to prayers and

thanksgiving, thinking himself not ill off.   He had had his breakfast.

And Tweed and Tyke, the beasts that perish, put their noses into the porridge-pot to see if Kit Kennedy had left anything.   There was not so much as a single grain of meal.

CHAPTER XXXI.

KIT'S CLASSICAL TUTOR.

ONCE fairly settled Kit carried out his intention of
letting his grandfather know of the situation he had
found, and his Uncle Rob was despatched to report.
Upon his return the young forester allayed the fears of
Kit's mother and the Elder.

"He'll hae his ain battles to fecht, and his troubles
will no be to seek. But the man is an honest man,
though the woman is an ill-tongued tairger. But I wad
let him bide a while. The boy wasna learnin' muckle
at the schule onyway!"

These tidings were duly conveyed to Kirkoswald, and in
her heart Lilias rejoiced that her boy was at a distance
from the district, and, as she hoped, beyond the reach
of Christopher Kennedy.

Had she known how at that moment Kit was lying
prone on his face on a pile of cornbags in the barn of
Cairnharrow listening to the tramp as, in a rapid, clean-
cut voice he ran over certain unknown words, Lilias
Mac Walter might not have been so easy in her mind.

It had happened in this wise.

Heather Jock's hint had borne immediate fruit. John
Rogerson, more commonly called in Galloway fashion
"Cairnharrow" after the name of his farm, had
got a "spelk of wood into his hand," which in the busy
season put him at a sore disadvantage. The tramp was
not strong and had had little experience of farm work,
but he was both cheap and willing, and at least well
worth a trial. So his sister said, and so also, after due
demur, Cairnharrow himself allowed.

In this fashion did John Smith become odd, or more

technically " orra," man about the farmhouse of Cairnharrow, a larger and better holding than that of Loch
Spellanderie.

Throughout the winter that excellent optimist, Kit
Kennedy, dreed his weird with Mistress Mac Walter,
and the work—indeed all work—came easily to him.
His mistress, it is true, had early stopped him from
attending the village school, nominally because he was
a hired boy and could not be spared, but chiefly because his quickness put to shame Saft Tam and Tatie
Rob, the younger children of his master. So, nothing
loath, Kit Kennedy abode at home.

It was not long, however, before he met the new odd
man of Cairnharrow. It was at the smiddy in the
village of Saint John, and the Cairnharrow man was
driving a cart in which he was to take back a plough
that had been repaired. Kit had come in with a coulter
which needed sharpening.

Now the " smiddy " of all Scottish villages is at once
local parliament and club-house. To its privileges
members are duly elected. They are also frequently
black-balled. They may even be expelled. Each man
has his place and privileges clearly defined. The miller
may no more sit in the joiner's place than Gavin Strang
the wright may usurp the broken anvil by the hearth,
which is the perquisite of the smith himself in his
infrequent spells of leisure.

Every one's character is discussed, their prospects,
temper, habits—if they lie abed in the morning, if they
are over-promiscuous in their nocturnal roamings, if
they look several times at a penny before parting with
it. All these peculiarities are referred to in the dry
allusive way characteristic of the humour of the Scottish
peasant—a saying a thing without saying it, as it were.

"Guid-een to you, laddie," said the smith, big Andro
Hutcheon, the most mighty son of Tubal in all Galloway, "ye come frae Loch Spellanderie. How do ye
draw wi' the mistress? Fine, ye say? Weel, ye maun
be an easily contented laddie. Ye dinna want to be
'prenticed to a fine smith business, do ye? This loon o'

mine is aye grumblin'. He should hae a tack o' Mistress
Mac Walter. But she's a fine woman, too—certes! They
tell me that she pared the nebs o' her deuks (her ducks'
bills) to a point so that they wadna eat so muckle meat.
It was a peety that they a' deed before she got time to
see hoo the plan wad work."

The Cairnharrow cart stopped at the door, and the
late tramp, now a very different figure from the one of
the Dornal quarry, looked gravely in.

"Is that pleuch dune yet?" he cried, in the local
speech, for he had an ear for languages, and a new tang of
rustic speech came as apt upon his tongue as if it had been
Greek dialect in the days when young Chris Kennedy
of Sandhaven won college medals by the handful.

"Come awa', man!" cried the smith, who was for
the moment seated on his anvil, "tell us what's a' the
news aboot Cairnharrow. The joiner there was juist
sayin' what an extraordinary fine woman he considered
your neighbour, Mistress Mac Walter, ower by at
Loch Spellanderie.'

"We are a' weel up oor road, except the maister," said
the "Orra Man," cautiously; "is the pleuch dune, smith?"

"What's your hurry? Stop and gie's your crack," returned Hutcheon, who took it almost as a personal affront
that any one should leave his smiddy under an hour.

"I canna bide the nicht," said the Cairnharrow man,
recognising the obligation and excusing himself, "I hae
to be hame to fodder the beasts and supper the horse.
The maister is laid up wi' an awfu' sair hand!"

"D'ye tell me sae?" cried the smith. "I missed
him oot o' the kirk—no that that's ocht to gang by.
But I haena seen him at the Cross Keys for a hale fort-
nicht, and the like hasna happened for thirty year. Ye
are no a drinker, I'm thinkin'!"

The smith turned to the "Orra Man" as he spoke.

"No," he answered, quietly, "I do not drink."

Something in the accent or the Englishy pronunciation of the words attracted the attention of the entire
parliament. Each man glanced at his neighbour,
though no man said a word. In that eye-passage the

whole smiddy compared notes, and were of opinion that, if the new Cairnharrow man liked to speak, they would listen to a tale worth hearing.

But it was not to be that night. For the messenger persisting, and the horse outside growing restless, the plough was lifted bodily into the cart, and the "Orra Man" made haste to set out. Suddenly he seemed to remember the boy from Loch Spellanderie.

"Will ye be lang, laddie?" he asked, looking back through the red comfortable door of the forge.

"Peter will hae the coulter dune in a minute," said the smith, and for once Peter proved as good as his master's word. He had the coulter finished, and Kit found himself seated in the red farm cart beside the tramp, both horse and cart clacking slowly up the road under the frosty stars of a winter's night.

Kit, in high spirits at the unexpected "lift" and the pleasant consciousness that it was yet a long way to Loch Spellanderie, chattered incessantly of himself, of his grandfather, of his grandmother, of Betty Landsborough, and somewhat more reservedly of Mistress Mac Walter and the household at the farm by the lochside.

The elder of the pair was a little uneasy till he reached the bright lights of the Cross Keys. The tramp drew up half unconsciously. Then he laid the reins on the neck of the horse, took them up again, and drove resolutely past. Kit and he could hear the murmur of many voices within, and the public rooms were bursting with lights. But the ex-tramp drove steadily on.

Then quite abruptly he addressed his first question to the boy.

"Is your father dead?"

Kit stammered, and in the friendly dark blushed also. This was a different thing to Mistress Mac Walter's voluble reproaches.

"My grandfather telled me that he was dead!" he said at last.

"And your mother—is she dead, too?" continued

the tramp, in the pursuit of his purpose ignoring any pain he might be causing.

"My mither is not dead," murmured Kit; "she is married!" But he said it sadly, as if the two things were much the same. As, save for a soul's continuing agony, they were indeed in Lilias's case.

The tramp thought a while and then continued, "Do you want to be a farm boy all your life?"

Kit explained that first of all he was not going to be a burden on his grandparents, and went on to tell how he had run away from home that he might be able to repay some of the money they had spent on him.

"Would you like to learn Latin?" said the tramp, as the snowflakes began to swirl in their faces, and the patient beast, hitherto jogging quietly between the shafts, tossed her forelock to clear the white drift from before her eyes.

"Aye, I wad that," cried Kit, eagerly, "but wha is to learn me? The maister here canna, and besides, the mistress wadna let me gang to the schule if he could."

"I will teach you," said the "Orra man," calmly.

"You!" cried Kit, astonished, "I didna ken that ye could read even. Are ye a learned man, then?"

The ex-tramp laughed a curious little laugh.

"You are thinking that it has not done much for me," he said.

"Oh, no," said Kit, politely, "I was thinkin' that my maister said ye were a guid worker, and he thocht Cairnharrow would be wise to keep ye!"

It was long since the tramp had heard any man, still one like John Mac Walter, praise his worth and faithfulness. The boy's words marked a distinct step in his upward way. He was glad now that he had driven straight past the Cross Keys.

"Listen," said John Smith, "put that sack round your shoulders. This way! Now come nearer me." He put his arm about the boy, and, after a moment of awkwardness, Kit felt strangely at ease. He wished the road to Loch Spellanderie had been thrice as long and difficult.

" You must say nothing of this to any one," said the
" Orra Man," in a voice which Kit could hear clearly
above the sough and rush of the storm, "I have wasted
my own chances. But if you are the lad I take you for
I am going to see that you don't waste yours. I will
teach you Latin and Greek."

" I ken ' *Penna*, a pen,' already," said Kit, whose ears
had been sharp while Duncan Duncanson took his one
" Latin boy " through a revisal of the declensions.

The " Orra Man " laughed a little.

" That is always a beginning," said he.

" But I hae nae buiks," said Kit, mournfully, " and
I'll hae juist to come to you when Mistress Mac Walter
will let me."

" We won't need books for a while, and I'll speak to
your master when I see him," answered the " Orra Man."

" When will you begin? "

" If ye please, I'll begin the noo," said Kit, nestling
closer to this wonderful " Orra Man " who knew Greek
and Latin and was willing to impart them.

So there amid the swirl and roar of the winter snowstorm Kit had his first lesson in the language, a knowledge of which is universally believed in Scotland to
unlock the doors of success in every profession. The
minutes sped all too rapidly, but he knew " *Penna* "
completely in all its cases by the time the mare stopped
at the loaning end of Loch Spellanderie, and Kit got
down most unwillingly, but with a strange upleaping
elation at his heart.

" Guid-nicht! " he cried up to the white-swathed
figure of the " Orra Man " which came between him and
the black sky, " till the morn's nicht at the Black
Sheds! "

" Good-night—think well over what I said about the
Accusative! "

It was no longer the voice of the " Orra Man " of
Cairnharrow which answered Kit from the red cart,
but the voice of Christopher Kennedy, B.A., formerly
classical master in the Academy of Cairn Edward, now
for the first time in his life acting as private tutor.

CHAPTER XXXII

"Penna, a Pen."

"Shake yoursel' weel, na, an' knock your great clamperin' feet on the door-step," cried the voice of Mistress Mac Walter, as Kit laid his fingers on the latch of the kitchen door. "Whaur hae ye been a' this time? D'ye think that I pay you good siller and feed ye up wi' the best of meat for you to gallivant aboot the countryside."

"*Penna*, a pen; *Pennae*, of a pen."

Kit murmured what he had learned in the cart like a kind of conjuration to ward off evil.

"What's that ye are sayin'—mutterin' ower ill words to yoursel', I'se warrant? John Mac Walter, I dinna ken what ye were thinking on to let siccan an ill-tongued wratch into your hoose, corruptin' your innocent weans and abusin' your married wife to her verra face!"

Kit went quietly to a seat at the end of the table, having deposited the coulter in the outer dark of the back-kitchen, a place filled with a dismal *débris* of pots and pans, dish-cloths, broken paraffin lamps, old boots, new blacking, iron girdles and wash-tubs.

"Come oot o' that!" cried the shrill voice of his mistress as soon as he had seated himself near the lamp, emphasizing the order with a cuff on the ear which made the water stand in Kit's eyes; "that's where Johnnie, puir lad, is doin' his lessons, as brawly ye ken. Ye wad like him to sit doon amang a' the wat snaw ye hae brocht trailin' in wi' ye, and get his death o' cauld. That's what wad pleasure the like o' you!"

"*Pennae*, pens; *Pennarum*, of pens."

"Gang and sit by the door and be thankfu' that ye

hae a meal o' meat to eat in a decent God-fearin' hoose, which is mair nor a nameless, kinless loon like you has ony richt to expect. And no a word oot o' the head o' ye, pervertin' the minds o' my innocent bairns and bringing disgrace on your maister, that may be an elder o' the parish in twa-three year, gin he keeps in wi' the minister and the factor ! "

Kit did as he was bidden, and sat humbly down on a low settle by the door, a place where he was little likely to be disturbed by Johnnie or any other, for there the winter's blast poured freely down the back of his neck round the open door which separated the inner from the outer kitchen.

Meysie Mac Walter, the eldest daughter of the house, now grown into a tall slip of a girl, brought him his porridge. This was, as usual, composed of the scraps and bottomings of bowls which had been left unfinished by the rest of the household. But when the mother's back was turned Meysie who had her own views as to Kit's merits, poured over all a generous " jaw " of new milk not unmingled with cream. So that Kit fared for that night likea prince—indeed, better than many princes.

And the fact that his ear tingled from the hard palm of Mistress Mac Walter was no more regarded by him than the buffet of the storm he had left behind him. Kit was of the bright nature which takes the universe as it rolls. And he was not unwilling to count the hardness of his mistress's hand as part of the scheme of things. He did not complain. He could take it out of the bag of chaff in the barn afterwards. And besides, was there not his new amulet of safety—" *Pennae, pennarum, pennis, pennas, pennae, pennis* " ?

Mistress Mac Walter thought that Kit did not care for reading, or she would have locked up every book about the house of Loch Spellanderie. And Kit, we may be sure, with such a privation before him, did not flaunt his accomplishments in her presence.

*   *   *   *   *

The proceedings of the " Orra Man " on the day after the snowy night journey with Kit were very peculiar.

It was market day at the town, and he went down with
his master from Cairnharrow. He wanted to buy some
winter things, he said. And indeed his wardrobe was
somewhat scanty. Mr. Rogerson advanced his "orra"
man some money on the strength of work yet to be
done, a dangerous thing in the case of many "orra"
men, who have mostly not been in regular places
before, and whose roots are therefore not set very
deep in the soil.

"Dinna be drinkin' it a'," said his master. "Better
buy your winter gear first!"

He knew the nature of "orra" men.

But John Smith did not at once proceed to buy winter
clothing. He skirmished this way and that through
the lanes about the Vennel till he lighted upon an old
dingy shop, in the window of which were several books,
a battered brass fender, some unmatched cups and
saucers, a pile of dingy carpets, and a paraffin lamp
without a globe.

The "Orra Man" entered and spoke thus to the
owner of all these. "Have you any Latin dictionaries
or grammars?"

The shabby old man in list slippers, who had come stumbling and snuffling out of a back room, shook his head.

"What ken I?" he said; "she's away frae hame
the day. Ye can look for yoursel'."

With this permission the "Orra Man," keenly
watched by the ancient long-coated guardian of the shop,
looked over the dusty books which were piled higgledy-
piggledy beneath the counter and behind the door,
mostly tied in bundles with string. He handled them
with the swift delicate art of a lover, blowing the dust
from the top, and running his finger along the right-
hand page to be ready for turning as he read.

The old man watched him for a little and then said,
"Ye are a queer ploughman to be seekin' Laitin dictionaries!"

The "Orra Man" did not hear him. He was
shaking his head over a doubtful note in an edition of
Suetonius.

"It will not do—clever—undoubtedly clever. But it will not do!"

"It winna do, will it not?" said the old man; "then maybe you will find something there mair to your taste, since you are so ill to please!"

As he spoke he threw open an upper glazed cupboard, and row upon row of classical books were disclosed.

"There," cried the old man, laughing senilely, "if you set up for a learned man, there's something to bite on. She bocht them at the sale o' a dominie that ran awa frae Cairn Edward a lang while since—made a munelicht flittin', that is. You'll see his name on the boards. He was just desperate for debt they say!"

And the "Orra Man," opening the nearest volume with a queer constriction of the heart, read the name written within. It was

CHRISTOPHER KENNEDY, B.A.,

on a neat blue-edged oblong, and on a flyleaf a Greek ode to Lilias Armour's eyes, which he had scribbled in pencil as he lay waiting for her one day high up on the Dornal moor.

"Are ye a buyer or are ye not? I canna bide a' day frae the fire on siccan a cauld mornin' as this, so I'm tellin' ye!"

The creaking tones of the old shopman awakened the "Orra Man." "I cannot buy them all," he said; "I have not the money. But I want to buy them one by one if you will keep them for me."

"Dinna fret; they'll keep themsel's easy eneuch in the toon o' Dumfries. There's nae run on the dead languages in Dumfries. Bibles are drug stock, and even Shakespeare—man, I dinna think we hae selled yin o' him for twenty year, except a big bound copy to Rob Veitch, the hosier, that he uses to keep his letters doon on his desk, and to throw at the dogs that come snuffin' aboot the wicks o' his shop door."

This being the state of the literary market in the neighbourhood, the "Orra Man" carried away on easy terms Riddle's Latin Dictionary, Dunbar's Greek

Lexicon, a couple of Edinburgh Academy's Rudiments (arid but unequalled schoolbooks), Cæsar, Livy, and (what was a sacrifice to his own desires), a pretty little Elzevir Horace which he had often seen in his dreams during the last sad years.

But John Smith went back to the yard where he had put up his beast without a farthing even to pay the hostler, and naturally without having added one stitch to his stock of winter clothing.

Yet the "Orra Man" was thrice wrapped in joy.

It was an unthought-of chance, though of course natural enough, that the old "general dealer" of Dumfries should have picked up the classical books which no one else wanted, and that he should have preserved them ever since in a dusty cupboard of his back-shop. But to the Classical Master it seemed of the best omen. It brought him, in his own esteem, within measurable distance of his old position, and he could hardly wait for the seclusion of his "stable laft" before turning to his favourite passages, and verifying the exactness of certain quotations which had been grains of gold to him in the dark ways of the underworld.

A somewhat shy and reserved man was the new "Orra Man" among his fellows, "a weel learnit man" they told each other when sizing up the new comer, "a great reader and juist wonderfu' weel informed—kenned nocht about farm wark when he cam' to Cairnharrow. But he was quick to learn—faith, there's little that he canna set his hand to noo!"

On the whole exceedingly well liked was the "Orra Man," but accounted to have a bee in his bonnet or such a learned man would never be where he was this day. Yet in such repute and serious respect is learning (or even the report of it) held in Scotland, that there was not a man but would have stopped half an hour longer or risen half an hour sooner to help John Smith with his work about the stables or in the fields.

"He's no used to it like us!" these kindly hearty farm lads would say; "what can a learned man ken aboot skailin' middens?"

CHAPTER XXXIII.

KIT GOES HOME.

THERE was one goal which his instructor always kept before Kit. Nothing was any use which did not lead to a university education. And the "Orra Man" had his own ideas as to how the matter was to be accomplished. He knew well that every three years there was a bursary open to the whole of Galloway—thirty pounds a year for four years was the amount. Not a fortune, doubtless, but capable, with the economy inherent in Scottish youth, of seeing him through his sessions at college.

The "Orra Man" resolved that his pupil should enter for this in three years. He would be fifteen by that time, and just within the standard of age.

"If I cannot train one pupil better than a man who has twenty to attend to my name is not—John Smith!" he said.

And though the terms of the affirmation were dubious, the training and discipline which Kit Kennedy presently began to undergo were of the most severe and drastic kind.

Both the "Orra Man" and Kit lived for these stolen hours, when by the light of a stable lantern they read together the solemn-sounding, grave-thoughted Latins, and after a while, with infinite stammering, the nimble-witted Greeks.

During all that first winter Kit met his teacher every night in the Black Sheds—certain ramshackle erections of wood on the boundary line of both farms. Here, wrapped in old sacks and by the feeble shine of a tallow dip set in a stable lantern, Kit mastered his verbs, regular and irregular, and so macadamised his way to the Latin version which he hoped one day to write.

One night, however, Kit waited long listening in vain for his companion. The storm beat outside, and the wind made eery noises among the tall ash trees overhead. Stray pieces of rotten branches struck the sheds at intervals, as if some one unseen were beating the roof with a stick. A loose clap-board knocked incessantly demanding admission. Kit's hair almost stood on end, but he conjured the ghosts aloud with " *tupto* " in all its moods, tenses, and voices. The incantation was perfectly effective, and gave Kit a better idea of the Greek language than he had ever had before.

But after all the " Orra Man " did not come.

The next night the boy again waited in vain in the tingling frost which had succeeded the rain, till his nose was blue and his fingers frozen to his palms. Long before nine he had lost track of his toes. But still the preceptor came not. Kit tried " *luo* " on the cold, but Greek, though excellent against the spirits that roam in the dark, was but a feeble protection against the bitterness of a Scottish winter, when the frost curls the very leaves of the evergreens inward, and the stars sparkle aloft in the seven prismatic colours.

On the third night the " Orra Man " appeared. His face was strange and drawn, his voice hoarse and whistled a little as he spoke. He had lost that straightforwardness of eye which had begun to distinguish him. He could not look his pupil in the eye.

" What's been the maitter ? " cried Kit, anxiously, as soon as he heard his foot on the threshold. " Hae ye been ill, Maister Smith ? "

" I have not been ill," said the " Orra Man."

" Hae ye gotten your leave frae Cairnharrow ? "

The absentee did not answer, and Kit, with the quick lightness of youth, accepted silence as a negative, and darted on to what he had been eager to tell.

" I hae learned a' the rules ye gied me and six pages mair. Will ye hearken me ? "

The " Orra Man " reached his hand automatically for the grammar, and Kit rattled his lesson off. But the teacher shut the book without remark, to the great disappointment of Kit, who had expected wonder and delight instead of this chilling silence.

"Is it no weel learned? Are ye no pleased?" he demanded, anxiously. The classical master did not answer. His head was bowed upon his hands, and when Kit looked closer tears were trickling between his wasted fingers.

"Dinna—dinna do that!" cried the boy, with the pained consternation of youth amazed before an elder's tears. "What gars ye do the like o' that?"

The "Orra Man" stilled his slow, painful sobs.

"Kit," he said, speaking with difficulty, "I am not fit to sit beside you—I—I—I have been drinking again. I was drunk the night before last, and was brought home in a cart. And Mr. Rogerson overlooked it, for the good fellows at the farm had done my work. They are all better men than I. If your grandfather knew the manner of man who was teaching you, he would never let me come near you again."

"Maister Smith," said the boy, "I yince heard the Doctor say that ye dinna get better a' at yince, o' a trouble that ye hae had for a lang time. Maybe ye hae had this trouble a lang while, and are no fairly better yet."

"Well," said the "Orra Man," looking at Kit for the first time, "let us go on with our work. I have promised, and I will keep. Till I see you Galloway bursar—I—I'll keep my promise. And then perhaps I shall be cured."

From this time forward Kit had long days of work and short nights of learning and sleep. Little by little he escaped from the domains of Mistress Mac Walter into the larger liberty of the work on the farm. And that made a great change in his circumstances, for John Mac Walter, though of no power or authority within doors, could make Kit's life infinitely easier without. He slept now in the stable loft, and as that opened above the horses in the stable Mistress Mac Walter dared not go in there to find out whether he was in bed or not, a habit which had embittered the first months of his scholastic career in the university of the Black Sheds.

Then Kit was growing rapidly, and being of a sturdy frame at a year's end he did almost a man's work. And, for his own sake, John Mac Walter insisted that Kit should have his meals full and regular. Even his mistress was quite alive to the advantages of getting a man's work for a boy's wage, and now mostly took it out of Kit with her tongue. So that he had no more to share his breakfast with the dogs out of the three-legged pot.

It was one of Mistress Mac Walter's pet projects "to mak' a minister out o' Jock.' Also it was about this time that she began to call her eldest son Johnny. Jock is not a suitable name for a minister in the making.

Jock was a soft, underhandish youth, lanky and stoop-shouldered, a coward by nature and a tale-bearer by education. For this last Kit would many a time have "knocked the head aff him" had it not been that he knew well that Jock would carry his grievances straight to his mother within the kitchen.

Johnny or Jock Mac Walter was accounted the best scholar at the School of Saint John's Town. He had a good memory, and his dominie was one of the ancient stamp who consider themselves disgraced if they do not send a scholar every year to the universities—and a bursar if possible. This old-fashioned pedagogue thought that he could make something out of Jock Mac Walter. "He's no what I could wish, nor what I hae had in the past. But he's a fair ordinary lad, and between me and the taws we'll maybe mak' a scholar oot o' Jock yet!"

Dominie Peter Mac Fayden, otherwise know as Birsie, had been dominie of St. John's Town for more than two generations, and he did not despair of yet living to tickle the palms of his earliest pupils' grandchildren.

He had the name of a "graund teacher"—he "brocht the weans on fine" they said. "He was maybe a wee sair on them at times. But he's an auld man, and his temper no juist what it was."

15

"Dod, gin it's waur than it was in my time thirty year since, guid peety the bairns! For a mair ill-tempered, thrawn auld runt there wasna in braid Scotland."

This was John Rogerson's opinions.

"I am glad I hae nae weans," he would declare, "but gin I had forty I wad send them a' oot o' the pairish before I wad pit them at the mercy o' sic a vicious auld curmudgeon. I declare ye canna gang within a Sabbath day's journey o' Peter's schule but ye will see a bairn a' forgrutten, haudin' its hand below its oxter, and the yells o' anither comin' frae the schule itself like to tak' the roof aff.

"'Ye are a great miss in a barn,' I said to Peter yince.

"'And what for that?' says he, glowerin' at me.

"'Ye wad do for flail and fanners too,' says I, 'for ye lay on like twa threshers on a sheaf, and gar the stour flee like a pair o' blue fanners new coft oot o' Andro Dobie's shop!'"

"The dominie wadna like that, I'se warrant," said his neighbour at the kirk door, where they were waiting for the minister.

For in the parish of Saint John's it was considered that lightning would immediately fall upon any head of a household or other responsible person who would venture to take his seat before the minister had gone into the vestry.

"Peter has a great name for bringin' on backward laddies, though," said Grocer Candlish; "there's Jock Mac Walter. I declare a stupider nowt than him ye wadna find between here and the back-shore o' Leswalt. He disna ken a turnip frae a patawtie except juist by the taste, and he has nae natural way wi' horse beasts ava'. But he can leather at the Latin till ye wad think somebody was swcerin' strange oaths doon by in the clachan."

"Oh, he's a terrible weel-learned craiter the maister," said the herd of Knockman, a hill farm at the root of Cairnsmore. "I hear he's gaun to sent Jock forrit for the next Gallowa' Bursary. His faither is to mak' a

minister oot o' him, I hear. Weel, I hae seen mony
queer-lookin' and unfaceable ministers, but gin they
mak' yin oot o' that callant, I'll say that the day o'
miracles is no bygane!"

"And what's the matter wi' Jock, na," said Grocer
Candlish; "he's a rael ceevil lad and eident at his
lessons?"

"What's the maitter wi' him—a ceevil callant, says
you. Aye, far ower ceevil. I wad like to see him
scoorin' the hills lichtfit like a wild goat, barefit and
bareleggit. Boy callants are best steerin'. But yon
laddie, he creeps to the schule, and he sits at the desk,
and he trembles for fear he's lickit, and greets when he
gets a cuff, and tells tales on the rest to sook in wi' the
maister. Oh, I hae been watchin' that laddie when I've
been aboot the clachan. Ye may mak' a minister o'
him, I will aloo, for the grace o' God is almichty. But
thae sort should be pushioned when they're young, and
that's my thocht o't!"

*   *   *   *   *

Every three months Kit got a day off, and went
through to the little house of Crae to see those whom
he had left behind. By the care of Betty Landsborough (or some one of her many admirers) it was
always a day when Walter Mac Walter was absent on
some of the mysterious business which about this time
more and more began to occupy him. Lilias came over
early, passing on her way the grass-grown courtyard
and closed doors, and regarding wistfully the barricaded
windows of the little farm of Black Dornal; then,
sighing a little she crossed the high-backed bridge of
Crae beneath which the water for ever rustles brown and
cool, striving with the green leaves and the jubilant
birds which shall have the meed of sweetest melody.

Then at the end of the little walk, which leads to the
left among the trees to the cottage in the wood of Crae,
Kit would fling himself into his mother's arms with a
little cry of joy.

"Oh mither—mither! But I am that glad to
see ye!"

And each time he would search her face to see if it had grown more weary, and her abundant hair for grey threads to pull out as if he had been her lover. And partly it was the anxious joy of a son's affection, and partly because he knew that the "Orra Man" would ask him so many questions about them all, but especially about his mother, when he went back to Loch Spellanderie and the Black Sheds.

Then in gallant procession they would return to the cottage, Kit leading his mother, looking radiant and almost girlish, the weary broken look for the moment quite taken away by the excitement of her son's homecoming, the flutter of her mother's bustling welcome and her father's stiller joy.

For early in the afternoon the Elder himself would come up the green walk between the pine woods carrying his stone-breaking tools—a little more bent perhaps than of yore, a little whiter of hair, but with all the old serenity of eye, the same straightforwardness of regard, the placid lip, the firm chin, the noble cliff-like brow.

At the same place each time, and ever with fresh apparent surprise on his grandfather's part, Kit would leap out upon him, and seizing the old man by the arms dispossess him of his hammers and leathern bag, crying out all the time, "Oh, grandfaither, are ye no glad to see me? I thocht ye were never comin'!"

Then with the old man smiling down upon him, and Kit circling like a jubilant collie round and round him, the pair would approach the door of the little cot. And Betty Landsborough would come out with a tin "bine" in her hands, and stand looking at them with that in her eyes which none of her admirers had ever been able to bring there.

Margaret Armour, her best "kep" accurately adjusted on her head in honour of the occasion, stood upon the spotless doorstep, saying nothing, but smiling observant, benignant as a motherly senior among her chickens.

"Kit, Kit," she would say warningly, as the boy, wild with getting home for a day would indulge in some surpassing prank, "dinna vex your grandfaither.

He will be tired. Did onybody ever see siccan a callant?"

But it was when they were all gathered in the little room, and the very window flowers seemed to turn inward to listen to their happy talk, that Kit's "headtime," as he called it himself, arrived.

Then he took from his pocket a purse which the "Orra Man" had given him, and from it he extracted his wages in dirty pound notes. Six pounds in the half-year was the figure. He carried them across to his grandmother with careless grace but inward swelling pride.

"Here, granny," he would say, cheerfully, "this is to help to pay the rent."

Then the same thing happened every time.

First Kit became conscious of a proud, beamy look answering his on his mother's face. Then the Elder would bow his head and give silent thanks. Thereafter the tears would well up into his grandmother's eyes, her lips quiver, and she would say, "I canna take it, Kit. 'Deed, I canna be takin' it frae ye, laddie!"

Mostly, while she was thus holding it in her shaking fingers and her hands were gripping her apron, with the glad tears "happin'" like rabbits down her black dress and white mutch strings, Betty Landsborough would come jauntily in.

"What's this, what this?" she would cry. "Never mair siller! I declare ye maun rob the bank. Faith, ye micht spare a note or twa for me to buy me a new goon, Kit—me that has aye been sae fond o' ye!"

For Betty Landsborough thought that there had been enough of the joy that brings down the tear, and with her rustic outspokenness, which in Whinnyliggate passed very well for wit, she soon brought the smiles back again to all the faces.

Ah, simple moods of simple folk, humour broad as the harvest moon that smiles in the September sky, pathos of the working field and kitchen, of the home-returning feet, the labour-weary body, the ageing face, the unageing heart—with the love so reticently shut within mostly, so suddenly revealed some day when the clouds rift—ye are precious every whit to me, but perhaps over-common for many others! Your manifestations may be unrefined, your words are often coarse, but the sin and the pain and the pardon ye reveal are those which each recurring generation has known since first the Wall of Eden was broken down, and man set to earn his daily bread in the sweat of his brow.

Then when Kit stood beside his grandmother, and Lilias still had that glorified look on her face, with a grandly simple gesture the Elder would rise to his feet.

"Let us pray!" I can hear him say. Then all rose as they did when the minister came to visit. At the Book night and morning they kneeled. But now they stood. For it was a family thanksgiving, and with a hand laid on the boy's shoulder the Ruling Elder prayed that the blessing of the Heavenly Father might rest on this lad who had no father on the earth, and that he who honoured his forbears, and obeyed the voice of his mother, might receive tenfold the blessing of the commandment with promise.

This was the time when Kit felt the tears flood up from his own heart to his eyes. His mother came nearer to him; he bent his head on her breast. Somehow the roof of the humble cot went off, and they seemed to be standing in a large place of shining beauty, as indeed well they might. For the cottage in the Crae Wood had become an antechamber of the court of Heaven, and the Elder's petitions the bridge between the poor human fact and the lofty human ideal.

Soon, all too soon, it was time to go.

Kit must be back at Loch Spellanderie for the suppering of the horses, and besides he had trysted with the "Orra Man" to meet him at the smiddy in Saint John's Town. With sad, reluctant foot Lilias must return to Kirkoswald to feed on the joy she had experienced and to await that which should yet be. She lived chiefly because of these visits of her son.

"Ye are no forgettin' the Book, Kit?" his grandfather would say, meaning the reading of his Bible.

"And your prayers?" his mother would add.

"And ye are keepin' oot o' a' bad company?" This from his grandmother.

"And you are no makin' love to ony o' the up country lasses?" would be Betty Landsborough's contribution; "mind that ye are trysted to me!"

Then Kit would ask for the foresters at Rob's Bothie, and comport himself so bravely at parting that smiles would be on every face. His mother usually walked a little way with him to a shady place in the wood down by the stepping-stones, where she took him in her arms, great fellow though he had grown, and kissed him and clapped his shoulder lightly with her hand, saying only, in a shaken voice, "My laddie! My nice laddie!"

Then Kit, first looking every way to see that no one was coming, would lay his cheek on his mother's brow and croon over her, saying, "Mither, mither, dinna greet! I am gaun to be a great man, and then I'll tak' ye away wi' me. And we'll hae a hoose in the toon and a hoose at the seaside. And ye shall hae silk to wear and a bonnet with gum floo'ers intil't, green and red and purple. And ye'll hae naebody to fret ye then, and nocht to do but to see that my sarks are clean to pit on —a clean white sark every mornin'. Dinna greet, mither, for it's comin'!"

His mother smiled through the fast running salt water.

"Be a good lad, Kit, and mind your prayers!"

"Aye, mither! And we'll hae twa servants, and ye'll gie them 'Scots wha hae' if they arena up at six o'clock and readyin' the porridge!"

"Kit, do ye aye mind to say a prayer for your mither?"

"Aye, mither, of course! But what need ye speak o' sic things. Somebody might hear ye. And the hoose will be three stories, and there will be canaries in every window——"

"Kit, ye never see ony tramp folk the worse of drink up your way, do ye?"

"No, mither. What for do ye speer? There's nae

tramps aboot the place, but I'll keep awa' frae them if ye say so, mither, gin that will please ye. Noo, I maun rin half the road to be in time for the 'Orra Man'."

His mother asked one other question with an anxious face.

"Oh, juist a kind man at a neighbour farm," Kit answered; "he is to meet me at the clachan—a ceevil man, and greatly thocht o' by his maister."

"Guid-nicht, mither; mind and no greet. And think on the clean sarks ilka day, and the twa servants and the canaries in every window."

So Kit would go off with his feet moving fast in the direction of Loch Spellanderie, but his face looking back over his shoulder. And he never cried a tear all the time—that is, not till he was too far from his mother for her to see whether he cried or not.

CHAPTER XXXIV.

Kit's Rival.

It was a great strain for Kit to keep the secret of the
"Orra Man's" lessons to himself, and only the urgent
remonstrances of his teacher, and the wonderful surprise it would be to every one if he succeeded, kept him
from telling his mother each time he bade her good-bye.
She had so little in life to make her glad. She seemed
to have suffered for everybody else's wrong-doings, and
to make up Kit wanted to give her all the joy he could.
But the "Orra Man" represented to him what it would
be when they saw his name in the papers.

And then Jock Mac Walter—and Jock Mac Walter's
mother!

Kit could not forego that revenge, and what he
suffered at Loch Spellanderie was perhaps as great a
factor in his desire for hard work and the acquisition of
knowledge as everything else put together.

For Mistress Mac Walter "rubbed it into" Kit after
her fashion. She informed him a thousand times that
John was to be a minister, and that he, Kit Kennedy,
was to be an out-worker about a farm, who might
indeed rise to handle a plough, but who could not be
trusted with a printed book.

Jock usually worked in the "ben room," or parlour of
Loch Spellanderie, a lugubrious apartment, with chests
of drawers and a best bed which retired itself as far as
possible into one corner behind curtains, and which
when company called they were expected not to notice.

His mother was in the habit of taking visitors down as
far as the door of this abode of the more learned muses.

"I think he's oot. Ye micht juist like to tak' a peep.

He sits there and learns a' the day through. Aye, that's a Greek buik or a Hebrew; I dinna ken what yin o' the twa. Jock is a fair neeger at baith languages, and as for Laitin, Dominie Mac Fayden says that he canna learn him ony mair. Noo, come awa! He'll be comin' in the noo, and he'll no like to think that his learnit buiks hae been disturbit by the likes o' us!"

"It's a preevelege to hae seen," his mother's visitor would say, diplomatically and solemnly; "I never kenned that there was sae muckle to be dune before ye could be a minister. I declare I'll think mair than ever o' the Sabbath's sermon noo!"

"Oh, Jock is no that length yet, but the fact is that he's gaun to win a grand heap o' siller that's called a bursary. It's gi'en to the best scholar. And though of course John disna need it—for his faither is perfectly able and wullin' to pay for his collegin'—forebye his rich uncle Walter (the laird, ye ken) that juists doats on him. But this bursary is an unco' honour, and it will be a great feather in Dominie Mac Fayden's cap. No but what John could win it by himsel'! It will be a fine thing to gang to Edinbra as the First Gallowa' Bursar. What think ye o' that for a name?"

So the privileged visitant would retire, awed and full of admiration for "that wonnerfu' callant o' Mistress Mac Walter's." But after she had passed the loaning end, and found herself safe on the broad unprejudiced King's Highway, she was wont to prophecy that somehow "siccan pride would get a sair doon-come."

But it was not from this that Kit suffered most, nor yet from having Jock thrown at his head at all times of the day. It was because he was not allowed to handle or even look at any of the favoured student's books.

It chanced that on one occasion John had brought an American edition of Virgil with him from Dominie Mac Fadyen's, a volume full of the most admirable translations and the most copious notes and explanations. So complete, indeed, was the volume, so all compact of helps and aids and informations, that it left the student nothing whatever to do—which, very naturally, was often just what he did.

But to Kit Kennedy, trained in the severe school of the classical master, to whom lexicon, grammar, gradus, and dictionary represented all the law and the prophets, this American royal road to learning was a revelation. He lifted it with brightening eyes and an eager hand. It was lying beside the bakeboard open. Jock had just been explaining to his scandalised mother about the doings of the heathen gods and goddesses.

"Tell me some mair about that shameless besom!" Mistress Mac Walter had been saying when mother and son were called out by a great outcry in the stable-yard.

It was at that very moment that Kit, all unconscious, came in by the door of the back kitchen, steering his way among the pots and pans.

There on the table open, no one near, lay the fascinating volume.

Kit had it in his hand in a moment. He turned up passage after passage, and ever his heart sank more completely into his hob-nailed boots. He could never hope to obtain from his poor barren dictionaries, and by the slow process of looking up every word, such a wealth of classical lore as lay open to the possessor of this volume.

He looked up line after line, in which he had encountered difficulties untold. Here they were all solved, with new and wondrous lights upon meaning, fresh and impossible felicities of translation, and rich store of allusions to manners and customs which made his heart flutter to think how little he knew.

Thus he stood wrapt and transfixed by the side of the bakeboard unconscious of all, till suddenly a tremendous box on the ear sent him reeling. The volume was snatched from his hand and the floury rolling-pin applied vigorously to his back. Kit's eyes watered with indignation more than with pain. But louder than the ringing of his smitten ear shrilled the indignant voice of Mistress Mac Walter.

"What do ye mean, ye ignorant wratch, ye nameless landlouper, by finger-markin' my John's learned buik wi' your great glaury paws? Did onybody ever see the like? A great muckle nowt like you, fresh frae the byre, to handle a dear-bocht buik like that, and be lookin' at it as if ye could understand a single word o't!

"What need hae ye o' eddication? What ye hae to mind is to haud the pleuch and count the beasts—that will tak ye a' your time, my man. Aye, and I'll promise ye that your maister shall hear this nicht, when he comes hame, baith how ye waste his time and lichtly me, his marriet wife, standing there wi' a mock on your face. I'll learn ye, my man. I'll gar ye lauch on the wrang side o' your heid gin I bring the roller down on your croon!"

It was with a very downcast countenance that Kit made his way to the Black Sheds that night.

"I think I had better gie it up; I can never be upsides wi' the like o' yon!" he said to the "Orra Man."

And with copious detail he told his master all the wonders of the American book. The classical master smiled a far-off, quiet smile.

"For once," he said, "Mistress Mac Walter did quite right. If ever I were to catch you with a book like that I would first throw it in the back of the fire, and then I would tan your hide from head to foot into the bargain!"

Kit opened his eyes wide indeed. What could his teacher mean?

"Listen, Kit," said the "Orra Man." "I don't know what Jock Mac Walter has learned, but I know what Dominie Mac Fadyen can teach. And—well, mind you your versions and never pass a word you don't know the exact meaning of to a shade. And when the day comes, we'll see what we shall see."

Walter Mac Walter did not leave Kit to his fate when he provided a home for him with his brother and sister-in-law at Loch Spellanderie. He was for ever passing to and fro on his now constant journeys. He drove a fast horse in a light dog-cart, and was understood to be engaged in extensive dealing transactions, the exact purport of which nobody but himself was acquainted with.

He did not personally pay much attention to Kit, contenting himself with seeing that he remained on the spot. But he obtained from Kit's master and mistress all information as to his doings.

"He's a decent, ceevil eneuch callant," said his master; "I hae nae faut to find wi' him that ye couldna find wi' ony ither callant, except that I wish he were a wee mair carefu' aboot the company he keeps."

"Ah !" said Walter Mac Walter, but asked no more till he had a chance of speaking with Mistress Mac Walter alone.

"What company does that boy o' yours keep ? " he asked.

"Him ? " cried Mistress Mac Walter, with her nose in the air; "the verra warst. But I dinna interfere wi' him. For I mind aye what ye said to me when he cam'. He taks up wi' naebody but the "Orra Man" ower by at Cairnharrow—a drucken wratch that I hae seen wi' my ain een brocht hame in the bottom o' a cairt after twa days' spree. And it's mair than suspected that he has been in the gaol twa or three times! "

Walter Mac Walter nodded with a satisfied air.

"And he goes a great deal with this man," he said; " what is his name ? "

"Oh, nocht particular. Some Englishy name he has caa'ed himsel'. The like o' thae craiturs has a new name ilka time they gang to the hirin' fair ! "

Walter Mac Walter smiled to himself, very well pleased, as he drove away.

Kit was safely out of his neighbourhood. He was fast becoming a mere rustic clod. He was already the companion of a drunkard and probable criminal.

"Providence is all very well," chuckled the laird of Kirkoswald, " but it pays better to depend on yourself for making things happen as you want them ! "

CHAPTER XXXV.

THE EXAMINATION DAY.

THE day of the great trial of scholarship came round at last. The secretary of the society had a considerable list of entrants. These, being a W.S.* and a man of exactitude, he had entered according to alphabetical order under their names, places of abode, schools at which they had studied, together with their present ages.

There was one entry which puzzled him a good deal. It came about midway his list of eleven or twelve as finally made out. It ran as follows: *Christopher Kennedy. Age, 15. Loch Spellanderie, Glenkells—Private Study.*

All the other entrants came from well-known burgh or famous parish schools, long celebrated for "sendin' up lads to the college." But here was a difficulty.

"It may be a practical joke!" said Ebenezer Fleming, W.S., and like a wary man-of-law he indited a letter to Christopher Kennedy asking for particulars and a certificate from his parish minister in lieu of one from his teacher. He got in reply a neat and clerkly letter, which would not have disgraced one of his own juniors at the office in St. Andrew's Square. And enclosed in it were two certificates, one from the parish minister of St. John's Town, and the other from his own maternal uncle, the Cameronian minister of the Kirk of the Hill in Cairn Edward.

"It will be some minister who has been teaching him —poor chap, I fear he will get a downcome when he tries himself against all these academy fellows. I got a

---

* *i.e.*, Writer to the Signet.

wonderful letter about one applicant—what is his name,
yes—yes—Mac Walter—John Mac Walter."

Now the Union of Galloway Associations held its
annual meeting in Cairn Edward at the time of the
examinations. And the unfortunates who had their
papers to write indited them in the assembly rooms of
the leading hotel, the Cairn Edward Arms, amid a
distant fusilade of popping corks, intermittent sounds of
revelry, and the constant trampling of innumerable feet
in the passages without.

Cairn Edward itself was new to Kit. That is, he had
been in the little town on Sabbaths when all the shops
wore their shutters—except the Apothecaries' Hall,
which had two down, and looked in its staid responsibility like a sportive parson who has lost a couple of
teeth, and who knows he ought not to be smiling under
the garish light of day. But Kit had never seen Cairn
Edward on a Monday. And that not a common Monday
either, but the red-letter day when the Union of
Galloway Societies met in the town and held its great
dinner in the evening.

The boy slowly took in the vision of the little whitewashed town with its smiling shops, broad streets, and
comfortable merchants all a-bustle behind their well-
polished counters. Red carts stood tilted here and there
with their shafts pointing to the sky, to the obstruction
of the thoroughfare. A ceaseless tide of grey-coated,
irregularly-bearded farmers and their more gaily-
attired women-folk poured up and down the one long
main street. There was quite a concourse at the cross,
and one could hardly elbow a way athwart the market-hill
(where the auction marts were) for men and dog-fights.

And in the midst of all this cheerful pother nine or
ten lads, crammed to the lips with knowledge, anxiously
awaited the examination papers which were to seal
their doom.

Kit was early on the scene. He was once more a free
agent. For he had given his notice and served his warning at Loch Spellanderie, as his monthly engagement
enabled him to do. Hit or miss, he knew well that he

could not go back there after the dread revelation that he had secretly put himself into competition with "oor John" for the great prize of the First Galloway Bursary.

But at the sight of him among the competitors John Mac Walter nearly fell through the floor with astonishment, with which indignation began soon to be at strife. It was in the big barren room where, during election times, meetings of the general Conservative Committee are mostly held that Kit first revealed himself as a rival to his mistress's son.

"Kit Kennedy, what are you doing here? This is reserved for candidates, don't you know?" said John Mac Walter, coming across the room to where Kit sat nervously fingering the rim of his Sunday hat, and running over a few propositions in the sixth book of Euclid about which he had qualms.

But Kit only smiled serenely. "Dinna you worry about me, John," he said, soothingly.

* * * * *

"Keep cool, never give your classics a thought. Read your paper through before you begin. Take the easy questions first. Keep a still tongue in your head, and, above all, think you are going to win!" These were the parting directions of the classical master in the street of Cairn Edward. He had ridden down from Cairnharrow with Kit in the farm cart in which he was bringing a number of calves for the market.

When the members of the United Galloway Societies arrived at the Cairn Edward Arms, they were taken as part of the entertainment to the hall where the eleven candidates sat hard at with nothing to depend on but their brains, a printed sheet of questions, and a plenteous supply of pens, ink, and paper.

"Lord bless my soul!" cried jovial Bailie Mowatt of Edinburgh, who had come down with the midday train to make the speech of the evening, "an' div ye mean to tell me that yon laddies ken a' thae things! And that they hae learned a' that for thirty pound a year! A declare A wadna do it for twunty thoosand. Landlord, see ye gie them the best dinner that is to be had

in your place. Bailie Mowatt, Bailie Mowatt, A aye
kenned ye for a dour ignorant body. But faith A never
realised the length and braith and deepth o' yer ignorance afore! Laddies, ye canna a' win. But ye are to
get your fares back and forrit to your hames frae Maister
Fleemin', that upsettin' lawyer body at tha heid o' the
table there, and a' your expenses, the same to be chargit
to Bailie Tammas Mowatt o' the Candlemaker Raw.
Enbra! Guid day to ye, callants!"

Kit had never sat in an examination hall before, and
the rustling of so much printed paper, and the scratching
of so many pens all moving rapidly forward, foundered
him for a little. But soon the wits came back to him,
and he remembered the classical master's advice—the
easy questions first, and keep cool.

Happily it was the Latin paper, and Kit ran his eye
over the prose version for translation with a wonderful
feeling of security, which began at his feet and spread
tinglingly upwards. It was a passage from Macaulay's
third chapter, one of his favourite pieces, and one which
he had more than once turned into Latin with the
"Orra Man." The excellence of the translation which
Kit sent in was quite hid from himself. He did not even
know that all the others were leaving their versions to the
last. It seemed to him that he was working very slowly.

Neither did he know that the examiner chosen by the
Society was an old pupil of Melvin's (prince of Latinists)
at Aberdeen Grammar school. If he had, he would
have taken even more pains with the version—and perhaps spoiled it.

The transactions into English proved the merest
child's play, and Kit wrote them off almost without
thought. Indeed, the whole paper was answered so
rapidly, and without a word wasted, that Kit was first
done, and presently found himself with a beating heart
watching the flying pens of the ten covering ream after
ream of foolscap. It seemed to him that he must have
missed out something essential. So he went carefully
over all his answers, recalling what the "Orra Man"
had told him, and putting down that and no more.

16

Then came luncheon and an adjournment, the youths rising pale and anxious at the call of their timekeeper, some even halting to alter some doubtful point even on the way up to the table; and then, after all was fixed, rehearsing in their minds some other method by which they could have answered or evaded a question and so made assurance doubly sure.

John Mac Walter kept at a distance from Kit, who sat in his corner shy and awkward, but relieved to find the work easy and simple thus far, and well within his possibilities.

A tall strongly-built Wigtonshire lad came over to where Kit sat and held out a horny hand with a friendly air.

"Hey, mon," he cried, heartily, "I think surely I hae seen you before. My name's Bob Grier. I come frae the Garlies. What's yours, and where d'ye come frae?"

Kit informed him gratefully, and straightway a fellow-feeling rose between them, as being alike far from home, and rough country lads among so many better taught and better clad.

"I misdoot neither o' us is like to get the siller," said he of Garlies; "there's a young lad frae aboot Balmaclellan that a minister tutored—a fine laddie, too, but a wee delicate. You or me, Kennedy, could twist him a' into knots. But I doot that at the learnin' he will twist us intil a cockit hat."

Kit smilingly admitted the probability, so far, at least, as he was concerned.

"What schule hae ye been at?" was Grier's next question. "What, nane since ye were eleven year auld! That's fair desperate. Ye'll no ken whether ye are richt or wrang, haein' naebody to tell you. Did ye do the version? What, every word o't! Let's hear!"

Kit ran over a sentence or two of his translation of Macaulay's periods. Grier turned about and called, "I say, lads, here's a loonie that has sent in a' the hale version, every word; and he can gie it aff his tongue like as if it was the Shorter's Quastions!"

Half a dozen of the candidates surrounded Kit.

" Say it again," said Grier, who, being a generous lad, wished his new friend to shine.

Kit repeated his version as accurately as possible.

" That's not classical Latin," said John Mac Walter ; "and what a funny way to speak it ! It's easy to see he disna ken muckle ! "

The smith from Garlies turned on the speaker. " Aye, my yellow-gilled dishclout, and what dub did they fish you oot o' wi' a worm ? What grand way do ye pronounce your words, that ye can afford to throw stanes at ither folk ? "

Jock Mac Walter wished he had his mother to answer for him, but managed to falter that "at ony rate that wasna the richt way."

" Man," said Garlies, " I wish sair we had you doon about whaur I come frae. There's a smiddy there that I work in whiles. Man, I could pit a pair of fine cuddy cackars on ye (iron shoes) that wad fit ye to a hair. And then ye could gang your ways up to the college o' Edinburgh and stand in the muckle " yett," and tell a' the professors hoo to pronounce the Laitin."

" Come to dinner now," announced the voice of the Secretary from the doorway ; we will take the mathematical paper in the afternoon."

And Kit felt a tremor like incipient rigor run through all his limbs. Here, if anywhere, he would disgrace himself.

   *   *   *   *   *

It was not to be so, however, for the old Melvin's pupil, perhaps conscious that he was not equal to modern reasonings and deductions, had confined himself mainly to the plain letter of Euclid and the honourable and intelligible highway of quadratic equations.

Kit ploughed through the paper without enthusiasm, but except that he had the " Orra Man's " trick of putting Greek letters at the corners of his figures, the Aberdeen LL.D. could find little to object to. And perhaps that very irritant trick, all innocently used by

Kit Kennedy, prevented his examiner from following the reasoning very closely.

But it was upon the afternoon of the second day that the phalanx of eleven encountered their Flodden field. Hitherto they had struggled on, no one of them acknowledging that he was beaten even to himself, except Rob Grier, who declared that "the minister loon frae Balmaclellan" was the winner. "And it's richt eneuch that the likes o' him should get it. For I can gang back and whack het airn in the smiddy at Garlies, and this hill tyke here can cut turnuts and clip sheep. But the like o' the minister loonie—faith, he's guid for nocht but to make mair ministers o'—to gie oot the psalms on the Sabbath, and tell folk on the street that it's a fine day a' the rest of the week! We hae a plaguit wheen ower money o' that kind doon aboot the Garlies."

Thus spoke Rob Grier, the smith-student, with the scorn of Tubal-Cain for them that only peep and mutter in that great sound heart of his. But Kit, having no liberty of prophesying among so many, held his peace.

Flodden began precisely at half-past two of the afternoon of the second day, when the Secretary handed out the Greek paper. Kit read it calmly over, and without observing the look of aghast surprise on every other face settled comfortably to his task of answering it.

Never before had he known the full capacities of the "Orra Man," and the worth of his stern drill in matching the Greek word and phrase, not with the English alone, but also with the Latin equivalent. He benefited by the list of words stuck on the barn door when at the threshing, the irregular verbs which depended from a point of the harness in the stable, the rules pinned above his candlestick, and the red and blue marks which decorated the grammars the classical master had bought for him from the general dealer in Dumfries.

So Kit began his paper with the same impartial succinctness which had marked his method of dealing with the others. The only difference was that on this

occasion he left the version to the last because, as he
said to himself, " the rest was so easy."   And so it was
—to a pupil of the " Orra Man." Kit finished his paper,
looked again at the tenses of the verbs, shook his head
at a construction which did not seem quite right, folded
the foolscap sheets neatly up, and carried it to the
Secretary.

"That will do; you can go now," said Mr. Ebenezer
Fleming, W.S.   "You will be present to hear the
announcement of the successful candidate made in this
room this day fortnight."

Kit looked back, and Rob Grier, sitting biting his
pen, waved a friendly hand.   But all the rest were too
deeply engrossed in making Greek bricks without the
necessary straw of grammar and vocabulary to be
conscious of his departure.

Their sole comfort was that all were equally bad.
Why, there was that muirland boy, Kennedy the name
of him—he had fairly given the thing up, and sent in
his paper without finishing it.

The candidates separated with a general idea that the
prize lay between the minister's loon from Balmaclellan,
who was delicate, and John Mac Walter, who declared
that he was sure to get it.   For in these things confidence always counts for a good deal.

Kit met the " Orra Man " at the smiddy on his way
to Cairnharrow.   So keen was his teacher to know how
he had done that he could hardly wait till they were in
the cart, rattling along the autumnal drift of dead
leaves which filled all the lanes.

" Well ? " said the " Orra Man."

" I dinna ken," said Kit, mournfully, for on the way
he had had time to think of all that he might have
done ; " there were ithers wrote far mair nor me.   They
fair covered miles o' paper.   And there was a verb I
wasna sure o' in the Greek."

" Have you the papers with you ? "

The hands of the classical master were trembling.
It was growing dark, so he lighted the stable lantern,
and master and pupil huddled under a sack in the

corner of the red farm cart, while Peggy, the sedate old white mare, jogged along, happily quite able to conduct herself home to Cairnharrow, for neither of her masters paid the least attention to her. She hitched her head occasionally when the "Orra Man" dragged on the rein which he had thrown over his arm, and which he was apt to pull upon in the extremity of his anxiety. This hitch expressed Peggy's contempt for the dead languages. Peggy did not mind going home all unguided, but she expected to have her head to herself when she was doing it.

"Now tell me all that you put down exactly—the Latin paper first."

The "Orra Man" frowned at one or two of the phrases.

"You should have bettered that," he said, without a word of praise.

"I ken," said Kit, humbly, "but it's no so easy when ye hear a' their pens racin' like the Skyre Burn comin' doon in spate off Cairnharrow!"

They were at the loaning end of the farm before the consideration of the papers and the criticism of the answers were half done. Then Kit went directly to the stable loft where he was to sleep with the "Orra Man," while in a sort of dream John Smith gave Peggy her supper and went in for his own. He had scarcely been gone a quarter of an hour when he was back again, and Kit could hear his feet rattling impatiently on the ladder at the end of the corn-chest by which access was gained to the "laft" where they were to sleep.

John Smith had a large "whang" of scone and cheese in his hand, which he gave to Kit for his supper. And the boy answered his master's eager questions as between alternate bites the "Orra Man" bent his keen face over the crackling examination papers. The whole work of the two days must be gone over again, and the light had begun to ooze up from the east like gravy through the crust of a pie before the "Orra Man" delivered his final judgment.

"Weak in mathematics, good in English, respectable

in Greek, and your Latin version about as good as if
I had done it myself."

And with this far from enthusiastic forecast Kit had
to be satisfied. He slept as soon as his head touched
the pillow. But several times he opened his eyes as he
turned over, and each time he saw the "Orra Man"
with the light of the stable lantern still upon the
papers, conning each question and estimating marks and
deductions upon the margin with a stubby lead pencil.

CHAPTER XXXVI

THE INNOCENCE OF BETTY LANDSBOROUGH.

DURING the next fortnight the "Orra Man" lost weight.
He did his work mechanically, and it was well that it
happened to be the end of the harvest and a wet uncertain season. For there was much to do at Cairnharrow, and that kept him from thinking. He had
estimated Kit's chances fifty times, and forty of these
he had made Kit out to be safe. The other ten it
seemed to him impossible that the lad should not have
slipped in some essential. Vague fears assailed him
whether he himself might not have lost his old taste
and knowledge, and be judging his pupil's performance
too high.

But at last the great day came, and the "Orra Man"
asked a holiday from his master.

At first Rogerson of Cairnharrow demurred.

"Smith," he said, "what's gane wrang wi' ye? Ye
are no drinkin', are ye? If ye are, for Guid sake gang
on a spree decently and hae dune wi't. For I canna be
doin' wi' thae off an' on ways—a drappie here and a
drappie there, and nae satisfaction ava'!"

With this permit and a number of commissions to be
executed in Cairn Edward, the "Orra Man" was
allowed to depart on a wet, gusty morning in late
September, when the winds were howling mournfully
up the valley with that desolate sound which is heard
only in late autumn, when the foliage, dank above and
sodden below, swishes hopelessly this way and that, and
when from far come the roar and sough of the torrents
off the hills, rising and falling, filling and thinning out
again with a certain large solemnity of note.

Kit had been at the Cottage for ten days, giving himself little anxiety as to bursaries and colleges. He went out each day with his grandfather and learned the whole art and science of stone-breaking. He broke his grandfather's spare hammer-shaft and manufactured a new and better one. Never was seen such a pile for one week's work as Kit and the Elder had ready on Saturday for the surveyor when he came along the road with his smart gig and little light-trotting nag.

His grandmother purred over Kit and contrived estoric dainties for him. His uncle Rob the forester took him to see the damage the wild goats of the hills had done the young trees, the big wasp's nest in the fir on the hill top (three stings), and together they harried six humble-bees' storehouses in the meadow (one sting each). Taken for all in all Kit had such a time as he had not had since he first went to school. He saw his mother twice for an hour at a time, down by the lochside in the place where he had promised her that he would be a great man.

He arranged with Lilias that upon the day of the declaration of the result he would put up on a certain high fir tree, which could be seen from the windows of Kirkoswald, a black flag in token of defeat and a white if he should be victorious. But he warned her that he had no expectations. He had indeed already made preliminary arrangements to winter as "boy" at Cairnharrow. But all the same (so he consoled her) he meant to keep his promise and be a great man.

The pleasantest part of the day was in the evening, when Betty Landsborough always asked him to go out for a walk. Kit was now fifteen, tall and well grown for his age. He had had his ideas as to love and the worthiness of girls considerably sharpened by a certain Vara Kavannah (she does not come into this story)* who had sojourned a while at Loch Spellanderie.

Betty always asked him which way he wanted to go, but as invariably turned up through the wood in the

---

* v "Cleg Kelly, Arab of the City."

direction of the bothies where dwelt Rob Armour and the other three foresters of the Crae Estate.

Betty was a pretty girl, and it was pleasant enough to walk beside her, especially when she kept her hand on your shoulder—the far shoulder, and did not resent it if (for convenience of walking) your arm went round her waist.

They talked about the bursary and concerning going to college and about Greek. But Betty's eyes were always roaming to and fro, and sometimes she would answer at random. Which was strange, considering that Kit was explaining so interesting a subject as the second aorist and when it should not be used.

"Oh, here's Frank Chisholm and Archie Kinmont, and—yes, I declare, there's Rob!" she would interrupt without the least compunction.

"What do they want? They are always prowling where they are no wanted," said Kit, discontentedly. He was getting on fine, and Betty was a nice girl.

Betty patted him on the cheek and leaned a little more on his arm. Kit would have drawn apart, but Betty said, very low, "Stay where ye are. They will think ye are feared."

So Kit, blushing a little, but feeling, as well he might, strangely flattered and elated, kept his place beside the wicked and designing Mistress Elizabeth Landsborough.

Then Betty, that arch traitress and tormenting gadfly, would sit down on a cut tree, either quite at the end or close against a branch so that the flank of the position was guarded. This done she would pull Kit down on the other side, leaving Rob and his mates to find accommodation where they would. This they did, either on the dry pine needles or with their backs against the trees themselves.

After this they all looked at Betty Landsborough and Betty talked to them, playing with Kit's crisp curls meantime, or resting a dimpled chin on his shoulder and looking over it at Rob Armour.

Kit would have preferred that these amenities had been accorded him in private. But Betty differed, and

Kit always made the best of things. The three young men sometimes glowered at Kit as if they could have choked him, but apparently that only made Betty fonder of him than ever.

It was curious how innocent and thoughtless Betty was. For of course it was bound to make the others, all grown-up men with beards and moustaches, very jealous. But Betty never thought of that, and took Kit with her every night when she went her walk. With her hand on Kit's shoulder, she coaxed, reproached, rallied, said daring things, and then looked modestly down after she had said them, always in case of need appealing to her protector in the sweetest and most seductive way.

"Is it no, Kit? Dinna ye think sae, Kit?"

And Kit always thought so. Then worst of all she had a way of picking up his hand and patting the back of it as they sat together, which was fitted to drive Frank Chisholm and Archie Kinmont, but especially Rob Armour, to a dancing distraction.

All three hitched in their seats as if they had been sitting on whin prickles, instead of good dry pine needles, and for half an hour their intentions towards Kit were murderous. But it was all Betty's surprising innocence.

Then they walked back as far as the end of the little loaning with Betty and her swain. They did not come any further for fear of meeting the Elder. Whereupon, taking leave of them, Betty and Kit walked sedately up the dusky little path till they came to the well by the wayside. In another moment they would be out of the shadow of the trees. Even as it was they were silhouetted against the clearness of the western sky, and it occurred to Kit that the three might be looking after them with their elbows on the topmost bar of the green gate.

But it was evident that Betty did not think so. For she always stopped here, and turning to Kit she whispered softly, "Ye can gie me a kiss if ye like, Kit!"

And Kit did so, since no better might be. It was all

done in innocence, of course, for Betty could not be suspected of purposely arousing bitter or envious feelings
in the breasts of those who had never done her any
harm. All the same it was curious how completely
Betty lost her interest in evening promenades so soon
as she was sure that the three foresters had gone up to
their bothies.

Kit thought it his duty, towards the close of these
ten days of idleness and bliss, to remonstrate gently
with Betty Landsborough.

" I dinna think they like it, Betty ! "

Betty smiled an innocent smile, and said, tenderly,
" But, Kit, what does that maitter to us if *we* like it ? "

Whereupon Kit intimated that in fact it did not
matter.

" Weel," said Betty, with an air of finality, " I am no
dry-nursin' Bob Armour and the ither twa that I ken o'.
Certes, they are auld eneuch and ugly eneuch to look
after themselves."

All the same Kit wished that Betty was not quite so
innocent, and a little more inclined to think of the
feelings of others.

Could he have listened to the conversation of the
three foresters as they went up the wood to their
bachelor quarters, with the cue owls mewing here and
there like cats in the dark green gloom, he would have
obtained light on several things that were as yet dark
to him.   For the words of the young men were
mysterious.

" She's a licht-headed, deceitfu' haverel," said Rob
Armour, bitterly.

" But she's bonny, Rob ! " suggested Frank Chisholm.

Rob groaned as he admitted it.

" I'll wager she disna care a preen for him. He's but
a laddie onyway. Betty may be deceitfu', but she's no
daft ! "

It was poor comfort, but the best that Archie Kinmont could minister to a mind diseased.

" Aweel," said Rob, with his hand on the latch of
the bothie door, " mean it or no mean it, I ken this,

that I'll hae nae mair to do with Betty Landsborough
frae this day forth.   Na, I have dune wi' her!"

"That's richt, Bob," said Frank Chisholm, consol-
ingly; "there's plenty will be glad to tak' the contrack
aff your hands as it stands, wi' a' drawbacks and
allowances!"

Rob Armour slammed the door in his friends' faces.
He felt that if Job had murdered his comforters it
would have been both a quicker and a more satisfactory
ending to that ancient drama.

CHAPTER XXXVII.

The Great Day.

In the room where the examination had been held, commonly called the "Muckle Commy-tee Room" of the Cairn Edward Arms, the candidates, their friends, and all whom it might concern were assembled. There was also what is called in local papers "a large and influential attendence of the general public," including as usual many whom the matter did not at all concern.

The examiner was not present. But he had forwarded his report with all the figures, which were there to speak for him. Mr. Ebenezer Fleming, W.S., Secretary of the United Galloway Associations, was standing behind the table, with the Provost by his side to confer a certain flavour of official dignity to the proceedings. These were understood to be the only two who knew the true state of the poll. This seems likely, for the Provost kept wide of his wife, to whom he dared not refuse to tell anything that he was known to know.

Mrs. Mac Walter of Loch Spellanderie sat with her son in the front row. Both wore their best clothes, and John had already adopted the sedate demeanour and style of address which is most consistent with the position of a First Bursar.

Rob Grier sat beside Kit, who was telling himself that he was not anxious, that he did not want to go to Edinburgh, and that he would be happier at farm work anyway.

"I wish I had a forehammer here and something to ding the sparks oot o'," said Rob Grier; "man, I canna keep my hands still. There's something gangs 'kittle-kittle' in my loofs."

In the remote corner, paler and more worn with anxiety than any of the candidates, the "Orra Man" was hidden away.

Nevertheless, the Provost eyed him and hunted his mind for a resemblance, which of course as soon as he tried to fix it as persistently eluded him.

"I have seen that face before somewhere," he said.

And so he had. He had been most of his life on the committee which appointed the classical masters to the Academy of Cairn Edward.

Then he called upon the secretary to read the report of the examiner. Now Mr. Ebenezer Fleming very properly believed in magnifying his office. All that any soul then present wanted was to know the name of the successful candidate, and then get away as quickly as possible. But Mr. Ebenezer Fleming was in no such hurry. The law has many delays, which is the reason why many lawyers are rich.

Therefore he entered into a good comprehensive review, heedless of the uneasy mutterings of sufferers scattered through the hall. He went over the history of county organisations, their feeble past, their magnificent prospects. He recounted the foundations of the United Galloway Societies of which he had the honour, and so forth. He gave the names of past presidents and secretaries. He went over the bequests which had been set aside for the purposes of this bursary. He furnished lists of past bursars and the honours they had obtained—omitting the third last, who had just got seven years for forgery.

The murmur in the hall steadily grew to a rumbling. But with dramatic effect the secretary produced complete silence and restored the former state of strained attention among his audience.

"But on the present occasion," he said in a clear voice, "the successful candidate is——"

He paused, and then deliberately began to take another cast back.

"But perhaps I had better read first what Doctor Mac Lagan says about the papers in general——"

But here he had overreached himself. His companion on the platform was on his feet.

"Tell the laddies," said the more humane Provost, who was not a lawyer, "gin ye dinna, I'll tell them mysel', and pit them oot o' pain."

The secretary looked a moment as if he would like to rebel, but the Provost was leaning forward with a name obviously on his lip, and the lawyer knew that he would be as good as his word. It would be a lesson to him in the future to keep all truly important matters to himself.

"The successful candidate on this occasion"—here he cleared his throat deliberately as a final irritation—"is Christopher Kennedy, who has obtained a total of 766 marks!"

There was a noise of feet, a gabble of voices. The words, "Oh, the deceitfu' vaigabond!" were heard from the vicinity of Mrs. Mac Walter. And with a loud clatter of iron-shod clogs the "Orra Man" trampled out of the hall.

Kit sat fixed and cold, thinking vaguely of his mother. Rob Grier from Garlies turned and gripped his hand as in a vice.

"Man," he said, "ye deserve it. Ye hae dune well. I'll hae to gang back to the forehammer (here a kind of dry sob caught him by the throat). But it's a' I'm fit for onyway. And wi' a' my heart I wish ye joy!"

Kit felt he was making a poor appearance beside the great-hearted smith, but for the life of him he could not think on anything to say. He only gripped his late opponent's hand, and the tears rose in his eyes.

"Hoots, man," said Rob Grier, "it's a' richt, and as it should be. I aye kenned that it was a' up wi' me as soon as I heard ye gang ower your Latin version as fast as a horse could trot."

By this time most of the people were on their feet to depart, but the secretary had more to say. He held up his hand for silence. "I do not wish to trouble you with the entire report, but there is one thing with which I must conclude."

"There is one name which comes next to that of Christopher Kennedy—some way behind indeed, but so far ahead of the others that the Committee of the Associations has resolved to give that candidate a subsidiary bursary of a smaller value. The name of that candidate is Robert Grier of Garlieston."

It was now Kit's turn to shake his friend heartily by the hand, and the words came back to him with a rush.

"I declare I am gladder than aboot my ain," he said, "but ye should hae had the best yin!"

The secretary read the other marks, concerning which the only notable thing was that the name of John Mac Walter came last. Then he added the very necessary rider, "If the bursar and the subsidiary successful candidate will apply to me at my office at 99, St. Andrew's Square (first floor, second door to the left), one of my clerks will pay them the moneys due to them, and they can forward to me, also at St. Andrew's Square, certificates of attendance at the close of each session."

Then the secretary folded up his papers in a glow at having so satisfactorily acquitted himself, and especially at having got in a little advertisement of his own importance and place of business in the most harmless and natural way.

For even Writers to the Signet are human.

Mrs. Mac Walter was at the hall door before Kit and in waiting for him.

"Ye nameless blackguard—you that for years ate the bread o' a decent household and then lifted up your heel again' them. A kennin' mair, an' I wad claw the e'en oot o' your face. This is the meanin' o' your carryin's on and your Black Sheds. I'll write to them that gies the siller, and see if they haud wi' sic' black ingratitude—that I wull!"

"Did I not do my wark, Mistress Mac Walter?" said Kit, very quietly, being anxious to get away and find the "Orra Man."

"Your wark—what has that got to do wi' it? Ye hae ta'en the bite oot o' my John's mouth, puir laddie.

17

l wadna wunner gin he was to do himsel' a mischief.
He's that upset aboot it?"

Kit passed on, but the voice of his late mistress
pursued him up the street.

"And I'll tell John Mac Walter, so I wull, that he's
richt served for takin' naebody-kens-whas intil his
hoose to deprave his lawfully-begotten bairns. And
I'll tell Walter Mac Walter that he can keep his wife's
misfortunes at hame after this—defraudin' honest folk
o' their just dues!"

"My good woman," said the secretary, suavely,
"pray do not fret yourself. Your boy would not have
got the money even if Christopher Kennedy had not
been successful. And the boy's character is without
blemish, as I have two ministers' certificates to
testify."

"Dinna 'Guid wumman' me," she cried in a louder
voice. "I am nae guid wumman, and that I wad hae
ye ken. What I say is that my Johnny didna get fair
play amang ye, and that I am weel sure o'. For the
Dominie says that there's no the like o' him in ten
parishes. Mair nor that, this Doctor Mac Lagan, he's
nae better than he's caa'ed, or he wadna hae alooed a
servant to be pitten before his maister, or his maister's
son, for that's the same thing. And gin the law was as
I would hae it, the siller should be my Johnny's even as
it is. For instead o' gieing the thirty guid pounds
to this ungratefu' blackguard, it wad declare that
Christopher Kennedy should hae spent his time learnin'
his maister's son, as it was his bounden duty to do.
What business had he to ken mair nor oor Jock, that
has aye had the best of book learnin', and him but a
chance-gotten callant keepit aboot the hoose out o'
charity, when a' is said and dune!"

But except in thus easing her mind Mistress Mac
Walter got no redress, but all the household had a
terrible time of it when she got home to Loch
Spellanderie.

Meanwhile, the new Bursar Designate was seeking
the "Orra Man" from public to public over the town.

He wanted to thank the man who had done this thing for him.

But it was five in the afternoon when, after being thrice turned from the door and thrice denied at the bar, Kit ran him to earth in the inner parlour of the Black Boar. He would have missed him a fourth time but for the eagle eye and trained legal intelligence of the Sheriff's officer.

But Willie Gilroy responded to Kit's questionings, "See your friend? Of coorse I saw him. He's drinkin' himsel' fu' in the Black Boar. They tell ye that he's no there? Man, ye ken little, an' you a learnit man they tell me, gin ye believe a single word that Becky Snodgrass wad say to ye. Gang richt in, I tell ye, and see for yoursel'. And if they try to hinder ye, threaten them that ye will bring a polissman! Faith, that will do your business if I ken Mistress Becky. She never could stand the silver buttons a' the days o' her."

Accordingly in the Black Boar, tumbled on a sofa of worn hair cloth, Kit found the "Orra Man"—dead drunk.

He did not heed the angry tongue of Mistress Becky. He knelt down before his friend and besought him to awake, for Kit had seen little of intoxication. But the "Orra Man" only groaned.

"Oh, this is terrible—terrible," said Kit; "I wish I had never gotten the bursary if I hae driven him to this."

It chanced that at this moment Mistress Mac Walter passed the door on her way "to change her breath afore she gaed into that cauld machine." She caught sight of Kit through the open door and cried out, "There a bonny bursar! Didna I tell ye? To think that the like o' him, that companies with a' the drucken and debauched in the countryside, should tak' the gowden guineas oot o' my innocent Johnny's pooch. I declare I'll juist gang this verra minute and fetch that secretary man to see this sicht."

But by this time Willie Gilroy was on the spot as a reinforcement.

"In the name of the law," he cried, grandly,

"woman, what is this disturbance opposite to my property? I will serve a notice on you instantly!" And Willie drew out his legal case. It is to be feared that like some other officials of greater authority, Willie somewhat traded on his neighbour's ignorance.

"There's nae disturbance, maister Officer," said the landlady Becky Snodgrass, with twittering anxiety. "I'm as desirous of getting this man awa' without a disturbance as——"

"Gang for his beast and cairt, boy, and I'll wait here wi' the body," said Willie, as if he were about to bury a fifth wife. "I dinna care gin I gang a bit of the road hame wi' ye mysel'."

Within ten minutes the red cart, with Mary Gray between the shafts, was at the front door of the Black Boar.

"This is your wark, Betty Snodgrass," said the Man of Law, "and gin he dies within twenty-fower hours—weel, there hasna been a woman hangit hereawa' since Mary Timny. It wad be a great occasion."

The unconscious "Orra 'Man" was brought out and laid gently in the bottom of the cart. Then with Willie on one shaft and Kit driving on the other they rattled away through the buzz and stir of the afternoon. Kit covered his friend from prying eyes beneath a couple of corn sacks. He himself enjoyed a popularity he had never known before, being pointed out as the "farm-lad that beat a' the ither laddies frae the schules an' academies."

Kit looked anxious lest the provost of the town, who shooks hands with him seated with his feet on the shaft, should wonder what freight he was carrying home.

"Weel dune, Whinnyliggate," cried the provost heartily. "I'll send ye a barrel o' herrin' to the lodgings when ye gang to Edinbra. They gang fine wi' a cup o' tea, and kitchen baker's bread so that ye wadna ken it frae soda scones."

But it were not till they were clear of the town, and driving up the long waterside of the Kells Water, that

Kit really felt comfortable in his mind. He wanted to get to the Cottage of Crae before the fall of the evening, for he had his signal to make to his mother. He knew that she would be watching eagerly from her lonely window in the red freestone front of Kirkoswald.

Willie Gilroy was every whit as eager as Kit. He wanted to see Betty Landsborough, and he had a question to ask of her. So Mary Gray had no rest for the soles of her four feet, and Kit urged her into a five-mile gait, a speed she had not attained for years.

Kit mourned over his friend and refused to be comforted.

" He's never been like this," he said. " I wad raither no hae had the bursary than that he said do the like o' this ! "

" Hoot," said Willie, " he shouldna hae tried to break himsel' a' at yince. The cravin' wad juist bank up like a water ahint a dam—and then—*whoosh*, awa' she gaed. This will maybe do him guid, gin ye can keep it frae the kennin' o' his maister. No that Cairnharrow has only richt to be very particular. I hae seen him gangin' oot o' the toon gye an' coggly in his gig himsel' ! "

In the meadow opposite to the Crae Cottage Kit pulled the cart up. " Bide you here," he said ; " I'll no be away a quarter o' an hour——"

" Bring me word what Betty Landsborough's doin'. And gin ye get a chance, tell her that there's a lad wantin' to see her at the loan end."

" What if she'll no come ? " suggested Kit.

Willie Gilroy closed an eyelid.

" Dinna tell her wha the lad is, and I'se warrant gin she's a woman ava, she'll come to see wha is it ? "

Kit shook his head. He knew that the Sheriff's officer was only preparing additional disappointment for himself. He remembered the three foresters and how Betty had treated them. He was glad he was not to be present at this new flouting of honest affection.

" Betty's weel and weel eneuch," he said to himself,

" but for the life o' me I dinna see what a' the fyke's aboot ' Betty this ' and ' Betty that ' ! "

He ran across the great stepping-stones, which time out of mind have carried the feet of home-returning men over the cool brown bend of the Crae water into the dusky woods, in which the tang of the cottage peat reek hangs like the peculiar incense of home.

The Crae stepping-stones ! Kit had crossed them on his grandfather's back when he was yet too young to stride the glossy interspaces of brown moss water. He had paddled with bare feet between them as he grew older. He knew the green stars of bottom weed, the little peeping whorls of water starwort, the tall rushes on either bank, which grew thickest where the water divides round a little ten-yard square island all over-grown with red purple willow herb. There are just ten stepping-stones big and little. You wade chin deep in the creamy spray of meadow sweet to get to them. Gowans tickle your chin as you turn up your trousers. The trout spurt this way and that as your shadow falls on the water. With what a pleasant sound the wavelets ripple about your legs as you mount Auld Cairnsmore, the big granite boulder in the middle. On rushes the Crae water with a little silvery water-break and a smooth glide over a stone which it has worn away till its head is beneath the surface. Then with three strides and half a jump you are on the pine needles, and the resinous smell of the firs sting your nostrils.

Verily it is good to be young and to taste these things. They are good to taste even if one is old.

CHAPTER XXXVIII.

The Flag Upon the Pine.

But Kit had no time to linger now. He went across at a run, and his appreciation of the rich twilight glow along the waterside took no other form than the drawing of a long breath as he ran up the path towards the cottage.

Now he must climb the tree for his mother's sake. She must know first. So up the smooth trunk of the tall pine on the top of the crag above the cottage Kit swarmed with the easy progression of a born woodland's boy. The flag was the handkerchief his grandmother had given him fresh and clean the day before. With a recklessness which would have shocked his uncle, the forester, he stripped the top of the pine that his flag might fly free. The sun shone out from behind a cloud; and Kit's signal took the air at the same moment.

What was his mother thinking now? Did she see it? We may be sure that she did.

It chanced that at that moment her husband, Walter Mac Walter, was amusing himself with taunting her, as was his custom when ruffled outside.

"I married you for your beauty," he was saying, "and how much of it have I ever seen? You go about drooping like a barndoor hen on a wet day. I cannot bring my friends to the house, for your face is like a death's-head at a feast. It is all that boy of yours. You think more of him—more of his blackguard father even now—than of me that made you mistress of Kirkoswald. Deny it if you can!"

Lilias his wife did not answer. She did not even look at him. His words did not hurt her, for in the household only the voices of those one loves have power to wound. He went on.

"Yes," he said, "I am nothing. I never was anything to you except a convenient means of paying your father's debts. But the day will come when the boy you doat upon shall break your heart with sorrow. He is his father's son, and already he companies with the lowest. In ten years he will be—well, what his father has become. You do not believe it, but I know."

"If you had your will I doubt not——" Lilias, the mother of Kit, was beginning. But in a moment she commanded herself and was silent.

Her husband laughed.

"You do well not to defend him. I tell you he will grow up an ignorant boor, a public-house sot, the companion of the vilest. Kit Kennedy by name shall be Christopher Kennedy by nature."

At that moment Lilias saw something far over the heaped masses of tree-tops down by the waterside. She was standing near the great wide window of Kirkoswald which looked to the south. She had her eyes on a particular fir-tree which, being perched boldly on a jutting crag, rose half its height above the wood. She often stood here and looked over the wide misty valley with eyes as full of luminous haze. But what she saw that night made her heart beat and the landscape waver before her face. The sun was setting, and shot a last level flood of rays up the glen from the west. A moment the top of the pine tree stood dark against the sky. The next a little white square flew out, danced in the unsteady breeze, and sank down limp by its flagstaff. Then it blew out again, and with a last expiring effort the sun caught and glorified it, so that it burned like a sparkle from the crystal river that is about the Throne.

Lilias the mother turned to her husband and smiled. And from that moment she heard not a word that he said. She only looked at him with the light of a new knowledge in her eyes. The man rose and went out, angrily slamming the door after him. He saw that somehow her soul had escaped him for that time, but in his dark heart he set himself more bitterly than ever to effect the ruin of Lilias's son.

* * * * *

From the pine tree on the summit Kit descended at a run heedless of his clothes, his Sunday suit though it was, and in due time to serve him at college through the winter. He left the handkerchief flying for his mother to see in the morning.

His grandfather was sitting on the seat before the door, putting a new shaft into a " knapping " hammer. At the Dornal Matthew Armour had been as he himself said "an auld done man," but with the renewed need for work his youth seemed to have returned to him in a sort of gracious Indian summer of unabated natural strength.

He did not hear Kit till the boy was quite near him. Kit stole behind the old man on tiptoe. His heart was now proud within him. It was worth while living for this. Kit had the same elation of spirit as when he joined the rejoicing uplift of Old Hundred-and-Twenty-Fourth in the Kirk on the Hill, a sort of high godward pride that was wholly impersonal. He had been an unprofitable son. He had run away from home. He had made them suffer, but now once for all this would make up. He stood looking at his grandfather, glorying in what he had to tell. He hummed the swelling notes of his favourite Psalm tune like those of a trumpet that sounds the charge when the enemy are already in full flight.

> Now Israel may say,
> And that truly—
> If that the Lord
> Had not our cause maintained——

" *Grandfaither — grandfaither ! I hae gotten the bursary !* "

* * * *

The words written and printed look like an anti-climax. They had even a ludicrous appearance. But not in the Cot in the wood, not to these simple folk to whom the chance of a good education comes next to a good conscience towards God.

The Elder rose and stood with his tall grandson before him. He did not look at Kit. His eyes were far over the tree-tops. He looked at the hills from whence had come his aid. He laid his hand upon the boy's head and lifted up the other.

"O Lord," he said, "I have loved the habitation of Thy House, the place where Thine honour dwelleth. One thing have I desired, not for myself but for this fatherless son of mine old age. Thou hast given me more than my heart's desirings. Now let Thy servant depart in peace, for mine eyes have seen Thy salvation!"

He paused a moment, and then said, quite naturally, "Let us go in and tell Margaret."

"And Betty!" added Kit, so happy that he could leave no one out.

Then who so made of as Kit Kennedy! His grandmother wept upon his shoulder, and Betty kissed him outright, again and yet again, in another fashion than she was wont to do for the painful benefit of Rob Armour and the two foresters.

"Oh, laddie, I wad gie a paper pound gin your puir mother could ken this nicht!"

"She kens! She kens!" cried thrice triumphant Kit.

His grandmother stood up aghast.

"Wi' boy, ye never dared gang up to that place to face that dreadsome man."

"I wad face him or onybody," said the valiant First Bursar, "that is, gin I didna think my mither wad hae to suffer for it after. But I dinna need to gang."

He led his grandmother to the window and pointed up.

"There!" he said, pointing to the fluttering scrap of white, "that's how my mither kens."

"Ye're a genius, Kit," said Betty Landsborough; "I wish I could wait for ye."

Then Kit remembered about the "Orra Man" and Willie Gilroy.

"I maun gang my ways up to Cairnharrow the nicht. I hae my work to do. I promised that I wad gang on wi' that till I was ready for the college."

"But no the nicht, Kit," said his grandmother; "bide with us this ae nicht."

"Aye," said Betty, "bide this ae nicht, and we'll no gang up by the bothie, but doon by the waterside, gin ye like."

But Kit could not for this time take advantage of the gifts of the gods.

He shook his head sadly.

"Na," he said, "I hae my work to do, bursar or no bursar. A man is nae better ·than his word, and Cairnharrow trusted me."

"The lad is right," said the Elder; "to me it is better than any honour or emolument that he desires this night to do his duty. Let him go!"

So Kit went down the path, and Betty came with him as far as the stepping-stones. She bade him good-bye in the shade of the last tree, and if Rob Armour and the two foresters had been within sight they would have had good cause for jealousy.

Betty was crying when she sent him off.

"Gang—gang," she said, pushing Kit away; "I am ower proud o' ye to hearken a single word. A laddie manna hamper himsel' wi' thae things at your age. But a' the same ye are a brave laddie! And—it micht hae been itherwise."

The cart was in the self-same place when Kit came across the stepping-stones, and Willie Gilroy sat very still and silent upon it.

He spoke, however, as soon as Kit came up.

"Was yon Betty Landsborough that was at the waterside wi' you?"

"Yes," said Kit, with eyes yet wet, "it was Betty!"

"Did ye—did ye mention the subjeck to her?"

"No," said Kit, smitten with remorse, "I clean forgot!"

Willie Gilroy bounded from the seat of the cart with an energy far more youthful than his years.

"Betty, Betty," he cried. "Oh, she winna stop for me. Cry you, Kit!"

"Betty, Betty Landsborough," cried Kit, touching up Mary Gray and plunging into the shadows of the Dornal Bank. He looked about him. The "Orra Man" had not stirred under his coverings.

The Sheriff's officer was absent a quarter of an hour, but just as Kit was taking the rising ground before the crossing of the Dee Bridge, where the high-backed arch strides across the turbulent rapids of the dark river, he heard a hail behind him. And lo! as he looked back, there was Willie Gilroy running with a little harvester's trot. He had made a short cut through the woods to overtake Kit and was out of breath.

"I'll come wi' you this nicht, Kit Kennedy," he said. "What like are the lasses aboot Cairnharrow? Are there ony o' them that a man might mak' up till?"

"But I thought that ye were fond o' Betty?" said Kit, astonished at Willie's proposition.

"Ow," said the Sheriff's officer, with a lofty contempt, "Betty Landsborough's no what I took her for. I consider her most michtily overrated—indeed, a perfect intak!"

"Betty's nocht o' the sort," said Kit, valiantly. "I'll no hae ye on my cairt, kind to me as ye have been, if ye miscaa Betty."

"I'm no miscaain' onybody," said the widower more soberly, "but I dinna think that she wad mak' an appropriate successor to Mary and Susan and Jean and my ain dear Margit. Na, it wadna look weel on my tombstone — *Eleezabeth Landsborough, dearly beloved (fifth) wife o' Weelum Gilroy, born* —— Na, na, it wad tak' up mair than twa lines, and letterin's desperate dear. Forbye, there wadna be room for anither, supposin' Betty to be taken awa!"

"What did Betty say to ye?" said Kit, anxious to improve his knowledge of the ways of women.

"She's an impudent besom. I carena what she said!" answered the Sheriff's officer, with suggestive curtness.

"But she's bonny," suggested Kit, even as Frank Chisholm had done.

"Beauty is but skin deep!" said Willie Gilroy, sententiously. "Even a bursar should ken that!"

"And what mair do ye want?" retorted the wise Kit; "for mysel' I care nocht for a woman withoot the skin!"

"Humph!" grunted his companion, "that's no what I wad caa' a pertinent observation."

Yet Willie Gilroy would in no wise reveal to his companion whether or no his offer had been well received by Betty. All that he would say was no more than that there were as good fish in the sea as ever came out of it —a proverb which must have originated with some fisher cousin of the fox who abused the sour grapes.

All the way to Cairnharrow the Sheriff's officer talked of nothing but Isobel Fairies, the dairymaid there, and Kirst Conchie the cook, weighing their several capacities, with various side hits at Betty Landsborough, always to her disadvantage. Kit, anxious to get the "Orra Man" safely bestowed, paid little attention to Willie's soliloquies, only answering a direct question after it had been asked half a dozen times.

They arrived at last at Cairnharrow, and Kit, who knew the ways of the house, made haste to take out Mary Gray and lead that steady-going mare to her stall.

Then, still hidden by the darkness of the winter gloaming, he and Willie Gilroy took the "Orra Man" in their arms and carried him to his "laft." He was breathing heavily and regularly.

"He hasna had muckle," said Willie the expert. "It's juist gaen to his head wi' his keepin' frae it sae lang. I'll wager he'll be a' richt in the morning.'

Then Kit went down again and did the "Orra Man's" work, stabling his horses and setting the yard and office houses in order. Finally, almost worn out, he went into the house of Cairnharrow for the supper which he had earned so well.

"Hello, Kit Kennedy," cried John Rogerson, the jovial farmer, "so Willie Gilroy tells me that ye hae won the bursary and are gaun to be a colleger. Ye hae dune weel, and whan ye gang to the big toon in the winter, I shall be a puirer man than I expeck to be gin I canna send ye a whang o' sweetmilk cheese and maybe a bit bacon ham to be kitchen to your piece."

Kit thanked the warm-hearted farmer, but Cairn-harrow cut him short.

"Did ye see ocht o' that daft craiter, my 'Orra Man'?" he said.

"He cam' hame wi' me in the cairt," said Kit, keeping carefully to a portion of the facts.

"And what for disna he come in for his supper!" demanded his master.

"He was compleenin' o' a kind o' sair head," said Kit, "and I'm thinkin' he will be aff direck to his bed."

"Humph," said the farmer of Cairnharrow, "this is no the first sair head that has come hame frae Cairn Edward on market Monday. And it's no like to be the last!'

Judiciously Kit said nothing, but retired early to the "laft," where the "Orra Man" slept serenely. He had not been long there when he heard a foot on the ladder.

"Are ye sleepin', Kit Kennedy?" said a voice.

"Na, I'm no sleepin' yet," said Kit, who had now for the first time a chance to think what the events of the day meant to him.

Willie Gilroy came in, dragging himself up by means of his long arms like a good-natured, black-bodied spider.

"It's a' richt, Kit," he said, confidentially, "it's to be Kirst Conchie the cook. I gaed to see Bell Fairies at the byre, and she had ways wi' her that I couldna stammach awa! What do you think, she actually put the guid coo's milk through a sile (sieve) afore she could pour it intil the bynes. Heard ye ever the like o' that? As if either butter and cheese were the ony the waur o' an odd hair or twa. Indeed, good judges even prefer a' wheen hairs. It's a sign that ye are gettin' nane o' your shop-bought crowdies, but rael Galloway stuff, when ye find a black curly yin or twa charkin' between your teeth.

"So I didna say a word, but I gaed awa ben to Kirst. The first thing I saw was Kirst pitten' on the parritch in the pot that she had emptied the pig's meat oot o'! That's the woman for me, says I. Nae fikey perniketty particularity aboot Kirst! Na, rough and ready, and no ill to please. Then she was gaun to dish the maister's porridge to gang ben. There cam' a flaucht o' soot doon the lum. Plap! Half a pound o't gaed in the maister's bowl. What did Kirst do, but gied it a bit turn wi' the dishclout, a bit rub wi' her elbow, syne turned up her druggit petticoat and dichted the delf dry. Then in wi' the porridge and awa to the maister. Certes! A thorough-gaun, tairgin', satisfactory kind of woman is Kirst!

"So I pat aff nae time, but says to her, 'Kirst, you and me's no sae young as we hae been. Gin ye are no particular wha ye get for a man, I'm no particular wha I get for a wife. Wull ye hae me?'

"So she said she wad, plump and plain as a woman should, though as ye can pictur' to yoursel' she was kind o' owercome at first wi' me speakin' to her sae affectingly. But saft talk o' that kind comes naitural to me. Ye ken I have aye had a wonderfu' way wi' the women fowk a' the days o' me."

   *   *   *   *   *

On the morning of the next day the "Orra Man" came to himself out of a deep sleep. Kit and Willie Gilroy were prepared to assert that he had hurt himself by falling at the door of the Black Bull. But the "Orra Man" listened to their stories with sad-eyed patience.

"It is kind of you two," he said; "I will not forget it. But I know well what happened. As soon as I knew that you had won the bursary it came over me like a Solway tide. For your sake, Kit, I had done it. But in a moment it came back upon me stronger than ever. It is no use, Kit, I am a doomed man! I have saved others, myself I cannot save."

"Nonsense," cried Kit, cheerfully, "it wasna the

drink. Ye had hardly touched onything. I ken, for I paid for it oot o' the siller in your ain pouch."

"The laddie's richt, man," asserted Willie Gilroy, with prompt friendly mendacity; "ye hadna even a smell o' drink aboot ye. Faith, I had mair mysel', yestreen, and I courted twa lasses till yin o' them promised to be my wife. Ye ken Kirst the cook. Ye'll ken her 'crowdie' onyway. Weel, she has gi'en her consent to lie beside Mary and Susan and Jean and my ain belovit Margit. I aye said the monument wad be the better o' anither line !"

The "Orra Man" went about his work in silence, and Kit helped him, but it was evident that he was revolving many things in his heart. Often he did not reply at all when he was spoken to. His eyes were far away, and several times he began to speak abruptly and then as suddenly stopped.

It was not till night that the "Orra Man" delivered his mind.

"Kit," he said, taking the boy by the shoulder, "you are on the right road now. So far I have been a help to ye, and you have given me happiness and fellowship such as I have not known for years. But the building is up, and it is time that the scaffolding should come down. I am no creditable companion for a young scholar and student. I will go away at once when you go up to Edinburgh. I am a derelict upon life's high seas, Kit ; your clipper ship is not to have my waterlogged hulk sagging and plunging behind her. So much at least of honour I have left me."

Then Kit answered with a light in his eyes. "You have done everything for me. I will not let you go. We have taken the rough together, now we will take the smooth."

The "Orra Man" smiled at Kit's boyish periods, but he did not smile when he saw the look in his eyes.

"Kit—Kit," he said, "you have done far more for me than I can ever do for you !"

CHAPTER XXXIX.

ENTRANCE INTO LIFE.

In due time Kit Kennedy went to Edinburgh. It was the dowie time of the year. November was just beginning. He said good-bye to his mother, who ever since she had seen the white flag flutter above the tree-tops had gone about with a little proud look on her face which Walter Mac Walter felt more than a strong man's blow.

His grandfather gave Kit his blessing. Mr. Osborne of the Kirk on the Hill bestowed on him a great deal of excellent advice, adding, "But, Kit my lad, you will just have to pay your footing like the rest of us. There is no royal road to experience any more than there is to learning."

Kit met Rob Grier at the end of Princes-street. They left their boxes at a call-office, and drifted southward looking for lodgings. The noise and stir of the city took Kit by the throat. And though from the point of view of the Strand and Fleet Street Edinburgh may be considered a quiet city, to a boy accustomed to the Black Craig of Dee it roared like Babylon.

Suddenly and quite unexpectedly they found themselves in front of the college, and here under the great gates was one Clement Sowerby, the Cairn Edward Academy lad who had tried unsuccessfully for the bursary. He was smoking a cigarette, the first that Kit had ever seen, and nursing a very big and exceedingly nobby stick under his arm.

Sowerby was the son of a comfortable tradesman in Cairn Edward, and had tried for the bursary more (as he declared) "for fun" than because he seriously needed the money.

18

"Hey fellows," he cried, "have you got 'digs'? Have you matriculated? What, never been inside the gates? Come along. I'll put you through."

Kit felt exceedingly lonesome walking beside such a mentor.

For though he had on his best Sunday clothes, they were already a little too short for him as to trouser leg and cuff. Somehow his limbs seemed to stretch a little farther through them each morning as he put them on.

The lads from Galloway presently found themselves in an elbowing throng of students, through which Sowerby pushed his way with the easy confidence of an old-timer.

"Here are your forms! Write your name there, and where you come from. Then put a pound note on the top, and shove the whole to that red-headed lunatic with the pen in his mouth. He'll give you your 'matric' ticket! That's all right. Now come on and let's find you 'digs.' There are some toppers near me."

But it was soon evident that the ideas of Sowerby as to "digs" and those which (from severely absolute considerations) governed Kit and Rob Grier could not by any possibility be unified.

After interviewing many landladies the two lads settled on a room high in a tall house in the Pleasance, the front of which looked down a long unlovely cross street, but the back windows upon the crags and grey pastures of Arthur's Seat. Mistress Christieson, their new landlady, was a widow whom penury had made careful and many lodgers suspicious. But from the first she took to our pair of Galloway lads. It was Kit who did the talking, and the terms as finally arranged were easy—three shillings a week each with coal and gas, no extras.

As Kit went up the stairs for the first time as a sort of householder he felt for his latchkey with a proud consequence, and blew the dust out of it as if he were blowing upon the trump of fame. A pretty girl, hearing beneath her his rushing feet, stood aside on one of the landings to let him pass. She was pulling on a

worn brown glove on her small left hand; as the
stalwart Kit went by she stole a glance at him.

Now the Galloway code of manners demands a
salutation from wayfarer to wayfarer as each crosses
each in the tranquil travel of life. So Kit smiled
broadly upon the pretty girl.

"It's a fine day!" he said, "but I wadna wunner
gin it cam' on a wee saft!"

A faint smile flickered on the girl's face. She
finished buttoning her glove with as much care as if that
were her only object in life. She did not reply, and as
soon as Kit had passed she began to descend.

"That's curious," said Kit to himself; "she never
answered me!"

He thought the matter over in his mind. It troubled
him not a little.

"Maybe the puir lassie's deaf!" he concluded within
himself.

    *   *   *   *   *

During these days Kit saw a good deal of Clement
Sowerby, the Cairn Edward lad proving unexpectedly
friendly. Bob Grier, however, could not abide him, and
wanted to "thraw the puir craitur's neck." But Kit,
being a natural optimist, would hear no ill of any human
being, least of all of one so friendly as Clement Sowerby.

So the dapper hat, the nobby rig-out, and the curly
stick appeared oftener and oftener at their joint lodgings.

Kit mentioned the matter of the pretty girl. Clement
Sowerby laughed.

"Some milliner," he said; "you must get to know
her—find somebody to introduce you."

"What's 'introduce'?" said Kit, to whom the word
had not occurred in translations of the classics.

"Oh, your landlady would do if she's a decent sort.
I say, I've a good mind to come and lodge here myself."

Rob Grier looked up with a belligerent air, but subsided again upon his books as Sowerby added, "But
really, you know, I could not stand the district; all
very well to come and look you fellows up, but it
wouldn't do at all to have to say "*160, Pleasance*" loud

out in the class when the Professor asked you for your address!"

In due time Kit lifted his bursary from the secretary, and made the necessary dispositions as to fees. He was attending three classes, but at first the work was less than nothing to a pupil of the "Orra Man." He ran off the versions in a quarter of an hour, and would do another edition quite different for Rob Grier, when that hard-working student would accept of the help, which, to do him justice, was not often.

Yet it would have been well for Kit if he had been kept closer to the grindstone during these first months of winter. Soon after his arrival Clement Sowerby had taken him in hand and introduced him to an outfitter, who made Kit a suit of clothes of a very different cut from those which had been the masterpiece of Tailor Byron in the village of Whinnyliggate the year but one before Kit came to Edinburgh.

The tailor tried to persuade the youth to run an account—"any friend of Mr. Sowerby's," he said with a smirk. But Kit's ingrained money sense kept him straight where so many are weak. He paid shilling by shilling on the nail, and saw that he got the largest discount too.

But there is no denying that in these days Kit did not fulfil the high promise of his start. The Professor, indeed, commended him again and again. The "Orra Man" had taught him to turn tolerable verses in the dead languages, and that being an unheard-of accomplishment among Scottish students, Kit leaped to a first place in his teacher's favour at a bound when he achieved a copy much more than tolerable. The Professor, standing up like Jove before the class, declaimed Kit's lines with a strong appreciation of their Horatian flavour. But that was Kit's Waterloo, for all unconsciously he had used the phrases of the "Orra Man." The next he gave in were hastily written, and the Professor looked disappointed.

He did not declaim the lines to the class on this occasion, but he called Kit into his retiring room, and had five minutes' talk with him, which the boy remembered all his life.

Three years afterwards he knocked a man down in the passage between the college and the museum for repeating a libellous statement about the Professor.

It was not long before Kit was "introduced" to the pretty girl. He was coming home one night along the Bridges. It was a wet, plashy night, tempestuously pleasant. The jets of the gas lamps were blown this way and that. Some had gone out. It chanced that in a quiet part of the street near the Surgeon's Hall Kit saw two or three fellows promenading arm-in-arm across the breadth of the pavement. A girl was walking quietly in front of him, but Kit had not noticed her much, for his hat was pulled low over his brow, and his coat-collar high about his neck. Suddenly, however, he heard a little cry above the whistle of the wind. The three youths had jostled the girl, and then swung round so as to enclose her in the centre of a narrow circle.

One of them had his hand about the girl's waist.

"Let me go!" Kit heard her cry.

Now Kit had no fear, and had been too much exercised in the heart of fighting among the country lads to think twice what he was doing. He was on the spot in a moment. And his strong ploughman's grasp was on the throat of one, while another, surprised by a left-hander on the jaw, went staggering into the gutter. There was no fight. The three bullies contented themselves with language of the foulest, but took themselves promptly off at the sight of the glowing belt of a city policeman, who came along, testing bars and shutters leisurely as he went.

With his natural quick imperiousness Kit took the girl by the arm.

"Come along!" he said, and hurried her southward.

They had gone a couple of hundred yards when it struck Kit that he had been hasty.

"I beg your pardon," he said, "if I have been rough!"

By this we can see that Kit had been learning many

things. At the same time they came to a better-lighted part of the town, and under the Bray burners Kit saw that this was the pretty girl he had passed on the landing beneath.

"Oh no," she answered, a little breathless with the haste at which Kit had dragged her along, "it is very kind of you. I was kept late at school to-night, and I never was spoken to before. My brother promised to meet me, but he must have been detained somewhere!"

The words were common words, but to Kit's country ear they seemed to be spoken with the accent of the nymphs and muses he read so much about in his shabby cream-coloured German classics. He wanted to tell her so, but did not quite know how to begin.

But he did nearly as well.

"Do you know," he said, talking as like the "Orra Man" as he could, "I always look out for you on the stairs?"

"Do you?" said the girl, in apparent surprise. "Why?"

"Because," said Kit, "you put on your gloves so nicely."

In Galloway they did not put on gloves in the pretty girl's way. Even Betty tugged at a creased pair of blacks, and left half an inch unfilled at the end of the fingers. But then gloves were only of acceptation from the kirk door as far as the end of the first psalm.

The pretty girl became prettier than ever, and if Kit had looked closely he would have seen that his frankness had brought a well-defined blush to her cheek. She was inclined to pass the words off as a compliment. But the eager freshness in Kit's voice told her woman's ear, inevitable in its appreciation of sincerity, that he spoke the truth.

"You live with Mrs. Christieson above us," she answered; "my father has seen you. He will thank you for being kind to me. He does not like me coming home by myself, and he will be very angry with Dick for not meeting me."

"I cannot be angry with Dick!" said Kit.

The girl evaded this.

"Dick is thoughtless and often stays out late," she said; "but I think you are often out too. We call your friend and you Box and Cox. He is Box."

"Why?" said Kit, wishing that the foot of the stairs were a score of miles away. They were turning down the street now which led to that dismal stone turnpike where they must part one from the other.

The girl laughed a little thrilling trill of laughter.

"Because," she said, "he keeps himself shut up——"

"And why am I Cox?" said Kit, interested.

"Well, because you are not Box!"

This was far worse than Greek to Kit, whose education did not include even the commonest of farces. But he was quite satisfied, and only sighed as the girl took down her umbrella at the foot of the stair. She did it so prettily too, with a little flirt along the pavement to shake the drops off the Fox frame knobs, and a sudden uplift of eyes in which consciousness of his admiration struggled with a desire to thank him for his kindness. But she saw too much on his face to risk many words in the dusk of the stair foot.

"I hope none went on you!" she said, lamely enough, referring to the raindrops which she had shaken from her umbrella.

"Oh no, thank you," said Kit, feeling unutterably coltish and stupid. He would have liked to tell her what he thought of her—that is, in the "Orra Man's" iambics.

"I suppose I must bid you good-bye," said Kit, slowly, stammering over his words. He was just beginning his education—if he had won a bursary.

"Not unless you decide to sleep in the cellar," said the girl; "we have three stairs more to go up together."

They went up one. The pretty girl paused a moment on the landing and looked at Kit, who was following somewhat forlornly behind her.

"You haven't told me your name yet," she said—"that I may tell my father," she added, hastily.

"My name is Kit—I mean Christopher Kennedy. I come from Galloway," said Kit, gratefully hoping that she would tell him hers.

The girl clapped her hands.

"Oh, 'Kit'—I like Kit ever so much better than Christopher," she cried. Suddenly she rushed upward and turned sharp to the right.

"Oh father," she cried, impulsively, "do you know what has happened?"

Kit caught sight of a thick-set man of middle height standing at an open door. He had a nose slightly hooked, prominent bushy eyebrows high in the middle (like a circumflex accent, thought Kit to himself), which gave him a look at once high and irascible. His face was thickly bearded with a short dense beard of the colour which the artist calls warm russet and the unthinking red.

The man in the doorway did not answer his daughter directly, but continued to gaze at Kit over her shoulder with an air of stern inquiry.

"The class was late and I must have missed Dick, somehow," she went on; "then just at Nicholson Square it was dark, and some nasty fellows spoke rudely to me —or rather would have done, but for this gentleman!"

She turned to Kit with an air of proprietorship.

"This is Mr. Christopher Kennedy," continued the pretty girl, blushing so red that she looked to Kit's eyes more engaging than ever.

The man did not speak, but bent upon Kit a look so searching that the boy felt as if he were entirely transparent to those bold, deep-set eyes.

"I did nothing at all," he faltered. "The fellows ran as soon as they saw me. Besides, there was a policeman coming, anyway!"

Kit was blushing in his turn.

"Will you come in, sir?" said the russet-bearded man, in no wise abating the severity of his glance. He had a deep voice, and as Kit passed him he noticed his enormous spread of chest—almost disproportionate, indeed, to his height.

Kit took off his hat and passed within. It was a simple kitchen that he was ushered into. A stout, matronly woman was bustling about a range, which shone in all its parts with winking brass and the polish of infinite black lead.

"Mother," said the man, "here is a neighbour of ours who has brought Mary home."

The woman turned upon Kit with a pleasant smile and held out her hand.

"Ye are welcome," she said. "What has come over that 'seefer' Dick that he didna meet ye, Mary?"

The pretty girl stood in the middle of the floor and explained. She drew one glove after the other slowly and daintily off. Kit could not help looking at her, though the action was clearly unconscious. He wanted to tell her that it was even prettier to watch her take off her gloves than to put them on.

"And, mother," she cried, for she had an impulsive way with her wholly unknown to Galloway, "if it had not been for Mr. Kennedy, I do not know what I should have done."

Whereupon the tale of Kit's heroism was again retold and again disclaimed, till that youth of parts was all quivering with excitement and throbbing with vague happinesses. He seemed to be setting his feet on the very threshold of the unknown. He began to sympathise all at once with Rob Armour and the two foresters who waited about the cottage gate to see Betty. Hitherto he had always agreed with Betty that it was very good fun.

But he was learning the other side of it while he stood fingering the brim of his hat, and watching the pretty girl drawing off her gloves so daintily that Kit dared hardly shake her by the hand, lest something so delicate should break in the stiff awkwardness of his countryman's fingers.

"Will ye no sit ye doon?" said the good wife of the house with cordial invitation. She was getting supper ready, and, though naturally heavy-footed, she wore such soft slippers and walked so springily that she

seemed to be in three places at once. The girl took off
her hat and went forward to help her mother. But the
elder woman pushed her from the fire.

" Gang awa' and sit doon. Rest ye, lassie. Ye hae
been a' day among the bairns in the schule, and then
at the nicht-schule as well. Your mither has dune
naething but plowter about the hoose."

" But, mother," said the girl, " I am not tired."

And to show how fresh she was, the young girl began
to take crockery from a wall-press and spread it out
upon the white cloth which was already laid. It was
pretty to watch her. She was so graceful, so innocent,
and so impulsive.

" I must be getting upstairs to my work! " said Kit,
a little mournfully. It would not be half so much fun
to sit and listen to the scrape of Rob Grier's pen doing
his Latin version.

" We are just going to have tea," said the taciturn
man, thawing a little ; " will you stay and drink a cup
with us ? "

Kit sat down, still, however, keeping his hat in his
hands.

The pretty girl came and took it away, smiling at
him as she did so.

" Poor thing! " she said ; " don't turn it round
and round like that all the time. You will make it
dizzy."

She disclosed a row of sparklingly white and even
teeth as she spoke. And Kit thought that he had
never listened to so witty a remark. Then, when the
table was set, she went and looked over her father's
head at the visitor, resting her elbows on the broad
shoulder and dinting her chin into his thick scrubby
bush of grey hair.

She was a very pretty girl. Her features were
delicate and regular, save for the slightest aspiration
on the part of her nose, which was set at a most pro-
vocative angle. Her eyes were a kind of blue, yet
never stayed the same for two seconds. She had
brownish hair with golden lights in it, and a dimple

played bo-peep at the right corner of her mouth each time she laughed.

She was not tall, but so slender that when no one stood beside her she gave the effect of being so.

Kit did not know what there was about this girl, of whose very name he was still ignorant, that made him think of all the beautiful things he had ever seen. Did she bend coquettishly down to her father so that the firelight was reflected in her hair, till the brown turned into red and the bronze to golden yellow—instantly Kit saw the Crae Hill sweeping back in stretch after stretch of red heather. It was morning's prime, and the sun was rising. Moor-cocks were crawing in the hollows, and the great gladsome day stood on tiptoe.

Or, she shook back her loosely clustering hair from her brow. The lights wavered across it from fire and lamp, and instantly Kit saw the thirty-acre field at the Dornal all awave with ripening corn. The wind came lightly from the west and drove it towards him in glinting swells. That was the most beautiful thing he had seen till he had met this girl of the city under the November street lamps.

Happily on this his first visit Kit did not need to speak much. The women talked both for him and to him, while occasionally the thick-set saturnine man put in a word.

Kit found himself at liberty to sit and look where he would. And the stern-eyed man watched the direction of his eyes.

Then they drew in to the plain deal table on which a fair and fine coth had been laid. Kit made a pretence of eating, but he was not hungry. It seemed a profanation toa eat in such a dainty presence; or, if not exactly profane, at least ill-judged and vulgar.

But the pretty girl herself had no such qualms. She was frankly hungry, and said so. So that it was not long before Kit observed with surprise that those white and even teeth were capable of being used for other purposes than suddenly aiding and abetting her eyes to break into a dazzling smile, like the sun peering through a tearful April sky. All healthily pretty girls must, as a condition of their beauty, eat well, and this one freely owned the necessity.

"I am a perfect piggie about supper," she confessed with frank unconcern; "I have it in my mind all day at school when I am drilling the infant class. I never think about anything else coming home, and then when I do get home I always look in the oven the first thing to see what there is."

At this moment a tall loosely-built lad, with short red hair, a weak mouth, and a freckled face came in. He wore a cutaway coat of smartish fashion and held a thin cane in his hand.

"Why, Dick!" cried the girl, rising to give him an impulsive kiss, to which he submitted rather than responded, "where have you been? I missed you, and if it had not been for this gentleman"—here she smiled at Kit, making his heart quiver strangely (again he saw the Crae hillside and the sunshine fleeting across it)—"I don't know what I should have done."

The stern-faced man continued to watch the youth, who did not seem to look at any one in particular, and who markedly avoided Kit's eye.

"I was out with Marmy," he said; "we went further than we intended, and I did not get back to the school in time. It's all nonsense about anyone molesting you, Mary. You are always so nervous. It is very silly."

"Dick," said his father, "take your supper and go to bed!"

The youth laid down his cane, put his hat carefully on a peg in the hall, and sat down at the table without giving Kit a glance.

The supper proceeded, but with something less of enthusiasm.

"You have not been long in the city, sir?" said the elder man, suddenly unbending and looking over at Kit with a friendliness in his eyes as sudden as it was unexpected.

How it happened Kit did not know, but a moment

afterwards he found himself in the midst of a full account of his life. He began by telling of his grandfather, of his grandmother, something even of his mother. He told of the Mac Walters of Loch Spellanderie. He entered into full particulars concerning Betty and the three foresters.

" I think she was a very cruel girl!" interjected the one at the table most able to criticise Betty's actions and motives.

From being silent Kit grew voluble, from the extreme of reticence he became almost confidential. And as he talked of the "Orra Man" his halting tongue grew oratory and the colour mounted to his cheek. While he talked he continued to look at the pretty girl, who blushed with contagious enthusiasm. But it was to the stern man that he spoke directly, and after a time he nodded quietly.

Suddenly, while Kit was speaking, the young man who had been called Dick pushed back his chair from the table, and, brushing the crumbs from his coat, he tramped noisily out and began to ascend the stair.

" Dick ! " said his father, in deep, quiet tones.

The feet tramped on.

" DICK ! "

The feet stopped on the landing. There was a moment's silence which somehow weighed upon all as though heavy with fate. The pretty girl's face lost its bright expression. It seemed to grow anxious, and she was obviously not listening to what Kit said.

The footsteps began slowly to descend. The head of the youth, more vapid and watery-eyed than before, was thrust within the kitchen.

" What do you want, father ? " he said.

The stern man did not answer in words. He only indicated the chair from which Dick had risen with a slight nod of his head.

Dick sat down.

" And now, you were telling us——" the face of the russet-bearded man was turned to Kit with the same unexpected smile of grave sweetness.

But the heart had gone out of the tale. Kit's glow of communicativeness had sunk like a blaze among whins.

"Must you go?" murmured the pretty girl, a little sadly. Kit liked the way she said that. He lay awake two hours trying to recall her exact manner of saying it.

"And be sure ye dinna gang by the door withoot lookin' in," said the motherly person at the foot of the table. "We hae aye supper aboot this time, and ye are welcome."

"I shall be glad to see you!" said the grave man, reaching out a hand.

"Good-night," said Kit, to the young man in the cutaway coat.

His father's eye was upon him, and he managed to emit a gruut which, on a liberal interpretation, might have been construed as an acknowledgment of Dick's salutation.

The pretty girl went with Kit to the door.

"You were very kind," she said, "we are all very— that is, we hope you will come back."

"You have not yet told me your name," said Kit, holding her hand till she should answer.

"Mary Bisset is my name!" she said, with a grave sweetness very like her father's.

CHAPTER XL

A New Acquaintance.

Kit's acquaintance with his neighbours underneath, to whom he had been so curiously introduced, continued and prospered. But a very strange element was introduced into it by Mistress Christison, Kit's landlady. Kit asked her about all the people on the stairs. Being a diplomat he took each landing in turn, beginning at the bottom. Mrs. Christison was standing in the doorway, an empty shovel in her hand, with which she was wont to deliver the coals in homœopathic doses, as if they had been pills which might disagree with the fire if taken too recklessly.

At last she arrived at the place to which Kit had been bringing her.

"Ow aye, the Bissets. I dinna ken muckle aboot them, nor do I want to. The woman is a decent woman, ceevil and sociable. But the man—he's yin o' your infidel lecturers or something o' the kind. He winna let a minister within his hoose. And no yin o' them ever sets fit within a kirk door. The lassie teaches weans in an infant schule. Bairns are sair mislippened noo a days. To think that in a Christian land they wad let the like o' her to learn them their A B, abs!"

Mrs. Christison divined the look on Kit's face.

"Oh," she said, "ye'll hae been meetin' in wi' the young man. He's the best o' the lot. No that I hae onything in particular again the lave o' them. But Dick is in a guid position, and wad do weel if he had better fowk at hame. But with his faither aye on this platform and that, tearin' at Christianity and the Toon

Council, the laddie hasna a fair chance. I wonder he disna change his name."

But, in spite of this censure, Kit haunted the Bridges at the hour when the evening schools were coming out. He had not much success. For Dick, perhaps acted upon by fear of his father, was unusually faithful. While more than once Kit, from the safe shelter of the Post Office pillars, saw Mary Bisset come across the street escorted by the square shoulders of the infidel lecturer himself.

But by changing his hours for going to college Kit did better. His first Greek class in the morning went in at nine, and Mrs. Christison's stair-foot lay exactly ten minutes walk from the college. The professor of that class was strict on roll-calls, if lax concerning everything else. But as usual he did not begin till five minutes past the hour, and he punctuated the whole with personal comments. Kit had been accustomed to leave the door at five minutes to nine, and be in his place by the time the professor had reached the letter " I " in the roll.

" Inglis ? " " Here, sir ! " " Ingram ? " No answer. " Where's Ingram ? Lazy boy, Ingram. Shall have three pages of Ossian to translate into Greek. What shall it be—that splendid passage where——What, Ingram's dead ? Very well, then, Ingram is excused from coming to my class. Johnson——Kennedy."

So hitherto Kit had always been in time.

But now the student left the house at half-past eight, just in time to see a pretty figure issuing forth from that gloomy, doorless, never-closed portal which yawned upon the street. Sometimes he would see Miss Mary Bisset stand a moment on the step, doubtful whether she should put up her umbrella, or daintily gathering her skirts with a little frown on her brow at the rain, reluctant as a kitten to cross the muddy road.

" Good morning, Miss Bisset."

" Good morning, Mr. Kennedy."

It was not " Kit " any more. Constraint had somehow fallen between them. Kit put it down to the influence of " that beast Dick." Dick evidently did not like him, and scowled when they met. He always had a low-browed, smartly-dressed man with him now who wore a tall hat and a heavy gold Albert—with other clothing to match.

But all the same Kit generally escorted Mary Bisset to school, and the young people thawed by the way. By the time they had reached the grim, square-windowed half factory, half church where she taught, they were again "Kit" and "Mary." And the young man felt that, if only he could take things up where he left them the day before, his friendship might prosper. For at this stage they speak of it, and think of it, as "friendship."

Twice a week there was no night-school, and Mary Bisset came home through the blue-grey early dusk just as the swift municipal Lucifers were lighting the lamps, and the long curves of the Bridges fairly undulated with the crawling, fiery serpents. There was a pleasant frosty hum in the air. Kit and she walked more slowly, and they spoke of books which she had read and he had not.

A fire was kindled in his breast.

" I will begin to-morrow. I will get the book out of the library." It was Gibbon's " Decline and Fall " of which they spoke.

"My father will lend it to you," she answered. "Come in for it to-night!"

And the student promised. At the same moment Kit, glancing up, met an eye, and with the courtesy he had learned since he came to the city he lifted his hat.

" Who is that ? " said Mary Bisset, looking also. " I did not know you knew any one in the city."

" It was—only a fellow from the town near my place," said Kit, evasively.

" He stared very hard," said the girl. "Perhaps he thinks you should be at your work instead of walking home with me when there is no need."

" It does not matter what he or any one else thinks ! " said Kit, loftily.

But the next morning Clement Sowerby ran all the way across the quadrangle to greet him, deserting a group of laughing, easy-mannered companions to speak to Kit.

"Hello, Kennedy, you're getting a gay dog for a raw hand! Where did you pick up that deucedly pretty girl I saw you with last night? I want you to introduce me, that's a good fellow."

"I do not know the young lady well enough for that, I am afraid," said Kit, shyly, wishing Sowerby at Jericho. "I should consider it a liberty."

"She wouldn't, I bet," cried Sowerby, cheerily; "why man, don't be afraid—I won't cut you out. I've got a girl of my own. But you were such an old sobersides that I did not tell you before."

*　　　*　　　*　　　*　　　*

That night, as Kit sat alone in the room which he shared with Rob Grier, he was surprised by the entrance of a visitor. The man from Garlies was out, engaged in the sort of penal servitude known as "coaching" at a guinea a month.

This consists in doing the lessons of High School and Academy boys for them, and if unremunerative is not exhausting, except to boot leather upon the hard sets of the Edinburgh streets.

"Mr. Richard Bisset!" announced Mrs. Christison, with a certain consciousness that her plain sitting-room, with the box-bed shut off by a panelled door and the dismal photographs of tombstones all round the walls, was somehow honoured by such a visitor.

Kit rose in surprise, erect and stiff as a pillar. The freckled youth had a tendency to wriggle upon his first appearance. But otherwise he made himself perfectly at home.

"Ah," he said, "you are surprised to see me. I thought I'd look you up. I was rather off it the other night—sort of chippy and hot about the gills, you know."

Kit did not know, but he smiled encouragingly as he offered his visitor the only armchair in the place. Dick

Bisset reached forward and took the poker. He stirred
up the fire which Kit, knowing that he had received all
the coal which his landlady could in justice to herself
afford for twice three shillings a week, had been carefully nursing against the return of Rob Grier.

"The fact is," said his visitor, "we don't know one
another well enough to be living in the same house. I
am obliged to you for your kindness to my sister. She
is a good girl, Mary, but I own it is no end of a swot
having to meet her. A fellow has so many things to do.
Not but what there are lots of fellows who would take
that job off my hands—eh, what?"

He tried to look knowingly at Kit, but that resolute
youth would not see, and as it were warded off the
glance with his shoulder.

"Oh, all right," said Dick Bisset, with a hurt expression, "I'm as particular as any one, and I tell you
frankly I didn't cotton to you at first. No more did my
friend, Mr. Marmaduke Styles. Marmy is a partner in
the big tailor's emporium at the corner of the Bridges.
You know the place, 'Try Styles's styles one guinea
the suit and an extra pair of trousers thrown in.' I
don't wear them myself, but it's a deuced paying
line!"

Kit had not a reply ready to this.

But the freckled-faced young man went on wholly
unabashed. "But I've come to my senses. And I'm
a chap that is not too proud to come and say so. I
don't mind owning when I'm wrong. I heard to-day
that you were a bursar and a swell at college. Well,
I don't go to college. I'm in an office, but clerking is
not my biz, though dad thinks it is. Ever bet? No!
Well, it's the best thing out. You can make a pot of
money in no time!"

Kit smiled, and said "that he had no money to bet
with."

"Oh, there's no risk," said Mr. Richard Bisset,
airily. "If you were in the know, and had Marmy
Styles at your back to put you on to real good things,
you wouldn't be lodging in a dog-hole like this."

"It looks very nice to me," said Kit; "I have been used to a stable loft."

"Don't know what that is," said Dick, still more flippantly. "Beastly place, anyway. But seriously, you should stand in with Marmy's crowd. There's only half a dozen of us, and we can make no end of money!"

"I have to do my work, and it will take me all my time to get through the session without running into debt," quoth honest Kit.

"Well, anyway, whether you do or not," answered the tempter, "you might come along with us to-morrow night; eight or ten fellows are going to have supper early and go to the theatre. Will you come?"

Kit had never been to a theatre in his life, and was about to decline, when Dick struck in, "I daresay my sister will be going. She'll come if I ask her, I know. There will be another girl or two there."

"Thank you," said Kit, definitely tempted this time, but still uncertain as to his duty.

Dick Bisset reached out a hand and shook Kit's heartily.

"That's right," he cried, "we'll make a man of you yet."

Kit's visitor did not sit down again. He mooned about the room as if he were looking for something but could not remember what. He examined the tomb-stones on the walls, and then the books on the table with a running undercurrent of comment, half muttered, half spoken.

"Poor place—poor place—tombs and epitaphs. 'Under the weeping willow tree.' That sort of thing. Books! What skittles! A + B − C. What blooming rot! Dick Bisset, I'm jolly glad that you are not a mug, and know better than that, if you do have to stick on to an office stool from ten to four."

Then he said half a dozen times, "Well, I must be going!"

But still he did not go, something else taking his wandering attention.

" Well, I'll meet you at the foot of the stair at half-past six—no, I'll come up for you here. And, I say, old fellow, I'm short this week, could you lend me a sov. for a day or two ? Till I get my pay on Saturday."

Kit wavered a moment, but the thought of Mary Bisset decided him. His heart sank, however, for he was uncertain about the value of Dick's promise and how he would manage without the money before the end of the session.

Nevertheless, he went to his little desk, and, unlocking it, he took out the roll of crisp notes he had received from the Secretary of the United Societies. He separated one and handed it to Dick Bisset without a word. Dick looked longingly at the roll in Kit's hand. He seemed on the point of speaking, but, apparently thinking better of it, he thrust the note carelessly into his pocket.

" Well, a thousand thanks, old fellow, he said; " you *are* a brick. You shall have it again on Saturday sure as fate, and a dozen of the same if you need 'em. Ta-ta ! Be ready with your best bib and tucker at 6.30 prompt to-morrow night."

At the door Robert Grier met him, coming tramping past in his rough way.

" It's a plaguit cauld nicht ! " he cried, slapping his hands together and getting as near the fire as he dared.

Dick eyed him with disfavour.

" Who's that beast? " he whispered to Kit after Rob had gone in.

It is somewhat curious that, when Kit came back to the little sitting-room, he found Rob Grier glowering at him with his back to the fire and his coat tails under his arms, ready to put a very similar question.

" What was that beast doin' in here ? " he asked.

And Kit, for the first time in his life, evaded Rob's honest eye. He could not bring himself to mention either the supper of the succeeding evening or the loan of the pound note.

CHAPTER XLI.

A Kind Brother.

Excitement, fear, and exultation walked patteringly to and fro all day in the heart of Kit Kennedy. He was called up in class, and, answering at random, he brought down on him the wrath of Professor Jupiter Apollo, who, standing by the hacked rails of the rostrum, hurled at him one decimating sentence, which rang long in Kit's ear, " Sir, the only creature on earth truly despicable is the man who can work and will not work."

Years afterwards, when Kit was ill with brain fever, he used to turn this into Latin in twenty-four different ways.

A month before Kit would have choked with shame to have had such words spoken to him. Now they seemed lighter than vanity to him. But Rob Grier, who was called up after him and who acquitted himself with the wooden perfection of the conscientious lexicon-rustler, shook his head sadly.

" Kennedy,"he said to Kit afterwards, " ye are cleverer nor me, but if ye dinna watch oot, faith, I'll beat you yet !"

But the anticipation did not appear to afford the blacksmith-student much satisfaction.

" Ye'll bide in the nicht and we'll work her thegither, when I get in frae my teaching," he said, almost imploringly, to his companion.

" Not I," said Kit; " I am going out to see some fellows."

So all day he walked to and fro outside the garden of Eden, and saw the tree of the Knowledge of Good and Evil glimmering ripe-laden through the pales.

Rather before his hour Dick Bisset came up the stair.
He rang the little bell which tinkled just on the other
side of Mrs. Christison's hall door, and with a condescending nod strolled past that lady as soon as she
had opened it, leaving a trail of cheap cigarette smoke
like incense behind him.

"Well," he cried heartily, "still at it? By Jove!
how you fellows do grind.   You'll be the better of a let
up.   Shut these books and come on.   We have to go
round by Mary's school.   I'm going to 'ask her out.'
I bet I know how to yarn her Johnny of a chief!"

Kit explained that the open books on the table
belonged to Rob Grier, his room-mate, and putting on
his hat the pair went down into the pale blue misty
twilight of the Edinburgh streets.   A frosty wind had
whipped them dry, and now drove a stray flake or two
of snow horizontally along the roadways which opened
out north and south.   Kit had never in his life been
conscious of so keen an elation of the blood as on this
humming lamplit evening of early winter.   A tingling
appreciation of life bubbled headily in his brain.   He
saw everything with a curious clearness, and seemed to
divine by instinct whither each passenger was going
and what drew him thither.

Kit did not know that this power of heightening his
own sensations by contrast with those of others was due
to a certain essential corpuscle of his blood inherited
from his father.   It was this which had ended in taking
Christopher Kennedy, B.A., away from Lilias Armour
early that autumn morning nearly twenty years ago in
the company of Nick French.

Kit only knew that merely to walk by the side of Dick
Bisset in the crisp frosty bite of the winter twilight,
through the exciting pour of well-dressed people, made
the Cottage by the Crae seem a thousand miles
away. It came upon him suddenly and not at all
remorsefully that for the first time in his life he had
that morning forgotten to say his prayers.   As the two
youths swung out of the defile of high houses on
the Bridges they emerged upon that astonishing

panorama, which, seen at the hour of gloaming, never fails to excite a thrill in the most hardened and most unemotional—in the lawyer escaping from the grinding monotony of Parliament House, and the engine-driver coming up from a twelve hours' spell upon the foot-plate.

The Waverley station was now no more a prosaic railway terminus. Common details were sunk in a pale, luminous, silver mist, through which burned a thousand lights, warm, yellow, and kindly. The blue deepened beneath the Castle rock. There it was indigo, with a touch of royal scarlet where the embers of the sunset lay broadly dashed in against the west. Princes Street, that noblest of earthly promenades, whose glory it is to be no mere street, lay along the edge of a blue and misty sea, bejewelled with scattered lights, festooned with fairy points of fire, converging, undulating, and receding till they ran red as blood into the eye of the sunset.

Above all towered the ancient strength of the Castle, battlemented from verge to verge, light as a cloud, insurgent as a wave, massive as its own foundations, etched bold and black against the spreading splendours of the west.

" Oh, look," cried Kit, laying his hand impulsively on the arm of his companion, " I did not know God had created anything half so beautiful ! "

Dick Bisset laughed.

" That's all very well," he answered, " but I'll lay you a crown to a tanner we'll better it for beauty before the night is out."

Ashamed to admit how much the scene had moved him, Kit was about to make a laughing reply, when he saw something burn a moment on the highest tower of the Castle. The sun had touched the flag in its final downward plunge. Like a flake of gold it floated a moment, and then vanished as a tongue of flame is blown upward from a conflagration.

And Kit Kennedy remembered that he had never taken down the white handkerchief from the top of the

pine tree above the stepping-stones.   His mother would
be looking at it that very moment from the dull windows
of Kirkoswald.

After this he was silent all the way to the factory-
like school in which Mary Bisset taught.   He scarcely
listened to her brother's declaration of his plan of cam-
paign.

"I know the Johnny who runs this show," he
confided; "he's rather gone on our Mary, I think.
Used to come up to see father (of course it was father)
when he was a student.   Mary was only a kitten then.
After, when he went up a bit, he got her this place.
He's a decent sort, but soft as they make 'em.   Lord,
it's like taking in a baby to yarn him.   I'm going to
tell him Mary can't wait to-night because she has to
recite to the sick kids in the hospital over at the end
of Laurieston.   Fact!   He'll believe it, too, right as
the mail.   It'll go, I tell you!   The only thing is
to keep Mary from giving away the snap to-morrow
morning.   That needs more savvy.   But I bet I can
work it!"

Kit was left without in the deepening dusk.   The
lamps no longer seemed to exist by sufferance of the
tidal glow of the sunset.   Now they burned with their
own proper lustre against the dusky bosom of the
mother night.   The mill stream of homeward-bound folk
ran more strongly away from the city.   Even Leith
Walk itself had grown picturesque in this light.   It was
no more a mere lane of communication between the mistress sitting aloft in a well-aired drawing-room and the
handmaid down in the scullery.   Its converging lines of
lights ran to a point which seemed to terminate in the
midst of a deep blue plain.   That was the northern
sea, off which the stray snowflakes had been arriving
one by one all the afternoon.

Kit stood waiting in the dusk, his heart beating with
a certain pride in living.   His lips tasted life, his eyes
were englamoured with vividest expectation.   Pretty
girls passed him on their way to the theatre, which
meant work to them.   Quietly, sedately, they went by.

Kit thought they were girls who had been at the
University Classes at St. Margaret's College.

Others passed arm-in-arm laughing and humming
gay airs. Kit looked longer at these. He thought
they were actresses. They were students of St.
Margaret's.

"This *is* nice, Mr. Kennedy," said a voice in his ear;
"it was delightful of Dick to get me off. And Mr.
Cathcart was so kind. He always lets me go when Dick
asks. But he generally puts such curious questions in
the morning. I don't know what Dick can say to
him."

There was Mary Bisset, prettier than ever. Kit
wondered that even for a moment he had considered the
girls who had passed to be nice-looking. Such a
light of release was in her face, such a sauciness of half-
defiant friendliness on her lips, that Kit could only
stammer and mutter commonplaces.

"Well, Dick, where are you going?" his sister
cried, putting her arm through that of the freckled
youth.

"First to supper and then to an entertainment,
sis! What do you think of that?" he answered
carelessly.

Mary clapped her hands. This time they were very
neatly gloved when she appeared.

"Oh, I am so tired," she cried, "so tired of children.
I don't think I ever want to see one again. Inky,
fractious little brats! And they were so extra fretful
to-day. I wish I had to teach the infant class. They
are sticky but dear. Where are you going to take us,
Dick? How nice it will be, just you and Mr. Kennedy.
I am so glad you have made friends. I am sure Mr.
Kennedy works too hard. It will do him good to get
out a while."

"That is not the opinion of my professor," said Kit,
honestly. "He thinks I do not work at all."

"Oh yes, I know," said Mary Bisset, looking up at
him with eyes that seemed to turn his vital parts to
lukewarm water within him, "they used to say the

same when I was a student—at Argyle House, you know. They never thought we did enough, however hard we worked for their old Quarterlies! And I was not very clever, you know."

"There are one or two others coming to-night," said Dick, "girls, too, so you won't be lonely——"

"How nice—girls whom I know?" asked Mary, a little more soberly.

"Well, no, I don't think so," replied Dick, "but you soon will. They are girls who are easy to get on with."

"Oh, yes, I remember," said Mary, with a relieved expression in her voice; "they are the girls who had stalls at that Charity Bazaar you went to so much last month. You told me about them. Didn't I guess right?"

Dick Bisset was palpably uneasy.

"I say," he cried, suddenly, pulling out his watch, "I did not know it was that time. I must go and fetch the others. I say, Kennedy, do you mind taking my sister a little walk and bringing her to Sponton's (you know Sponton's—well, ask then) about half-past six—that is, in half an hour? But be sure not to be late, for we have to go to the entertainment afterwards."

"Oh, Dick, don't be gone long," said Mary, definitely distressed. "Mr. Kennedy will not know what to do with me ages before that time. And suppose you were not there when we came, it would be dreadful. What should we do?"

"Why, wait; that's all you would have to do. But I'll be there right enough, so don't worry, Mary!"

Dick vanished up the steep little hill which led to St. James' Square, while Kit and Mary walked leisurely down the garden verge of Princes Street. They were silent for a while, moving side by side with a curiously pleasant sense of proximity.

CHAPTER XLII.

THE sunset had burned itself out. The Castle was now only a denser mass of blackness against the dark grey sky. A light haze of snow-cloud obscured the lesser stars. The city seemed roofed in for the night, but the brilliance of the stretching miles of lights was not dimmed.

"This is better than the schoolroom," said Mary, suddenly, with a little effort and a long indrawing of her breath. "Do you know I have never been here before after dark? Dick is always so busy."

"I—I am glad you see it first with me," said Kit, fighting with the difficulties of speech. Had it been Betty he would have talked easily enough, but this dainty marvel of the city froze him into silence. Yet the girl's happiness at her unexpected deliverance was childlike and unrestrained.

"It is so lovely to have a whole evening to myself, and so kind of Dick. I wonder what made him think of it. He has been a great deal at a charity bazaar—to buy a field for his athletic association or football club—or something. It has taken a lot of time and trouble. I wish I could have helped and had pretty dresses to go selling things in."

Mary Bisset sighed and looked down at the plain black dress and trim quakerish mantle which outlined her slender figure so clearly against the reflected lights of the pavement.

Kit cleared his throat to speak. It had suddenly become dry, and when his voice did arrive it came in volcanic bursts and had a strange hard quality. The girl looked up expectantly.

" You were going to say——? " she suggested.

Kit tried again, still it would not come. But just when he had almost given up hope of ever being able to utter another articulate word his voice came back with a suddenness which made him start.

" Will you take my arm, Miss Bisset ? "

Kit actually looked round to see who had spoken. It was certainly not his own voice he heard.

The pretty girl gave a little skip.

" Of course I will. How strange it seems to be called ' Miss Bisset ' out of school. I shall expect you to snap your fingers like this and say, ' Please, Miss Bisset, will you wipe my slate for me ? ' "

" May I call you ' Mary ' ? " Kit ventured, beginning to be astonished at himself. Her little gloved hand was on his arm by this time. It seemed to nestle there. It looked exceeding small and smooth, while the glove itself fitted without a crease. This was not at all like walking in the woods with Betty. The lad drew a long breath.

" You are getting tired," said the girl, evading the boldness of Kit's question ; " let us go back ! "

" Oh, no, not yet—Mary," said Kit, who, having now overcome the resistance of his voice, resolutely pursued his advantage with all the adventurousness of the truly bashful.

But there is little use in chronicling over again these eternal and unvarying tentatives of young and innocent hearts—how he teased her to call him by his first name ; how he used hers in every sentence for the pleasure of hearing it spoken unreproved ; how she, shying from the adventurous recklessness of " Kit," presently condescended upon the halfway house of " Mr. Kit," with which the hero had in the meantime to be satisfied ; how, having uttered it once, the pretty girl blushed and would have drawn back.

" I did not say it," she said, and then with wayward irrelevance she went on, " Well, you made me say it, you know you did. I will take away my hand and go home by myself if you say I said it."

It was all very charming and delightful to these
simple unstaled souls. But such moments speed fast,
and Mr. Dick Bisset was waiting at Sponton's. Kit's
heart was rippling like a river over pebbles in a water-
break, so quick and continuous was its beating. His
eyes were feverishly brilliant, his brown face a little
pale under its weathering, and he walked not on Caith-
ness flags chilled by the north wind, but rather upon
rolling clouds and the viewless air.

Suddenly, after Kit had reached his right hand over,
and rested it on the smooth brown glove long enough to
feel the warmth strike upward into his bare, frost-bitten
fingers, the pretty girl started, and light as a falling
snowflake her glove ceased from his rough tweed sleeve.

She clasped her hands tragically as she did when she
recited at the children's hospital.

"Oh, what shall we do? It is seven o'clock already!
Dick will be so angry. There, it is striking from St. Giles.
Listen! How could we have been so careless, *Kit?*"

It was the first time she had ventured it, and the
monosyllable fell with a sharp sting of exceeding plea-
surableness upon the lad's ear and vibrated long in his
heart.

She did not put her hand back again on his arm, but
he did not care.

"Kit—Kit!" he said softly to himself; "she called
me 'Kit.'" Then he smiled.

But he had the good sense to know his limit, the
guarded bounds of the night, and not to try for more.

*   *   *   *   *

"Sponton's—yes, this is Sponton's," said the sleek-
haired, tightly-buttoned epicene boy who stood behind
at the swinging glass door. "Mr. Bisset's party?
Yes, sir—upstairs, second on the right."

Sponton's had been a famous place in the beginning
of the century. In it had sat Scott and Jeffrey, talking
ceaselessly, while with clear-cut cameo face Lockhart
had listened. Earlier still one Burns (lately Burness)
had come across the new bridge and tasted the
Scottish stone ale, "virulent as a tass of raw brandy."

It had been the rallying-place of the New Town wits against their natural enemies, of the "Sports" and "Jeremies" against the bookish haunters of Old Town printing presses and stationers' shops.

But of late Sponton's had fallen on evil times. Great warehouses had walled it in. A domed public department had overshadowed it. Its once commanding site had narrowed with the years to a shy, many-angled lane, affording unrivalled opportunities for quiet approach in several directions. Many douce Sunday-plate citizens knew Sponton's. When men rubbed shoulders there, oftentimes they did not recognise each other. There was something in the air which provoked after-reticence.

Yet there was nothing definitely wrong about Sponton's—nothing that might not have been set up in type and printed in the morning paper. Only when after a dinner there a well-known author was found tumbled into an area with a broken neck, there was a black mark against Sponton's in most serious men's minds.

Needless to say neither Kit nor Mary Bisset had the least idea of this as they went upstairs. But the consciousness of it accented the look of surprise on the face of the befrizzed, powder-tinged attendant, who came forward to say, respectfully enough, "Will the lady take off her hat?"

"Oh, no," said Mary, quickly, and a little breathlessly, "I will leave my cloak and go in as I am. Dick won't mind!"

There was no difficulty in locating the room where Dick Bisset and his friend Mr. Marmy Styles were holding their select little supper party. A hum of brisk talk, a popping fusilade of corks, told that Kit's loan could not go far in such a place. It was well that Mr. Styles was a partner in the "This-style Nineteen and Eleven" shop at the corner of the Bridges.

Kit and Mary were hailed clamorously by Dick from the other end of the room, as they stood tremulously hesitating in the doorway.

"Here you are—we thought you had bolted. Wherever

have you been ? 'A starry night for a ramble'—that sort of thing, I suppose. Come and sit down !"

Kit was stunned at what he saw, and Mary Bisset stood poised and quivering, with a look on her face as if she meditated flight.

But Dick pulled her round by the arm, talking all the time.

"Here is a lady friend of mine who wants to know you, Mary. My sister, Miss Violet Clifford. Sit down, Mary. Here, Kennedy, do your duty !"

Somehow Kit found himself in a chair. Presently Mary was seated by his side, removing her gloves. He saw a folded white napkin on his plate, and he had not the least idea what to do with it. The glitter and hum dazed him, and he started violently when a hand was laid on his shoulder.

"Hello, Kennedy," said a familiar voice, "I did not know you were up to this sort of thing! Congratulate you on your pace, my boy. But what would they say up in the Kirk on the Hill—eh, what?"

Kit turned, smiling stupidly, and there behind him, easy and cool in evening dress, was Clement Sowerby.

Instantly Kit became conscious that he alone of all present was attired in tweed. Some were in black morning coats, for the affair had a very informal air. But Kit felt inconceivably miserable. He thought that Mary would despise him. He knew the other fellows would. He seemed to recognise amusement in the half-smile on Sowerby's face.

Yet he could only vacantly stare and look at the dazzling front of Sowerby's shirt.

"Bisset lives on the same stair," he said, awkwardly, "and he asked me to bring this young lady—his sister !"

Sowerby bowed slightly as Mary glanced shyly up at the mention of her brother's name.

"Very pleasant duty," he said; "see you again! Ta-ta !"

But as he fell back Sowerby, who was a better fellow than he gave himself credit for, muttered, "Beastly shame to bring his sister to Spouton's—what a sweep!"

CHAPTER XLIII

His Father's Son.

WHEN Kit had time to distinguish persons he noticed that there was a general forcing of the note among the ladies of the party. Their colour was generally a trifle high and unusually permanent. Not like Mary's, which (Kit thought was a strange elation) paled to lily clearness one moment, and the next grew pink as the inner rose leaves where the dew lingers longest in the morning. Their voices were mirthful, but they lacked the woodland abandon of Betty's when she was tantalising the foresters, or Mary's gay ripple when she had clapped her hands and said, " Oh, ' Kit,' that is a nice name—so much better than Christopher."

The general style of dress was also a little extravagant, but Kit thought that no doubt some of the costumes were parti-coloured because of the late fancy dress bazaar.

But his eyes rested with a curious pride on the plain black gown of the girl beside him.

" No one of them is the least like her," he summed up his observations, and many of the men about the table seemed to think so too. Mary kept her eyes on her plate, and after the first stun of surprise seemed to draw nearer to Kit, talking earnestly and quickly all the time.

Kit's heart beat faster than ever at this subtlest flattery. He sat up straighter and looked more boldly about him. He found no difficulty in doing as the others did, and he emptied again and again the curious wide-mouthed glass which was set before him. A stronger tide of life ran through his soul. Life became

20

suddenly wider, richer, fuller. Every day he had to live seemed another promissory note of thrilling experience. He began to talk, and with the eloquence of the natural observer he told Mary Bisset of the beauties of his own Galloway.

He warmed as he spoke of the delicate flushing rose bells of the heath in early June "till the wild moors look like a pretty girl blushing," he said, and he looked at her as he said it.

The girl's knife and fork trembled on her plate with the vibration of the lad's voice in her heart.

He described the great forty-acre corn field with its roods of rustling oats, and the wind waves coming and going across it.

"It shines just like the sun on your hair, Mary," he said.

There had been a hush at the table. Several had been curiously regarding the rough tweed-clad student with the pale, eager face. Among others who did so was the rubicund old proprietor, successor to the original Sponton. To him age had not brought reverence nor the hoar hair respect.

So that, without Kit being the least aware of it, his voice was heard all over the room in the hush before the rising of the ladies.

"Yes," he repeated, for the pleasure of seeing Mary Bisset's cheek turned a little towards him, "it is true; I will say it again. The wind on the corn at home is just like the sunshine on your hair, when you go down the street on a windy morning!"

A roar of laughter ran round the table.

"Bravo!" cried Clement Sowerby, clapping his hands, "Kennedy can 'see' us all and 'raise' us at this game. Bravo, old man! Galloway for ever—in love or war!"

In the laughter which followed all rose and the ladies trooped out, Mary Bisset following with a crimsoned face. The girl Violet Clifford came and took her by the arm kindly and went out with her. Then all the young men regrouped themselves and began to talk

quite differently. Kit did not understand a tenth of
what they said. But after he had sat looking about
him for ten minutes the old proprietor of Sponton's
came up and, with his usual familiar courtesy to his
guests, bent his dyed moustache over Kit and said,
"May I have the pleasure, sir, of knowing your name?
You remind me so strongly of a face I used to see here
thirty years ago."

"My name is Kit—that is—Christopher Kennedy!"
the lad answered. The rubicund man stood back to
take another look at him. "Bless my soul! Well—
well—well!" he muttered. "Most strange——"

"What is strange?" said Kit, absently enough,
with his eye on the door at which he expected to see
Mary Bisset reappear.

"Nothing—nothing," replied the proprietor, with his
fingers on his chin—"a coincidence, nothing more. I
once knew a man of your name!"

"Now then, pay the shot!" cried Richard Bisset,
jovially. "I'll take the chink now, if *you* please! For
you fellows won't have a rap on you by to-morrow
morning. Come, shell out. Ten bob each for your-
selves and five for the lady."

Kit rose gasping, but had the presence of mind to
show no surprise. Yet his heart fairly sank within
him. Another of his few pounds gone—the precious
pounds which were to see him through the session.

More as a precaution than anything else he had put
one in his pocket when he came out. He handed it to
Dick.

"All right, you're a blooming Crœsus," said he; "I
saw this fellow with a pack of these last night in his
'digs'; the other five shillings will just do for the
entrance money to the Elysium."

And Mr. Richard Bisset thrust Mr. Secretary Fleming's
second crisp bank-note into his pocket.

At this moment Miss Violet Clifford put her head
prettily in at the door with her hat on, a rather flam-
boyant composition of yellow satin and white feathers.

Well, lazy fellows," she tinkled, "we are ready if

you are. Perhaps, though, you don't want to come. If not, there are others in plenty who will ! "

Opening the door wider she came into the room, and assumed the dignity and port of a sergeant-major.

" '*Shun !* " she cried. " Stand at ease ! Order arms ! Quick march ! "

And she waited till all had passed her. Kit was last, and as he went by she took him by the arm and detained him a moment.

" See here," she whispered hurriedly, " take that girl home. She is a teacher in a school, and though there's no harm for us —or you either perhaps—there may be both harm and trouble for her. It's a shame for Dick to have let her come."

" How can I ? " said Kit. " I have promised. She expects it."

" Nonsense," cried the girl, angrily. " I tell you, you do not know. It will do her harm in her profession to be seen at the Elysium."

They had moved out now, and Kit, looking down the narrow hall which formed the private entrance to Sponton's, saw Mary Bisset standing near the door as if meditating flight. As soon as she saw Kit, she made a slight gesture as if to go to him. But seeing Miss Clifford's hand on his arm she stopped suddenly, and somewhat ostentatiously resumed her conversation with her brother's friend, Mr. Marmaduke Styles.

" Now go," said Miss Clifford, giving him a little imperious push ; " do as I tell you ! "

Somewhat unceremoniously Kit took possession of Mary, ousting Mr. Styles without apology, and they were on the doorstep and going down the steps before he knew it. The Elysium was quite near to Sponton's, and as the night was fine the party had elected to walk to the boxes which had been reserved for them.

Mary was very silent, though she suffered Kit to take her hand and put it on his sleeve. But there was now no warmth in the pressure.

" Mary," said Kit, as soon as they were out of hearing of their companions, " do you think we should go

with the others to this place? Would your headmaster
like to hear of it?"

"I am not responsible to him for where I go. Nor
to you either, Mr. Kennedy," said Mary, with considerable asperity. "I am with my brother."

Kit wondered what was the matter, but had not the
tact to find out without asking.

"I think you should let me take you home," he said,
lamely enough.

Mary instantly removed her hand from his arm, and
turned to look for Dick.

"You are at liberty to go and find that girl with the
dyed hair if you like," she said, with a pretty spiteful-
ness. "I will accompany my brother."

"Why, what's the matter, Mary?" cried Dick Bisset,
who was coming along after them. "What's this?—
Kennedy wants to go home! Oh, nonsense, of course
not—unless you would rather. Well, make up your
own minds."

And he passed on with Miss Violet Clifford upon his
arm. As the latter went by she cast a look backward
at Kit over her shoulder which happily Mary did not
intercept.

Mary stood a moment, secretly relenting at the sight
of his dejected countenance.

"Are you sorry?" she said, severely.

"I am sorry you are angry with me," said Kit.

"Well, let's say no more about it—come along!"

And putting her hand more confidently than before
on his arm she said, "Kit, I did not like that man with
the watch-chain. He frightened me a little. But I
feel quite safe with Dick—and you!"

There was nothing left for Kit but to obey. So now
the pair, left last of all, silently followed the others
in the direction of the famous Elysium Theatre,
Auditorium, and Music-hall—as it was named in
the advertisements.

At that time the entrance to the better places was
not through the present spacious hall, with its bunched
electric lights and countless palms and statues. The

entrant to the boxes or stalls had to pass along a narrow lane, half of which was occupied by a concreted channel, down which in the winter rains a stream flowed towards the subterranean levels of the Cowgate. It seemed to Kit that, as he turned down here with Mary on his arm, he caught a glimpse of a dusky figure flitting before them.

But he saw no one, and he was just making up his mind by which of the three inscribed doors arranged side by side he was to enter when out of the darkness, straight in front of him, a figure stepped into the glare of the gas jets, a man haggard, worn, emaciated, scarce of this world, a figure which struck shame and gratitude and fear all at once into Kit's heart. It was the man to whom he owed all, yet upon whom since leaving Galloway he had scarcely bestowed a single thought.

The "Orra Man" stood before him, between Mary Bisset and the door of the Elysium.

Kit disengaged his arm with a quick cry, and ran forward with his hand held warmly out. The "Orra Man," instead of shaking it, put his own right hand behind him.

"No," he said, "I will not shake you by the hand till you tell me what you mean by going in there."

He pointed with the index finger of his left hand to the brilliant portals of the Elysium.

"Why," said Kit, a sort of quick chill obstinacy coming over him, " I am taking this young lady to join a company of whom her brother is one. Nothing more!"

"No," cried the "Orra Man," tragically, "but it *is* something more! That for you is the way of death, with Hell following after. Others may try it unharmed, but not you. And if this girl is as innocent as her face proclaims her, as I think her to be—I pray you—I command you—take her to her home. She will thank you one day."

"I owe you much," said Kit, doggedly, "but you have no right to dictate to me what I should do. No, nor yet to this young lady. I tell you I am taking her to her brother."

"Brother or no brother," cried the "Orra Man," "you do not pass here while I can stop you. Listen, I have a right to prevent you. I myself have flaunted it in such companies as you were led into to-night. I have tasted the tree of bitter knowledge. I have eaten the apples of Sodom that grow thereon. The ashes are under my tongue now. Kit Kennedy, that way is death to you. I have seen the worm that dieth not. The germ is in your blood. I knew that it would grow, and that I alone could save you. For this I left Galloway. For this I came to Edinburgh, that you might never know what I have known, the utter agony of having dragged the innocent down with you to the pit—the remorse, the bitter unavailing regret for the past. I tell you, turn and flee! Stand not on the order of your going. Go!"

"I will not," said Kit, excitement and anger towering in his brain. "Stand out of the way! What right have you to say where I should go, or with whom?"

And with his strong young man's arm he would easily have swept the frail body of the "Orra Man" out of his way, but all at once a white flame seemed to pass across the countenance of the ragged man who withstood him. It was as if his features had suddenly been lit up by a flash of lightning which shone on them.

"I will tell you, Kit Kennedy," he cried, "the right I have to withstand you—*I also am Christopher Kennedy and your father!*"

THE strange revulsion of feeling which came over Kit at the "Orra Man's" words, the new light shed back upon the past, his mother's warnings, the half-understood taunts of schoolmates, his own vague questionings, all combined to compel belief. Why else should this man spend laborious days and sleepless nights in teaching him—whence came his indubitable learning, if this were not the sometime classical master of Cairn Edward Academy whose name he bore? Besides, there was something else, a reverberating string in Kit's heart which told him the man spoke the truth.

"I will go," he said, brokenly. "I will go home. Come, Mary!"

And the girl, with that sense of being bound up with great occasions which more than anything dominates women, turned away from the door of the Elysium and walked southward with Kit without a word. The "Orra Man" did not follow them. He stood still on the steps from which he had spoken to them, the garish lights shining steadily down on his pale face and ragged attire.

Kit and Mary were just vanishing into the darkness when Dick Bisset came to the door. He peered up and down the lane, and a liveried official also looked out behind him.

"Kennedy—Mary," he cried, "hurry up! We are waiting." Then to himself he muttered, "They are not in sight. I guess they have grown chicken-hearted and gone home. All right! I've got the yokel's dollars and they can please themselves!"

The official, a fatted bull of Bashan in livery button

and gold braid, caught sight of the " Orra Man " standing at the foot of the steps.

"Hey, get away from there," he cried. "You are
here after no good. I'll bring a policeman to you in a
minute!"

And the elder Christopher Kennedy also turned and
went out of these dusky Elysian Fields into the keen
frost-bitten, lamp-lit cheerfulness of the town. Kit and
Mary were already out of sight before him. A light
snow was beginning to fall, and the broad, far-sailing
flakes blew in their faces. Mary Bisset did not speak.
She knew instinctively that Kit's heart must be a
whirling chaos. But she did what was better. She
put her left hand up and joined it to her right so that
the fingers of both lay lightly netted upon the lad's
arm. And the slight action healed and stilled Kit's
heart more than any words.

By the time they turned from the glow and clatter of
the main thoroughfare, up the long defile of the street
at the end of which loomed their door, both were
calmer. But it was the girl who spoke.

"If you can tell my father anything, he is a wise
man. Many come to him for advice. He does not
believe like others, perhaps. He does not go to church.
They call him an infidel. But he will tell you what
to do."

"Thank you," said Kit, "perhaps I will. But not
to-night. I think I will go straight home to-night."

"Come in with me," pleaded the girl; "they will ask
me where Dick is and I shall need you."

Kit silently acquiesced, and the pressure of the little
smooth brown glove on his arm was more than sufficient
thanks.

When they went in Mr. Bisset was bending his dark
brows over Rawlinson's " Five Monarchies " and making
copious notes in a ruled notebook. He looked up with
a sudden brightening of the eyes as his daughter came
in. Then the girl, without taking off her hat, ran over
to him and installed herself on his knee.

"At it again, Dad!" she said, brightly. "I declare I

think it is you who are the student and not Mr. Kennedy here. He never seems to have anything to do. I don't believe he is a student at all."

Mr. Bisset looked over at Kit soberly, and said with a certain characteristic sententiousness, " Mr. Kennedy is getting a great opportunity—an opportunity for which I would have given ten years of my life. I am sure he is profiting by it. I also have attended classes at the university. But I could not compete with striplings from the High School or even with such well-trained youths from the country as himself. My mind, matured in many things, lacked the easy suppleness of youth. It was more difficult for me to acquire, easier for me to let slip, more difficult for me to summon my knowledge at call. From what school did you come, Mr. Kennedy? There are, I hear, good schools in Galloway."

Kit blushed crimson.

"I did not come from any school," said Kit. "I was taught privately by—by a friend."

The Infidel Lecturer glanced keenly at Kit.

"He must have been a fine scholar, sir," he answered; " did not you win a bursary?"

Kit nodded and looked at the floor.

"He is ashamed of this teacher," thought his questioner, for the first time disappointed in the lad. "I will find out if this is so. And if it is——"

Kit's welcome in the house of the Bissets hung on his next words.

"He was perhaps not a very desirable acquaintance after you had finished with your studies?"

The clouds cleared instantly from Kit's brow at the question.

"Oh, no," he said, eagerly, "you must not think so. I was only sorry that he would let me do so little for him. I have not been in the least worthy of his help and friendship."

Kit glanced over his shoulder. Mary had stolen quickly and quietly out of the room. He was alone with the stern-browed man, who seemed to wait for him to say more.

With all his natural impulsiveness Kit dashed at the difficulty.

"He was my father, sir, but I did not know it till to-night."

The dark man nodded without manifesting any surprise. He was accustomed to hear unexpected things, and so when Kit rushed headlong into his story, not sparing himself nor blinking the facts of his idleness and neglect of college work, he merely sat still and listened. Kit could not enter into the events of the night without implicating Dick. But he said enough to give Mr. Bisset the clue. The Infidel Lecturer heard him to the end without comment, and then held out his hand across the table.

"I thought you were a featherhead like Dick," he said, "but I see you will make a man yet."

Then one of the things happened which are called providential. There came a ring at the little tinkling bell, and presently Mrs. Bisset, who had been busied in the kitchen with the preparation of supper, ushered in a visitor.

It was Mr. Cathcart, Mary Bisset's headmaster.

At the sound of his voice Mary herself came forward with somewhat heightened colour.

He was a tallish, dark, official-looking man, with a formal manner and a rather melancholy address, as if the responsibility of so many children had taken all the youth and boyishness out of him.

"Why, Miss Bisset, then you did not go to the hospital after all!" he said at the sight of her.

"No," said Mary, a little breathlessly, "I knew nothing about it till Dick told me, and then after all he was called elsewhere!"

Kit somehow felt a strange, angry resentment against this man begin to steal over him. He noted jealously the flush on Mary's cheek when she spoke to him, and he did not understand that she was trying to preserve the balance between truth and the reputation of a brother like Dick.

"I did not expect to find any one except your father,"

said the schoolmaster, "but I thought I might have the benefit of some conversation with him."

To this Mr. Bisset did not answer. There was the sound of another voice at the door, one anxious and a little querulous. The Lecturer was listening with straying attention, and did not hear Mr. Cathcart's last words.

Presently his wife came to the door of the little parlour.

"William, you are wanted," she said.

The Infidel Lecturer went out and almost immediately returned.

"Mother," he said, quietly, "do not wait up for me. I am needed over in the Grassmarket. I may not be home all night."

"Very well, William," said his wife, evidently accustomed to such an event.

"Will you walk a little way with me, Mr. Kennedy?" said Mr. Bisset, going to the corner to take a great oaken staff in his hand; "we will talk as we go. I am sorry to bid you good-night so soon, Mr. Cathcart, but a sick man wishes to see me. Such things happen even to a pastor without a church, an apostle without a creed!"

He smiled slightly and held out his hand. The schoolmaster took it with an alacrity which was not lost upon Kit. He on his part could do nothing but prepare to obey. He shook hands with Mary without looking at her, and though there was a slight smile upon her lips, her eyes followed him sympathetically down the stairs. When Kit thought that she had gone in he stole one swift glance back, and lo! there she was still, her arms on the rail, looking down on him. Her face lit up quickly as if she were saying, "Tell him!" She waved her hand gracefully and kindly towards him, and somehow Kit went out into the whirling snowstorm strangely comforted. Though he had left the schoolmaster in the little lamp-lit parlour alone with his sweetheart, Kit somehow felt that he had taken the soul of Mary Bisset out with him into the storm.

The Infidel (as Mrs. Christison most unjustly called him) was wrapped in a huge Inverness cloak of grey frieze, with a collar which stood up about his ears. Kit, who had never possessed a great coat in his life, simply buttoned his stout tweed jacket up to the neck and strode on beside his friend.

It was a strangely altered world into which these two emerged, the first snowstorm of the year, and already it had wrapped all the city in a white clinging mystery. The wind from the north still kept the pavements fairly clean, but a thin and steady drift blew low along them which banked itself deeply at every turning. And there were growing wreaths piling themselves in swirls at the angles of the narrow alleys through which they made their way steadily towards the Grassmarket.

"Now tell me about your father," said Mr. Bisset, kindly.

And Kit told all he knew. He spoke of his grandfather, the ruling Elder in the Kirk on the Hill. He told of his mother's marriage, and of all the unhappiness which came after, of the loss of the Dornal, and the stone-breaking by the roadside. Then, softening the details as much as possible, he told of his first sight of the "Orra Man," of their compact, and how it was carried out. He related the story of the long nights of three winters in the Black Sheds, of the early summer mornings that broke ere they had finished their work, and of all the growing knowledge which had ended in the winning of the First Galloway Bursary.

And as he talked the hand of the Infidel Lecturer fell upon his shoulder and remained there. William Bisset heard Kit to the end and then he spoke.

"We'll make a man of you yet," he said; "but first we must make a man of your father!"

They were crossing the wide space at the higher corner of Candlemaker Row, now tortured and tumultuous with whirling snow. Greyfriars' Bobbie, coated white as he must often have been during his lonely vigils on his master's grave, looked down upon them as they turned down into the dark trench of houses.

"I will think over this and find your father," said
Mr. Bisset ; "no one can long be hid in this little city,
though there are some queer places in it, too. But I
can go where the police dare not. It is my one
privilege. Now, do you turn back!"

"Let me come all the way with you," said Kit,
impulsively.

The Lecturer seemed to hesitate a moment.

"Well," he said, "you may see some strange things
and observe what you call religion from a new angle.
Still, if you wish it you may come. Walk straight after
me, and keep your eyes only on that which immediately
concerns us."

The two men crossed the white-sheeted causeway of
the Grassmarket, and at the further side dived into a
dense rabbit warren of houses. But Mr. Bisset did not
hesitate a moment. As they went down the steps a
policeman turned his lantern into their faces inquiringly.

"Beg pardon, Mr. Bisset," said the man, "I thought
it was a pair o' my 'lambs.' It's no a time to be out
on pleasure. And them that's in the Grassmarket this
nicht has a reason!"

"All right, Fergus," said the Lecturer, "I have a
reason!"

"I'll wager that!" answered Constable Fergus, and
shut off the light of his lantern with a snap.

"Now take my hand," said Kit's guide ; "it is scarce
canny walking here."

He went down many steps, and then with equal
confidence went up. He passed dark doors and wound
round spiral staircases, through whose iron-barred
windows the wind whistled and the sparse snow drifted.
Halfway up a man opened a door and held a candle into
their faces, going in again with a muttered curse of
disappointment, and leaving the darkness more complete
than ever.

At last Mr. Bisset stopped. He paused a moment as if to
listen. But it was as silent within as it was dark without.

A smell of chloride of lime oozed from under the
door. Mr. Bisset rapped. A faint light stirred inside,

filtering round the ill-fitting frame, and shooting illuminated arrows from latch and keyhole.

A woman stood within barring entrance, a tall gaunt woman with a wisp of grey hair across her brow.

Sullenly and silently she drew back at sight of Mr. Bisset, who passed austerely in as if unconscious of her obvious ill-will. He strode straight along a narrow passage, his great shoulders brushing either wall equally, and Kit followed at his heel.

Both worlds were growing bigger before the First Bursar of the United Galloway Societies.

His guide entered a small kitchen room, clean and carefully tidied up. The tiles of the fireplace had been recently whitened, and the ribs of the grate were blacked and polished. A kettle sang thinly on the hob. There were two closed and curtained beds along one wall, and upon them small heaped mounds told of the sleep of childhood. As Kit stopped one of the heaps moved a little, and he caught the glint of a black eye and a tossed elf lock that fell over a thin inquiring face.

On the other side was a larger bed, also let into the wall and curtained with faded chintz. The latter had been so often washed that the colour and pattern were almost indistinguishable. Nevertheless everything was clean as country linen.

A man, small-featured, haggard, hollow of eye and cheek lay sunkenly on the bed. His thin hand drooped over the coverlet. He had a brush of stubbly grey hair like a dragoon's helmet on top of his head. A shoemaker's bench and stool in a corner betrayed his occupation. His face wore a querulous, almost acrid expression in moments of pain, but at other times a certain unwilling nobility crept into it. There was at least no doubt that his eyes lit up when they fell upon his visitor.

The cobbler held out his hand, lifting it from the patchwork as if it had been a dead weight.

" Ye hae come ! " he said.

" You are very ill, Bartholomew ! " said Mr. Bisset, touching the man's wrist lightly, and as it seemed mechanically, in search for his pulse.

"I am going, sir—going to find out!" He smiled as he said it.

"Ah, Bartholomew, I envy you to-night if that be so," said the Lecturer, sadly, "that is the best after all. They have called us Agnostics so long—Know Nothings. You have your chance now to prove them wrong."

"I would not be sorry, sir," said the cobbler, "but for these."

And a slight movement of his hand included his wife and the sleeping children. Kit caught again the restless black eye out of the heaped coverlets in the other bed.

"Don't go hard because o' me, Bartholomew," said the woman, coming to the bedside. "I have kept the poor children from starvation before and I can look after them again, praise God. It will be better telling you now to think of your immortal soul."

She cast a savage glance at the Lecturer, which however seemed to be absorbed by the mild persistence of his glance.

"To be faithful, honest, diligent, owing no man anything—these are no bad recommendations to any true God," said Mr. Bisset, gently, "and Bartholomew need not fear to meet such an One on his journeyings."

"Be soft with her, sir," murmured Bartholomew the cobbler, "ours is the sterner, the more barren creed. It is not fit for her; she is a woman."

"It is best so," said Mr. Bisset, "I would not have it otherwise. Let every man be fully persuaded, did not the Tarsan say?"

"Who is this young man?" said the cobbler, looking across at Kit with a strange look. It was as if death were in speech with life, one world hailing another.

"He is a young student who lives beside me; I brought him to talk to on the way. It is a very stormy night."

The dying man smiled.

"Aye," he said; "I wonder if in half an hour I shall be looking down on the house-tops? It is a rough night to be going so far."

As he grew feebler he motioned the Lecturer nearer to his lips. And Kit, seeing that they wished to speak privately together, moved over to a scrubbed white-wood chair by the side of the bed where he had twice seen the black beady eyes and the tangled elf locks.

Kit had a penny in his pocket. He took it out and stealthily held it on the edge of the mattress. There were two black eyes watching him now. The tall woman moved gauntly and mechanically athwart the fireplace, and rubbed a brass knob here and a piece of iron there. Kit held the penny a little higher. A hand almost like the beak of a bird shot out from under the torn blankets and pecked it away.

"Yes, Bartholomew," Kit could hear the voice of the Lecturer, "she shall be cared for. We of the Many Minds are poor, and it would not be well for her to be among us, at any rate. But I know a man——"

"What, not a minister?" cried the voice of the cobbler. "No minister would trouble himself with the widow of a dead unbeliever."

"You are no unbeliever, Bartholomew. Only fools are unbelievers. And, at any rate, Alexander Strong would not care what you were. I promise you your wife and bairns shall not want."

Mr. Bisset rose.

"You are right," said the cobbler, his eye painfully bright. "Let there be no farewells on the platform when the train goes out into the night. It is better so. Good-bye, sir. Wife, see that the children are covered. It is a bitter blast outside. And I want you to lie down. You must be tired. I am going to turn my face to the wall. I must try to sleep."

And as Kit followed Mr. Bisset out he looked back. The cobbler had already turned his frail body away from them. The gaunt and silent wife was arranging his pillow gently, and from the bed on the other side Kit caught sight of the dark head of a girl of eight. The penny was fitted into one of her eye sockets, and she was regarding him with a haughty and even indignant stare.

21

CHAPTER XLV.

THE BROKEN HINGES.

THE Lecturer and Kit walked rapidly through the white deserted streets till they reached a tall house in a fashionable quarter. Mr. Bisset stopped before it. The windows were dark, but a little faint light came from the hall, filtering through the ground-glass of the fanlight and revealing the number. It was 52, and the figures will recall things high as heaven, warm as the Forgiving Love to many hearts. There are hundreds of us who will never forget Number Fifty Two till the sods rattle down above our breasts.

From this point Mr. Bisset's proceedings were not only singular but even suspicious. He went off into the middle of the road and groped about in the thin snow till he had collected a handful of pebbles the size of peas. These he began to throw up at the range of unlighted windows with but indifferent success.

" Which window do you want to hit ? " said Kit, feeling that here at last was something that he could do better than his companion.

" The second on the left above the porch," said the Lecturer.

" Whose house is this ? " said Kit, making the pebbles rap regularly on the glass of the window which Mr. Bisset had designated.

After a little a light sprang into being behind the blind. The window was thrown up, and a face appeared dimly white against the dark behind.

" Well, who is it ? " said a voice, as if quite accustomed to such midnight summonses. " Oh, Bisset,

bless you, man—come up directly! Here is the key.
I keep it tied to a string on purpose."

"I can't come up, Mr. Strong," said the Lecturer.
"I have to go on elsewhere. There's a woman and her
children would be the better for seeing you. So I came
along to tell you. The man is dying or dead. He was
one of my people. But the wife is a Christian and
needs you. Last house on the right in the Tinkler's
Close off the Grassmarket—you know the place."

"All right! I know it!" said the voice, cheerily.
"I'll be down in a minute. Any use taking wine and
things?"

"None," returned Mr. Bisset, "but something from
the poor's-box would not come wrong."

Kit and his friend stamped about for a minute or
in the roadway to keep the blood moving in their veins.
Kit saw Mr. Strong for the first time under the fanlight.
Then the minister came out, a tall squarely-built figure
with a leonine head and a countenance grave and
kindly, capable, too, of kindling into an Isaiah fire upon
occasion—a man affectionate in private, tender of heart
above most, but dangerous to cross when charged with
his message and when the decks were cleared for action.

"Come along, Bisset—talk to me as we go," said
Alexander Strong, swinging a rough-checked shepherd's
plaid about his shoulders and thumping the pavement
with his unshod staff. "But who is this with you?"

"Another of your people," said the Lecturer, "a lad
from the country, recently come to the city with a
bursary, a clever head, and an ignorant heart. Let him
come and see you. You'll do him no harm. He has a
father, too, he was telling me. But I think I can best
look after him."

"Come and see me on Saturday about lunch time,
and we will have a talk. That is my hour!" said
Alexander Strong to Kit.

Then to the Lecturer he said, "And now for your
friend's wife. What had we best do for her?"

And there in the black deeps of the night, under the
canopy of the drifting snow, the Agnostic Lecturer and

the Christian Teacher conjointly laid their plans for the helping of poor human creatures.

In this fashion they came again to the cobbler's house. Once more they went up the darksome twists of the stair, Alexander Strong trampling between them with his vigorous hillman's stride.

As they opened the door they heard the sound of a woman sobbing. The cobbler's wife was straightening the limbs of the man who had been her husband.

"He's gane—my Bartholomew's gane withoot a word!" said the woman. "Oh, if my man is lost because of unbelief, I want to be lost too!"

"And you are the man that did it, too," she cried with sudden fury, turning sharply on the Lecturer. Then she saw Alexander Strong.

He came forward and took her hand gently. Without a word he went across the floor to the bed, and stood a long while gazing down at the serene face of the dead.

The Infidel Lecturer drew Kit away, and as they closed the door they heard the voice of the Preacher of the Gospel saying gently, "Fear not! It is written, 'To his own Lord he standeth or falleth. Yea, he shall be made to stand, for the Lord hath power to make him stand.'"

And his hand was upraised over the dead face as if in benediction.

"Come away and leave them. That is his work, not yours or mine!" said Mr. Bisset as they went homeward.

*　　　*　　　*　　　*　　　*

When Kit arrived at the door of his lodgings he found Mrs. Christieson still out of bed. He expected, and perhaps deserved, a word of censure for his late hours. But his landlady had something else on her mind.

"Oh, Maister Kennedy," she said, as soon as she saw him, "sic a turn up as there has been here since ye gaed oot."

She paused for breath, though she had not been

climbing the stairs. Then she went on, " Maister Grier
didna come hame till eleven. He had met in wi' somebody frae his ain countryside, and stayed crackin'.
And then there cam' a tramplike man and wad be in
to see you. I said him nay, but he wadna be said nay
to. And faith, but there was something commandin'
aboot the craitur too. Sae I took him ben, thinkin'
that every minute Maister Grier wad be back, for he
was never late before. I gaed doon to the baker's to
get the loaf-bread for the breakfast. The stupid body
hadna sent it. And wad ye believe me, when I cam'
back the door was open to the wa', and there wasna a
soul in the hoose. Oh, gang and see that a' is richt!
For I'll no sleep this nicht gin ocht has been ta'en
through my fault."

Kit went into the room where Rob Grier was
already in bed sleeping the sleep of the physically
tired and constitutionally healthy. He went directly
to his little desk. His heart stood still when he saw
that it had been burst apart at the hinges. He un-
locked it and the lid fell off. The remaining eighteen
pounds of his Bursary money were gone !

The Universe ran round and round as he stood
staring, and had he not grasped the back of a chair
he might have fallen. Nevertheless, Kit was no
weakling.

In a minute he had gripped himself, and walked
steadily to the door, at which appeared the agitated
face of Mrs. Christieson.

" Was the man who asked for me tall and thin, with
grey hair and a cut across the forehead ? " he asked.

" That's the man," cried Mrs. Christieson, much
relieved ; "and bless me, sir, when I look at ye, he
raither favoured yoursel'. Maybe he was a relative ?
Then ye hae fand a' richt in your room ! "

" All is right—perfectly right, Mistress Christieson,
thank you ! " said Kit Kennedy.

" The Lord be thankit for that, for I was a feared
woman this nicht ! " said his landlady, as she closed the
door.

And then the First Galloway Bursar sat down amid
the ruins of his prospects to think what he should do.

He could not stop attending his classes and go back
to service because he had taken the money of the
Societies, and was under contract to finish his session
and forward his certificates to the secretary.

He could not go on living upon Mrs. Christieson
with no prospect of paying his bills.

Still less could he accuse his teacher, his benefactor—
his father, of the theft.   If he had taken the money, he
was clearly not accountable for his actions any more
than he had been that night of the declaration of the
prize-winner, when Kit had found him in the parlour of
the Blue Boar in Cairn Edward.

So, throwing his plaid about his shoulders, and
putting down the gas he had no longer the right to
waste, Kit Kennedy went and stood in the window.
And all through the watches of the sombre night the
white flurries veered and swirled, and the lamp shadows
wavered forlornly across the sidewalks of the snow-
shrouded city.

CHAPTER XLVI

THE PRETTY GIRL GROWS PRACTICAL.

KIT had ten days before him during which to make good the loss of his bursary. Then he must settle with Mrs. Christieson for his fortnight's board and lodging. His college fees were paid, so that, save for the buying of class books, he was safe in that direction. But in ten days he would be more than a pound in the debt of the honest woman, while all that remained to him was sixpence, which he discovered in the corner of his waistcoat pocket.

It was the afternoon of the following day before Kit saw his father. The student had struggled through the day somehow. His classes had hummed themselves away. Rob Grier had propounded starting posers on the rules of Greek composition, which Kit had answered at random.

But it was Professor Aitchison who stung him into a sort of temporary interest, and that more on account of his province than from any personal feeling.

Professor Aitchison embodied patriotism to the university. Picturesquely Bohemian himself, he encouraged all manner of vagabondage among his students. If these fortunate youths did not learn much Greek, at least they never forgot their acquaintance with that fine, impulsive, clean-thoughted, noble gentleman Professor Angus Aitchison of the University of Edinburgh.

But without doubt the man of genius could be excessively trying at times.

Entering the class-room like a whirlwind, he was halfway through the Lord's Prayer in Greek before the men could rise from their seats. Then still in a

blind hurry he would dash into the subject nearest (for
the time being) to his big bairnly heart.

"Gentlemen, I have unfortunately come without my
lecture this morning. But that is the less to be re-
gretted that I find in this morning's *Thistle* the most
truly diabolical article, sufficient to bring a Sodom-
curse, a very Gomorrah-brimstone-cloud upon this city.
I will now make a few remarks upon the *Thistle*-man!"

Then Angus Aitchison waved his oaken staff round
his head and declaimed for forty eloquent minutes.

When he had calcined, pulverised, and finally dis-
persed the *Thistle* miscreant he would return to his
class.

"Dear me, we have only a few minutes left. Mr.
Fred Stewart, what do you mean by sitting there idle
all the day long? You are an unprofitable servant,
sir! That's a bad translation, but a good fact. Read
the first ten lines of our lesson for the day, and be quick
about it!"

This morning it was Kit who, at ten minutes to the
hour, was called upon to read a page of the Iliad.

Kit translated with his mind upon the burst hinges
of his little desk. But sheer instinct led him through.

The Professor stopped him.

"You are translating like a saw-mill, Mr. Kennedy.
Yes, with about as much heart and genius as a saw-
mill."

Then like a flash came the question, "Have you read
my translation of the Iliad into ballad measure?"

"No, sir," said Kit, who had not so much as heard
of that great work.

"No!" cried Angus Aitchison, throwing back his
head, "no porridge-fed Gallovidian ever read anything
half so good as my translation of Homer. Sit down,
sir. Mr. Fred Stewart, do you go on."

Kit listened to the laughter of the class with a
curious detached coolness.

A week ago he would have blushed and subsided.
But he was both older and wiser now. And whether
he remained at college or went back to the plough-

tail, he did not purpose to be called "the porridge-fed Gallovidian" so long as one stone of that class remained upon another.

So he continued to stand up.

Fred Stewart was half through his page before the Professor noticed Kit still on his feet. He was declaiming a noble speech and marking the time with his hand as he trampled his way pridefully through the sonorous polysyllables.

"Sit down, sir. Sit down!" he cried. "What are you waiting for?"

"I am waiting for your apology, Professor Aitchison," said Kit, calmly.

"My apology—mine—what—why?"

Halted in full career, Angus Aitchison rose to his feet and stooped in a thunder-cloud of black gown and silvery hair from the rostrum upon Kit.

"Your apology for calling me a 'porridge-fed Gallovidian,' sir!"

And Kit kept his stand, respectful but determined.

Then that very fine gentleman Angus Aitchison approved himself greatly. He dropped in a moment the outer cloak of eccentricity, and rose to the height of his own true heart.

"Did I call you that? I had no right to call any man that. I do beg your pardon most heartily, Mr. Kennedy."

Then the Professor bowed to his student as the cheers of the class rang out.

"And now, Mr. Kennedy," he continued, "will you do me the honour to breakfast with me to-morrow morning?"

Verily it was a training in high-mindedness to sit under two such men as Jupiter Olympus, Professor of Humanity, and Angus Aitchison, Professor of Greek in the University of Edinburgh. From them the students learned everything but roots. And these they could acquire well enough from a couple of assistants at £100 a year apiece.

As Kit returned from college, the loss of his money

aching in his heart without remission, he met his father at the foot of the stairs which led to his lodgings.

The " Orra Man " was now dressed in a black frock coat, which buttoned tightly about his spare form, grey trousers, and well-made boots. His linen was clean, and the slight misfit conveyed no more than an impression that the wearer had been long ill, and had not again grown familiar with his own apparel.

" Will you come up ? " said Kit, and led the way up the grimy stair.

The Classical Master followed, so completely altered, that Mrs. Christieson, at gaze round the edge of the kitchen door, failed to recognise in the pale scholar of the afternoon the dreaded tramp of the night before.

When they reached the fifth floor room these two stood looking at each other squarely.

" I missed you last night," said the elder, " but I am not sorry, for we will talk more soberly and fitly to-day."

" He does not remember ! " said the son. And in his sick heart he rejoiced.

" Kit," said the Classical Master, sitting down and looking across at his son, " I did not intend to tell you last night. It was perhaps ill-judged and wrong, but the words sprang from me unawares. They are true words. I am your father, and because you know that, my life shall begin newly from to-day. Or else I will not live it at all. I met a man this morning who put the matter clearly. I knew him when I was a lad at Sandhaven. He is a friend of yours—Bisset, a city missionary, I think."

" Yes," said Kit, " a kind of missionary."

The Classical Master went on without appearing to hear.

" Now I see clearly that if I cannot use life well, at least it lies within my power not to misuse it to the hurt of others. More than that, Mr. Bisset has put me in the way of earning my bread honestly. I am to have three hours coaching every day at a crammer's, which will leave me time to look after your work also."

The eager look had come back to the eyes of the

" Orra Man." Once more the eternal hope was dawning for him, and Christopher Kennedy, B.A., was as
keen as ever on the scent of the ideal. He picked up
an exercise which lay on the table.

" Pshaw ! " he said, " wooden—wooden. We must
do better than this, Kit. Where were you in the last
class-examination ? "

" Fourth ! " said Kit, hanging his head.

" And first at the entrance—that will never do.
There has been slackness somewhere. We will change
all that. I am free at six. Expect me to-morrow, as
soon after that as I can get lodgings. I bid you good-
bye now."

He paused on the stairs and beckoned Kit to approach.

" One word," he said, softening his voice. " You are
not altogether in want of money, I hope ? I happen
to be temporarily in funds."

" I am not in need of money," said his son, lying to
his father with a clear and steady eye.

And then with jaunty carriage and alert air the
Classical Master went down the stair. He regarded the
public-houses with a proud look. He even walked twice
past the first, smelling with disgust the mingled odour
of bad tobacco and stale beer which trailed out from its
open door.

" Thank God, that is done with ! " he said.

 * * * * *

Kit breakfasted next morning with Professor Aitchison, and had it proven to him, as it were out of the
whirlwind, that Gaelic was the finest language in the
world, that Greek came next, that English was not a
language at all, that a song was better than a sermon,
that Episcopacy might be the religion of a gentleman,
but that Presbytery was the religion for a man—and,
lastly, that personal vanity was the only deadly sin.

He went away in the clear brisk sunlight of the winter
forenoon, carrying with him a warmth about the heart
which lasted all day from the mere contact of Angus
Aitchison, gentleman, scholar, poet—and play-actor.

And it says much for his entertainment that he was

half a mile from the plain little house at the corner of Frederick Street before he remembered the dark cloud which had shut so suddenly down upon his soul.

Kit was naturally reticent of trouble. He called on the Reverend Alexander Strong, who sat in his study with a paper-covered volume of Barbera's Dante in his hand. A cup of cold tea was at his elbow and his feet were on the table.

"Ah, I have been expecting you—I thought you would never come," cried the minister, heartily. "Do you smoke? No! It is a bad habit. I am going to give it up—ah, *next week*."

And he lighted a black and polished clay as he spoke, shifting a red coal dexterously between his fingers and looking calmly at Kit all the while.

The house in Melville Street, occupied by Alexander Strong as a kind of barracks, impressed Kit with a curious sense of brotherhood. He felt instinctively that it was all the same to this man whether he was a chimney-sweep or the owner of millions, famous or infamous, witty or stupid, saint or convict. At best and worst he was a brother to Alexander Strong, and—he had a soul to be saved.

But the minister did not ask him to come to church. He did not even recommend his Bible-class. He had no panacea save the strong, comfortable shake of his right hand. He talked gravely and confidentially of books and men and things, and having asked Kit's opinion he considered his reply, not as a compliment, but respectfully and as equally worthy of attention with his own.

As they went down the stairs the minister put his hand on Kit's shoulder.

"You are a bursar, I hear, as I was," he said, "so you won't want money yet. But if you do, you know where to come. You would probably like better to take a lift from a poor man like me than from any one else."

"Thank you," said Kit, choking a little; "I don't know why you should say that to me. But I am not in want of money."

"Very well!" said the minister, "but all the same don't forget if the thing should happen."

But the pride which the scholar-gentleman and the man-and-brother could not overcome was broken down by a girl.

Dick Bisset looked in early on the afternoon of the day after the supper at Sponton's.

"Good biz that you did bring Mary home last night," he said; "her chief came along, and if he had found out she wasn't at the Hospital, it would have given away the whole blooming show. But it is all right. He's gone on Mary no end, and I tell her she had better marry him and have done with it—position, tin, and all that. But there's no hurry. Let her have her fling first like yours truefully, Richard Bisset."

Kit said nothing. His heart could not well be sorer. He fingered a slim Tacitus, red-covered and with "Capio lumen" upon it. With all his soul he wished Dick Bisset would go.

"Say, Kennedy," cried that hero, suddenly, "do you want to get on to a winner? I can put you straight. A sov. will do it. I tell you I copped a quid or two yesterday that the old man don't know of. It takes it all to go the pace. Best girls aren't run on soft sawder these days!"

Here Rob Grier trampled in, and, with a brief nod to Dick, and taking no notice at all of Kit, he pitched his wet hat on the sofa and drew in a chair to his books.

"Well, so-long, Kennedy; you're going to be lively, I can see," said Dick, "so am I. I wish you joy of 'Hocus-pocus-saveloy-sap'!"

And he laughed — for, strangely enough, Dick considered this funny.

"The examination's only a week off now," said Rob Grier, with a kind of entreaty in his voice; "you are going to stop in and work, aren't you?"

"No," said Kit, "I feel curiously unsettled to-night. I think I shall go for a walk."

Rob Grier threw himself back in his chair, a sort of darkly angry look on his plain strong face.

"Now I tell you, Kit Kennedy," he said, dourly nodding his head, "you had a long way the start of me. But if you don't look out I'm going to come in ahead."

"All right," answered Kit, smiling sadly; "I for one shall not be sorry."

"No," thundered Rob the Smith of Garlies, "*you* won't be sorry! Who said you would? You haven't enough sense. But there's an old man down in Galloway that you told me was breaking whin-stones on the roadside for your sake, and thinking of you as he cracked every one. He'll be sorry. And you've got a mother, haven't you? And if you are the man I take you for, there's a girl somewhere that'll be sorry. Besides (he was speaking truculently now) I don't want to have to doctor the certificates that I send in to that Secretary-duck over in St. Andrew's Square. I want the credit for what I do. And I sha'n't take it unless you are before me, as you ought to be. So now, there's for you!"

Kit started up and held out his hand. The ex-blacksmith gripped it in a vice.

"That's all right," he said, the anger cooling out of his voice, "but what's up anyway? You are striking off the iron somehow. You can't have got through all your money? Any bad news from home?"

"No," said Kit, "it's all right."

Rob Grier shook his head.

"You are a dour dog," he said; "you won't tell me, of course. Now mind you, I haven't much, but if you are in a hole—well, ye ken Rob Grier by this time."

And Kit rose quickly and went out, for the kindness that ringed him round made him afraid of that bugbear of youth—the making a fool of himself.

Kit ran downstairs. It was a dank, softish night, with greasy pavements and an unfulfilled promise of the frost breaking up. The wind, which since the morning had been sweeping the streets clean of snow, had died away, and the city was full of the damp exhalations of steaming tramway horses and sodden half-slaked ash-bins.

Kit turned moodily into the current of the main southern thoroughfare. There is a tide along it which runs strongly north all the forenoon, and as strongly back again in the late afternoon and evening. He was breasting its later flood now, and the sight of the lighted shops and garish shows of Christmas cards in the newsagents' windows jarred upon him. The world was very black just then, and Kit withdrew himself deeper into his own soul.

It was when passing the barred and ballustered front of the Surgeons' Hall, where he had first met Mary Bisset, that something in front of him caused him to lift his head. Hitherto he had been looking at the ground and mechanically avoiding the passers-by. But now he looked up alertly.

For there, not a score of yards from him, was the Pretty Girl marching along with a little sheaf of books under her arm caught in an elastic band. She was carrying herself, thought Kit, with even more than her usual inimitable lightness. He stopped and held out his hand. She began at once to tell him how Mr. Cathcart had waited till her mother was deadly weary, and had even disgraced herself by yawning in his face. But Kit did not answer. He only turned and walked slowly back with the girl, as if it were a settled and accepted thing that he should do so.

Presently Mary Bisset stayed the current of her gladsome gossip. "What is the matter, Kit?" she said, looking intently into his face.

"Nothing," asserted Kit, more gloomily than before.

Mary smiled a little private smile confined to the side of her face furthest from her companion. She thought that he was sulky about the visit of Mr. Cathcart. And being a sensible girl she was not a bit sorry that he should feel that way about the matter.

"It will do him good," she said to herself; "they are all apt to take things too easily."

It is curious that she never thought of connecting

Kit's gloom with the man who had claimed him for a son, after stopping them both at the door of the Elysium.

To Mary Bisset, innocently conscious of her own attractiveness and of Kit's admiration, only one subject appeared likely to influence his moods.

At last Kit burst out.

"This is good-bye," he said.

"Good-bye!" faltered Mary Bisset; then with a slight smile she continued, "You are angry with me—you are joking?"

"No," said Kit, blurting out his trouble at last, and glad to be done with it. "I am disgraced, whatever I do. I have lost my bursary money. It was stolen out of my desk late last night. I cannot stay at college and run more deeply into debt. Yet I have to send my certificates to the secretary because I have taken their money."

As he spoke Mary Bisset's face grew pale, and her sweet lips fell pitifully away from each other.

"But why," said she, breathlessly, "why do you not apply to the police?"

Kit smiled grimly, thinking neither of his sweetheart nor yet of her words, but of his own sick heart.

"Because the only two who entered my room were my own friend Rob Grier and—and my father! That is the reason."

"Your father!" cried Mary, incredulously; "the man whom we saw at the music hall—he was really your father?"

"I have no choice but to believe so," answered Kit.

As Kit spoke they had been nearing the defile of houses, down which they were wont to turn in order to reach their homes.

Mary touched Kit's arm.

"Don't let us go in yet," she said; "let us walk across the Meadows and talk it all over!"

Kit, wrapped in his trouble, gloomily acquiesced. It had begun to rain a little, and Mary Bisset wanted to pick up her skirts before venturing through the grimy needle's eye of Archer's Hall.

"Will you hold my umbrella for me?" she said, glancing up at Kit.

Kit reached a hand for the closely enwrapped, lady-like article of protection, which he held like a toy. He himself walked brow forward in all weathers and took the rains of heaven as they fell. But the girl's practical words awoke him out of his selfish sorrow.

He held the umbrella over Mary's head.

"It is kind of you to mind," as he spoke he stumbled in his speech; "why should you care that I am ruined —disgraced?"

He said the last word with a sort of sob. He thought of going back to his mother and those who had been so proud of him. The white flag would still be flying on the pine tree on the lochside slope, and he knew that his mother would look towards it at morn and even.

Mary Bisset's lips were pressed closely together now. They denoted a kind of womanly determination equally foreign to the soft childish curves of her cheek and to the sweetness of her eyes. She was rather longer than she need have been in settling the swing of her skirts to her mind. For there was that in her eyes which Mary did not care to trust even to the gloomy November night. Then at last she laid her hand on Kit's arm and drew him away to the right, along the little walk through the Meadows, with the bare boughs dripping overhead and the lights of the city winking mist-blurred through a pale bluish haze.

"Kit Kennedy," she said, sharply, "you call your-self a man, yet you are ready to give in at the first obstacle. I have been going to speak to you for some time. I am glad the chance has come now. You have been taking things far too easily. You tried for a bursary. You won it. And—well, you have done nothing since. I know, for there is one of our teachers attending your classes."

"Mr. Cathcart!" said Kit, gloomily.

"No—not Mr. Cathcart," Mary went on, "but it does not matter if it were Mr. Cathcart. The thing is so. And I dared not tell you. But now, when you speak of meanly giving up—why, I can speak, and I will."

"What can I do?" said Kit, who was becoming a little sulky. He had not been so spoken to ever since he began to think well of himself.

"Why, at the very first check you would cast all to the winds. I tell you, Christopher Kennedy," she flashed round upon him so swiftly that Kit stopped. The pretty girl stood fronting him, one small gloved finger pressed peremptorily into the palm of the other hand, with the action she used when emphasizing a fact to a stubborn class (and the inspection day was near). "I tell you plainly, I am twice the man you are. You think I am only a girl, and in one way I am. But I have kept myself and helped my father and mother with the rent ever since I was thirteen. Then they would not take me as a pupil teacher, because my father was an Infidel Lecturer. But I became a pupil teacher all the same. Parents would not send their children to be taught by me for the same reason. They took them from school. I went and saw them—and—the children came back again. Then I could not be admitted to the training colleges here because they were denominational. I went alone to London at seventeen and got through my two years there. With worse than no influence I gained an assistantship in a school where influence does nearly everything."

Mary was talking swiftly now, still standing in front of Kit. Both of them had forgotten all else. And more than one passer-by turned and smiled at the tableau. Kit, a tall awkward lad, stood holding an umbrella over his own head, while this slender, emphatic little person demonstrated fiercely into the palm of her gloved hand.

"A lovers' quarrel!" they said to themselves, and retailed the matter as a joke at their cosy tea-tables on the other side of the Meadows.

Kit was dumb before Mary's outbreak. Yet even in the turmoil of his thoughts he could not help being stimulated and quickened. Mainly, however, he was

thinking how pretty she looked. The light of one of
the rare lamps fell directly upon her piquant face and
flashing eyes. The sweetness seemed gone from these
last, and in its place there was such a flashing contempt
for cowardice, such an ardency of resolve, so pronounced a snap and glitter of belligerence, that Kit
could do nothing but stare.

"You are lovely !" he stammered, as if ignorant that
he was speaking at all.

Mary Bisset stamped her foot.

" Pshaw," she cried, " that proves it. I speak to you
for your good. I tell you my heart as I have not done
to my own father, and you have nothing to answer but
that ! Did I not tell you that I was twice the man you
were ? You ought to be ashamed of yourself, Kit
Kennedy."

But all the same, because no woman can stand and
look at the admiration in the eyes of a man who—
well, who is worth taking the trouble with that Mary
Bisset was taking with Kit, the sharpness oozed out
of her declamation, though the earnestness remained.

After all, Mary Bisset was a pretty girl as well as a
very practical person. And she knew her merit on
both scores.

But she was not going to be less practical because
Kit admired her, and because even in the midst
of her tonic indignation she could see (as it were)
her own quite satisfactory person reflected in the
mirror of Kit's eyes. Still Mary was conscious that
she ought to have been annoyed, and this made her
more than ever determined that Kit should pay for
the feeling.

"And now," she said, with a vicious snap of her
white and regular teeth, " instead of standing up to
trouble like a man, you would basely turn your back
on it as soon as the wind blows. You mean to dis-
appoint your friends and break their hearts, to rejoice
your enemies—and—I shall be sorry. I am sorry now
—that is, unless you have something more in you than
running away."

Kit had thought specially well of himself in this matter. He had hidden his trouble successfully from his father, from Mr. Strong, from Rob Grier. Hitherto his conscience had continuously applauded itself. But this was decidedly looking at the matter from a new stand-point.

"What am I to do?" said Kit, yet more mournfully.

"First, give me a share of my own umbrella," said Mary, still indignant, "and then walk along like a reasonable being."

But within herself she was saying, "I am doing it all for his good."

Which process is rarely pleasant for the beneficiary.

"*Do?*" said Mary, suddenly losing patience as the helplessness of Kit's question came back to her mind, "well, first of all—try. What does your companion do—teach in the evenings. Why cannot you? Get some work to do out of college hours. Your preparation, by your own account, does not take so much of your time. My father will get you some, if you are not too proud to take what turns up."

"God knows I am not proud," said Kit Kennedy, earnestly.

"Well, then," said Mary, relenting a little, "I am sure you will do very well. And you will never speak any more of going away or giving up college? Now we must go home. They will be wondering where I am. And besides (as if the state of the elements had occurred to her for the first time) it is raining and my hat is soaking. More than that, I have talked to you as no girl ought to do. And they were quite right to try to stop me teaching in the schools. For I never do what I ought. But all the same, they did not."

Thus Mary talked on as they left the twinkling gloom and converging lamps of the Meadows alone in the misty "haar." * She did not want Kit to say any more. She could see perilous things—things for which she was not ready, things which were better unsaid for

* Haar, i.e., the soul-chilling, body-freezing, easterly mist off the German Ocean.

the present—hovering in his eyes and trembling upon his tongue.

They got to the foot of the stair. Kit paused to take down the umbrella.

"Mary," he began, in a thick, suppressed voice, speaking with more than his old difficulty.

"Good night," she said, lightly, "there is my father waiting for me. But you are not going to keep my umbrella to yourself now, if you have done so all the time we have been coming home. Deliver it up! And mind what I have said to you!"

So with a flash of admonitory finger, and a kind glance which she left Kit as a salve to his feelings, she tripped up the steps, leaving the young man standing limp and dazed by the greasy lintel of the common stair.

"Why," said Kit to himself after a long pause, "I thought she was only a girl!"

But at that moment Mary Bisset, who after all was only a girl, or at most only a woman, was lying on her little white bed with her face to the pillow.

"Oh, what shall I do—what *shall* I do?" she was saying in accents that were sobs. These are words that do not vary with rank or age, wisdom or experience, when women are in trouble.

The only difference is that after the storm is overpast some do know what to do, and upon such descends a time of clear shining after rain. And Mary Bisset was of those who do not spend long in fruitless mourning. For by the time her mother came knocking at the door she had risen, dabbed her eyes twice with *eau de cologne*, and begun to make up her mind for a second and more bitter interview. For as yet only the easier part of her work was done.

CHAPTER XLVII

MARY IMPROVES DICK'S ARITHMETIC.

" DICK, I want you ! "

"All right — plenty of time. I'm getting up," grumbled the voice of Dick Bisset from the little corner room which he occupied next Mary's. Then he lowered his tones, "Mary, go into the kitchen like a good girl and get a fellow some baking soda without letting father see you. I was on an awful tear last night, and I've a head on me as big as the Castle Rock ! "

Mary did as she was asked. Her father had already gone out. Her mother was putting the finishing touches to breakfast.

"Dick will need more than soda," Mary remarked to herself, "when I have done with him."

"Now be quick ; I'm all ready for school and I want to speak to you in the parlour ! "

Dick groaned audibly within his locked chamber door.

"It's no use taking trouble with me, old girl," he said ; "I am not your sort—nor yet father's. But, I say, I must have had a grandfather who made things hum in his time, though ! "

The last sentence he confided to his mirror, in which he regarded his swollen and discoloured face, his pale watery eyes, and closely-cropped reddish hair.

"Dick, you're not an Adonis," he admitted, shaking his head ; it's well you are smart, and can get the rhino together where another would starve. Or Violet, good girl as she is, would never look at you for your beauty."

Meanwhile Mary Bisset was walking up and down swiftly in the chill of the fireless parlour. It was the

early morning of a northern winter and grey with the
usual dampish haze. The streets gleamed a little and
the pavements appeared brighter than the gloomy sky.
A stray light or two blinked belatedly in the otherwise
blank front of the houses and was reflected on the greasy
pavements. A policeman drew his cloak closer about
his shoulders and looked eagerly out for his relief. He
smelt many breakfasts and stamped his feet. Shutters
were rattling endwise on the flags, being clattered into
bundles and made to disappear swiftly behind shop
doors. A maid with an untidy "bang" low on her
forehead was sweeping out the baker's shop opposite.
The policeman looked over at her with a friendly expression. But she slammed the door and went in. She
despised policemen. She hoped she was a step above
that. She was engaged (or the next thing to it) to a
clerk in an office at eight shillings a week.

Mary had a book in her hand, and was supposed to
be looking over her lesson for the day. Half a dozen
note-books, roll-books, and bundles of exercises, blotted
and scrawled, but interlineated in red with her own
neat and business-like writing, lay under the broad
indiarubber band which she used to keep them together
on her way to school.

Presently Dick came in grumbling. He rubbed his
hands together.

"Beastly cold," he muttered. "Say, old girl, spit
it out quick! Get it up off your mind whatever it is,
and let's get into the Christmas fireside. This sort of
thing don't conduce to moral resolution."

Mary stopped opposite her brother. The table with
the old-figured table-cloth was between them. The
light from the large double window fell greenish-grey
upon his face. He looked as unwholesome as possible,
a strange brother for Mary Bisset to lay claim to.

"Now, Dick Bisset," the sibilants fairly hissed,
driven forward by the impulsion of scorn and disgust
which was behind them, "will you give me the eighteen
pounds you stole from Kit Kennedy upstairs, or shall
I bring in a policeman?"

Dick had been stamping, shuffling, rubbing his hands disconsolately, and generally dragging himself frowsily together to face the actualities of the day.

But when Mary's words, as clearly enunciated as if spoken to a class, fell on his ear, he seemed to tumble inward upon himself like a collapsing house.

"Eh—eh?—what—what's that?" he gasped, gripping at the edge of the table and almost barking across at his sister as he thrust a suddenly whitened face nearer to her.

Mary Bisset repeated her request still more clearly.

"I allow you five minutes to make up your mind. Either give me the eighteen pounds you stole out of Kit Kennedy's desk; or I will go down and fetch up that policeman there!"

And with her hand Mary indicated the cloaked figure standing sentinel opposite the baker's shop.

"Hush—for God's sake, hush! My father will hear you," whispered Dick.

"My father is gone out—my mother is busy. We can talk!" said his sister.

"I didn't, Mary—by heaven, I didn't do it. I wasn't in his room a moment. He lent me the money," gasped Dick. "He lent me a pound—I own that, but I did not steal his money. What do you mean, Mary Bisset," he spoke louder now, "by charging your brother with being a common thief? I'll let you know, madam——"

Mary fixed him with the eye wherewith she subdued an unruly class or kept at bay a demonstrative admirer.

"Richard," she said, straightly, "where were you going when I opened the door to let out Mr. Cathcart? I saw you run upstairs into Mr. Kennedy's room. I waited till I heard you come down again. I knew you must have come home early from the Elysium on purpose. But I thought you wanted to see if Kennedy had got home. I know better now. Give me the money."

Then the face of Mr. Richard Bisset became pitiful to see.

"Don't tell my father that," he said; "he always

sides against me. I couldn't help it. I had to do it
or be disgraced. I was owing money at the office.
Besides, the 'swot' upstairs has plenty of money and he
thinks his pal took it—that smithy-shop chap with the
Roman beak. Mary, as you love me, as I am your
brother, don't say a word."

He came round the table and tried to take his
sister by the hand. His weak mouth was working, and
there was a gletty foam gathering about the wicks.

"Give me the money," repeated Mary Bisset,
implacably.

"Be merciful, Mary," he cried, sinking on his
knees; "see, I beg of you. You and I have always
been pretty good friends, haven't we, Mary?"

"Get up, you pitiful coward," cried his sister;
"stand up to your crime like a man. Give me back
every penny you stole from Kit Kennedy, without
which he is disgraced."

"I cannot—before God I cannot," groaned Dick,
still on his knees; "see here, sis, I had to put in ten
pounds yesterday morning into the till before the boss
came along to check my petty cash. And I spent the
rest—I gave some to——"

"No more lies, Dick; you couldn't spend eight
pounds in a single day even if the first part were true.
Come into your room!"

Mr. Richard Bisset raised himself to his full height
and endeavoured to assume a dignified expression.

"What if I bid you do your worst," he said, in a
bullying tone. "I can see the country swine has been
blabbing to you. How will it look if it comes out to
Mr. Cathcart and your managers that you suppered
that same night at Sponton's with the loser of the
money? How can he prove that he did not spend the
money himself, or take it in his pocket and get eased of
it on the way—aye, or give it to you himself? Oh,
such things have been before, young lady, and they can
be again. And your good name ain't quite——"

"I want the money," said Mary Bisset, so coldly and
bitterly that Kit Kennedy would not have known her

voice had he been in the next room; "whatever may come of it after, my word and his will be better than yours in court. Kennedy and his comrade will swear to the money being in the desk. I will swear that I saw you take it—that will be enough."

It would. Dick knew that it would be much more than enough. Besides, the fear of consequences which served him as conscience was in arms against him. That Mary was rather overstating her case did not occur to him. He collapsed all at once.

"As I live, Mary, I have not got more than a pound or two left, and I need the money badly."

"Turn out your pockets, and then I will see what I shall do."

"You shall have every penny if you won't split," said Dick, eagerly ladling crushed cigarettes, loose tobacco, matches, coppers, silver, and stray half-sovereigns out of his pockets.

"Open that case." Mary pointed to Dick's only lock-fast place—a little jewel-case she had once given him on his birthday. Her brother scowled at her with an almost murderous look in his eyes.

"I sha'n't do anything of the sort. There's nothing in there that concerns you—no, nor your precious friend upstairs either," he said, with an ugly sneer.

"Very well," said Mary Bisset, beginning to walk towards the outer door.

Dick saw the wet waterproof cover of the policeman's helmet still sentinel beneath the window.

"Don't go," he said, weakly; "I'll open it."

He fumbled in his waistcoat for the key, then fumbled a little longer with the lock. It opened quickly, and a torrent of letters and notes, on pink and other fanciful papers, tumbled out and slid with a soft rush upon the floor. They were mostly strongly scented, and mono-gramed in several colours.

Mary stirred these contumeliously with the point of her small but very practical boot. Then she lifted the lid of a little velvet-lined compartment. Two pounds in notes lay there, together with a white-wrapped jeweller's box. Mary coolly lifted and counted the money and slipped it into her pocket. Then she possessed herself of the jeweller's box and a receipted bill which lay beneath it.

Dick swept forward again.

"Leave that alone!" he cried, hoarsely; "that has nothing to do with you or with the money. I swear to you that it has not!"

Mary coolly stood her ground and opened the bill. It was dated the day before, and the date stamp attested the fact that it had been paid the same day to a firm of jewellers on the North Bridge.

Then she thrust the whole into her pocket.

"Go to your breakfast, Dick Bisset," she said, "and thank your Maker that you have a sister."

Dick made a final appeal.

"Mary," he said, in a shaky voice, "you and I have always been pals. I've never told about your going to church. I've never let on that you don't think as father does. Give me the money now. I'll pay that fellow upstairs as soon as I can raise the cash. I will —I promise it. I'll swear it if you like. But I need the money now, and I must have it."

"All I have to say to you I have said, Richard Bisset. Now go!" quoth this determined little lady.

Then the fellow's sudden anger burst into sudden fury.

"You call yourself a sister. You think yourself a Christian. I hate such sneaking. You will favour anybody but your own brother. I don't believe you are my sister at all. I've seen my father's papers, mind you. I know more than you think. You are no sister of mine. You're a foundling picked out of a hedge root!"

"Well," said Mary, careless of his raving, "at any rate I know more than father knows about some things. And if you don't take care I will tell him what I know."

"Take care! Take care yourself." Dick stood before his sister with clenched hands and injected eyes. "What would your father say if he knew that you went regularly to church—sneaked off to communion when he thought you were a walk in the park with me. And I've screened you for years, and expected you to stand up for me in your turn. More than that, suppose I split about your walking in the Meadows with Kennedy, and his meeting you every night on the way home. What would your father say to you then, Miss Immaculate Straightforwardness!"

"You can say or leave unsaid exactly what you please," said Mary; "perhaps my father knows more of these things than you imagine. At any rate (she added, looking meditatively out at the window), there always remains the policeman!"

"Children—children—what are you arguing about," cried Mrs. Bisset through the shut door. Then, dusting the meal from her hands, she opened it, and saw Dick standing at one side of the table and Mary on the other near the window with a book in her hand.

"Oh, I suppose Dick is helping you wi' your arithmetic," she said. "Ye were aye a kennin' weak in that, Mary!"

"No, mother," rejoined Mary Bisset, calmly walking to her breakfast in the kitchen, "this morning it is I who have been improving Dick's arithmetic!"

CHAPTER XLVIII

THE PRETTY GIRL TAKES CHARGE.

MARY made a very hurried breakfast in spite of her mother's anxious protests.

"Eh, lassie, ye are eatin' juist naething, and I trudged a' the road to the Cross Causeway for the kippers. Henderson's is the only shop for them in the Soothside. And ye hae plenty o' time. Dick, gar her eat something afore she gangs oot. The lassie will starve by dinner time. And then she will as like as no tak' nae mair than a biscuit or a 'bap' to her milk."

But Dick appeared preoccupied, and his whole contribution was a sullen, "Oh, let me alone!" in reply to his mother.

Mary rose, and having collected her books and methodically furled her umbrella she went out.

She had nearly an hour to spare. This was not one of her early mornings at school. She had time to visit a certain jeweller's shop in the North Bridge where she had business. A smart assistant was dusting a long array of glass cases, enclosing objects which the printed cards displayed above termed "Bijouterie," as unsympathetically as if they had been the legs of chairs.

An older man, with a look of responsibility upon his face, was taking off his coat in leisurely fashion before hanging it up in a little glazed office open at the top.

"I should like to return this ring," said Mary, opening the box and displaying its contents to the assistant. The youth smartened up noticeably at her entrance and greeted her with a bow, which, however, was half-checked when he heard the object of her visit so abruptly stated.

"You wish to return this ring," he repeated a little uncertainly, as if he could not have hear aright. "Is it not satisfactory?"

"Perfectly," said Mary. "But my brother bought it under a misapprehension. The money—the money he paid for it was not his own. That is, he had no right to spend it, and I want it back!"

Mary was conscious that she was not doing herself justice. But the case was difficult. So she smiled. That smile "wandered" the assistant. He promptly lost grip, but with a last instinct of self-preservation he fell back on his reserves.

"Mr. Ashton!" he said.

The responsible looking man, now delivered from his *surtout*, came out of the office with a letter open in his hand and a quill between his teeth. He removed the latter and also the frown from his brow at the sight of the pretty girl, and passing his hand automatically over his thin hair with the action of making sure that it was not standing on end, he came forward to the counter at which she stood.

"Well, madam, and what can I do for you?" he said, bowing to the early customer.

His face grew graver, however, as Mary stated her case.

"I don't think we can; in fact, I know we cannot," he said, very excusably.

"Mr. Ashton," said the girl, earnestly, "I do not ask you to do this thing as an ordinary business transaction. But the circumstances are peculiar. I must return the money my brother spent with you. I am the daughter of Mr. Bisset—the—the Lecturer, and I am only a girl (with a little gasping sob), but—I am trying to set things right!"

The sob took the responsible man by surprise. He stared at the pretty girl. There were tears in her eyes. He thought he had never seen anything quite like it— at least not for five-and-twenty years. Then suddenly Mary Bisset smiled at him through her tears. He had once, very long ago, seen something like that.

"But I am foolish to trouble you with it!" she said.

The responsible man smiled in his turn, and rubbed his hair-parting in some perplexity.

"It is gravely irregular, and I don't know what my partner will say. But let me see the receipt."

With the money in her pocket, all six pounds ten of it, Mary walked erectly down the North Bridge, and out upon the arches by which that fine highway swings itself contemptuously across the screeching, snorting underworld of the Waverley Station.

The tears were still wet in her eyes, but it might be the wind that kept them there.

Back in the shop on the North Bridge there was a smile on Mr. Ashton's face which something else than the snell bite of the North-Easter had brought there. He held Dick's receipt in his hand and examined it meditatively.

"This been crossed out on the stock book?" he called out, suddenly.

"No, sir," said the smart clerk, looking out from behind the window case shutters.

"Ah, well, see here," he said, tearing it up into fragments, "put the ring back in the show-case and write a new ticket. And, ah—you can have Wednesday afternoon for a holiday. You need not mention the transaction to Mr. Merrylees!"

The clerk said aloud, "Thank you, sir; certainly not, sir."

Then, having retired behind some high show cases, he coughed discreetly behind his hand.

"And at his age, too!" he said to himself.

*   *   *   *   *

It was five o'clock of the afternoon. Kit Kennedy had been at home twenty minutes, after having waited in vain for over an hour at the Surgeons' Hall in the hope of meeting Miss Mary Bisset. He had not lit the single flaring jet of gas which his agreement with his landlady permitted him to use at his pleasure. He did not even close the shutters, but sat staring out into the gloom of the long uninteresting street. He had dulled the edge of his remorse with a day of such hard study as he had not done since he came to Edinburgh. With the zeal of the reformer he had performed much more than his appointed task, and had, in fact, gone on reading an English translation of a recently translated German treatise on Greek accents till the reading rooms of the University had been closed. Now he had neither the heart nor the necessity to begin any futher studies.

Rob Grier had not come back from his guinea-a-month tuition, and the fire was smouldering under the roofing of black slate with which Mrs. Christieson covered it every time her lodgers went out.

Kit could hear that lady shuffling about in her little kitchen and he smelt the odour of burning toast. There came a sharp knock at the door, not loud and indignant like the postman's when he has come all the way up four flights of stairs with a postcard, but light and decisive.

He heard Mrs. Christieson open the door, and then a voice said clearly in a tone and accent that thrilled him to the heart, "Is Mr. Kennedy at home?"

"Aye, he's at hame. At least I think sae!" returned Mrs. Christieson with reserved suspicion.

"Will you tell him that Miss Bisset has a message for him?"

The landlady came in muttering. "Did ye ever see the like?" And with a countenance indicative of the gravest disapproval she opened the door of the sitting-room and announced Kit's visitor. With a quick spring Kit closed the door of the little close-bed where he and Rob Grier passed the night in exceedingly close quarters.

"Come in, Ma—Miss Bisset," he said. "I am sorry I did not see your father when I called. I meant to have told him about my visit to his friend Mr. Strong."

Kit thought rather well of himself for his tactful interpretation of Mary's visit in the presence of this hostile third party. But Mary was uncompromising.

"I wanted to speak to you myself," she said. "I did not know that you had called for my father."

Kit stood with the door knob in his hand while Mrs. Christieson lighted the gas and stirred the fire.

"I shall not need tea till Mr. Grier comes in," he said. "Thank you, don't trouble about the fire any more!"

For Kit had learned other things besides the classics from the "Orra Man." For instance, he made sure now that Mrs. Christieson had retired to her own domains by the simple process of looking down the passage, and then turned to shake hands with Mary Bisset.

But that young lady was in an exceedingly business-like mood.

"This is yours," she said, quietly handing him a roll of notes. "Will you oblige me by counting them?"

Kit stared and gasped in his astonishment. But his hand being still outstretched, he mechanically took the bank notes and turned them over helplessly.

"What—what is this?" he said. "How did you get—where?"

"I will put the matter plainly, Mr. Ken—Kit," she said, relenting a little, "and then you must decide what you are to do. One thing I am decided, that you must have no more to do with any of us. My brother broke open that desk in your absence and stole this money. I return it to you. If you are inclined to prosecute, I can give such evidence as will be sufficient to convict him."

Kit sprang forward to take her hand.

"Mary," he cried, "as if I could! What does it matter? Dick is nothing to me. It served me right for listening to him. I should have known better than to have taken you to his wretched supper party. But I only care for you, and I wanted to see you."

"You must not see me any more," said Mary, compressing her lips at the end of every sentence; "you have your career to think of and your reputable companions. I forbid you ever again to speak to me!"

"Mary," cried Kit, catching at a hand that evaded

23

him without its owner appearing to notice the attempt, "you do not mean it!"

The pretty girl nodded determinedly.

"I have learned many things during these last days," she said; "the world is not given us to get what we want in. Good-bye—Mr.—Kit."

The Christian name was a compromise, and carried with it the weakness inherent in all compromises.

There came a little throbbing quaver into her voice as she turned towards the door, saying, "It is a shame. And we might have been such friends!"

"And so we shall, Mary," cried Kit, following her eagerly; "I do not care——!"

But his visitor was already in the narrow passage outside, and Kit was sure that Mrs. Christieson's ear was glued to the crack of the kitchen door. He could only follow his sweetheart silently to the outer landing.

"Good-night, Mr. Kennedy," said Mary Bisset, without again looking at him.

"Good-night!" said Kit, dropping her hand in a dazed way and watching her down the stairs till she was lost in the gloom of her father's doorway.

"And wull ye hae your tea noo, or wull ye wait for Maister Grier," said his landlady, putting her head out at the door of the kitchen. "At ony rate, come in an' shut the door!"

"I don't want any tea! I shall never want tea again!" said Kit, seizing his hat and rushing downstairs.

Mrs. Christieson lifted up her hands and stood looking after him.

"Lord sake, is't as bad as that?" she cried.

And having shut the outer door with a bang she returned within, muttering that "it wasna sae in my young days, the idea! 'Miss Bisset'—no less, and 'I have a message for Mr. Kennedy,' as bold as brass. And then when she tak's her leave, the puir laddie wants nae tea and gangs fleein' doon the stair as if he was oot o' his mind. It's a crying shame and a disgrace, and sae I wull tell Mistress Mairchbanks when she comes up the stair to hear the news."

But Kit was not long before he returned. He had brought a small cashbox with a lever lock, and to this he consigned the bank notes which he had so wonderfully recovered. He noticed that nine of them were new and crisp, but he did not know the reason. He only knew that she had given them to him. So as he was stooping over the great red painted box the Whinnyliggate joiner had made for him to hold his books and clothes in, he looked shamefacedly around, and then with a swift furtive action he kissed the paper which her hands had touched. But he did not know what these rustling sheaves had cost the girl. Then he placed in the cashbox besides the money the tassel of an umbrella, which somehow had found its way mysteriously into his pocket in spite of the fact that he had never owned an umbrella in his life.

Down in the room below Mary Bisset was surveying herself in the glass. She had been dabbing her tear-stained eyes with a handkerchief after the immemorial manner of women, and was now "seeing how she looked" before going into the kitchen to her mother.

"I did it for the best," she said. "And I am very glad. But I did want a new dress and cloak this winter. I suppose this will turn. And at any rate he will never know—I shall never, never let him speak to me again!"

But at this point somehow she could not dab fast enough, and had to sit down and bury her sobs in the pillow lest her mother should come in and ask her what was the matter.

The late post brought to Kit in his fifth floor chamber two letters and a visitor. The first letter was from his mother and the visitor was his father.

CHAPTER XLIX.

KIT'S MOTHER'S LETTER.

DEAR SON [*so the letter began*], I know not when I shall get this letter written nor yet how I shall get it forwarded to you. I must depend upon the opportunities of a kind Providence.

God knows I would not distress you unless there were need. But so sore has been my trouble and my need so pressing that I have no other resource.

You know, dear Kit, that I have never complained, but have been rather thankful that life held so much for such an one as I. But now I cannot bear very much longer.

My husband is grown so troubled in mind that he is often quite past himself. I say not that he can help himself, for his mood comes upon him like a possession, and at such times I go in hourly fear of my life. He has shut me out from the sight of any human creature ever since he heard of your winning the college bursary, at which I could not conceal my joy.

Now he speaks of taking me to Sandhaven, there to spend the winter. I know not what he has in his mind. But as we are to pass through Edinburgh, I hope to see you, though I know not how. We put up (according to present intention) at the Tabernacle Hotel, which is, I believe, situated in a street called Leith Walk.

Be diligent at your lessons, dear son. And, Kit, do not forget your prayers. The day may come when they and the hope of death are all that remain to you in this world. Pray for your mother also, that soon she may have that rest which is the alone desire of her heart.

But first she would like to see you through the college and established with credit in some profession. I hope you will choose the holy ministry.

*   *   *   *   *

The letter ended sharply, without leave-taking or signature, and to Kit's mind, now sharpened by hatred and suspicion, this suggested that the remainder had been cut short by the necessity of concealment, or perhaps in order to take advantage of a chance to have it forwarded.

The other letter was from Betty Landsborough. It ran more briefly.

DEAR KIT,—I write to let you know about your mother. Walter Mac Walter is, Rob and I both think, plainly going out of his mind. And we think something ought to be tried to get her away from him, lest he do her a mortal mischief. He locks her up in a room at Kirkoswald and keeps the key, letting none go near her but himself. Heather Jock brought the word, but Walter Mac Walter has threatened to shoot him if ever he catches him about the house again.

Dear Kit, they say that you collegers have holidays at Christmas time. Come home if you have to walk all the way, and Rob Armour and you and me will try to get her way from that man. It is not safe. We are all in some measure of health here. Your grandfather and grandmother are well at time of writing. Laziness is all that is the matter with Rob, also conceit of himself.

Kit, I hope you are behaving yourself among the Edinburgh lasses, and have not forgotten your old friend,

BETTY LANDSBOROUGH.

*   *   *   *   *

While Kit perused his letters the "Orra Man" sat looking at him with a hungry look in his face. He had noticeably improved in appearance since the day after the Elysium. He now wore, not a spare suit of Mr. Bisset's, but a well-cut overcoat, frockcoat, and grey trousers. His carefully-brushed silk hat lay on the table brim upwards.

He continued to gaze wistfully and eagerly at the letter in Kit's hand. Kit laid it on the table whilst he read over Betty's.

"Well?" said Christopher Kennedy, B.A., a white and quivering anxiety settling down upon his pale face. He frequently smoothed his hair, now liberally sprinkled with silver, and pulled at the moustache, which, however, still remained black and long.

An impulse came over Kit. It was an old adage of his grandfather's, which he had but lately begun to understand the meaning of, that nothing steadies a man like responsibility or women like children of their own.

Impulsively he thrust both letters across to his father and sat looking at him as he tried to peruse them.

Christopher Kennedy laid the papers down, gravely drew out a double eye-glass, carefully adjusted it upon his nose, and lifted Lilias MacWalter's letter with shaking fingers.

As he read his head drooped on his hand, and the letter was laid down on the tablecloth, with a fast-falling rain of tears falling upon it.

Kit sat silent and waited.

At last his father looked up. He read both communications more than once.

"Kit," he said, in an almost inaudible voice, "do you think you can trust me with these letters? I have too long stood apart as unworthy and allowed this iniquity to go unchecked. Now, thank God, by the help of my two friends and fellow-townsmen, Alexander Strong and Daniel Bisset, I am depending upon strength that is not my own. There lies upon me a responsibility of which you know nothing. Will you trust me a little longer, and do nothing in this matter till I have laid these two letters before them?"

"What has Mr. Strong or Mr. Bisset to do with my mother?" said Kit, with sturdy Scottish unwillingness that such troubles should be spoken of outside the family.

"Mr. Strong nothing, save as one in whom I have confided, and who has helped me as it does not often fall to one man to help another. He has put power and purpose into my poor life. But as to Daniel Bisset and his daughter! That is another matter! They are most intimately connected with all that concerns Walter Mac Walter."

Kit felt that he was beyond his depth. But the look of power and dignity on the "Orra Man's" face was so surprising that he suffered him to carry off the letters.

Christopher Kennedy rose with the two papers in his hand.

"I will return as soon as we have decided upon a plan of action," he said. "Fear nothing. God has given Walter Mac Walter into our hands, and the wronged woman who has been so long in the valley of the shadow shall again walk in the light."

He passed through the door and went downstairs.
Kit, sitting silent over his books, could hear the door
of the Bissets' flat open and shut. Then in a while it
opened again, and presently looking past the edge of
the blind he could see the broad shoulders of Daniel
Bisset and the tall slender figure of his father striding
down the windy street arm in arm. And he knew that
the exdrunkard and the Infidel Lecturer were on their
way to take counsel with that eminently noble gentleman and Christian minister, the Reverend Alexander
Strong, of the more than Metropolitan Church of Saint
Laurence.

Rob Grier came back in the highest spirits and
slapped Kit on the back.

"I've got a berth for you after the New Year," he
cried. "What do you think of that? There's a
cousin of my cub's who is going in for his medical
'prelim.' He has yarned his father that he has passed
already, and now the old man is on the war-path and is
coming up at the end of the session to prospect. Besides he is ready to take his first professional, and he
can't unless he has passed his preliminary. So I've
promised that you will shove him through."

"Why don't you do it yourself, Rob?" said Kit,
smiling up at him.

"Oh, Rob Grier kens his place,' said the ex-smith,
dropping into the vernacular. "It's mainly Laitin and
Greek that he wants. Besides, I hae as muckle afore
my nose as I can manage!"

The two lads rose and shook hands without words on
either side.

"Now," said Rob, "just cast your blinker ower my
version, and tick the howlers wi' a killivine."*

For this is the sort of macaronic speech produced by
a few months of college life acting upon a base of rich
Galloway Doric.

An hour afterwards, in the great bare study of
Alexander Strong, three men sat round a table. Their
host was summing up.

* That is to say, "Underline the bad mistakes with a lead pencil."

" What you have to do is plain. You, Bisset, must keep some of your people on their track from the moment they reach the city. If Walter Mac Walter is a madman, he is most certainly a madman with a plan in his head. The brother of the dead Mary Bisset may have his own idea what that plan is."

" And you, my old college mate," he turned to the Classical Master, " you have also your part to play, ' in the strength of a man,' as Bisset might say ; ' by the help of God,' as I would put it. Right is on your side. We will support you in that right. If Mac Walter shows fight I will bring poor Nick French with me. But he will not fight. At all hazards and at any cost we must get this wronged woman out of his hands."

" Then," said Daniel Bisset, " it is agreed that we go to Sandhaven and take Kit Kennedy and Mary Bisset with us. That is, in the event of Walter Mac Walter taking his wife there."

The others nodded, and then, standing up, they all shook hands solemnly upon their compact.

CHAPTER L.

BAXTER'S FOLLY.

THE old inn of Port Baxter lies high up on the tall cliffs between Sandhaven and Arbuckle on the east coast of Scotland. The memory of the aboriginal Baxter is not yet quite forgotten. The oldest inhabitant has endless stories to tell of his eccentricity, his startling wealth, and yet more startling tales of how he acquired the latter. Baxter of Baxter's had been an overseer and afterwards a master in the West India plantations in the pre-emancipation days. He was known indifferently as the " Auld whupper-in " and the " Slave-driver."

Nevertheless, his descendants had fallen upon evil times, and the most prominent now drove the Sandhaven dustcart. But a certain awe and respect still accompanied Baxter *tertius* on his rounds. Though not naturally dusky, the nature of his profession gave some colour to the universal opinion that he had some " slaister o' the tar-brush " about him.

In the days before railways there could have been no safer investment than the inn of Port Baxter. In itself the port was nothing—a mere fringing hamlet along a sandy bay far below ; a dozen fishers divided into three quaintly intermarried families, engaged chiefly in producing albinozed babies in thatched cottages and cherishing odorous lobster-pots upon a tiny quay. For all that, when first built " Baxter's " little deserved its nickname of " Baxter's Folly."

But, like Baxter's descendants, Baxter's had fallen upon evil days. For the coaches had vanished from the roads and the bicycles were not yet. Still there was a certain traffic, carriers between the three notable towns from which Baxter's lay about equidistant, shepherds driving to or returning from Fairport market or Falkirk Tryst, many sea bathers in the summer time—an over-press of them indeed, sleeping in tiers in the barn and on the dining room table of Baxter's, so, at least, they said in Fairport. At all events, custom sufficient there was to make a fairly rich woman of Mistress Meysie Conachar, the plump and rosy hostess, who with her own shapely hands served the liquors in the bar and clinked the money into the till.

It was a dullish December evening that Hoggie Haugh, hostler and factotum of Mistress Conachar, was engaged in sweeping out the stable-yard of Baxter's. Hoggie had obtained his wonderful Christian name ("if shape it could be called that shape had none") upon the ice at the play of the curling stones. He suffered as a player from a chronic inability to pass the "hog-score," a sort of great gulf fixed upon the rink, those failing to overpass which abide in a kind of limbo, unclassed and uncounted at the game's ending. As for Hoggie's other name it was seldom heard, but on these occasions was pronounced with the exact sound of some one impolitely clearing his throat.

Now Hoggie was a stout fellow, shrewd, not uncomely to look upon, and accounted to be "far ben" with his mistress. There were those who even paid a kind of provisional court to Hoggie, as not unlikely to stand behind the bar some day himself and rattle the coin into the till, the coppers into one sounding compartment and the tinkling silver into a place by itself.

Hoggie communed with himself as he swept his besom steadily to and fro—or rather, to be exact, to, but not fro:

"It's saft like, but it's gaun to be safter afore a' be dune," he confided to the clouds. He looked up at the leaden pall which had spread above and sniffed at the light breeze, which came from the south-east. It smelt moist in his nostrils. And Hoggie soliloquised as he leaned upon his broom:

"Snaw," he said, nodding his head, sagely; "an on-
ding o' snaw—wreaths and drifts o' snaw—a close cover
for Christmas, a white and sleekit New Year. And
packs o' veesitors in the hoose, or on their road. Guid
send that they be storm-stayed on their way, for I kenna
what they will do wi' themsel's. It's a blessin' that the
mistress has flour an' meal, hams in raws and raws, and
saxty hens on the baulks—every hen o' them guid layers
even in winter time!"

He sniffed the air again. "It's aboot tea-time,
Hoggie," he said; "I wish ye could smell the ham
fryin'—Lord, here they come!"

As he spoke a high dog-cart whirled past and drew up
in the corner of the yard with a spirited clatter and a
spraying of the sand and gravel from the tense forefeet
of the black mare between the shafts.

A tall dark man leaped down, and throwing the reins
carelessly to Hoggie he turned to assist a veiled lady
from the other seat. She was clad in black, and
wrapped from the cold in many folds of shawl.

"Here, take the ribbons, don't stand malingering
there!" cried the dark man to Hoggie, "and if you
don't let her cool slowly and feed her well, I'll tan the
hide off you, my good man with the bullet head!"

"The bullet head—very well," said Hoggie, under
his breath. "I'll mind that! Tan my hide, master,
will ye? Hoggie Haugh kens a gentleman and a
a gentleman's words. And he neither sees ane or hears
the ither."

This to himself, and then with a sympathetic glance
at the silent figure standing waiting in the snow he
murmured, "Eh, the puir thing, I'll wager she has
nane o' her sorrows to seek wi' a black-a-vised Turk like
that! Tan my hide, will he? Let him try 't, that's a'!"

And Hoggie Haugh, having led the black mare into
stall, turned about and "squared up" scientifically at
the back of the visitor which was just vanishing into
the bar, the silent woman following meekly behind.

"Eh, puir thing!" said Hoggie again.

Hoggie went back to his sweeping, but now with a

more perfunctory diligence, owing in about equal
measure to the broad flakes of moist snow, which had
begun to fall lightly and airily, with many upward
liftings and side swirlings in the winds that blew
before the snowstorm, and to the fact that Hoggie had
an eye to keep on the kitchen of Baxter's and an ear to
direct towards the frizzle of the pan.

But before he had time to reach his desired haven
of a sonsy meat tea he discerned through the drift,
which began thinly to veil the face of the bleak moorland, a number of dark figures advancing on foot up the
long steep ascent.

At this Hoggie threw down his broom with a justifi-
able expression of disgust.

"Mair and mair! They may be wantin' to stop ten
days like you drawing craiturs that cam' at the time o'
the snaw-storm three year syne, and nearly ate us oot
o' hoose and hame. At the best they'll be bidin' for
their tea, and Hoggie will hae to wait till the mistress
and Meg has them served. May the black deil tak' a'
stravaigers and run-the-countries that are sae far left
to themsel's as to forsake their ain comfortable firesides
in sic weather."

Hoggie was at the gate by this time, and the stoutest
of the party of four came forward to speak to him.

"Are you the master of this inn?" he said, politely.

Hoggie shook his head with a curious little smirk.

"Na," he said, "I wadna tak' that upon mysel'—
juist yet. But the mistress is busy ben the hoose, and
—weel, ye may say onything to me that ye hae to say
to her."

"We are three friends out from Edinburgh on a
walking tour in our Christmas holidays. At the last
moment my daughter wished to accompany us. I fear
there is a storm brewing. Could we have any accommodation, however humble, at your inn?"

Hoggie scratched his head.

"Weel," he said, "ye'll hae to gang into the auld
hoose. For there's a lady and"—Hoggie paused—he
could not conscientiously add "a gentleman"—"a man

here already, and they hae engaged the best rooms and
the parlour. They hae had them bespoke mair than
three weeks. Sae gin ye want ony accommodation,
ye'll e'en hae to gang to the auld hoose."

"A double-bedded room, and a small one for the
young lady, will be all we shall want, and we are willing
to go anywhere you can put us. Whe e is the 'auld
hoose' of which you speak?"

Hoggie turned on his heel, and pointed to a long,
straggling, single-storied thatched house, whose small
windows looked into the quadrangle of outbuildings at
the back of the larger inn.

"That's the auld hoose," he said; "it was here before
ever there was a Baxter."

The two seniors—who were, of course, the "Orra
Man" and Daniel Bisset, looked at each other.

"That will suit us admirably," said Mr. Bisset.
"Can we go in now and take off our wet boots, and
ease the straps of our knapsacks?"

"Ye maun hae been ill-fixed at hame that ye cam' aff
on a walkin' tour, an' wi' a lassie too, in weather like
this! But I suppose ye'll be English, an' the Almighty,
if He has gien them siller, has surely withhauden a'
common sense frae the puir craiturs. Come your ways
ben. I bide in the auld hoose mysel'—for the present.
And I'se warrant ye'll no be waur dune to there than
if ye had the best bedroom in Baxter's. Come ben!
Come ben!"

CHAPTER LI.

"How Long, O Lord, How Long?"

Lilias Mac Walter sat in a little chillish sitting-room, in the contracted grate of which a fire of wood and peat was reluctantly burning up with a maximum of smoke and a minimum of flame. She had thrown down her shawls and bonnet upon the sofa, and now she sat in the armchair by the fire looking straight before her, a dull and hopeless ache wrenching stolidly at her heart. She had suffered so much that the acuteness had gone out of the pain itself. Death and life seemed now very much alike to her. Walter Mac Walter grew every day more sullenly enraged. Sometimes he would sit and watch her for hours with hateful, malevolent eyes.

Again, without any apparent occasion, he would hector and rage, threaten and bully, till only the dulness of weariness and indifference preserved her sanity.

On this occasion he strode restlessly up and down the narrow apartment. He had the whip still in his hand clutched in the middle, and every other minute he would stop at the window and curse the snow, which appeared somehow to irritate him past endurance.

"But for this I might have had it over to-night," he muttered. "Pshaw! nothing goes right with me! But I am glad, though, that the place looks different."

He stopped before his wife.

"Woman," he said, "rise up and look after the fire, and see that the idle people bring us something to eat."

Lilias stooped obediently, and began to arrange the smouldering peat and dying embers. She blew ineffectually till the man, laying his hand upon her shoulder

with a sudden fierce access of anger, thrust her rudely
aside.

"Stand away from there!" he cried.   "You blow all
the ash into the room.   Get the dinner laid, and leave
me to attend to the fire myself."

Lilias moved listlessly towards the door.

"No," thundered her husband, "did I not tell you that
you were not to go out of my sight on the peril of your
life? Dare to disobey me on your peril! Ring the bell!"

And as the woman did not at once see the bell-pull,
which was hidden behind a deep curtain, he rushed
thither himself and pulled it till the cord came off in his
hand, and the released lever sprang back with a wheez-
ing screech.

Mistress Conachar of Baxter's Inn appeared a
moment after at the door of the private parlour, a little
flushed in the face, partly from the shortness of breath
natural to her years and manner of life, and partly from
an excusable anger at being summoned thus imperiously
in her own house.

As she entered Walter Mac Walter threw the green
cord of the bell-pull on the floor.

"Can you not bring up dinner at once? I ordered
it to be ready upon my arrival. Is three weeks too
short notice for you?"

"You are nearly an hour before the time you speci-
fied in your letter, sir," said Mistress Conachar with
dignity.   "But I will spread the cloth."

"Yes, spread it and be done!" returned Walter
Mac Walter, striding to the window, and standing
there a tall, gloomy figure, the whip still clutched
nervously in his right hand.

Mistress Conachar erected herself, and sailed out
with the stately port of a galleon before the wind.

"Indeed," she said, indignantly, "is this the King o'
Muscovy that we hae gotten at Baxter's? 'Spread the
cloth and be done!' It's not likely that Elspeth
Conachar will bide where her conversation is not
esteemed a privileege.   Where's that guid-for-naething
Hoggie Haugh—oot at the auld hoose, ye say, wi' mair

tourist bodies? I wonder what's ta'en the hale warld to travel at Christmas. Never was sic daft-like ploys heard o' in my young days. Babbie, tak' ben the second best service. Guid kens what sic a monster micht no do to my best cheena. Faith, I'm heart-sorry for yon puir peetifu'-lookin' thing that he has for a wife. She appears no to be lang for this warld. An' gin I was her I wadna muckle care, wi' siccan a girnin' Hottentot for a man!"

When Walter Mac Walter was left alone with his wife he sat down opposite her.

"You do not ask why I have brought you here," he said; "I know your play and pretence of meekness. But, my lady, I learned from a source you cannot guess at of your letters to the old stone-breaker, your father. I doubt not they were the means you took of sending my money to the drunkard's son. Now it seems that I cannot watch you closely enough in your own house at Kirkoswald. But I can here. I will not once let you out of my sight. You shall see your old father on the parish before you die. And I will make of your son just what his father was. I cannot say more than that!"

Lilias had eaten nothing, and now sat with her head turned away from her tormentor, looking into the fire with an expression of more than mortal anguish.

"*How long, O Lord, how long?*" she was saying within her own heart.

And it was not to be long. For so the Lord of the snow and of the sea and of the heart of man had decreed.

Walter Mac Walter went on. His cord was lengthened yet a little.

"And let me tell you that now you are in a place where you can do nothing to help your beggar's brat or alter that which is coming to him. I saw Sowerby of Cairn Edward, the other day, and he told me that the brat was already proving the blood he came of. He is spending his bursary money like water in the vilest places. He will soon come to the end of it and be disgraced. That is why I will take good care that you do not send him any more. In a year I will see him back at the hedge-root, where I have seen his father lie. I shall live to have him sent to gaol, and you shall go to the trial—Lilias, pretty Lilias that once flouted and despised Walter Mac Walter. Have not I paid my debts in full?"

And the sound of his voice reached the ears of three who listened beneath in the snow, and was heard also by a fourth, who stood a little way behind.

"Aye," this last communed with himself, "oot o' his mind, I wad say sae. That's never the voice o' a man in his seven senses. Ye may coont on Hoggie Haugh to keep an e'e on him. I'll never tak' a wink o' sleep this nicht wi' that puir thing in his poo'er."

For the excellent thought had come to Mr. Bisset, so soon as he had heard Hoggie describe Walter Mac Walter as a "black-a-vised hyena," that they should take the ostler partly into their confidence. A crisp and "crunkly" pound note wonderfully assisted the process, and the "Orra Man's" discriminating appreciation of the horses in the stable beneath the auld hoose o' Baxter's bought Hoggie Haugh body and soul.

"He's gane to his ain bed and barred his door, flingin' it to wi' a brainge that shook the hoose!" was Hoggie's last bulletin. "I'll listen whiles at the puir lass's window through the nicht, and gie ye a cry if need be."

"I also will watch with you!" said Christopher Kennedy, B.A.

CHAPTER LII

THE NIGHT WATCH.

LILIAS MAC WALTER had long known her husband's essential insanity. For years he had dwelt morbidly upon her past. The boy Kit Kennedy was to Mac Walter the outward sign and token of her former love for his father. Of a cast of mind originally coarse and brutal, without mental or moral reserves of power, Walter Mac Walter had grown to believe that his chances of happiness depended upon the removal of the boy out of his path, and for this purpose he had systematically endeavoured to separate Lilias and her son. But recently an idea far more dangerous had taken its place. He had made a mistake. The wife herself was the barrier to happiness. The son must be ruined. The mother would die of grief. He himself would be free—or, if this failed him or proved too slow, he must discover other means to free himself.

His return to places familiar to him in his boyhood, his fits of alternate kindliness and brutality would, to a medical man accustomed to cases of delusion, have indicated influence and homicidal mania, and have diagnosed Walter Mac Walter as belonging to the most dangerous class of lunatics.

Yet he was a man of money, power, and responsibility. It was impossible to restrain or confine him. His mental states were not noted save by his wife, and she, wearied and made even indifferent by long-continued cruelty, mistook his moods for the natural bias of a perverted jealousy, though a specialist on the alert would rather have noted them as strong evidence of dementia. There are lunatics who, being sane

in the ordinary affairs of business and the outward
relations of mankind, and having no one in any sort of
authority over them, cannot be proved to be insane till
some overt act of mania suddenly startles their world
into dreadful knowledge of their condition.   Such
maniacs are perhaps the most dangerous of all.

It was, for instance, no unusual thing for Lilias to
awake in the night to the affrighting consciousness that
her husband had entered her room and was standing
silently by her bedside with arms folded across his
breast.   Hour after hour he could remain so, never for
a moment removing his gaze from her face.   And then
as the grey light of the morning stole into the fearful
chamber, and the blinds edged themselves with
brighter light, he would steal back to his own room
on tiptoe and fling himself upon his bed, still fully
dressed, only to repeat the performance the following
night.

It was a vigil like this, for the first time spied upon
by other eyes than those of the persecuted woman, who
had borne her trouble so silently throughout the years,
that Walter Mac Walter kept that stormy night of
midwinter in the inn of Baxter's Folly high on the
cliffs of Sandhaven.

The two men, watching at the edges of the blind
through which the feeble glimmer of the night-light
shone like an illumination, saw Walter Mac Walter
come in and stand by his wife's bed.   Motionless for a
full hour they watched him.   Their hands were on the
window sill ready to throw up the sash and spring into
the room if he should lay hands upon her.

Presently Lilias moved in her sleep and moaned restlessly.   The watcher by the bedside drew back a little
into the shadow of the curtain.   Then, as she became
still, he again approached and, swiftly stooping, glided
his hand under the pillow.

He brought out in his hand a withered spray of
heather which once had been white.   At the sight of it
a kind of fury took possession of him.   He stamped his
stockinged foot on the threadbare carpet, and gnashed

his teeth as he tore the dried fibres apart and scattered the dust-like leaf meal upon the floor.

Lilias Mac Walter turned over at the sound, and opened her eyes upon the startling apparition of the anger of her husband.

"Walter!" she gasped, not yet fully awaked from sleep. "Walter!" And could say no more.

And still the men at the window watched with their hands tense upon the chill wood of the window frame. The Classical Master put his hand behind him to feel his revolver easy in his hip-pocket. But without a word, or once removing the terrible fixity of his gaze from that of the woman, Walter Mac Walter backed to the door and so disappeared.

And Lilias lay thus hour after hour, staring at the blank black oblong of the door through which her husband had disappeared, her lips and throat not only parched but dissicated, her brain almost paralysed, her soul under the influence of such deadly fear that she could not even pray the prayer so familiar to her—the eternal appeal of the sufferer to Him who, sitting at the helm of the Universe, yet permits the suffering to continue. "How long, O Lord, how long?"

But now it was not to be so very long.

The light came clearer. The day broke. It was Lilias Mac Walter's Christmas morning.

    *   *   *   *   *

That morning was Christmas morning over all the world. With the dawn the air had grown keen. The soft breath of the cyclone had quite passed. Glittering frost had fallen with the dropping of the wind upon the hardy hollies and stunted laurels around Baxter's Folly. The snow had not drifted deeply, and especially on a slope so wind-swept as that of Baxter's Ness it was nowhere more than a crust; while save for a wreath or two behind dykes, the edge of the great cliffs which stand out into the German Ocean all the way to Sandhaven were blown wholly clear.

It was twelve of the clock on as fine a December day as ever lighted up the white face of this northern

land before life or sound appeared in the rooms occupied
by Walter Mac Walter and his wife. Breakfast had
been served at nine, but at eleven the dishes had not
been touched. For Babbie Mac Gregor, the maid-of-all-
work, had given so terrifying an account of the dark-
faced man who sat at the table-end crumbling the
"dottle" of his pipe upon the tablecloth and among
the very dishes, and had growled at her to "let
that fire alone for a meddlesome fool" when she
went near to sweep up the scattered ashes, that it was
thought best to leave everything alone for the present.

Hoggie, who did not seem to have anything to do on
Christmas morning, wandered to and fro near the
windows of the New House. He was prepared to assert
that he was pruning the rosebushes, that is, if any one
had asked him what he was finding to do there. But
no one took any particular notice of Hoggie.

The "Auld Hoose" lay apparently untenanted, save
for a pew of reek which rose straight up into the
windless air. It was so still that when Mrs. Conachar's
Brahma rooster crowed suddenly in the yard it brought
a trickle of snow sliding down the roof of the stable.
Only a low growling *sough* very far away could be
heard, which was the sea calling restlessly at the foot of
Baxter's Heuchs.

Punctually at twelve the door of the New House
opened, and a little wreath of snow with a wavy crest,
which had been making a Cambridge blue shadow upon
itself, collapsed inwards on the mat. Walter Mac
Walter held the door open for his wife to pass. And
Lilias came out, looking slender and even girlish in her
plain black dress outlined against the spotless snow.

The pair turned into the high road together, watched,
however, from every window of the inn. The "Auld
Hoose" stood blank and silent without apparent
observer. Only a black lump sped seaward behind a
dykeback where the snow was lying thickest. It consisted of the hunched shoulders of Hoggie Haugh.

"This way!" said Walter Mac Walter, cheerfully.

And his wife turned obediently at his word.

They had not proceeded far, however, when the snow grew deeper in the hollows, and the progress of Lilias became so painful that her husband, who strode on before, waxed irritable and impatient.

"Cannot you go faster than that?" he growled. "Here, take my hand!"

But she shrank from the touch of his fingers and struggled on, sinking to the knees at every step.

"This will never do," he said; "turn back and we will get the mare and trap."

"Here—fellow," he shouted at the entrance of the yard, "where is that drunken scoundrel of an ostler?"

But Hoggie was far out of sight or hearing.

"I will put the beast in myself!" he said, angrily.

And striding from door to door round the yard he soon found the black mare, and began with the strong assured fingers of an expert to harness her.

The dogcart was sheltered in the wide bare house which in its time had held many a snowed-up coach with His Majesty's Royal red and gold on the panels. Walter Mac Walter drew it out by the shafts, and had the whole turnout ready as quickly and as neatly as any professional yardman.

"Get in!" The order to his wife came like a military command.

But this was too much for one of the watching contingent behind the blinds of Baxter's Inn. Mrs. Conachar came out at the back door, a silver platter in her hand and a paper folded upon it.

"Will ye be pleased to look at this, sir, before ye gang oot o' my yaird. It is the custom of the hoose!"

"What is this?" The words came gruffly as Walter Mac Walter tied a new knot upon his whiplash.

"The accoont, sir, if your honour pleases!"

Walter Mac Walter erected his head with a certain gesture of surprised contempt.

"I am not a trickster," he said, very proud and high.

"It is a custom o' the hoose, sir," repeated Mistress Conachar, fearless and implacable where money was concerned. Babbie Mac Gregor said afterwards that she was "fair feared to hear her mistress speakin' that gate to him, and the muckle black hyeny lookin' as if he wad hae etten her. Oh, if I had only jaloused!'"

"I am going for a little drive with my wife," said Mac Walter. "To look at the view from the cliffs. I am not going to run away!"

"Na, but I dinna ken but your horse micht!" said the stout-hearted landlady, still extending the silver salver.

Babbie remarked that a "*reesle-reesle* ran up her back like pittin' a clean sark on" at her mistress' words. She "couldna describe it itherwise, but she kenned it was a warnin'!"

Walter Mac Walter pulled a thick wad of bank notes out of his pocket. He selected a couple, throwing them to Mrs. Conachar with scorn, and crying, "There, woman, will that content you?" he helped his wife into the dogcart.

"For the present, sir, I thank you!" replied the landlady, with strictly non-committal curtsey.

"I'll gie him 'Spread the cloth and be done'! Na, na—the black-a-vised gorilla doesna breathe that can say the like o' that to Elspeth Conachar, though her Jeems, puir man, is dead and in his restin' grave thae fourteen years come Martinmas!"

CHAPTER LIII.

BAXTER'S HEUCHS.

During their short drive to the heights of Baxter's Heuchs, Walter Mac Walter talked to his wife as he had done during the first months of their married life. He even pointed out places of interest familiar to him from boyhood. There was Sandhaven itself, glittering in the morning light, a water-colour in white and red as the wet tiles took the sun and the warmth beneath melted the thin snow. The smoke was blowing blue and gossamer fine from it. He showed her the fishing boats bending their sails to fare forth from the harbour mouth, and the distant lighthouse, a pillar of cloud by day, of fire by night, rising from the sea as the low sun of winter shone down on the myriad glasses of its crystal crown.

"Now we will go across the fields to the finest view of all! We have not had a holiday like this for a long time!" he said, cheerfully, leaping down and tying the reins to a stone gate-post.

Though the mare had scarcely come half a mile, he slung the bag of oats over her nose, and left her to feed at the entering in of the bare field which divides the high road to Sandhaven from the yet more bald and windswept cliff-edge.

"This way, Lilias," he said, reaching his wife a hand to help her over a great wreath of snow which undulated behind the dyke and rose into a final swirl that pushed a white nose a yard or two through the gate itself.

It was the first time he had spoken her Christian name in kindness for ten years.

She did not reply, but gave him a gloved hand, and

they went up the field without a word. A curious kind of amazed apathy had come over her. She even smiled to think how little she cared what should happen to her.

They reached the highest part of Baxter's Heuchs, from which the cliff began to drop, first in a little short slope of bare grey turfage to the brink, and then in a four hundred foot fall, sheer down upon the myriad flashing facets of the restless winter sea.

There was haze to seaward, like the moonlight which dwells in a large opal when you hold it so that the prismatic colours are not seen. The sea was blue and calm beneath, the waves the merest dancing dimplings. But an intermittent heave and growl told that a swell was running far into the caves which undermined the huge headland of Baxter's Heuchs.

Lilias shivered a little. She put the shawl, which she carried across her arm, about her shoulders. She felt somehow that the sea looked chilly.

"Yes, the view is fine," said her husband, looking out underneath his hand, "but I know a spot where you can see the mouth of the Guillemots' Cave, with the sea running straight into it. I have not seen it for twenty years. But I think I can find the place. It should be just by that little pinnacle on which the raven is sitting!"

Lilias shrank back a little, as if unwilling to go any nearer the verge.

"I am tired," she said; "I think I would like to go back to the inn."

"Nonsense," he cried, hilariously, without, however, looking at her. "It is a glorious morning, and I am going to show you all the places I knew as a boy. I remember walking here with——"

He broke off short.

"Give me your hand," he said, abruptly, with a quick change of voice. And he seized her fingers in a grip like a vice.

There was a noise near him, a stone dislodged itself from a crevice and trickled slowly down the bald grey slope. Then with a quickening leap it sped over the utmost cliff edge and fell—fell—fell—far out of sight and hearing into the deep gulf below.

Walter Mac Walter held up his left hand and inclined his ear to listen.

He listened in vain. No splash came up, nor any sound save the low booming from the caverns under.

"Four hundred feet," he said, with a kind of mounting exultation, "four hundred feet—and then!"

They went on, Lilias with her fine boots growing wet and discomfortable as the sharp slats cut them and the snow sifted in. Afterwards it appeared to her strange that at the moment her chief thought was a feeling of regret that she had not put on a stronger pair.

The edge of the cliff was thrown up in a sort of bluff like the crest of a breaking wave. A little wind-worn gallery ran beneath, aided in the task of keeping its position by the original backward thrust of the strata.

Walter Mac Walter had been holding his wife by the arm as they went up the last steep ascent. Now they paused on the very edge. The world seemed suddenly to grow hollow beneath them. And the heart of Lilias —nay, all her body seemed hollow also. Her instinct was to clutch the arm of her companion, and only an intense personal loathing kept her from yielding to it.

"Come here and I will show you the mouth of the Guillemots' Cave!" he cried, in an excited tone.

He almost dragged Lilias to a lower jutting pinnacle. "See," he said, pointing downwards into the gulf with his finger, "they are flying out and in like spirits—like ghosts of the dead, while the sea calls beneath. Four hundred feet! Look—look! They are beckoning us!"

His voice rose to a shriek and he compelled her to look over the verge.

As she did so he loosened his hold on her arm, and appeared to stumble with all his weight against her. She fell forward—outward—downward—and knew no more.

CHAPTER LIV.

WALTER MAC WALTER MEETS MARY BISSET.

WHEN she came to herself Lilias found that she was supported in arms which clasped her firmly about the waist. Her head lay on some one's shoulder. This was very strange, yet somehow, as the buzzing in her ears ceased, she seemed to find herself in some strangely familiar place. She felt an incurious content steal over her. She was quite ready to stay where she was for ever.

"Mother," she said, "is that you?"

But even as she said it she knew that her mother was not there.

Then her eyes opened upon a world of dazzling whiteness, upon the blue of a brilliant sky infinitely removed.

Then her eyes lighted upon Walter Mac Walter. He was standing above her bedside looking at her as she had seen him do last night. She shrieked aloud.

"Oh, take him away—do not let him come near me!"

Then a voice spoke in her ear, a voice she knew, yet could not remember whose it was. It said, "He will never come near you any more."

She perceived that two men whom she had never seen held her husband by the arms, while her son Kit, very hale and strong, stood behind with a strange, alert, triumphant look on his face.

But the voice behind belonged to someone else.

"Who are you?" she faltered, trying weakly to turn her head.

"Lilias, I am your husband!" said Christopher

Kennedy, laying her gently back on the grass and looking down into her eyes.

*　　　*　　　*　　　*　　　*

Joy does not kill, as the story-books aver. Perhaps for the reason that when it comes suddenly and unexpectedly like an angel from heaven, it is not at first believed in.

Slowly Lilias became aware that the elder of the two men who held her husband was speaking. The sense of his words seemed to come to her from an infinite distance.

"Listen, Walter Mac Walter," he was saying. "You know me. You have known me all your life. I am Daniel Bisset, brother of Mary Bisset, your dead—your murdered wife."

Walter Mac Walter tried to thrust his guards from him, but they held him fast, Hoggie Haugh hanging upon his arm with the grip of a giant, and Kit Kennedy standing behind ready to assist in case of need.

"Yes—murdered," said Daniel Bisset, solemnly. "We suspected it before. We know it now. From the place from which Mary Bisset fell you would have thrown Lilias Kennedy to-day, even as twenty years ago you sent my sister to her death."

"Lilias Kennedy!" The words came scornfully from the lips of the baffled madman.

"Aye, Lilias Kennedy, no other," said the Classical Master, coming forward—for his charge was now sufficiently recovered to sit up (and, after the manner of women, begin to arrange her hair). "She is my wife, not yours. Alexander Strong, of Edinburgh, has found poor Nick French whom we thought dead. He has kept the original marriage lines of Christopher Kennedy and Lilias Armour. So long as I thought her happy I would never have come forward. I would have kept myself where she would never have known. But now——"

"It is a lie—a lie—a devil's lie;" cried Walter Mac Walter furiously, foaming at the mouth.

Then Daniel Bisset spoke again.

"It is a truth which the judges of the land will

believe, as they will believe the witness of us four men
—when you, Walter Mac Walter, are tried for the
attempted murder of Lilias Kennedy and the accomplished murder of Mary Bisset, my sister and your
wife!"

With a quick access of maniacal strength the prisoner
cast his guards this way and that from him. Even then
he would have sprung upon Lilias, but for the shining
tube of a revolver which looked at him from the right
hand of the Classical Master. He heard his guards
rushing at him from behind. With a quick swing
he turned, dashed between them, knocked Kit down
flat on his back, and ran along by the edge of the cliff
in the direction of the gate at which he had left the
black mare tethered.

But at the first dip of the ground, in a little sheltered
hollow, he came upon a girl sitting. She held her
hat in her hand as if enjoying the winter sunshine, and
as he ran towards her she rose with a startled look on
her pale face.

The maniac stopped dead in his career with a strange
gasping cry.

"Mary Bisset! In God's name, Mary Bisset!
Touch me not. Out of my way, fiend!' he shouted.

And swerving to the left to avoid the wraith of his
victim, he stumbled upon the imminent verge of the
cliff, and fell outward and forward. He clutched at
nothing as he fell, and as it were wrenched himself
round, till his distorted face looked up at the accusing
phantom who had confronted him so startlingly. That
face vanished like a falling stone.

And from below there came an agonised cry of
"Mary Bisset! Mary Bisset!"

Then silence.

The fragments must be briefly gathered up. Lilias Kennedy began a new life from that day forth. Her husband, long tried in the fire, had come forth refined. These two went to the South of England for the winter, and Daniel Bisset accompanied them "for his health's sake," he said. But the Classical Master knew better.

"I thank you, Daniel," he said; "next year I shall be able to walk without swaddling bands—by the blessing of God!"

"Amen to that!" said the Infidel Lecturer.

Mary Bisset gave up her situation and went with them, but her mother refused to quit Edinburgh.

"I will keep the house open and the fireside warm against your return!" she said.

Dick listed in the Scots Greys which were quartered at Piershill, and his father refused to buy him off in spite of his mother's many prayers.

"It is his one chance!" he said.

Kit went back to his college course, and when he came in spring to the Cottage under the Crae Wood he had two medals to show the Elder. But he had heard news that had saddened him. With one of the curious freaks of violent and passion-driven men Walter Mac' Walter had left all his property to Mary Bisset, the only daughter of his dead wife. Kit felt that now Mary was separated from him by a great gulf fixed.

He said this to Betty, to whom he communicated all his woes.

"Nonsense—try her," said that experienced person; "Rob tried me a score o' times afore I wad hae him. Only a fool ever takes it for granted that a woman will say 'No'!"

And Kit took Betty's advice.

*   *   *   *   *

It was the bright heart of May when Mary Bisset came to Kirkoswald with her adopted father. Mr. and Mrs. Christopher Kennedy were already there, putting the place in some sort of order. They had refused to remain, however, in spite of many invitations.

"I can maintain my own wife, thank God," said Christopher Kennedy, Senior, with some pride. "I have been appointed Classical Master at the Edinburgh Athenæum. It is not a great school, but it is better on that account for one so long out of practice. Lilias and I have taken a house, and we start work after the holidays. Daniel will be near us."

Mary Bisset was infinitely distressed that Lilias would not consent to receive any of the inheritance of Walter Mac Walter.

"I am not his widow. I never was your father's wife. I will have nothing that ever belonged to him. It is yours by right and by gift. But if you put my father and mother back in the Dornal they will die happy."

And so it was arranged, Rob and Betty jointly and severally agreeing to work the farm for them.

"But I wad like to see the Rob or the Betty that will mak' me ither than mistress o' my ain hoose," said Kit's grandmother.

"Fegs," said Willie Gilroy, who had come to see them comfortably settled, "ye are o' the same mind as my wife."

"What, Willie, ye are never married again?"

The Sheriff's officer admitted the accusation with a shake of his head.

"Wha is 't, Willie?" cried Betty Landsborough, who was naturally much interested.

"It's juist Meg Patterson frae Clairbrand."

"But she's surely no young. Willie, hoo auld is she?"

"God kens," said Willie. "I misdoot she'll never

dee decently, this yin. I think I'll hae to shoot
her!"

* * * * *

Kit found Mary in the renovated drawing-room of
Kirkoswald. She was looking prettier than ever before,
though very simply dressed. But the radiance of her
eyes seemed somehow to fill the room, even as once it
had filled Kit's heart under the Edinburgh gas-lamps.

He took her hand and bent his head towards her.

"What is it, Kit?" she said.

"You are a great lady now," he said, very low.
"You are the owner of all this!"

The pretty girl was silent a little, looking up at his
drooping head with a singularly sweet smile. Then she
went a little nearer to him.

"Ask me if there is nothing else I would like better
to be!" she said at last.

Then Kit asked, and found that there was.

THE END.

W. Speaight and Sons, Printers, Fetter Lane, London.